M000074120

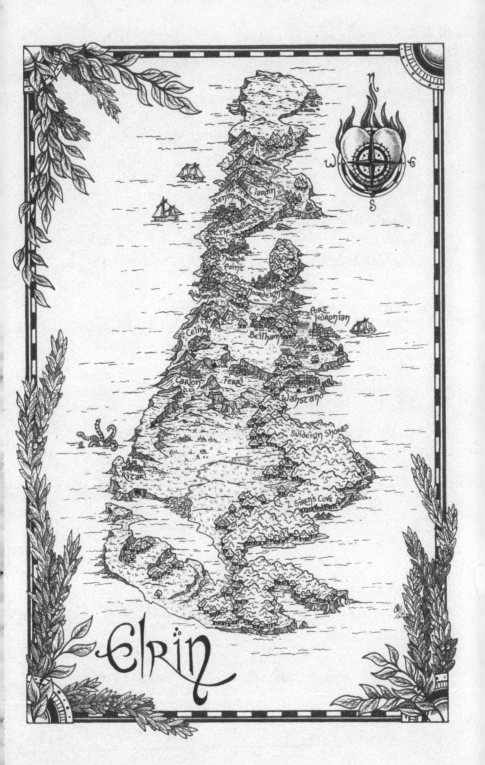

Legend of the Huntress

K. GODIN

LEGEND OF
THE HUNTRESS
K. GODIN

Print edition ISBN: 9781777880507
E-book edition ISBN: 9781777880507
Hardback edition ISBN: 9781777880514

First edition: December 2021
10 9 8 7 6 5 4 3 2 1

WWW.AUTHORKGODIN.COM

This is a work of fiction. Names, characters, places, and incidents either are the product of the author's imagination or are used fictitiously, and any resemblance to actual persons, living or dead, business establishments, events or locales is entirely coincidental.

Copyright ©2021 by K. Godin. All rights reserved.

No part of this publication may be reproduced, stored in a retrieval system, or transmitted, in any form or by any means without the prior written permission of the publisher, nor be otherwise circulated in any form of binding or cover other than that in which it is published and without a similar condition being imposed on the subsequent purchaser.

Cover Design and Interior Layouts by Miss Nat Mack
Map by Amy Elizabeth Sayers
Editor Beth Attwood
Editor Lottie Clemens

Legend of the Huntress

K. GODIN

LEGEND OF
THE HUNTRESS

K. GODIN

Print edition ISBN: 9781777880507
E-book edition ISBN: 9781777880507
Hardback edition ISBN: 9781777880514

First edition: December 2021
10 9 8 7 6 5 4 3 2 1

WWW.AUTHORKGODIN.COM

This is a work of fiction. Names, characters, places, and incidents either are the product of the author's imagination or are used fictitiously, and any resemblance to actual persons, living or dead, business establishments, events or locales is entirely coincidental.

Copyright ©2021 by K. Godin. All rights reserved.

No part of this publication may be reproduced, stored in a retrieval system, or transmitted, in any form or by any means without the prior written permission of the publisher, nor be otherwise circulated in any form of binding or cover other than that in which it is published and without a similar condition being imposed on the subsequent purchaser.

Cover Design and Interior Layouts by Miss Nat Mack
Map by Amy Elizabeth Sayers
Editor Beth Attwood
Editor Lottie Clemens

To those who search for an escape in the pages,
I hope you find a sanctuary here.

Chapter 1

Death.

The air was heavy with the scent of it and the smell made my eyes water. Breathing through my mouth, I ducked my face away from the stench that wafted off the pile of bodies just a few yards away and lowered my eyes to watch my leather-covered toes as I scurried through the village. Lifting the deep green wool hood of my cloak up over my head, I glanced behind me for any observing eyes. My size had often made it difficult to remain unnoticed; my long legs and wide shoulders were not easily concealed amongst the typical small statures of the northern folk of Noorde Point, and I curled myself inwards in fear of being caught as I made my way to the boundary.

I had grown up here in the tight walls of the village, never venturing far past the tall wooden barrier that surrounded the lowly community. Instead, I had become rather fond of the way the giant line of trunks cast its shadow across the small worn-down sheds and houses in the afternoons, and truly, the line of bark was the only thing in the village that ever really made me feel small. Even now I had to lift my head while I rose on my toes to scan for the sharpened tips of timber that pointed to the sky. I was still a few strides away, and with one last glance at the pile of corpses that were covered in a thin white sheet, I lumbered through the narrow back street that led to the opening I had made at the bottom of the wooden wall.

Finding the hole easily, I tucked my long fingers into the soft, worn leather gloves I had stolen from the tavern and dropped to my knees in front of the thick wooden barrier. I winced at the icy sludge that now soaked through my breeches, and my hands grasped at my pack before shoving it through the opening. Certain it was sitting safely on the other side, I slid my way through the hole on my stomach, doing my best to shuffle my massive length under with whatever grace I could muster.

Belly crawling the last few feet, I immediately regretted not bringing more clothing with me as I tried to keep as much of my torso out of the mud. I had been in too much of a hurry to pack accordingly, trying to make a swift escape while my parents had been distracted with the small remnants of the fall harvest. It had been a dry summer and a worse autumn, the cold roaring in faster than it ever had, and no one had been prepared for the onslaught of frost and frigid temperatures. Least of all my family. Our crops would not last us through this winter, though now it was the least of our concerns.

What had brought our village to its knees was the fever that had torn its way through the community. It shook us to the core; it was unlike anything we had ever seen. Most infants succumbed to it overnight, and the elders had not managed any better. The councilmen said that it had come from a travelling ship that had docked south in Port Gordian, that the strangers from the west had brought it, and from there it had spread across Elrin before finally reaching us in the north.

Noorde Point and our neighbouring villages had been greatly affected and received little help from the immortals of Wahstand, who were unchanged by the disease. In fact, when we wrote to them in desperation, we received only a single letter back from the capital. It had been full of empty well wishes and a retelling of a similar fever that had swept through Elrin hundreds of years ago, just before the war. Perhaps it was a cautionary tale, or maybe a harsh reminder that humans did not fare well when a sickness overtook the lands. Either way, it was obvious that they would not send aid for a community of lowly mortals.

For weeks we had gone without any remedy until gossip had begun to spread of a witch in the west end of the Swallows, a legendary marsh that was hidden away in the trees. It was said that she was a Healer's halfling and had the ability to craft a tonic to fight the fever. Of course, I had initially mocked the whispers, but as the fever spread through the townspeople, I grew more desperate, willing the quiet chatter to be true. I had discussed my idea with Elizbeth, who had originally argued with my rashness, but as more and more of us perished she was forced to agree. We were willing to try anything at this point, and so, I found myself leaving my home in search of a cure.

Now kneeling, I took out the long wool scarf Elizabeth had made me in preparation for this journey. She had been insistent in helping me in any way she could, and with the gusts of wind blowing into me, I was grateful for her thoughtfulness. The landscape this far north was unforgiving, with more wilderness than settlements, though it was beautiful. Northern Elrin was filled with dense forests and high hills and cliffs. In the summer some may even call it paradise, but now, as I pulled myself to my feet ankle deep in mud and old leaves, it felt like a wasteland. A wasteland I had decided to journey across based on the gossip circling behind closed doors.

Trudging through the darkening woods, I shivered from the icy wind and eerie silence as I set a strong pace. The air was oddly still, and the only noises heard were my footfalls and heartbeat that rang in my ears. Tugging my hood closer, I tried to pretend that the light of the day was not disappearing between the thick branches of the cedars that towered above me, ignoring the way the limbs of green reached for the last glow as if they were desperate for any taste of sunlight.

Pausing in the darkening woods, I pulled my compass from my cloak and remained still while I waited for the needle to point me towards my destination. But my eyes narrowed as the dainty piece of metal in the centre of the glass just spun and spun so quickly I couldn't tell the ends apart.

Tipping my chin, I searched around me for any sign that I was heading in the right direction, but everything looked the same. I could have been walking in circles and I would have had no way to tell. I balled my fists and my eyes filled with tears of frustration. I had no idea how long I had been walking; the shortage of sunlight had thrown me off and now I was disoriented. I tucked the compass away, my fingers sliding across my leather belt until they found purchase on the cold handle of my dagger. I grasped it in my fist tightly before pulling it from its sheath and continuing on.

"Skylahr."

My name was whispered through the trees as if a nymph spirit was taunting me from afar, slurring my name through drunken, lustful lips. It was a quiet voice, full of wanting, and it sent shivers down my spine, making my stomach drop in panic.

Lowering my hood to give myself better vision of the area surrounding me, I hurried my pace, but the change of speed and adrenaline made my feet unsteady, and I had taken only half a dozen strides before I was slipping on ice and tumbling to the ground. Lifting my hands to catch myself, I forgot the cold steel clasped in my palm, and the sharp edge of metal clipped my right wrist, making a clean, narrow slice through my sleeve and into my skin.

"Shit!" I hissed and lifted my arm to inspect the wound, the harsh sting too distracting to ignore. Blood oozed sluggishly, the crimson bright against the pale skin that surrounded it. However, it was not deep enough to seriously harm me, and I sighed with relief.

"Thank you, Jester," I murmured to the God of luck. An inch over and I would have cut through the prominent blue vein. Pulling my sleeve back up, I sat back on my heels and took in my surroundings. There were still no sounds or signs of another living creature, and it soon became obvious that I was ill prepared for this excursion. I would be very lucky if this spill was my only one while I crossed the icy forest floor, and I was close to venturing past the point of no return. And though I had not located the Swallows, I knew I needed to go back home and figure out a better way to make the journey. Next time I would have to bring more supplies with me and apparently find a new compass. I made a mental list as I turned to follow the footsteps I had made in the damp soil, but as I searched the ground, three were all I counted. Apart from those prints, there was no other sign I had been in the forest. It was as if someone or something had come in behind me and swept away my trail, and the thought had the hair on the back of my neck standing on end.

Cursing angrily, I sheathed my dagger as a precaution before I pulled my hood up and began to run. My long legs covered the ground swiftly, however, I was not fast enough. The years spent hunting with my father had taught me to follow my instincts and if they were right, whatever whispered my name had found me and I was no longer the hunter but rather the prey.

Darting rapidly to the side, I found the closest trunk that would hide the bulk of my size and ducked behind it, kneeling to make myself less visible. Holding my breath, I leaned against the bark while listening to the air around me and closed my eyes to focus. To my right, I could just make out the sound of wet, frozen soil squishing beneath a heavy weight.

Four even steps, I thought to myself.

So not human then, but a beast, and a beast of considerable size— something small wouldn't be so noticeable. Bent low to the ground, I waited and waited for the animal to make an appearance, but I was still alone. Whatever it was had left, or it was observing me—I couldn't be sure which. Anxiety punched through my chest while I tried to come up with a strategy. I could run and pray to the Gods I would make it, or I could sit and wait it out, which could inadvertently make me an easy catch.

I remained still for two more heartbeats before I took my chance.

Bolting left, I twisted and turned as I attempted to dodge whatever attack was coming, not taking the gamble to look back, even when my lungs burned from exhaustion. Instead, I ran faster, pumping my arms while I willed my legs to carry me. I ran for what felt to be miles but found no light, no clearing, and the trees never seemed to end.

Even when my hair matted against my sweat-slicked forehead and my chest ached, I was still in the cover of darkness. If anything, it felt as if I was running deeper into the woods, like the world had turned on its side and everything was backwards.

Skidding to a stop, I doubled over and braced my hands on my knees while I gulped in the cold air. The frost burned the back of my throat while my legs wobbled, knees knocking in the effort to hold my weight. My cheeks were damp from the tears that had escaped, and I wiped them away roughly before pausing. For a moment I heard nothing, but then the four dull thuds were inching closer and closer.

Consumed by my panic, I hadn't even noticed the unfamiliar warm tingle that had started in the base of my spine until it had grown into a flame of heat that burned through my veins. Gasping in pain, I cried out as the inferno crashed through me, certain that this was what it felt like to die.

"Huntress, protect me," I prayed to the dead Goddess, and then my world went black.

Chapter 2

Pain was the first thing I was aware of when I awoke. A deep throbbing ache echoed through my head, like my heartbeat had been given occupancy of my skull and began to pound away in there. Squinting my eyes open, I turned to my side and retched onto the floor. My throat burned as I emptied my stomach, heaving and spluttering until I had nothing left to give. I wiped my mouth with the back of my hand as I pulled myself up, taking deep breaths before looking around me.

I had been prepared to find myself in the middle of those damn dark woods, ready to try to patch my skin together and accept my fate. But none of those things came to pass. Instead, I was perched on the edge of my bed back home in Noorde Point.

"How in the hell?" I whispered as I peered down at myself. I still wore the same breeches and tunic I had on the day before, though they were filthy. Glancing down at my feet, I noticed my boots too were covered in dried mud, ending the trail of dirt that was scattered across the floor from the doorway. Closing my eyes, I pressed my palms against the lids to soothe the hammering in my skull while wondering if it all had been a nightmare.

But as I cradled my face, I remembered my fall and I tensed, waiting to feel the inevitable stinging pinch from the scratch on my forearm, and yet, no pain came. Lowering my arms, I winced at the morning light before tugging my sleeve down. There was indeed a rip right through the rough material, but the skin underneath was smooth, not even so much as a scratch blemishing the skin. However, the relief of being uninjured only added to my confusion. If I had indeed dreamt the entire thing, why was there so much evidence to the contrary? Had I reached the point of exhaustion that I had been delusional? Was that even possible? Or was it the fever? Maybe I had finally fallen victim to its clutches.

My head spun and the feeling of acid bubbling up my throat came back to me in heavy waves. Swallowing the bitterness down, I stood on weak legs and stumbled blindly to the wash basin that was perched on the dresser. Holding the edges of the wood in my hands, I took a deep breath before wringing out the cloth that was folded next to it. I wiped the sweat and grit from my face before tearing my tunic off over my shoulders. My breeches and boots came next, piling onto the floor in a heap, and I made myself as presentable as I could, watching my reflection move in the dusty mirror that hung in front of me. My round face was pale, and the only normal colour left was the splash of freckles over my nose. My eyes had deep blue shadows under them, making my appearance even more unappealing than it usually was. My wide shoulders were hunched, and I looked sickly with my bronze waves in disarray.

Perhaps I had caught the fever after all and it was all an illusion, even last night.

I quickly pulled on new clothes, searched for an alternate pair of boots, and cleaned the sickness from the floor before throwing my door open. Racing forward, I had managed only two long strides before colliding with a slightly smaller body in the hallway. The other person was sent sprawling to the ground in a tangle of long, thin limbs. I blinked down at them only to realize it was Liam Roy, the blacksmith's son. His mop of mousey-brown hair was a tangled mess as it blocked his plain dark eyes from me. Awkwardly, he pulled himself up, his head coming just to my brow bone before he looked sheepishly at my face.

"Skylahr!" he greeted cheerfully but his voice cracked, causing crimson to fill his cheeks.

"How are you? Are you alright?" Liam paused, looking over my shoulder into my room before prattling on. "What happened last night? You were acting so strangely, I wanted to be sure you were well." He stuffed his hands into his pockets while he shifted from one foot to the other nervously, talking so quickly I was unable to respond.

Recently, I had even less patience for Liam than normal. He had spent the majority of last winter chasing me around the village, insistent that we should marry. His only reasoning being that it would give me security that most women desired at my age, and it would help me avoid the scrutiny I was often on the receiving end of. Little did he know, however, I was fully aware that his father was longing to get a hold of our lands, and a union between us was the easiest way to secure them. I had refused to be a bargaining chip then and now I refused purely out of spite. I had too much pride to give in.

"What are you going on about?" I asked, finally focusing enough on his words that I was able to register them. What could he possibly mean? Had I said something about my travels in the forest? Would I be reprimanded for sneaking out through the wall?

"You don't remember?" he asked with a tilt of his head, eyes lingering on my chest too long for my liking before he glanced away shyly. "I had called on you earlier, but your parents didn't know where you had gone, and Elizabeth would not tell me either, so I waited for you."

Ignoring the shiver that ran down my spine at the thought of Liam lurking around my house, I let him continue. "Then when you finally appeared, filthy and covered in mud, I called out for you, but it was as if you couldn't even hear me."

I stood in front of him for only a moment longer before pushing my way past and out the front door. Given that the entire night felt like a fantasy my mind had conjured, I had imagined that the outside world would have been different in some way. However, standing in the entrance of our home, I realized everything seemed as it should be. The smells wafted from the market two roads over, and the sound of the blacksmiths shoeing echoed in the air. The only things that were unusual were the glances and stares thrown my way. I had grown used to the looks of those who disapproved of my wardrobe or looked at my height and build with aversion, but these were neither. The people who I caught glancing at me turned away in what could only be described as fear, and some of the villagers went as far as to turn their heads towards each other and whisper quietly before scurrying away. Liam was right; I had obviously made a spectacle of myself even if I couldn't remember doing so.

Sighing angrily, I dropped my chin down, my shoulders caving in on themselves in an attempt to make myself smaller before I began a brisk pace with Liam close on my heels. Pausing at the chicken coop, I heard the voices of my parents arguing in the barn, and I waited until I was certain I would not be seen before I hurried up the hill towards Elizabeth's.

Watching my feet until I reached the top, I was seemingly unaware of the person approaching Liam and me until she was too close to avoid. I recognized her as the baker's daughter, though I could not place her name. Was it Millie? Maybe Molly? We had only one formal introduction at the summer festival earlier in the year, and her cold eyes and twisted grimace at my large appearance had been all the information I needed.

She tugged up her skirts as she quickened her steps to reach us, and when she was an arm's length away, I noticed her eyes had not been set on my face but rather Liam's. She reached a hand out to rest on his elbow before smiling sweetly at him.

"Liam! Hello!" She waited for his answering grin before narrowing her brown eyes at me, and I lifted one brow while glaring back. Seeing her as my opportunity to make my escape, I turned to Liam and attempted to excuse myself. However, he was pushy as ever and tried to pull his arm away from Millie-Molly in order to follow me. The girl huffed in irritation before setting her attention back on me. I watched as her face went from hostile to puzzled, her eyes holding my own, looking from my left to right, studying them closely.

"What?" I snapped angrily, growing impatient with her gawking.

"Your eyes…" She paused, now looking more nervous rather than confused. "They're hazel."

I slid my gaze from her over to Liam and back, waiting for either of them to elaborate, but in Liam's defense he looked just as perplexed as I was. My hazel eyes had always been the only feature of my face that was worth taking notice of. They were not just a light brown with a mix of grey, but rather a combination of emerald greens, golden hues, and flecks of what could only be called silver. They stood out from my awkward plain face and were difficult to miss.

"Yes." I nodded dumbly, confirming what I already knew.

"But yesterday they were…blue." She whispered so quietly I could barely make out the words over the cold wind that blew around us. Liam took a step closer to her in what seemed to be concern, his brows pinching.

"Mabel, what are you talking about?" Oh, Mabel. Right.

"Liam, I saw her come through the gates last night." She paused before throwing a suspicious glare back at me. "And her eyes were blue. A striking ice blue."

Liam and I looked at each other, neither of us saying anything. Perhaps she had been too far into her wine? Or had the fever taken her too and these were the early symptoms?

Liam was far more concerned than I, and as he studied her carefully, I saw another opportunity. Using his worry as an opening, I firmly excused myself again, watching as Liam cupped her elbow to spin her towards her father's bakery with a reassuring hand on her back. When they had disappeared from sight, I continued on my way, though my mind was spinning at her odd reaction. Although I could not recall the night before, there was no possible explanation for what she had dreamt up. She was obviously mistaken.

The familiar narrow path that led to Elizabeth's modest house was a comfort. I knew my friend would be able to aid me in my confusion; she had that way about her. Always logical and full of reason. She would most definitely have an answer for my missing memory, or at least a theory of some sort.

Lifting the latch on the solid wooden door, I entered. The home was warm, the fire burning hotly in the far side of the small kitchen, and I could hear her humming in the back room where the spices and flour were kept. I crept around the corner and waited patiently, listening to her light footsteps pad their way closer until I had the perfect time to jump from behind the wall. Her shriek echoed around us loudly before she threw the cup of wine she was holding in her hand at me.

"You asshole!" she swore while her pale, delicate face regained its pretty colour. Elizabeth's deep brown eyes narrowed up at me as she tipped her head back to study my face carefully, her gaze taking in the blue shadows that hung tiredly under my lower lashes.

"What happened?" she asked while ushering me to take a seat at the feeble wooden table, glaring at me when I tried to refuse. Elizabeth was small but mighty; she barely came to my shoulder, but on a bad day even I was afraid of her. Unwilling to argue any further, I dropped into the chair while she observed me carefully.

"I don't know. That's why I'm here. I have no recollection of last night, and I was hoping you would have some insight." I shrugged.

"Nothing whatsoever?" Her forehead wrinkled in concern.

"This morning I woke up in bed, covered in mud, and the final memory I have from last night is getting lost looking for the Swallows. Something had been following me and I had run as far as I could and then—" I paused, searching for some way to explain what came next. "And then nothing."

"Nothing," she repeated, frowning at me.

"That's it. Just black nothingness."

Unfortunately, Elizabeth had never mastered the skill of concealing her feelings and her disappointment was evident. I knew she had hoped that I would return with answers or even better—a remedy. The last thing we had anticipated was an entire night forgotten and nothing to show for the trouble of my journey.

The fire burned and cracked behind us while we sat in silence, neither of us certain what to say next, and I sighed as I trained my eyes on the glass window that looked out into the street. The roads had been less crowded with the fever spreading, but it seemed even more empty than usual today, and the vacancy only echoed my failure while the feeling of hopelessness filled the room. Now that the fever was rampant, we would all succumb to it eventually, that was for certain.

My chest filled with grief, and as I sat there beside the fire, I bowed my head and prayed, silently begging for someone or something to hear me. But the Gods were silent, as silent as they had been for the last five hundred years, and the familiar pressure of desperation fell on my chest again.

My voice broke the quiet.

"Tomorrow." I swallowed, decision made. "Tomorrow I go back."

Avoiding my parents had been easier than anticipated that afternoon when I returned. I knew that they had to have learned about my sneaking off, but they did not speak of it. In fact, the only thing my mother mentioned was the mud I had trudged through the house. If only I had been so lucky with the rest of the town. Try as I might, I could not avoid the whispers that echoed behind me on the winds when I passed through the streets leaving Elizabeth's. Peering eyes and judgement followed me wherever I ventured for the rest of the day, only confirming my bold entrance through the gates the night before had drawn more attention to myself than normal. So much so that the tales of my whereabouts that night had grown as the day wore on, some theories surprising even me.

It was said that I had a lover, tucked away past the village limits. Though the more believable rumours said I was scouting beyond the walls to find my family new land in hopes of escaping the fever, only to be shunned by the creatures of the forest. Or perhaps I had lost my mind to the disease and had gotten lost in the delusions. That particular rumour had struck a chord, leaving a sick feeling in my gut. After all, had I not come to that same conclusion? Pushing the whispers from my head, I waited until my parents turned in for the night before heading back to Elizabeth's.

In the cover of darkness, I slipped into her home carefully, and we sat ourselves in front of the fire again, devising a strategy while we slurped on watery broth and tea. When the details were finalized, Elizabeth had taken my empty pack and filled it with all that she could spare before hugging me tightly and sending me off into the night. We knew waiting until the dawn of the following morning was not an option any longer; I needed a time where I would not be seen. And now that people had a reason to observe me more carefully, daylight would no longer be practical. Not to mention the guards that had been stationed at the gate.

Although we were not prisoners in our homes, we were expected to report our travels, and I was sure busting through the wooden entrance in the middle of the night would not bode well for me. Nor would escaping through the secret jagged hole in the wall for a second time. Additional chances were not freely given by us people of the north. It was not what we were taught.

So, although I was thankful for the darkness that kept me hidden from prying eyes, I couldn't help but long for the warmth of the sun as I crawled my way through the opening. When I had finally made it clear through the border, I jogged into the cover of the forest before pulling Elizabeth's compass out of my pocket. This time I wanted to make certain that the needle did in fact sit and settle one way before I entered farther into the looming woods.

Having a clear indication west, I tucked the compass back safely under my cloak. The forest was nearly black and I tried my best to keep my breaths steady. Panic would not be a friend to me tonight if things did turn badly again, and I needed to keep my wits about me if I wanted to have a chance of making it to the Swallows. Luckily, once I was through the threshold, the trees were not as intimidating this time around, and I wondered if it was because something had changed or if I was more prepared for them. Moving quickly through the dense forest, I willed myself to look back only once, making sure that the light from the village behind me was gone before I was truly surrounded by blackness once again.

I had managed to walk a distance before my shoulder began to burn and tingle where the strap of my sack hung, its heavy weight swinging back and forth with every stride, and I was cautious of the strong movement. The added bulk could easily tip me over if I lost my footing, resulting in a worse injury than a minor cut to the wrist. Mindful of that, I switched shoulders and observed the woods. They were still just as silent as they had been, but the sour taste of fear was absent from my tongue. Feeling more at ease, I walked with purpose, this time sure of the direction. However, in case my compass had steered me wrong, I made sure I would be able to turn on my heel and walk straight back. At one point I had thought to leave clues or a trail, but I could only imagine what may be lurking in this place, and I could not risk the chance of leading anything back home. If I were to die, I could take comfort in knowing my family's safety would not be jeopardized by my poor judgement.

Continuing my straight path, I realized all sense of time disappeared as my surroundings grew darker, and had it not been for the burning in my legs, I would have thought I was a mere few yards from the village. My thighs were strong from farm work and labour, but covering this amount of distance at such a strong pace for so long made them ache to my bones. Finally, when I could no longer ignore the cramping, I searched for a dry clearing where I could rest.

The air came through my dry lips in little bursts, the steam swirling around my eyes, and I tucked my cloak tightly around me before kneeling on the small patch of dry ground that I had found. I would rest for a moment and then continue, I promised myself as my pack slid from my shoulder onto the soft soil, giving my body immediate relief. Pulling it across my lap, I struggled to open it with my cold, stiff fingers.

"Shit," I cursed under my breath while my fingers slipped over the freezing metal buckle half a dozen times before I brought a gloved hand to my mouth. Pinching a leather fingertip between my slightly crooked front teeth, I tugged the material off. Exposed to the air, my fingers flinched before finally getting the buckle open, and I grasped at the stale bread and the wool scarf before taking both out. I wrapped the wool up and around my hair to protect my ears from the cold, then quietly snacked on the crust of the bread while I regained my strength. Swallowing loudly, I finished the crust before closing the buckle tightly and swinging my bag up over my shoulder once again. When I was sure-footed, I tucked the wool tightly against my chin before readying myself to continue.

Falling into a steady pace, I again took in the seclusion of the forest. Though tonight the quietness and isolation were a relief. The attention I had received the previous day had been unwelcomed and the gossip ate at my nerves. I had always been different, never fluttering my lashes at the men or gossiping with the girls my age. My physical appearance was not one of beauty, and I was often found to be too intimidating to welcome the attention of my peers. In fact, I was regarded as unpleasant looking; my shoulders were wide set, my arms were heavy with muscle, my hips were awkwardly placed, and I stood at least a head taller than the men. But being in the forest now, I finally felt small compared to the trees around me. They dwarfed me completely and I was strangely giddy with the feeling. Being in the wilderness of the north had always brought me peace and I was pleased that tonight was no different. It was so unlike the day before.

Losing track of the distance I had covered, I noticed that the woods had begun to thin. The cover was no longer the thick darkness it had once been, and I realized dawn was near as the golden hues of sunlight peeked through the branches. I wished I knew how close I was to the Swallows. There was no definite path; the legends of the magic marsh had been passed through the northern villages for years. But no one had any actual idea if the place existed, and as I walked on under the bright morning sun, I felt defeat sink in my stomach like a rock.

Basking in the warmth of the light, I stopped in my tracks and closed my eyes. I had been walking for hours and there was nothing to

show for it. In fact, I couldn't help but feel that this had been a fool's errand. There was no known evidence of this witch's existence besides idle gossip and I wished I had found another option. Especially now that I had travelled an entire night only to find nothing. There was no sign of any marsh, be it magic or not.

And now it was time to turn back.

Spinning on my heel, I moved forward only to stop midstep as something caught my eye to the right of me. There tucked behind two ancient oak trees sat a small house. It was made of stone and clay with wild bushes covering the front, and up along the sides, vines twisted like some sort of growth. Initially I thought perhaps it had been abandoned, but on the back corner sat a chimney with clouds of smoke slithering out of it.

I grabbed at my dagger and approached the house, taking each step cautiously while I waited for some sign of life. But as I was about to reach the entrance, the door slowly cracked open with a loud groan. Examining the opening, I could just make out one single cloudy eye peering at me from around the wood, its brown colour diluted by a film of grey, and I swallowed before stepping back and raising my dagger in front of me.

Holding my position, I waited as a husky chuckle came from behind the wood and the cold sound of it sent shivers down my spine. Slowly the door swung wide and the motion stopped my heart as I took in her appearance. Before me stood what I thought was to be a woman—she was small and terribly thin. Silver hair hung limply past her shoulders and her face was pale, almost grey, with a purple tinge to her lips. I had seen features like this only once before, the same colour of skin belonging to a woman who had tumbled into the sea only to be pulled out a day later. She too had brown eyes with a fog painted over them, staring blankly into space. But this creature in front of me appeared to be very much alive.

"Skylahr Reed." Her mouth had barely opened but my name was loud and clear, her voice a terrifying hiss that churned my stomach.

Narrowing my eyes at her, I braced my weight in my knees. If she were to approach, I had to be ready. Her murky eyes watched me carefully, and she smiled, noting my defensive stance, but did not come any closer.

"I have come from Noorde Point. I need your help." My voice shook as she laughed at me, her lips curling over rotting teeth.

"You come asking for my service and yet hold that knife as if I am some pig to slaughter?"

I exhaled loudly before lowering my arm. I knew I could not trust her, but I dropped my hand anyway. I had come all this way and to turn back now would be an act of cowardice.

"Please. I've been told you could help me. A fever has spread like fire through my village and people are dying." I lowered my chin hoping to appear smaller, to appease her in some way. "Please, I need your help. I will do anything."

She studied me closely, and it seemed that my change in posture and my pleading had been all the action needed as she glided towards me, her dirty skirts swirling around her feet. Watching her warily, I clenched my jaw shut and closed my eyes, bracing myself for contact as she lifted her pale, thin fingers towards my face.

But just as I felt her freezing touch graze my skin, a deafening roar shook the earth I stood on. The noise was so loud it forced my lashes to flutter open just in time to see her sneer as she glared over my shoulder.

"You brought a friend." It took seconds for her words to register and then I too peered backwards.

There, within arm's reach, stood a massive beast—a wolf larger than any horse I had ever seen. He had black fur that shimmered in the sunlight, and I watched as he moved his paws shoulder width apart. Bracing himself on his forehand, he lowered his head in a snarl, his black lips pulling over massive white fangs as his growl rumbled from his chest.

Keeping my eyes on his muzzle, I grabbed at the hilt of my dagger with shaking fingers and turned my back to the witch, blocking her from the monster.

"What a surprise," she mocked over my shoulder. *"She thinks you are here for her."*

I shot a glance behind me before sliding my eyes back to the wolf, but his own cool silver orbs were solely focused on the woman, not even blinking my way.

"Behold, a gift from our mighty God the Protector."

Chapter 3

The Protector.

Did I hear her correctly? This massive beast was a gift from the God of old? My eyes flickered back to the witch, my face drawn in confusion before another snarl burst from the beast's teeth. The sound was nothing short of vicious as he crept closer.

He ignored me while he held the witch's stare, and I watched in fascination as his body stalked closer, moving silently until he was so near that I could feel the heat of his breath against my face. His snout moved slowly, bringing his wet nose to graze against my cheek before sliding it over my shoulder, and I stared straight ahead, not daring to look into his mouth as it opened in a growl. Spittle sprayed from his jaws and landed against my cold skin, forcing my pulse to quicken, and I became acutely aware of just how close those teeth were to my jugular. Teeth that were twice the length of my middle finger.

With one last deafening roar that made my ears ring, he sat back on his haunches, his eyes never leaving the witch, and the message was clear. He was not leaving.

No one moved while his cold silver eyes shifted to mine and I realized they were more human than beast. Holding his gaze for a long moment, I blinked at him stupidly before turning to the witch as her voice gurgled out from her throat.

"I heard you, you great beast. I will not harm her," she snarked at him

before raising her eyes to mine.

"You can communicate with him?" I asked, eyes wide, baffled. Her answer was a sharp grin before she jutted her chin out at the wolf.

"Well enough. He is worried I may take advantage of the lost lone trespasser. Rest assured you will leave my home alive."

Immediately I noticed she did not say unharmed, only alive, and my nerves grew when she opened her front door wide and gestured for me to follow her in. With one last glance at the black monster, I ducked through the doorway.

Folding myself into the chair she had kicked in my direction, I took in the dark room around me. The little house was filled with cobwebs and dust, and bits of rotting food lay on the floor, leaving the stench of the room so strong I felt the bread in my stomach turn. There were a dozen shelves hung on the wall, each one holding glass vials filled with brightly coloured tonics and concoctions, and I prayed to the Gods that one of them was to be my remedy.

"I am the Lady of the Swallows. You will address me correctly." Her voice was cold as her eyes held my own, and I nodded my head silently before dropping my gaze. Watching her slippered feet peek out from beneath her skirts, I noticed she moved around me with grace that could not be human, and I waited as she wandered back and forth across the room until finally her toes stopped just inches from my own booted feet. Lifting my eyes, I looked up into her grey face, waiting for some sort of instruction.

Her eyes were narrowed, her head nodding down, and I followed her gaze to her hand that was outstretched. Not understanding, I sat stock-still until she grew impatient and her fingers motioned for me to lift my own. I slipped my rough, warm hand into hers, and she twisted it so my palm faced up and then ran a finger across the callouses that coated the flesh. She gazed into my face, and her mouth opened in a horrifying smile before she yanked my limb in front of her eyes, her cold breath tickling my palm. I had been entirely enthralled by the way her clouded brown eyes followed across the skin that it left me distracted and totally unprepared for the yelp that came from my throat when her teeth sank into my flesh.

The pain was sharp, and as I tugged my hand away, she growled at me before biting down with more force. Blood seeped down my arm, running to my elbow and onto the floor, and outside I could hear the roar of the wolf. Surely he had heard my cry of pain, but could he smell my blood? Did he know she would do this? Finally, she lifted her mouth from my palm, her dark teeth now maroon in colour and her purple lips shining with my blood as she smiled at me.

"Delicious. It has been many years since I have tasted the blood of a maid so untouched," she purred at me, licking her lips slowly as if to emphasize her delight. Holding my hand to my chest, I ignored the blood that now was seeping into my tunic as my heart raced. Turning away, she grabbed a piece of cloth and held it out for me to take. My fingers hovered over the fabric uncertainly for an instant before I carefully took it from her grasp and wrapped the wound.

"You just—why?" My words stumbled out of me as I leaned back against my chair, creating as much space as possible between her teeth and my flesh.

"You came for a remedy, did you not?" Her voice was wet and clogged, her throat coated with my blood.

"Yes, my lady," I answered in a whisper, my injured hand curling in on itself while I watched her carefully.

"I had to be sure the trade would be worth it." She selected a large glass bottle filled with what looked like melted silver from a shelf and my eyes widened in surprise. The witch remained silent as she tipped it towards me, but just as I lifted my hand for it, she snatched the bottle away with a dark, taunting laugh. *"I still need the rest of your payment, child."*

Her skirts swirled as she strode to the mantel of the fireplace, her fingers tracing the dusty surface until she reached the middle of the ledge. There sat a dark wooden box, which she opened, pulling out a clean silver blade that gleamed in the glow of the fire. Spinning it around in her fingers gracefully, she then stood before me, her hand reaching for my own once again.

When my jaw went slack, she flashed me a predatory smile. *"You look like a rabbit caught in a snare. I don't want all of it. Just another taste."*

Unwrapping my hand, I gave her my silent agreement and watched while she dragged the blade across her teeth marks, widening the wound. I bit my lip to keep from gasping in pain, and I instantly knew I had been right about the smell of my blood when I heard another snarl come from the other side of the stone walls. Choosing to ignore the imposing threat of the beast, I trained my eyes on the blood that slowly trickled past the glass rim. The smell of rust and salt was strong and filled the space around us, and as soon as the jar was filled halfway, she pushed my hand back to my chest, obviously deeming the amount enough. Grabbing at the forgotten fabric, I rewrapped the palm and then watched as she slid the tonic towards me before pointing to the door.

Taking the cue to leave, I stood quickly, feeling light-headed but unwilling to stay a moment longer. However, just as my fingers touched the steel of the lock, I heard the witch come closer. Her cold fingers grasped the fabric on my shoulder as she pulled herself an inch away from my ear.

"A warning, child. I see crimson banners covering the hills and violet eyes that search for you. And with her hatred comes destruction and death. Those of half blood will finally perish. There is no stopping the Seductress. May the Gods protect you."

A shiver ran down my spine as she released my tunic, and I dared not look back at her as I pushed the door open. Squinting at the light that flooded my senses, I blinked to recover my sight before gasping when the wolf stood in greeting. His size once again forced my heart to stutter in my chest as he took a cautious step towards me. His black muzzle lowered, the wet nose snuffling at my arm until it pressed against my wrapped hand. Fearful that the smell of blood might provoke something in him, I shielded it against my chest before stepping out of his way.

The witch had called him a gift from the Protector. She had spoken as if the God of old had summoned this creature. But looking at him now from the corner of my eye, I was certain he was just a wolf. A beast who held magic I was sure, but a beast all the same.

The legends of the Gods had depicted the Protector in many ways. Some spoke of a great being with strength, others said he was humble and cunning. But one similarity they shared was that of his fierce protectiveness and loyalty and his love for the Goddess the Huntress. However, not one mentioned that he would have the power to call on monsters to do his bidding; I had never heard a tale such as this.

Walking slowly, I held my breath as my back turned to him. If he was going to kill me, it would be the perfect opportunity to do so now, and I waited for him to seize the chance. However, he chose instead to stroll quietly behind me, keeping a small distance away as if not to frighten me. I managed to wait until we were in the cover of the deepest parts of the forest before I stopped and turned to him. His silver eyes met mine as he tipped his head to the side, ears flickering in question.

"Are you going to hurt me?" I asked out loud. If he could understand the witch, perhaps he could communicate someway with me as well. Holding my stare, he dropped his head low and to the side and I waited for any other indication. When none came, I took that for my answer and decided to carry on. Keeping a safe distance from his long snout, I rubbed at my wounded hand.

A warning, child. I see crimson banners covering the hills and violet eyes that search for you.

The witch's words filled my mind as I put one foot in front of the other. The Seductress was once said to be the Goddess of love and truth and at one time she had fancied herself in love with the Protector. However, the God had turned her away for the Huntress and that had been the beginning of the end.

The Seductress's insane jealousy and rage over the Protector's mate had resulted in the War of the Gods, and it was said that she went mad with power, resulting in the creation of the Crimson army. The scriptures alleged that she had gifted her soldiers with immortality for their alliance and servitude, and they would be her defense against the Protector and his own immortal army, the Lupines.

She was the villain in our stories, and thus her name was rarely spoken. So why would the witch speak her name now? And what did she think the Seductress wanted with me?

Deciding it was just a tale to frighten me, I pushed all thought of the Goddess to the back of my mind and peered over my shoulder to glance at the wolf. His eyes were still watching me thoughtfully, and I wondered if he would follow me to the village. Would he be a threat there? I decided that if he did turn, I would slide the tonic through the gate and meet my end fighting. My fingers moved of their own accord as they felt under my cloak for my dagger. It wouldn't do much but if I aimed precisely, I could wound him enough to slow him down.

Completely focused on creating a plan in my mind, I had not noticed that the smell of the village had filled the air, and I squinted my eyes to see the smoke above the tree line. Blinking in confusion, I realized that the time it took to get out of the woods was a mere fraction of the journey I had going into them, and I knew then it must be magic. I wondered if it was the wolf's presence, but when I turned to face him I was met with an empty forest. His massive black body had disappeared in the space behind me, and my confusion twisted into relief as I bowed my head in prayer.

"Thank you, Huntress," I whispered before lifting my face and searching out the route to the wooden barrier. I confirmed I still had the tonic, and refusing to linger a second longer, I crawled through the hole before creeping my way to Elizabeth's, never pausing until I slid through the back door.

"I know you did not bring your mud into my house." My heart jumped before I turned around on my heel, my eyes wide as I blinked at my friend. Elizabeth was leaning casually against the wall, an apple in her hand while she watched me with a smug grin, her perfectly straight teeth gleaming with mischief.

"Ass," I hissed at her before sinking onto the bench next to me. She smiled before coming to perch at my side. Biting into her apple loudly, she waited for me to say something but instead I opened my cloak and handed her the glass bottle filled with silver. Her brown eyes widened at the sight of it before she took it from my hand. Studying it carefully, she turned to me.

"You found the swamp witch?" Her voice was filled with wonder as she ran a finger over the smooth, cool surface of the glass.

"I did, though there was very little swamp."

"And you lived. Colour me surprised," she joked, all while watching the silver liquid swish in its bottle.

Elbowing her sharply in the ribs, I sighed in exhaustion before tipping my head back and closing my eyes. I could tell she had a thousand more questions on the tip of her tongue, but I was too overwhelmed by the whole ordeal to answer any. Instead, I kept my eyes closed, not even noticing that she had stopped fiddling with the tonic to stare at me.

It wasn't until I felt her small hand touch the palm covered in blood that my eyes fluttered open. Gazing down at my hand, I took in the bare skin and realized the rag was missing from its place. Puzzled, I turned my hand over in her fingers, wiping the dried brown crust away. But there in the pale grasp of Elizabeth lay my own uninjured skin. The teeth marks were gone, the wound closed, and I was left with only a small pink line.

"How the hell?" I whispered before scanning the room for the piece of cloth that would be coated in my blood. When there was no sign of it, I rushed from the house and traced my steps back, ignoring Elizabeth as she called my name in worry.

Reaching the wooden wall, I crawled through the hole and marched back to the forest. I needed some proof that I had in fact been wounded. I did not want to wake tomorrow and question the events I knew to be true today. Not again. I could not handle it for a second time. And so, as my eyes searched frantically for the piece of cloth, I retraced my steps as best as I could.

When I had just barely entered the forest, I noticed something blowing in the wind. There, in the threshold of the trees, hung the fabric tied in a neat bow. Knowing there was no possible way the breeze could have done that, I checked my surroundings first before walking to the branch and gingerly untying the deep red cotton from the bark. Bringing it closer to inspect it, I knew it was in fact the same one, and I slid my gaze around the trees as if I was waiting for something unknown. But the forest was as quiet as it always was, and I stood stubbornly in place, refusing to move in hopes that some magic being would once again make an appearance.

Minutes passed slowly with no sign of another creature, but when I turned for home, I realized something moved behind the shield of branches and I lifted my head. Examining the green, my hazel eyes clashed with those glittering silver orbs again. But this time they were not sitting on either side of a long back snout. No, instead standing before me in the shelter of the bush was a man.

He was striking, not only impressive in height and build, but unworldly beautiful. And as I gazed at him, I knew there was no possible way he could be of this earth.

His torso was naked, the tan golden skin left bare for my eyes to trace, and they moved over his extraordinary chest to his thick arms and back up to his face. His chin was lifted in confidence, and I followed the sharp line of his jaw to his high cheekbones, then over a straight nose, not stopping until I circled back to the piercing silver eyes.

He watched me carefully, his own stare roaming over my form before he lifted a hand in greeting, and when the air left my lungs, he smiled, his perfect white teeth blinding against his full mouth. I remained rooted in my spot, and a horrid squeak pushed past my lips as I watched him take two long strides towards me. His head was held high as he closed the distance only to stop when a sudden howl echoed around us. Swinging his attention towards the sound, his brow furrowed, he looked back at me for an instant before disappearing suddenly into the dark.

I stood in a daze, my mind spinning as my desperation for answers grew. And as the feeling gnawed at me, the forgotten red cloth blew from my hand and tumbled in the wind.

Chapter 4

My dreams were filled with a chiseled face and stormy silver eyes the month following my visit to the Swallows. I dreamt of the rough voice that would accompany those features and what answers he may hold. But something dark and dangerous was lurking in the back of my subconscious, bringing the night terrors to the forefront of my mind. The swirling silver eyes and sharp jaw always melted into ruby-painted lips and violet eyes that were so deep they filled my lungs with terror, drowning me in my fear. The dreams always started the same way—I would be ripped from my bed, dragged into the town square, and forced onto my knees. Her eyes would stare down at me as I knelt in front of her, those lips lifting as she watched a sword swing down onto my throat. However, they didn't end there. I was then forced to watch as my parents met the same fate, their bodies crumpling to the ground while their blood soaked the snow. And as more time went on, the vision became more and more real, always resulting in my own panicked heartbeat startling me awake. By the third week, I was afraid to close my eyes, the fear of what I may envision keeping me from nodding off each night.

I did count my blessings though, thanking the Gods that the drama of my abrupt return the month prior had all but died down, and I was relieved no one had been aware of my second journey to the Swallows. I had not spoken a word of it to anyone but Elizabeth. However, I had kept the details of the strange man from her knowing

I had already piled too much onto her with little explanation, and I couldn't continue to expect her to hold my secrets when I had no answers. Luckily for me she had seemed happy enough with the remedy I had brought, choosing to ignore my weak lies and feeble attempts to change the conversation anytime it steered in the wrong direction. I had figured it was gratitude or maybe she was just too distracted with caring for the sick.

Elizabeth was a skilled healer and had taken it upon herself to dose out the potion any time someone new became symptomatic, and it would seem that our prayers had been answered. Though the silver liquid did not cure those who were too far gone, it did work wonders on the rest. And though I should have felt a weight lift as the fever cases declined, the pressing worry and terror of my nightmares had only taken up the extra space in my mind.

Sighing tiredly, I focused back on my task, lifting my pitchfork and tossing the soiled straw into the heap before wiping my sleeve against my brow. My tunic was damp with sweat from my efforts of keeping distracted with the chores rather than the lingering fear that followed my every move. I had already managed to clean the yards, chicken coop, and feed shed, and yet it still was not enough. Each time the air around me settled, an unnerving feeling lifted the hair on the back of my neck, and I was sure someone or something was watching me. Watching and waiting to strike.

Consumed by my paranoia, I had kept a careful eye on my parents and Elizabeth, always ready to shield them if the time came, but my silent hovering had begun to annoy them and I could see the suspicion in their eyes. Deciding it was best to busy myself, I willed my mind to believe I truly had nothing to worry about.

Finishing the stalls, I wiped my hands across my breeches and attempted to tidy my hair into a braid. Once somewhat organized I made my way through the fields, taking in the light snowfall that had covered the ground in a whimsical crystal dusting. It was the kind of snow that glimmered, untouched and perfect, the type that made the winter enjoyable. Relishing in the scenery, I unfolded the cloak that I had draped over my arm and placed it over my shoulders before picking up my pace. The fields were oddly empty, not a single person in sight, which was peculiar for this time of day, especially with the nice weather.

Ignoring the panic that had begun to set in my mind, I turned to the path that led into town but became more and more puzzled when I realized I was the only one around. Since the fever had slowed, Noorde Point had been bustling with newly acquired energy, so the calm made me eerily suspicious. My feet crunched over the snow as I hurried to the main road, and I quickened my pace when I heard the low murmured voices in the centre square. Pulling my hood down, I stood at the back of the group that had assembled, for once thankful for my towering height as I peered over the heads of those in front of me.

Moving my gaze, I searched the crowd until I realized what they had gathered around. There in the centre of the circle that had formed was the head of my family's bull, and my vision began to blur as I blinked at the dismembered head. Noticing movement to the right of the bull, I slid my attention and recognized my father's large frame folded in half as he knelt in the snow. And with shaking hands he rolled it over, inadvertently aiming its face directly into my line of vision. Gasps echoed around me in unison as we all took in the letters carved into the flesh between the unseeing eyes, but I remained frozen as I reread the word over and over.

SKYLAHR

My heart stuttered and I jumped when I felt a hand grab at my shoulder. Turning my dazed vision to focus on Elizabeth's eyes, I watched as her skin paled with worry. Lifting my attention to the people around us, I felt my own blood drain from my face. The entirety of the crowd turned their eyes to me in accusation, and my mouth opened but nothing came out. The world felt like it had spun sideways, and warm fingers grabbed at mine, tugging them harshly until I blindly followed her back from the mob.

Elizabeth's hand was firm while she dragged me through her front door and into the chair that was placed in front of the fireplace. Her hands fumbled as they struggled to light the fire, and she cursed quietly under her breath before peering at me through her long, thick lashes. Finally managing a spark, she blew on the kindling until the heat grew and then grabbed another chair to set beside my own.

"Sky." Her voice was hoarse and we both winced as she cleared her throat. "Skylahr." But what could she say? What was there to say? The bull had been a message, there was no argument about that. But from who and why?

Violet eyes flashed across my mind and my stomach turned in fear while my heart raced under Elizabeth's scrutiny. Pulling my cloak tighter around me, I leant forward and put my head between my legs as I blinked down at the floor under my boots.

"Sky?" Her voice was barely a whisper and I felt her small hand rub soothing circles over my shoulder.

"I need to leave." I had meant to keep the words in my mind but now it was too late to take them back.

"Leave? You can't leave." I had never mentioned the warning from the witch and now to do so, to even speak of it felt like putting a target on her back. Especially after the square.

Instead, I sat up and grabbed at her hands, cradling both in my own. I couldn't explain my reasoning, I knew that, but I prayed to the Gods that she would trust me in the same unwavering way she always had.

"I need to leave. You saw what was carved, I need to leave." Elizabeth's pretty face melted into a deep-set frown as she searched my eyes, her brown irises moving back and forth between my own.

"It was probably just a cruel jape." She winced and I knew she could hear the doubt in her own words.

"That was not a jape, Elizabeth. The girls can be cruel, and the men may dislike me, but no one would do that."

Her eyes flashed angrily at me; she knew I was hiding something. "Then who did?"

"I don't know, truly I don't. But I've obviously enraged someone, and my parents cannot risk anything more. That bull was one of our only animals left and now they will suffer for something I have clearly done."

Before she could ask me anything else, we were interrupted by a strong pounding on the door. I released the breath I had been holding, watching as Elizabeth smoothed her skirts before greeting our visitor. I could see my father's dark gaze as he searched the room, his face softening when our eyes met. Striding past Elizabeth, he squeezed her shoulder in comfort before he reached out to cradle me in his arms. I had been taller than my father since the age of five and ten, but I still felt small when he squeezed me tightly in his embrace. Even now my shoulders were almost as wide as his and my arms and legs nearly as strong, but I still felt like a little girl when he clutched me close to his chest.

"Oh, my sky and stars." His deep voice rumbled around us and I felt my eyes mist over with tears. He pulled away, his large hands wiping my cheeks before he directed me back into my chair.

"Da, I'm so sorry." I ducked my head as I folded myself into my seat. "I don't know who did it or why, but I promise I will find a way to buy another bull."

My father's brown eyes were gentle under his thick grey brows while he reached for me. "Sky, that is the least of my concern. All I need is to know that you are safe, that no one is going to harm you."

What could I say? That a witch had bitten me and I had traded my blood for a potion? That I had been warned and could have anticipated something like this? No, he would think me mad, or worse, he would believe me and want to protect me the way he always had.

"I promise, Da, I'll be fine."

Elizabeth's eyes narrowed at me over my father's shoulder and I quickly looked away. She knew there was more to it; I had not fooled her.

"Your mother is worried sick; I think we need to head home and put her at ease. Thank you, Elizabeth, for getting my Sky here so quickly."

Her eyes swiftly moved to my father as she smiled warmly at him, nodding her head. Leading me to the door, my father gave Elizabeth a firm hug before walking out the entrance, leaving us alone.

Thankful for the privacy, I glanced back at my best friend, my face hopeful that she would let me leave without any more prodding. Her dark eyes were suspicious, but her mouth stayed in a firm line and I took her silence as momentary acceptance of my story. Hugging her tightly, I made my escape home only peering back over my shoulder once. And as I gazed at her pale face, I prayed this would not be the last time I saw her.

Chapter 5

The sunlight that peeked past the curtains was warm against my face as I hugged my knees closer to my chest. My night had been filled with terrifying visions, so unbearable that I had woken dizzy and nauseous. The fear had forced me to empty my stomach thrice before I finally gave up on sleep, and even now my small clothes clung to me, still damp from sweat. With exhaustion blurring my mind, I calculated my next steps. If there was any chance of my dreams being a warning, if the bull had been a message, I needed to leave before my family was truly put at risk. Before all those horrid visions became real.

With one last deep exhale, I unfolded my body and stood on weak legs as I hurried to dress, before finding my warmest cloak and boots. Preparing myself for the frigid temperatures, I added a deep green jerkin and leather gauntlets before I took a moment to scribble out a note for my parents.

I'm sorry I did not say goodbye. I will miss you.
Love your sky and stars

It pained me to leave without so much as a quick embrace, but I had to gather the rest of my things and the glimpses of my dreams that flashed through my mind kept me from delaying. After placing the note carefully on the kitchen table, I finished packing and rummaged through my parents' wooden chest. If I was to travel on my own, I needed more than my dagger, so I began searching for my father's blade. Finding the blue wool cloth that shielded the metal, I pulled it from the trunk. The cover had been a gift from Elizabeth to my father on his last birthday and I stroked the fabric fondly before removing it and fastening the sword to my hip.

With one last glance around my childhood home, I picked up my bag and lifted my hood. Sneaking out of the village had almost become second nature after the last two times, but this felt different. It felt final.

My escape would have to be perfectly timed if I wanted to avoid my parents. They had buzzed around me worriedly all evening, the scene from yesterday scaring even my mother, who had always been too proud and stoic to show fear. Thankfully though the work that would be needed for winter was more pressing than supervising me and both of them had left at sunrise to organize our farm. Creeping around the back of our house, I waited silently, praying to the Jester that I could somehow luckily make it to the wooden wall before being seen. Hitching my bag up higher over my shoulder, I made a mad dash towards the wall, not stopping until I was sliding into the rough bark and crawling through the gap.

Rather than travelling north into the forest, I crept around the wall and followed just off to the side of the road that led west. I would journey to Carlon, the western city that had been built in honour of the Jester. It was said that the Temple of Fate and Fortune had been the resting place for the scriptures, and if I truly wanted to understand the warning from the witch and the history of the Seductress, it was the best place to begin. From there I would go to Wahstand, Elrin's capital. I knew that there was a chance that I was being paranoid, that my dreams really had nothing to do with the bull and that it was all just coincidence. Maybe I had been fooled by an old woman who longed to play with the minds of the unsuspecting and the village men had found a new way to torment me. But something in my gut told me there was truth to her words, that my name carved into the carcass had been a warning of what was to come. And if that was true, the capital was my best option to find answers.

Wahstand was home to the Crimson army and the remainder of the Seductress's supporters who had been tasking themselves with preserving the capital and their bloodlines. Surely, they would have heard whispers of their once-followed Goddess if she truly had been conjured again.

Following the pathway to the main road, I noticed that it had remained empty and I walked at a brisk pace, for once grateful for the fever for it had scared most travellers off. Not needing to worry about strangers gave me the opportunity to observe the landscapes around me in peace. Northern Elrin truly was beautiful beyond reason. It was lush and green, the forests filled with cliffs and hills, crystal-clear lakes and waterfalls, and the smells of cedar and pine were always heavy in the air no matter where you were.

Completely distracted by the view, I had not noticed a group of five or so travellers off to the side of the road. They were huddled in a closed circle and I wondered if perhaps they were not used to the cold and were sharing warmth. Crossing to the other side, I kept a wary eye on them though they seemed oblivious to my presence. However, as I passed, I noticed a scuffle between the group that was rapidly growing in noise, and I chose to pick up my pace to avoid conflict. That is until I heard the shrill scream of a woman.

Stopping in my tracks, I watched as she broke free through the circle only to be grabbed and dragged back behind the men closest to the road. The woman's wide, frightened eyes caught mine over one of the men's shoulders and I knew I couldn't leave her. Placing my hand on the pommel of my blade, I prayed I would be strong enough and charged at them in hopes of breaking their hold. He collided harshly with the smaller of the men and tumbled roughly to the ground, causing his friends to turn sharply at the interruption. Using the distraction, I managed to knock another's grip off the woman but was caught unaware as a hand was tangled in my hair before it pulled my head back sharply. Groaning at the harsh sting, I swung my elbow roughly into the soft middle of my captor and a gruff curse was shouted at me while another hand reached blindly in my direction, only to be knocked away by my own. I had speed and size on my side, but there were so many of them and I had lost track of the woman during the chaos.

Praying that she had seized her opportunity to escape, I watched as the man who had been knocked to the dirt staggered back to his feet while he pointed his sword at me. The gleaming metal made me pause, giving two of the men a chance to seize my arms and pin them at an awkward angle behind my back.

"Ye stupid big bitch!" the man with the blade spat, his hand shaking. "Ye'll pay for this!"

The cold steel was held to my throat, the tip pressed with just enough pressure to break the skin, and a warm trail of blood rolled down my throat only to pool into the dip of my clavicle. Ignoring the sting, I watched the armed man with narrowed eyes and spat at him.

"Fuck you!" I snapped before kicking a leg out.

This only enraged him further. He lifted his free hand, closing it into a fist before slamming it down with enough force to split my cheek open. I hung my head while white speckles danced across my vision, and my world spun until fingers were in my hair again pulling my neck back. Anticipating the throbbing pain in my cheek and heaviness in my hair, I was left confused when my mind began to solely focus on that strange heat licking up my spine. It coursed through me rapidly, filling my stomach before it bubbled up into my throat and then my mouth opened wide as if I had been possessed. And in the back of my throat a noise so loud, so inhuman, built and built until I could no longer hold it in.

My roar shook the trees, causing the birds to flee from the sound and the men who were behind me to release my arms. I was free and yet the fire continued to spread, its flames licking at every inch of skin. I had just managed to watch the blade drop from the stranger's hand before the heat consumed me.

When I came to, I was sitting cross-legged leaning against a rough trunk of a tree, and with a pounding head and queasy stomach, I rubbed at my eyes. But the movement caught my attention when I felt my tunic stick to me and my vision dropped down before I gasped sharply at the sight.

My chest was soaked, coated in a spatter of blood that splashed across my front. It reached from waist to neckline and it covered both hands, caking under my nails. My breeches were also saturated and the strands of my hair closest to my face hung wetly, the normal light bronze now darkened to a brown.

With shaking hands, I opened my jerkin and lifted the hem of my shirt searching my skin for any sign of damage, but my palms slid across the flesh and found none. I then moved to roll the sleeves up to my elbows, still only finding smooth skin. The panic turned into confusion as I leaned heavily against the bark. Breathing deeply, I searched for my pack and it was then that I noticed where I was. Once again, I was back in the forest of Noorde Point. In the same damn forest I had travelled through just the month before.

"Why?" The words broke from me as I sobbed in frustration. Why was I back here? I had been a half a day's journey away from this spot and yet here I was.

Wiping at my nose, I stood as the smell of rust made me gag but I fought down the urge to vomit. I would not succumb to that weakness; I had no time for it. I needed to find shelter and build a fire after locating a place to wash the gore from my skin.

Moving quickly, I tried to ignore the wind that blew against me, its force causing the fabric of my clothing to cling to my body, freezing the blood to my flesh. I crossed my arms and tried to shield myself as I scoured the forest for a way to clean myself off.

Finally finding a stream, I unclasped my cloak before I knelt at the water's edge, taking a moment to stare at the face that shone below. My normally pale reflection peered up at me, but this woman was not one I recognized. My round cheeks were coated in burgundy making my normally berry-coloured lips look pale, the scattered freckles were not visible under the blood that painted my long nose, and my eyes were wide and dazed.

Unable to look at the carnage any longer, I dipped my hands into the river, splashing my face before I scrubbed at the skin until it was numb and raw. I then moved to my arms and torso, but gave up after a long minute and instead chose to lie on my belly and let the river soak through. When the freezing water around me went from crystal clear to a swirling pink, I moved back up to my knees. I trembled, the cold eating at my skin, but I pushed the sting away and bowed my head as I basked in the silence. Holding my face in my hands, I remained in that position until the sound of splashing broke my concentration.

Whipping my head up, I came face to face with a long deep grey snout and two dark eyes, and I sat frozen as the wolf sniffed at me loudly. His face moved, his muzzle snuffling at my cheek before he took a step back. His eyes continued to study me closely for another long second and then he threw his head back, howling so loudly I had to duck my face and cover my ears with my hands.

When the howl finally cut off sharply, I raised my eyes. The grey wolf was still there, observing me, but just behind his flank I could make out the shape of a familiar black body. He approached me slowly, pushing his slightly smaller companion out of his way before crossing the river to stand next to my side. I watched him carefully, my breath stuttering in my chest as warm air blew across my face down my neck, and I could hear the gentle snuffling as he searched my body. Lifting my hands in surrender, I cleared my throat.

"It's not mine." I wasn't sure he would understand my meaning, but I held my hands in their place as he circled around me. Focusing on his grey friend in front of me, I willed my heart to calm when I felt the snout poke into my ribs. What started as a gentle push grew into a forceful shove and I was knocked off my knees.

Scrambling to my feet, I created as much space as possible as the two wolves circled me only to be ushered between them. Confused by their herding, I began to walk, ignoring the two fur bodies that pushed me forward with low growls. We had made it a mere few yards before my feet had grown uncoordinated and I stumbled again. My clumsiness obviously irritated the wolves and the black beast huffed at me before pressing against my side. Not understanding what he wanted, I shuffled back only to have him push closer again. But this time his front half bent in what would be a bow, and he nudged his ribs against my hip.

Finally, it dawned on me.

"You want to carry me?" I questioned. His response was a short bark in confirmation while he pressed tightly against my torso. Resisting the urge to move away, I weighed my options. I had no pack, no weapon, and surely, I would die from the cold before I felt even an ounce of hunger, and he had protected me once before. Perhaps the Jester would gift me the same luck once again.

Making my decision, I ever so slowly reached out to run my fingers through the silk fur of his scruff. Twisting my hand around it, I hoisted one long leg over his withers before settling easily.

"Like riding a horse, right?" I whispered under my breath but caught the backwards flicker of his right ear.

Naturally, I gripped his barrel with my calves only to have his head swing back at me with a snap of his jaws in warning, and I shivered at the thought of those fangs grabbing a hold of me. Softening my seat, I stroked his shoulder in apology while doing my best to not shiver and shake on his spine. Finding my balance with practiced ease from years of riding, I gave him a gentle nudge of encouragement and then we were off.

The trees sped past us in a blur, but it was obvious that he kept his pace slow for my benefit as his pack mate had raced off as soon as I had mounted. Petting him again in appreciation, I noticed that the heat of his fur had begun to dry my breeches, however my body still stung from the cold. I leaned forward carefully, pressing my front against his warmth. His coat was the softest thing I had ever touched, warm and dense but not rough, even against my cheek.

The cheek that should have burned with any contact no matter how gentle it was. Sitting up to run my fingers over the bone, I felt no tenderness or pain. My fingers pressed harder in search of the open cut, but it too did not exist. Confusion swirled in my mind as I lay my chest back down, burrowing into the fur before allowing the gentle rocking of his gait to lull me into a daze.

I had no idea when I had nodded off nor how I had managed to stay on, but sometime later I became very aware that we were no longer in the forest. Instead, we were quietly passing through a small brightly lit town. The buildings were old but well taken care of and the streets were clean. Cobblestone covered the roads, and I was taken aback by its simple beauty. The wolf below me seemed unaware of my awe and appeared to be at ease walking through the gorgeous town, as if he had done it hundreds of times.

Lost in the village's finery, I had not noticed that we were now heading towards a massive set of stone stairs until I had nearly toppled backwards when the angle had changed. Leaning forward, I peered at the space between his ears and gaped at the most beautiful castle I had ever seen. It was perched on the edge of a cliff overlooking the town. It was tall and intimidating, and its walls were made of stone with big bright glass windows and high doorways. It was not overly done like the portraits I had seen of the manors in Wahstand but was rather simplistic and mighty in its splendour. Behind it stood the massive mountains, their tops a brilliant white, and I knew then we were in the Lupine territories. The home of the Protector's immortals, the place of legends.

Leaping up the rest of the stone steps, the wolf stopped and bowed at the entrance, waiting for me to dismount, and a woman appeared from behind the great wooden doors. Her frame was tall but slim and delicate, and she had rich, deep brown hair that reminded me of Elizabeth's. Though her eyes were cold as they watched me, and the soft golden skin of her face paled as she took in my bloodstained clothes.

Trying to ignore her gaze, I slid off the back of the wolf but before I could take a step towards her with an introduction, the other beast skidded to halt in front of her and opened his mouth wide.

I sprinted forward at her in terror, sliding to a stop when his wet, slobbery tongue lolled out his mouth and licked across her face. Her harsh scowl was replaced by a bright smile and a husky, deep laugh broke from her chest.

"Keyno!" she chastised before throwing her arms around his massive neck.

The beast seemed to nuzzle her back before his body vibrated, his bones shortening until the grey furred beast was replaced by a tall naked man and I gasped at the sight. I had never seen magic at work, and I was stunned while I watched the couple. Paying no mind to his nude tan skin, the man swept the woman into his arms and kicked the impressive-looking front door wide open. I gaped after them for long moment before spinning back to the black wolf.

However, when I had turned, the massive creature was gone, and my eyes focused instead on an eerily familiar muscled chest, which was even more glorious up close. The bronzed skin was smooth and tight across the bulging shoulders, and my mouth hung open as I traced his collarbones with my eyes before sliding them up his thick neck. Full lips were pulled into a smirk just below the strong, straight nose that was framed by high cheekbones. But just as last time, the most remarkable feature was his luminous silver eyes. In this proximity, they were bright but molten, like liquid steel, and I inhaled sharply when one black brow lifted while he leered back at me. Yet, before I could bristle at his expression, his lips parted and a deep voice that reminded me of a strange combination of smoke and honey rumbled from his chest.

"Are you enjoying the view, love?"

Chapter 6

My mouth hung open and I watched warily as he approached me. He had an air of arrogance that surrounded him, and it made me irritated and touchy. I had met men like him before, not nearly as handsome but just as overconfident. Narrowing my eyes, I studied him as he lifted his arms to cross in front of his chest, leaving the rest of him bare to my gaze. I huffed under my breath.

The urge to drop my eyes became stronger, and I struggled to instead lift them to stare just above his shoulder. I blinked into the space, and my attention focused back on him when I heard a warm chuckle break loose before he tried to come closer. Anticipating his pursuit, I dodged his forward step and spun to the left, distancing myself a few feet away.

He held his hands up in surrender and crooked one long finger for me to follow before turning to the open door. With his back left exposed, I took the opportunity to study him, but I had been left unprepared for the gruesome sight. There across his massive shoulder blades ran a jagged scar that reached all the way down to his hip. It was darker than the rest of his flawless skin, and the injury would have been fatal to any normal man. Realizing he must have heard my swift inhale, I watched as he stopped and turned his chin to his shoulder, his dark silver gaze flickering towards me before he lifted his head and continued inside. I, however, hesitated, wrapping my arms around my middle while I shifted from one foot to the other.

The light that glowed from the open door was warm and inviting, so tempting that my body almost betrayed my resistance when the smell of meat and bread wafted out in waves. Biting my lip as my mouth filled with saliva, I tried to remember the last time I had smelt such a meal. But it had been so long, I couldn't even recall the occasion. My stomach rumbled with hunger. I was dizzy with want, and yet my stubborn nature kept me in place, although I couldn't tell if it was due to fear or my pride. However, my determined absence must have been rather comical to the strangers, and I watched their shadows pass by the door with quiet laughter and whispers just loud enough for me to hear. Refusing to be seen as a joke, I stomped my way through the entrance.

"No need for all that now, you're shaking the roof right off this place." The words purred out of him in an annoyingly beautiful way, and he was in front of me again, this time in a deep black tunic embroidered with silver designs and a pair of dark charcoal-coloured breeches, leaving his feet bare. Doing my best not to react to him, I lifted my chin with a tight jaw and focused on the figure approaching us.

"Kalian! That is not how you speak to a lady!" She now stood directly behind him, and my breath caught when I took in her beauty. She was also tall in stature and had dark features like the rest but with pronounced curves and the posture of a true highborn lady. Her plain black dress fit her snugly but was astoundingly elegant as she glided towards him only to lift a hand to swat at the back of his head before pushing past with a hand out for me to take.

"I apologize for my son. He's more gentleman than beast, I assure you." She paused, gripping my fingers while gazing into my eyes kindly. Something about her put me at ease instantly. "I am Isla, welcome to Denimoore."

Son? She looked just a few years older than my own two and twenty years, and I would have thought they were siblings. Realizing they were most definitely immortals, I gaped at them until I noticed her expectant stare and I cleared my throat in response.

"Skylahr." My name sounded like a croak in comparison to her smooth voice, and I blushed as her other hand lifted to pat our joined palms before she turned to her son.

"Kalian, take her to find some fresh clothes and let her clean up a bit." She smiled sweetly before glaring at the massive man. "And do try to behave yourself for once. Please."

Turning back my way, she ushered me towards her son, who had the decency to look a little embarrassed by the scolding from his mother. It was then that I noticed just how immense his size was, even compared to my own towering height. My eyes came just to his shoulder and I had to tip my head back to see his face completely. He nodded at Isla sheepishly, and his silver eyes caught my own. The intensity had my gut swooping while heat rose to my cheeks.

"Dear?" Isla asked while placing a hand on my forearm.

"I'm sorry?" I asked in confusion, turning to her. She smiled at me with laughter and Kalian's own snicker echoed around us. Gone was the fleeting embarrassment on his face only to be replaced with the cockiness that was rapidly becoming all too familiar.

"I asked you if you preferred dresses to your tunics, but it appears you were...distracted." His deep voice rumbled, and my cheeks flamed while my jaw clenched.

"Tunics," I spat at him, not seeming to surprise him with my temper.

Shrugging at me, he stuffed his hands in his pockets before sauntering down a long hallway, whistling as he did so. Following behind, I winced when my footsteps seemed to echo loudly on the stone floor while his own padded so quietly you could barely hear them in comparison, and I watched my feet more closely. Too concerned about trying to remain quiet, I lost focus and collided sharply into his solid back. He had stopped in front of a room and I had been too busy awkwardly striding with my head down to even notice.

"Easy there." Kalian laughed while bracing my shoulders with his large, warm hands.

"Don't touch me," I snarled, pushing out of his grasp.

"Are you always so pleasant or do you reserve all of this fury for someone who saved you from freezing to death?"

"I didn't need your help," I growled through my clenched teeth.

"Of course not. I'm sure you had a handle on the whole situation. Covered in blood and freezing as you were."

I took a step closer to him, peering up at his face in anger. "I didn't ask for your aid."

Kalian smirked down at me, one brow lifting while a smug smile stretched across his mouth. He dipped his head down so close to my face that I could count the blue flecks in his eyes, and his breath was sweet as it fanned across jaw, making my lashes flutter.

"You didn't have to," Kalian whispered deep and low. My eyelids lowered as his voice swirled around me and I forgot to breathe. Completely in a daze, I hadn't noticed that one large palm rose to cup a shoulder, his thumb just making contact before the burning heat broke the trance I had been put under.

With speed I did not know I possessed, I snatched his wrist and tore his hand from me, watching as his own eyes widened in surprise at the movement.

"I said," I paused, inhaling deeply through my nose. "Do not touch me."

"So spirited." He tsked under his breath before pulling his arm away.

Kalian took a step back, straightening to his full height again before cocking his head to the side to study me. He must have found what he was looking for as his eyes softened into a look of pity that had my hackles rising. Sensing my annoyance, he blinked twice, replacing the sympathy with a cocky smirk I assumed he usually wore, and then he gestured with a hand for me to enter the room we stood in front of.

I pushed the door open, and my jaw dropped in awe as I took in the large bright room that was sprawled before me. Its walls were a light blue in colour with grey drapes that framed the window, which took up the entirety of the back wall, and in the middle stood the biggest four-poster bed I had ever seen. It was decorated in sheets that looked plush and soft and my body ached to crawl under them.

"This will do, I assume?" Distracted by the elegance before me, I had forgotten momentarily about Kalian's presence.

"Yes," I whispered under my breath. "But am I to stay?" I asked carefully.

"Only if you wish to."

"And if I don't?" My voice shook with uncertainty.

"Then you will change into dry clothes, and I will take back to where I found you." His voice and face seemed sincere, and I was so exhausted that I was unwilling to challenge him, though I knew it was because I truly did not have anywhere else to go.

"I'll stay, but just for the night."

He nodded in agreement as he entered the room and walked to the wardrobe tucked against the wall. He tugged the doors open and sorted through the clothes quickly before pulling a few choices out.

"They'll be a little small, I'm guessing." He paused, eyeing me, his smile lifting as his eyes lingered on my body. "But will work." Just as my mouth opened to snarl at him, a woman's voice called out from down the hall, and I craned my neck over my shoulder to glance behind me.

She glided towards us, one long golden leg pushing through the slit of her crimson dress with each step, the flesh exposed right up to the highest point of her thigh, leaving little to the imagination. Red silk clung to her wide hips and tiny waist, curving up over her ample chest with a deep, drooping neckline. Her black hair was slicked back away from her stunning face, and when her black eyes met my own, they widened in surprise before narrowing. She obviously had expected him to be alone.

Kalian, who had ignored her greeting, finally acknowledged her presence and came forward. He stopped at the entrance, his eyes catching mine before moving down the hall to the woman in red.

"Ah, Nadine." He nodded his head politely, his nonchalance causing a falter in her step. Her shoulders hiked up higher towards her ears while her long fingers balled into fists. Then she turned her murderous eyes at me. Kalian, however, paid no mind to her animosity, and his hand cupped my shoulder before pushing me into the room with a gentle shove.

"Get clean and change," he barked out at me before turning away, and I stood dumbstruck as the woman embraced him tightly, her fingers sliding into his hair before pulling his face down to her own. Kalian responded by loosely wrapping her in his arms before bending his head to meet her lips for a kiss. A kiss that was so intense, I couldn't help but feel that it should have been had in private. Caught by surprise, I was unable to look away and I heard her groan into his mouth before her eyes slid open. The black irises immediately found my own and she narrowed her eyes at me only to close them again a second later.

My embarrassment of being caught watching them had my face feeling as if I had been in the sun too long and I took a step farther into the room. Blindly reaching out for the cool brass knob, I looked anywhere but at the couple directly in front of me. Finally finding the metal, I curled my fingers around it and used more force than necessary to slam the door shut.

"When your mother said you had brought a woman home, I had expected something else. She's rather…odd. So tall and plain and that ridiculous scowl on her face," Nadine whispered just loud enough to be sure I heard.

Kalian's response was too low for me to catch, but I was certain it would have made my heart sink. *Giant. Plain. Better suited as a man.* I had heard it all before and had grown used to it from years of torment at the hands of my peers.

I knew his opinion really should make no difference to me. He may be glorious and handsome, everything young maidens dream of, but I was not so weak or petty.

Oddly irritated, I pulled my soiled clothes off and quickly replaced them with the clean set that was laid out for me. The tunic tugged at my shoulders and pressed tightly against my breasts, exposing a decent-sized sliver of my midriff. The breeches clung to the muscles of my thighs and were easily five inches too short, the hem landing midshin, leaving my ankles exposed. My boots would help conceal that, but the tunic was hopeless. I felt the frustration build as I tried my best to tug at the shirt, but there was not enough give in the fabric to stretch it out. Pulling again at the wool, I cursed when a knock rang out through the room.

My fists rubbed tiredly at my eyes and I opened the door, grimacing as

Isla's eyes dropped to the pale skin that peeked out above my breeches. She was graceful in handling her judgement of my appearance, doing her best to hide her reaction, and I was grateful for it.

"They're rather small." I sighed while wrapping my arms across my stomach, ignoring the sound of the fabric protesting as it stretched across my shoulders.

"That was thoughtless of me. I apologize, dear sweeting." She grabbed my hand and led me from the room and down the hall. We stopped in front of a pair of doors and she threw them open before moving around the massive room with practiced ease. She gathered a bundle of clothes into her arms, steered me back down the hall, and waited for me to change into what she had picked out.

The tunic was a deep green, fitting loosely down my arms, forcing me to roll the sleeves into cuffs. The pants, though long enough, were snug on my hips and thighs, obviously not made for a woman's body. But Isla seemed pleased with her choice, her brilliant smile warming her dark eyes as she clapped her hands together.

"Much better, but we must hurry, sweeting. Dinner is waiting for us." She looped her arm through my elbow with ease, and we walked linked together towards the main hall.

Her black skirts rustled as she pointed out the paintings and sculptures that lined the walls, only proving that the castle was just as impressive inside as it had been out. There was obvious pride in Isla's voice as she went on and on, and it was difficult not to be pulled into her warmth as she smiled so kindly at me.

Rounding a corner, we entered the dining hall and it too was just as impressive. The ceiling was high with paintings of what I assumed to be their ancestors covering the walls, and the table was long and dark, filled with dishes of meats and breads. The sight forced my mouth open in wonder, which had our spectators laughing quietly.

Snapping it shut in embarrassment, I let Isla steer me to an empty seat next to hers. Kalian was placed beside her at the head of the table, and on the other side of him was the man who accompanied us through the forest, though he was human and clothed this time. To his left sat the woman who had greeted us, her face still pulled down into a frown though the deep blue of her dress distracted me from it. There was an empty chair beside her and then Nadine, who was still glaring at me as she took in my appearance before quietly laughing behind the rim of her wineglass. While I was doing my best to ignore her, Isla patted my arm gently in reassurance. The woman adorned in navy watched this carefully before scoffing under her breath then swallowing a mouthful of red wine.

Feeling out of place, I stabbed at the meat sitting on my plate before cutting it roughly. But my force caused my knife to slip and the metal clattered against the dish noisily, which drew all eyes to me for an instant before everyone continued carrying on with their conversations. Nadine, however, smirked at me before whispering to herself, too low for me to make out. Though whatever she had said, however, had been loud enough for the woman two seats over to hear.

Slamming her fist against the table, the woman turned to Nadine. "Shut your mouth, *puore*," she snarled. Looking around the table in confusion, I realized I didn't recognize the word, but it made Nadine's face pale and her eyes drop.

"Leena!" Isla warned, and for the first time her voice held none of its usual warmth.

"She has no place at this table. Having Kalian between her thighs regularly isn't an exclusive privilege. She has no more importance than the others."

"Enough, Leena," Kalian's calm, deep voice commanded. "I choose who is a guest at our table and you can either shut your mouth and eat or you can leave."

If Leena was going to challenge him, the anger simmering in his silver eyes stopped her as he stared her down for a long moment while waiting for her response. When he received none, he picked up his fork and began to eat once again. The room was silent and uncomfortable as I picked at my food, and although my stomach begged me to eat faster, I couldn't muster the courage to draw attention to myself while everyone sat on edge.

Dinner passed without so much as another word, and once the table was cleared, Isla vowed to show me more of the family's treasures. Too grateful for the full belly to refuse, I stood from my chair and nodded my head to the rest of the table before following her out. Moving quietly behind her, I tried my best to ignore Kalian's watchful gaze as it burned across my back.

Isla led me in the opposite direction as before, taking her time to show me the corridors and rooms. The castle was massive and yet it felt warm and comfortable, not at all what I would have thought a building this size made of stone would feel like. Turning around a corner, she led me to a wide hall, its windows stretching from floor to ceiling, giving the most spectacular view of the town down below. The roofs were coated in snow that gleamed under the light of the stars and moon, their shine only being outdone by the glistening tops of the mountains that surrounded the village. It was breathtakingly beautiful, and I could feel Isla's smile as she observed my wonder.

"Where are we?" I had never seen a place so peaceful and perfect, its magnificence seeping into me the longer I stared.

"Denimoore." Isla's skirts swished as she took a step closer, her own gaze settling on the streets below. "The Lupine capital."

Tearing my eyes away from the window, I glanced at her fond smile as she regarded the view with pride. I wondered if they ever truly got used to the loveliness of their home; I never would. Turning back to the glass I noticed that the dark sky had clouded over, the air now filling up with single perfect flakes as they danced in the winter breeze, only adding to the mystical vision.

"Come now, sweeting, you look dead on your feet. We can come back tomorrow." A gentle hand touched my elbow and she steered me back to my room in a motherly fashion. Isla was right, the longer we walked the slower my pace became, and I was all but asleep as we finally reached my door. Pushing the heavy wood open, I paused in the doorway, turning to Isla in gratitude.

"Thank you for your generosity, I can never repay you, your—" I paused, racking my brain for the proper title of a highborn lady of a capital. "Grace." Her smile was sly as she watched me bow my head in what I hoped was a graceful move. I had never mastered the curtsy and truly could not manage a best attempt when I was so exhausted.

"Now, Skylahr, please stop with all that. Isla is fine. After all, my son is the lord of this house, not I." Her warm hand reached out to squeeze my shoulder before she bid me goodnight and continued on her way down the hall. Waiting until she was out of sight, I shut the door gently and crawled onto the massive plush bed, falling asleep before I had even managed to take off my boots.

Chapter 7

Though the bed was the most comfortable I had ever been in, it still could not keep my anxiety and nightmares away. I had tossed and turned after a particularly vivid dream had startled me awake, and though I was exhausted, sleep still never came back. Rolling over for the fifth time, I finally gave in and stood from the warmth of the bedding.

Turning to the window, I noticed that the snow was still falling delicately from the sky, and the light from the moon was just visible through the heavy clouds. As I stood there in the soft glow, part of me wished I was back at Noorde Point. I wished that the past months had never happened, and my biggest concern was how I would avoid Liam Roy and his attentions. I had been lucky then; a boring life would have suited me just fine, and now I felt foolish for spending so much time wishing for more.

The regret and the lingering nightmares made me antsy and I closed the curtains, blocking the winter sky from my eyes before exiting my room. The hallways were dimly lit, only a few candles flickering every yard or so, and I took the opportunity to explore on my own. Tiptoeing through the halls, I tried to remember my way back to the wall of glass Isla had shown me, wishing for a distraction from the visions that remained in my mind. But the dark halls confused me, and when I heard a muffled whimper, I realized I was not only lost, but I was also no longer alone.

Turning towards the noise, I froze. Nadine's crimson skirt was hoisted up around the golden thigh that had curled around the strong hips pinning her against the wall. Her head was tossed back, the black hair creating a curtain against the stone. Tilting her chin, she offered Kalian her throat, and whatever he was doing pushed a groan out of her perfect lips and my eyes widened in fascination. I then watched as he grabbed at her hands, lifting them above her head, before pushing them against the wall with enough force his knuckles turned white.

"Please," she begged, her voice breaking with need, and the sound finally brought my focus back to my position. I was standing, right in the middle of the hall, watching the lord of the castle fuck his mistress, and I did not have the decency or intelligence to stealthily leave.

Still frozen in place, I watched as Nadine cried out for Kalian again but this time the noise forced panic to flood my veins, and I turned on my heel to dive back behind the corner I had just rounded. Managing one step, I then lost my footing and knocked into one of the stone statues that littered the wall, sending it to the floor in a shattering crash. Everything slowed and I felt my face become unbearably hot as I watched the pieces of stone scatter across the ground. Standing stupidly still, I gaped at the mess I had made, unwilling to turn around and face the couple I had interrupted.

"That was my grandfather." I squeezed my eyes shut when I realized how close that voice was to my ear, and I willed myself to disappear somehow.

"What are you doing out here?" His voice was warm, lacking any sort of true anger, but I was too flustered to answer.

"Are you mute or just stupid?" Nadine barked at me, her perfectly even voice still beautiful as she humiliated me. Turning to them, I kept my head bowed and wrung my hands together nervously but remained silent.

"Your lord was talking to you." Her tone grew nastier, and a spark of heat slid up my back before I lifted my face to the couple.

"I wasn't aware he needed his mistress to speak for him," I barked just as viciously before covering my mouth. I had spent my life being teased and prodded and I rarely snapped that way, and yet in a matter of moments this woman had forced me to lose sight of my patience.

"How dare you——" Her gaze had narrowed, and she looked ready to strike me, but Kalian too seemed to sense her next move and grabbed her by the elbow before steering her away from me.

"Enough, Nadine." His voice was firm and when her lips pulled into a pout he sighed before gently pushing her away. "Go to bed."

When it looked like she was about to argue he shot her a glare that sent a clear message, and Nadine tossed her hair over her shoulder before straightening her skirt and glaring at me. I held her gaze until she finally turned away and sauntered back down the hall.

"That will not bode well for you." The anger in his voice had faded and I finally had the courage to meet his eyes.

"What won't?" I asked, confused, though the rage still lingered.

"Making an enemy out of Nadine."

I rolled my eyes, dismissing his concern immediately. I had spent my fair share of time around ladies just like Nadine, and she was no more intimidating than the rest.

Meeting his eyes with a raised brow, I shrugged. "She doesn't frighten me," I paused before addressing him correctly. "My lord."

"No, she does not." It was a statement of agreement, and his gaze roamed my face for a moment before he looked back down at the floor.

"That really was my grandfather."

I followed his eyes to the broken statue and felt instant regret for my clumsiness. I hoped Isla would not be too upset. Bending down to pick up the scattered pieces, I felt his silver eyes still peering at me, making me feel more annoyed than unnerved.

"Is there something else you wished to say, my lord?"

"Only that you really have no right to be wandering the halls at night." He was right; I was a guest and had been welcomed warmly, more so than I deserved, and now I had taken advantage of that hospitality. Sighing, I stood back up, cupping the pieces of stone in my hand before nodding my head.

"I'm sorry, my lord. I will head back to my room as soon as I have cleaned this."

"Oh, leave it." He brushed me off before clearing the pieces from my hand and discarding them back onto the floor. "And stop calling me that. I fucking hate it."

His warm hand cupped my arm, guiding me in the direction of my room, and it stayed there for the entire walk back. Once we were in front of the door again, he pushed me into the threshold of my room before his large hand grabbed the knob. Slowly inching it closed, he paused when the opening was just wide enough for me to see half of his face.

"If I find you in these halls again, I will have to punish you." His expression was stern, mouth tight and brows drawn, and the look forced my face to pale as I realized how serious he was. My tongue refused to move as I opened my mouth to reply, and I was horrified as I spluttered out a noise rather than words.

"Speechless? Good, maybe you will listen. I don't want to have to take you over my knee, but I am a true believer that a good swatting is sometimes needed."

Whatever fear I had disappeared the moment his lips lifted into that blasted smirk and I knew I could not stop myself when the next words hissed through my teeth, consequences be damned.

"Bastard." I grabbed at the door, slamming it in his face before sliding the lock.

"Fucker," I cursed again only to growl when I heard him snicker from down the hallway.

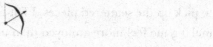

Isla had not been angry about the statue the next morning, but rather thanked me for finally destroying that "ghastly old thing." We had eaten together in the dining room, making idle chit-chat but never truly talking about anything of importance. Any time she asked about my family or travels, I shied away from the topics and redirected her attention to something else. It was obvious that she knew my tactics but still allowed me to control our conversation, and I was grateful for her kindness. When she excused herself from the table, I made my escape back to my room, hoping to avoid another run-in like the one I had the night before.

Perched on my bed, I gazed out at the mountains that lined the horizon, awed by their beauty and size. I wondered how far they went and what it would be like to stand at the very top and take in the view. Would my eyes be able to see all the way to Noorde Point? I sighed sadly as I thought about my parents and Elizabeth, silently praying that they were well and not too angered by my departure.

My musings were interrupted by a firm knock on my door and I tried to hide my displeasure at being found as I greeted my visitor. Leena's own face looked just as displeased as she leaned against the door frame, her dark eyes sharp as they peered up at me.

"My mother says you're a good shot."

"I'm sorry?"

Huffing at me impatiently, Leena pushed herself away from the door. "You've mastered how to use a bow, have you not?"

"Oh! Yes!"

"Good, then come with me." Without another word, Leena spun on her heel, her dark braid nearly whipping me in the face, and I watched her for a moment before pulling on my cloak and following her.

She led me through the front entrance and down the steps where two servants were waiting with bows in hand. Grabbing hers, she tossed the spare to me before ordering the two men to set out the targets. Leena widened her stance, her body sure as she took aim, and then she let her arrow fly, nearly hitting the edge of the middle mark in the target that stood several yards away.

She was good, very good, but kept too much tension in her shoulders and was holding her breath when she aimed. I watched her repeat the same mistake another four times before she turned to me expectantly. Smiling tightly at her, I kept silent about my observation and took my place.

My first arrow flew slightly to the left, hitting closer to the middle than Leena's had but not where I wanted. Though I was disappointed, the spectators who gathered seemed impressed as they watched me wide-eyed. Isla and her son stood on the steps, followed by Keyno and three other males I did not recognize. The strangers seemed the most stunned as they looked back and forth between me and the target.

Ignoring their wonder, I relaxed my shoulders and fired off the next four arrows in rapid succession, each one hitting the middle circle, the final piercing the canvas with a dull thud, its noise echoing in the silence around us.

"Well, boys, with her size and aim it looks like we won't be needed here," a voice called and Kalian snickered along with his friends.

"You're right! Someone find out what they're feeding their young down south, I could use a few sons her size," the shortest of the group japed while elbowing their lord in the ribs.

"Perhaps she'll find a pretty husband, give her children a fighting chance." The way the third man spoke those words so confidently had forced the air from my lungs and I dropped my gaze, too humiliated to meet their eyes. Turning to Leena, I watched as she glared back at the group of men, her lips lifting in a snarl. Isla, who had been focused on me, also turned to glower at the rowdy bunch before her eyes landed solely on her son.

"Enough." Her voice was not raised but the anger was still there, and I appreciated her coming to my aid. Her fingers lifted towards me and I smiled softly before taking her hand and following her into the castle.

"Ignore them, they're jealous of your skill," she whispered once we were in the safety of the solid walls. My mother would have tried to use the same theory to reassure me once, and I was touched by her attempt.

"I have heard it all my life, it doesn't bother me anymore." I shrugged, willing her to see my façade rather than admit that those taunts would always sting just a bit.

"That may be so, but it doesn't mean you don't believe those words to be true."

"There are worse things in life than being ugly and tall." My voice was unwavering as I smiled at her. "Besides, being a good shot makes up for it."

Isla's answering smile was full of pride and I felt that much lighter watching as she nodded in agreement. "So it does, sweeting. So it does."

Chapter 8

I had promised myself over and over that I would leave for Carlon that morning and yet hour after hour passed and I still could not find the courage to depart from the castle. Instead, I found myself wandering the halls in the afternoon light, my eyes drifting across the paintings and views the windows offered. Isla had disappeared after tea, and Leena had not been seen since our archery match that morning. Left to my own devices, I took it upon myself to explore the halls though the castle staff watched me with wary eyes. Their distrust was obvious in the way they gazed at me before they whispered to each other as they passed.

Doing my best to ignore their attentions, I finally found my way to the glass wall and I was not disappointed. In the bright afternoon sun, the snow sparkled, and the town seemed like it had been conjured by one of the artists who had painted the other landscapes that hung on the walls. The view was picturesque and pristine, and I was fascinated by how crisp the white made the village look.

"Ah, there you are, sweeting." Isla was adorned in a deep blue dress that would have been plain on anyone else, but her tan skin and beauty changed the simplicity of the fabric to something more as it danced around her feet. Her hair was brushed back on one side, held there by a delicate metal comb that was adorned with delicate gold leaves and white pearls. It was something my mother would have adored, and the thought made my chest ache.

Isla's grin was warm as she looked down at the village. "I guessed this was where I would find you."

"The view really is marvelous." I shrugged before my eyes widened as I watched one of her delicate hands reach for my bronze waves that hung in a disarray. Her fingers were gentle as they combed through the tangles that had knotted at the ends, and I felt embarrassed that I was not more put together.

When one finger snagged on a particular unruly knot, she withdrew her hand before patting my shoulder. "Let's get you cleaned up, shall we?"

I really did not want to follow her, but her face held no room for argument, and I was silent as I trailed behind. We passed the room I had been given in our journey, and I had been so distracted studying the blue silk that swayed across the floor with every step Isla took, I had not noticed that both of her offspring were waiting for her.

"Why did you ask for us, Mama?" Leena grumbled, looking bored as she watched our approach.

"I only asked for you, dearest." Isla paused before turning to her son. "Kalian?"

He was even more unbearably handsome in the bright daylight, his golden skin glowing in the sun while his silver eyes seemed to blaze under the thick black lashes that framed them. His lips lifted on one side, smirking, and I realized he had caught my admiring.

"I wanted to know why you needed Leena, and I thought perhaps I could be of some assistance."

Isla rolled her eyes at her son, not believing his excuse for even a second, and when she noticed his reluctance to leave us, Isla huffed in agitation before smiling at me in apology.

"Kalian, why don't you and I go find some more clothing that will fit our guest. Leena, wait here."

Leena's eyes narrowed at me while the two made their way back towards Kalian's room, and I immediately missed the buffer Isla provided between me and her daughter.

"You know, my mother has a habit."

My head swung back to the beauty who leaned against the wall, her eyes gazing at her fingernails in boredom.

I had no idea what she was talking about and felt my brows drop in confusion. "Habit?"

"Yes. She has a habit of taking in strays, so don't feel special. She has lost three children in her life, and I think you may just be another distraction to fill the void. It won't last. They never do."

I had not even known these people for an entire day and yet the words still cut me deeply. I had only one single ally here in this mysterious place and it hurt to think I may lose her.

"I'm not looking to be saved nor cared for." My voice was weak in my own ears and I winced at how unsure I sounded.

"Good. You aren't wanted here. You have been enough of an inconvenience, and I won't have my mother become attached to a mortal like you." With that Leena stood straight and turned to meet her mother, who had returned with a pile of clothing in her arms. Isla faltered in her step as she noticed the tension between us, pausing only long enough to glare at her daughter before pasting a smile across her lips.

"Now then, let's get that hair taken care of." I smiled awkwardly before following them into the room.

The women spent a length of time on my thick hair, both brushing through it before they twisted the stands into a long, neat braid. Isla then forced me into a more formal green tunic, one that was covered in sparkling silver embroidery. The beauty of it felt lost on me and I wished she had allowed me to wear a plainer one.

Happy with her work, Isla sent me on my way back to the dining hall where we would all gather for dinner, and while I walked through the castle, I prayed that Leena would not tell her mother about our conversation. I didn't need any more pity.

Finding my way through the halls, I finally stumbled upon someone other than the servants. In a room to the left sat Kalian, who was surrounded by his friends, each one sprawled across the couches and chairs, drinks in hand. I could hear their heavy laughter from my place in the hall and I ducked my chin, making myself smaller for my escape.

"Did you see her? I hear your mother stuffed her into a fancy tunic and braided her hair, as if that would help." I winced at the laughter in his voice and peered into the room. Keyno looked at the man with disgust but said nothing as he waited for his lord to speak up.

"Oh, come on, Keyno, don't look at me like that. The girl is a sharp shot but my Gods she is a beast of a woman." The other two strangers laughed for a minute until they realized both Keyno and Kalian remained silent. Unwilling to hear their retort, I turned on my heel, not caring that my boots echoed off the floor as I fled.

"Skylahr!" It was a mere moment before Kalian's stern voice bounced off the walls and I slowed my pace until I stood. Promising myself I would not run from him, that I would not be a coward, I waited. After all they were just words, nothing I hadn't heard before.

"Skylahr!" he called again, this time his voice much closer than I had expected. Turning to him, I lifted my chin and glared.

"What can I do for you, my lord?" I snapped at him, emphasizing his title in pure rage.

"Don't be like that." He dismissed my anger with a roll of his eyes, and I clenched my fists, my fury growing. "It wasn't me; I didn't say anything."

I scoffed at his excuse before narrowing my eyes as I peered up at him. "Trust me, you didn't need to. I know exactly what I look like. I'm not delusional and I know those words are true but that does not mean I deserve to be mocked!" The volume of my voice rose as fire bubbled in my veins.

Sighing, Kalian tried to defuse the situation by lifting his hands before dropping his gaze. "You're right, it was unkind, and I shouldn't have allowed it to happen."

I was furious at them for their words but watching this magnificent man cower in my anger just made me more so. I knew it was an act, all in hopes that I would forget what I heard and carry on the way a lady should.

"Stop that. I don't need your protection or your apologies," I snarled at him, watching as his eyes lifted and widened, the heat slowly seeping back into them as his jaw clenched.

"Bloody hells, girl. Then what do you want? Kindness or honesty? You cannot have both." My body moved on its own as I took a step closer, my chest brushing against his as I glared up at his face.

"I want my worth to be seen and I deserve decency and respect! My value goes beyond my looks!" Without giving him a chance to respond I turned away from him, storming down the hallway before slamming my door behind me.

Chapter 9

I had skipped dinner that night and only managed to hide in my room for another hour the next morning before Isla came to find me again. Unable to escape her clutches, I was stuffed into a fur cloak and a scarf before being pulled onto the back terrace where a large breakfast was spread out before me. If it hadn't been for my queasy stomach, I would have indulged my sweet tooth with the fresh pastries but instead, I sulked in my chair. However, Isla paid my poor attitude no mind and rather turned her face towards the sun as if the winter air wasn't a bitter sting against her skin.

Sipping my tea carefully, I studied the sprawling grounds that were coated in a thick cover of snow. The acreage was impressive, and it was obvious that the land was immaculately kept, even in the winter months. Taking in the views, I could feel Leena as she watched me, her dark eyes full of judgement. Though they were nowhere near as cold as they had been when she had snapped at me in the hall, so I took this as a good sign.

Finishing my drink, I excused myself from the table, hoping to walk the grounds before finally asking for an escort back to the Noorde province. Isla dismissed me with a wave of her elegant fingers before asking Leena to accompany me. The younger woman groaned at her mother but agreed before leading the way down the back steps.

Stepping onto the snow-covered grass, I took in the land around me. The cluster of mountains behind the castle seemed as if they were close enough that I could reach out and touch the white tips, and the forest was bright and shining with the ice that melted from the branches. Once I was finished scanning the area, I turned to Leena with a timid smile in hopes of easing her discomfort, but she narrowed her eyes at me before sighing in resignation.

"Are you trained in the sword as well then?"

I appreciated her effort to find common ground and tucked my cloak tighter around me before answering. "Yes, my mother used to say I learned to use a blade before I walked." Nodding her head, she turned from me and waved a hand in my direction as a cue to follow.

Silently trailing her, I noticed we had entered a training yard. Stuffed dummies were perched on their mounts to the far left, there were targets lining the right side, and a fight ring in the middle. She grabbed a wooden training weapon and tossed me another before walking into the ring, taking up a defensive position. I shrugged out of my cloak before following her into the circle. The wooden hilt felt familiar in my palm, my callouses lining up perfectly and my blood singing with adrenaline.

The woman remained still, and I took a deep breath before I made the first move and lunged forward. I was quick but my blow was blocked easily and for the first time a smile fell across Leena's lips. Rocking back on my heels, I brought the blade down again at a different angle, only to be blocked once more. This continued, blow, block, blow, block until I felt my lungs begin to protest. Leena, however, seemed unbothered, not even a sheen of sweat could be found on her face.

I took in her stance, looking for any openings she may have. Focusing on the left, I noticed that although she had the speed and stamina of an immortal, she was not careful, and her arrogance left her vulnerable for an attack. Biding my time, I backed off and allowed her to pursue me while blocking her aggressive offensive attacks. We covered the space of the ring again and again as we circled each other, and Leena's smile had grown bigger with each swipe at me as she had assumed she would come out of this spar victorious. Little did she know, however, she had walked right into my plan, and three jabs later, I had kicked out her feet from under her before pressing the wooden tip of my weapon against her golden throat.

"Do you yield?" I asked, my voice coming out breathlessly as sweat dripped from my brow.

Her eyes blinked up at me in a daze and she slapped my faux blade away from her before gracefully pulling herself to her feet. After dusting herself off, she bent to retrieve her own blade from the snow and snapped it as easily as she would a twig as she stormed out of the ring. My eyes were wide in shock, and I watched her retreating figure, completely unaware of our audience until I heard the slow clapping echoing behind me. Turning on my heel, I spun to face Kalian and Keyno, who were both leaning against the wooden fence of the ring. Meeting my gaze, Keyno stopped clapping before he jumped over the barrier and approached me. He paused, bending over to pick up the broken sword from the ground before straightening to his full height and clapping me on the back in a brotherly manner.

"Well, Hazel." He paused, smiling to himself at his new nickname for me as my head tilted in confusion. "I have never seen anyone besides Kalian beat my Leena at the sword." He laughed again before casting a glance back at Kalian.

Following his gaze, I was struck by the intensity that I found. Kalian was watching me with blazing eyes; his jaw was tight and shoulders stiff as his eyes scanned me from head to toe. The heat of his stare left me feeling as if I was naked under his gaze. Swallowing roughly, I turned my eyes back to his pack mate only to find Keyno studying me with amusement.

"Am I interrupting something?" He laughed to himself before falling silent at the warning growl that came from the fence. Holding his hands up in surrender, he smirked at Kalian.

I decided it was best to ignore the two males, so I walked over to my discarded cloak and draped it back over my shoulders. Fastening the clasp, I turned back around only to find both Nadine and Isla waiting with the men. Isla was smiling proudly at me but the beauty at her side still looked at me as if I was the scum of the earth. She had laced her arm through Kalian's and was obviously trying to direct his attention back to her. Ignoring the couple, I grinned at Isla before bypassing the group and making my way back up the stairs.

Walking quickly, I managed to find my way back into the safety of my room. I shut the door behind me before I tore the damp clothes off and padded into the adjoining room where a deep tub full of sweet-smelling warm water waited for me. Carefully climbing into the bath, I sank into the water with a sigh as my tense muscles relaxed, and I tipped my head back against the rim and closed my eyes.

In the silence, my mind wandered to my village. I wondered how my parents were faring. How was Elizabeth? Picturing their faces, I prayed to the Gods that the tonic had continued to work, and that the village was still on the road to recovery. Tucking my chin into the water, I pulled my knees to my chest before blowing bubbles into the bath while I brooded in privacy.

My hands were pruned by the time I pulled myself from the water, and I dressed into a change of clothes before walking to the mirror on the wall. Focusing on my reflection, I traced the freckles across my nose with my fingers and my wide lips parted as I tried to imagine what I could have looked like had I been blessed by the Gods. Fingertips pushed at the roundness of my cheeks and I searched for a way to make myself more appealing.

"My mother used to tell me that my face would freeze if I kept touching it like that." At the sound of his voice, I peered into the mirror, my eyes drifting to the space over my shoulder. He was leaning against the wall, arms crossed, shirt ruffled as if he had just thrown it on and yet he looked extraordinary.

Although it was difficult, I didn't turn around. I was still too angry about the night before, and I had promised myself to hold strong in my annoyance. As if he could sense my resolve, Kalian lifted his lips. It was not a smirk, but a true smile, and his perfect white teeth were blinding as his fingers combed through his hair. The motion lifted his tunic just enough for me to catch a glimpse of the flawless muscled stomach and my mouth dried at the sight of it. Hating that my skin pinkened under his watch, I cleared my throat to break the growing tension and focused back on my reflection. But silver eyes continued to study me and when my own hazel flickered to him, I noticed that he had focused on my lower back. Narrowing my gaze, I waited for them to move away from the spot but instead his lips parted, and his throat bobbed as he swallowed.

Turning to face him, I crossed my arms before glaring at him. "What are you staring at?!" His tan skin deepened in a blush and he averted his gaze quickly but never answered. The silence only made my confusion grow.

Coughing into his fist awkwardly, he walked back to my door. "I was hoping you would be willing to help me."

My head tilted to the side in question and I waited for him to explain. For the first time he looked truly uncomfortable in my presence and I was delighted in the realization.

"Help with what, my lord?" My voice was sugar sweet and mockingly pleasant as I blinked at him in the way I had seen other ladies do. However, I was not nearly as convincing as I'd hoped, and Kalian rolled his eyes at me in annoyance.

"I was going to the armoury to sort the weapons and polish the blades. I could use your help, if you felt so inclined."

I eyed him warily.

"Why would the Lord of Denimoore be doing the work of the blacksmith's apprentice? And why would he want a woman's help?" I asked in the same girlish voice, enjoying the nasty look he shot my way only to realize I had pushed his patience too far. He took three long strides towards me.

Suddenly nervous of his approach, I slid backwards until my shoulders were pressed against the glass of the mirror. My hands fanned against the cool wall and I braced myself as Kalian continued to advance, not stopping until his solid chest grazed my own.

I tried to ignore the way our tunics brushed against each other with every heaving gulp of air I took in and instead turned my chin away. My lashes had fluttered closed at some point, but I knew he was closer now. I could feel the heat of him on my exposed neck and I gasped in surprise as his voice purred into my ear.

"Because I enjoy working with my hands." He paused, his breath fanning across my skin, his lips grazing the delicate flesh of my lobe. "And because then I could show you what my fingers can do." My knees trembled as the blood roared in my veins and my belly swooped. It took a long moment for me to finally regulate my breathing and when I opened my eyes, I realized I was alone.

I never did make it to the armoury; I was too much of a coward to face him after I had peeled myself from the wall and was forced to splash cool water over my heated face before searching for Isla. I had found her in the drawing room, perched in a chair while she flipped through a book. She was the very picture of perfection, and I wished I had half of her elegance. She greeted me warmly as I folded myself awkwardly into a chair and offered me a delicate teacup. I had never really enjoyed afternoon tea, but I knew it was rude to refuse, so I lifted the fragile dish and sipped the brown liquid carefully only to gag as it burned my throat.

"Bloody hells!" I coughed as Isla snickered at me. "What is this?"

"Sweet licur, you'll get used to the burn. Just hold your breath and take a big swallow." It was then that I noticed her face was flushed and eyes looked hazy. Taking her advice, I tipped my head back and swallowed the contents in one gulp and it burned all the way to my belly where it settled.

Giggling quietly, she grabbed at my empty cup, filling it again before pushing it to my lips, and I swallowed it in one mouthful. Isla nodded her head proudly at me before she stood from her chair and grabbed my hand, encouraging me to follow.

"Come, sweeting, it's time for dinner."

We entered the dining room, arms linked, and I ignored the nasty look I received from Leena as I sat across from her. Keyno was much more pleasant as he smiled at me, nodding his head in welcome before pressing a kiss to his mate's cheek.

The table was filled with a lavish meal, and our cups were filled with wines. It was quiet with only Leena and Isla truly conversing with each other while Keyno and I ate peacefully. We were nearly finished when Kalian's massive frame strode through the doorway as he towed Nadine along. Upon their entrance, Leena snarled at the couple, her displeasure evident in the aggressive way she stabbed at her plate. Keyno glanced at me before lowering his gaze. A safe decision I guessed and did the same.

"Leena, grow up." Kalian's voice was harsh as he pointed one long finger at his sister.

Leena glared back at her brother before flicking her long hair over her shoulder. "She has no place here."

"I am the alpha's concubine and have been so for two decades. Surely I have more right than her." My eyes lifted swiftly, and I realized Nadine had directed that jab at me. Blinking at her dark gaze, I remained silent as I had a feeling that this was just the beginning.

Sure enough, Leena stood from her chair with enough force that the solid wood toppled backwards. Her hands slammed down onto the table as she leaned forward, her body tense.

"She is my mother's guest. *You* are one of many fleeting distractions for my brother. You warm his bed, but you have no more importance than that."

Isla's attention swung to her daughter as she too rose from her chair. Her face spoke volumes and the air around us grew cold.

"Skylahr, I apologize for my children. I think it's best we retire for the evening." Nodding, I followed her back to the drawing room, not saying a word until we were settled in our previous seats. The air was still tense, and I opened my mouth to find some way to distract Isla from her anger only to be interrupted by a knock at the door.

Turning, I noticed Leena poke her head into the room. She eyed me with disdain before softening her face at her mother. Waiting for an invitation, she hovered at the doorway until one finger was crooked at her, and she ducked her head, looking at the floor before entering.

"I am sorry, Mama, for what I said at dinner."

Isla hummed under her breath before opening her arms to her daughter. Leena tucked herself into her mother's embrace for a second while Isla pulled back to smooth her hair.

"Have you apologized to Nadine?" she asked the younger woman.

A sour look crossed Leena's face before she smoothed it out in a quick, well-practiced move. Rolling her eyes, she pulled away from her mother's arms, picking at her nails like she was disinterested in the topic.

"No."

"Well, there is no sense in apologizing to me, I am not the one you hurt with your words."

Sighing at her mother, Leena stood before turning to sink into a chair with an exaggerated sigh. "Even if I wanted to—which I don't—she's with Kalian."

"Even better. You can apologize to both then."

"No, Mama, *with* Kalian. I'm surprised you cannot hear her screams and moans all the way down here." To my shock, Isla had no reaction. My own face, however, burned in embarrassment. I had never heard those matters discussed so openly by a woman before. Drunken men, sure. But never a lady. However, Isla only laughed softly before shaking a finger at her daughter.

"If I remember correctly, I just caught you and Keyno this morning in the library."

My throat tightened as I swallowed my shock, forcing a spluttering cough from my lungs. The noise caused Leena to glare at me before turning her pink face away. I wished a gaping hole would open beneath me, if only to avoid this conversation. I had no experience with the opposite sex and here I stood while a mother and daughter discussed such intimate details like it was the weather. My awkwardness was evident in the way I shifted my weight and Leena took notice.

"Oh, don't be such a prude!" Leena seethed at me while flicking her hair back over her shoulder, and Isla snickered before straightening her spine and shooing her daughter away, offering me an apologetic smile.

"Leena has a quick temper but do not let it fool you. She has a kinder heart than most." I felt a brow rise on its own before I could stop it, and Isla burst into a fit of giggles before patting my arm gently.

The rest of the evening was spent talking about my own childhood and memories. Her eyes focused solely on me with interest as I spoke of my parents, my mother's tough love and will, and my father's kind heart. We talked about my hunting and lessons in archery and sword fighting. She asked about my favourite hobbies and my friends. Only one was worth mentioning and she praised me for the loyalty and love I had for those I cared about. We sat comfortably in silence until late evening, each holding a glass of wine to sip on.

The alcohol made my cheeks prickle and burn but left a lovely fuzzy feeling in my chest, and by the time the sky had darkened, I could barely hold my footing without laughing a girlish giggle I did not recognize. Isla stood with her arm out for me to grasp before we left the room. I swayed this way and that, bending over in fits of laughter before straightening and sucking my cheeks in to attempt a look of composure. We giggled like young maidens all the way to my room before she pushed the door open and bid me goodnight.

Leaning against the wood, I watched Isla's skirts swish around the corner of the hallway in fascination. I had always dreamed of being like her. So poised and delicate, a true lady. Sighing to myself, I rested my forehead against the carvings that covered my door and dreamt of what my life would have been like had I been so fortunate.

"Ugh, Kalian! Please!" A high-pitched wail echoed from down the hall interrupting my musings and I felt my eyes widen at the sound. It had been hours since Leena had come into the drawing room. So long it had not crossed my mind that they would still be...occupied.

"Oh!" Another moan came and then another and another. So constant it became like a melody of sorts. Having enough, I pushed into my room, slammed the door, and leaned back against it, while my heart hammered in my chest. I had once heard similar noises coming from the brothel in our village but none of the girls had ever sounded so...

Lustful. Wanton. *Needy*.

Even with the wood barrier, I could still hear her calling for him, begging. I cupped my hands over my ears before growling in frustration and diving into my bed. Snuggled under the thick covers, I placed one of the plush pillows over my head until the only thing ringing in my ears was my own heartbeat. I kept my head like that until I was sure I could not hear their coupling any longer.

After a long moment of silence, I took a chance and poked my head out from the cloth barrier I had burrowed under, holding my breath while I listened. When all remained quiet, I released the air slowly, sinking down into the plush bed before blinking up at the ceiling willing myself to sleep. And just as I was about to sink into a deep slumber, I heard him call out.

It was a great, deep guttural groan. Almost primal sounding. And I had heard nothing like it before.

A wave of heat scorched my body, forcing my toes to curl involuntarily, and my lower belly felt as if it was full of butterflies. It was the same feeling I had when he backed me against the wall. But the wine had made it feel a thousand times stronger.

Losing all of my inhibitions and propriety, I took a deep breath while pure unadulterated wanting left me panting in my bed. For the first time I wished I had more knowledge of the opposite sex. Maybe then I would know what she had done to cause such a reaction from the proud, arrogant man I had quickly come to know. The first man to ever truly pique my interests.

The wine had given me the courage I had always previously lacked, and I closed my eyes tightly while I tried to conjure the face he would have made when that sound broke out of him. His eyes would be closed, that magnificent jaw shut tightly, and his lips left open for me to kiss and bite. His head would tip back, and the cords of his throat would pull so tight I would be able to see the pulse that surged through them.

With one hand, I lowered my breeches before running my fingertips across the smooth skin of my legs, my fingers trailing up the inside of my thigh, discovering new territory in their journey as they soothed my desire. Would his fingers be gentle in their grazes or would he grab and pull roughly, only to leave me wanting more? Would he kiss me? Whisper in my ear as those deep silver eyes watched every hitch in my breath? Would he be satisfied to watch me beg for him as Nadine had?

My own fingers moved towards the apex of my thighs, finding moisture and slickness covering the delicate skin. But still my fingertips searched until they found that spot, the bundle of nerves I had only ever heard about. Though surely others' pleasure dulled in comparison to this. With a few dozen exploratory swirls and circles, the heat that had been boiling in my belly spread through my veins and down to my toes only to loop back again. It was as if I was no longer in control of my body and that something else entirely had possessed me. With a low, breathy cry, I felt my pleasure burst and my back bowed.

Falling back against the mattress, I blinked through the daze of my mind. Focusing on my shallow breaths and my heartbeat that pounded through me, I waited to hear another noise from down the hall before my humiliation slammed into me. For the first time ever, I had sought pleasure, and from my own hands at that. Turning onto my side, I stared out the window in front of me. I barely knew the man and yet after just a mere two days my self-control was non-existent.

"Stupid beautiful man," I grunted before pulling the covers over my head again and falling into a restless sleep.

Chapter 10

My mouth felt like cotton the next morning, the wine and licur mixing into an acid that burned in my stomach. Although I had slept well past dawn, I still felt exhausted, and my head was pounding as I rolled onto my back. Closing my eyes, I prayed that the embarrassing memories from the night before were just a figment of my imagination. I had been close to almost convincing myself until I realized that the tightness around my calves was in fact my breeches that had been pushed down. Running my palms over my face, I slowly sat up before the spinning of the room had me pinching the bridge of my nose.

"You, Skylahr Reed, are an embarrassment," I huffed to myself.

"Well, I wouldn't go that far, at least not yet," a deep voice rumbled, cutting through my wine sickness like a blade.

Opening my eyes, I squinted over to the chair that was usually tucked beside the vanity, and there, sprawled across it like he had been posing for a portrait, sat Kalian. He wore a white cotton shirt under a black and silver coat. His breeches were dark and fitted, tucked into his boots neatly. One brow lifted at me with a smirk and I wished I could slap it off his face.

Noticing my temper, he took his time tracing my features before slowly moving his gaze down. First glancing at my collarbone and shoulder, which had been exposed during my tossing last night, then following the visible pale skin down to the neckline that just managed to cover the swell of a breast. Realizing the state of my undress, I pulled my sleeve up with a growl and ran my fingers through my long bronze waves that tangled down my back before glaring at him.

"What the hell are you doing in here?" But my anger only seemed to please him, and he leered at me, his eyes flashing with heat.

"Why I thought after all the ruckus last night, I would come check on you. You were calling for me after all."

He tilted his head before grinning and the realization dawned on me. He had heard me. Eyes wide and cheeks pink, I dropped my gaze to my lap, which was thankfully covered by the pile of blankets, and I swallowed twice before regaining my composure.

"I have no idea what you're talking about," I lied while watching him with a blank face.

"Of course you don't, love." He winked at me before standing. Lifting his arms in an exaggerated stretch, he let out a loud groan. One somewhat similar to what I heard the night before.

Watching me with those silver eyes, he lowered his arms before sauntering to the door. He pulled it open only to pause and turn back around to face me. Biting his lower lip, he gazed at my chest before dropping his voice into a smooth, deep timbre.

"Don't worry, I dreamt of you too."

My hands were not fast enough, and he easily dodged the pillow I sent flying in his direction. With one last wink, he turned on his heel and strode down the hallway while his laughter echoed behind him.

I had remained in my room for another hour, my eyes gazing out the window as I blinked at the scenery while the anxiety began to brew in my chest. It had been days since I had arrived in Denimoore, and I knew that it was time to continue on. Gathering my freshly washed clothes, I found a blanket to tie into a makeshift pack before making my bed as neatly as I could and scanning the room for anything I may have forgotten. Certain I had everything, I closed the door behind me quietly and ducked my head as I wandered through the magnificent halls, searching each room for Isla.

I had hoped I would have the chance to say goodbye before leaving for my journey south, but the lady of the house was nowhere to be found, and I worried I would have to ask her insufferable son for help on my own. Poking my head through the entryway of the dining room, I found the smug prick sitting in his chair sipping on tea.

"Hello, love," he purred, setting his glass down to smirk at me. "Need something?" His voice was full of taunting while he glanced at my pack and cloak, obviously understanding I was planning to leave.

"I was looking for your mother," I snapped at him before crossing my arms.

"Yes, well, she's currently occupied being the lady of the house. The duties are endless, you know. But I'm sure I can be of some assistance." His eyes dropped to my chest then moved to my legs before slowly climbing back up to meet my own.

Asshole, I thought as I pictured slamming my fist into that jaw of his. He was playing with me, I knew that. He had no real offer, nor did he actually want me. But my obvious lack of experience made for a clear target. It was an easy opening to get under my skin and he so enjoyed toying with me.

Just as I was about to curse at him, his mother came through the room in all her glory. Looking between my displeased face and her gloating son, she narrowed her eyes at him.

"Kalian! What did I tell you about teasing the poor girl?" she scolded.

"Look at her, she is far from a helpless little maiden! She could probably take down Keyno with a body like that. Honestly, Mother, you are always so concerned for the wrong person. I'm the victim here."

My glare hardened at his insult, and I suddenly felt self-conscious of my lumbering size. I knew my showing off during the spar had worked against me, only giving him more material to use in his jokes at my expense. Isla also took his jest seriously and slammed her hand down onto the table with a violent slap.

"Kalian. I will not have your taunting and prodding today." She pointed one finger at his face and their eyes clashed violently, neither willing to look away.

Clearing my throat, I took a step towards them, waiting for an acknowledgement, and when I received none, I crept closer, placing my hand on Isla's shoulder in reassurance before retreating. "It's fine, Isla. Nothing he said is a lie, I can handle myself."

Not looking away from her son, she reached back behind her and gripped my hand. Giving it a squeeze, she slowly turned to me. Her eyes had immediately softened, and she smiled gently.

"Of course you can, dear sweeting. Of course. But he also needs to be kind and welcoming to my guests. This is not how the alpha behaves." She shot another look over her shoulder before patting my cheek gently and then her eyes focused on the pack in my hand.

"Is that the quilt from your room?"

"Yes, I'm sorry. I had nothing to carry my clothes in and I was hoping to keep the ones I'm wearing if that wouldn't be too much to ask." I paused, clearing my throat before continuing. "I'd like to head to Noordeign today, though I would not expect anyone to take me that far," I reassured her.

"Oh, sweeting, of course you can keep them, but I really wish you would stay another night."

I had a feeling that Isla would be set on me staying for longer, but I just couldn't find it in myself to put off my departure. I was concerned for my family's and friend's well-being, and I wanted to be sure there was no trace of truth to the witch's warning. Seeing my steely resolve, Isla sighed before turning back to Kalian.

"Keyno and Leena are on watch, are they not?" she asked.

Kalian threw back the rest of his drink and stood from his chair. He pulled one arm through his coat then the other before folding it gently. His shoulders were clothed tightly in a navy-blue tunic that emphasized the gold hues of his skin.

"Yes, we had some trouble south of the border. They are leaving for another watch momentarily, so they can take her back."

I let a sigh of relief escape me, knowing I would avoid a journey south with him. He, however, smiled at the sound, and his face had my stomach filling with dread.

"Of course I will come along. Just to be sure everything goes smoothly. Looks like you will get to mount me again, love."

Rolling my eyes at his poor attempt at a joke, I looked to Isla. "There is really no need for him to come."

"Unfortunately, dear, that is not my call. He's the alpha here." Her smile was sympathetic as she caught my wince. Nodding my head in defeat, I followed closely behind him as we exited the castle.

I did my best not to picture beating him with a sword or pushing him down one of the nearby cliffs as we crossed the front yard and followed a narrow pathway that led into the forest. There stood the great grey beast that I knew to be Keyno, and beside him was a deep tan and black pack mate. It was smaller in size and appeared to be female, almost more delicate maybe. However, the look in her deep eyes was anything but, and as she watched me with those dark irises, I knew it was Leena. Standing awkwardly under her scrutiny, I waited for an invitation of sorts, but none came.

"There is no chance in hell my sweet sister will let you sit on her husband." Kalian laughed. "And if you even think about asking her, she will probably rip an arm off."

"I can walk," I huffed before turning to face him, wincing at my poor timing. Kalian had pulled off his tunic and was right in the process of stripping his breeches down his long muscular legs. Turning my eyes to the sky, I exhaled, watching the fog of my breath disappear into the air. I waited for a sign that he had finished, looking back only when I felt his black fur rub against my thighs as he pressed against me impatiently. Mounting him without making it a spectacle, I squeezed his sides gently before bracing myself for the swiftness of his gallop.

The trees passed us in a blur just as they had the last time, but I was rested now and could take in our surroundings. The pack of three were stealthy and quiet in their travels, and I noticed that the animals around us did not flee in fear. Feeling my awe, Kalian lowered his head and picked up speed, his gait opening as it became a smooth four beats rather than the rocking it had been. Holding on to his fur tightly, I felt a laugh bubble up from the chest. The speed and freedom made me feel as if I was drunk on giddiness, and Kalian responded with his own bark of laughter before charging ahead.

Keyno seemed pleased by the change in pace. His mate, however, growled loud enough for me to hear over the wind whistling past my ears, and I looked over my shoulder at her only to be thrown off balance when Kalian skidded to a stop. At the sudden change, my body lurched forward, and I nearly went headfirst over his shoulder and barely managed to catch myself in time to avoid that embarrassment.

Righting myself, I looked around the forest and tried to locate the reason for the sudden change, but Kalian had his nose up in the air for just a moment before lurching forward again. This time, however, his speed filled me with fear.

The wind grabbed at my hair and cloak, pulling both with such force it caused my neck to ache from craning forward in order to keep my balance. I blinked the water from my eyes when a sharp, stinging warmth filled the space just above my brow. I could feel hot blood fly out of the cut and into the gust of cold air, and I looked back behind me, noticing one single tree branch sticking out just far enough to make contact. Lowering myself down over his shoulders, I attempted to avoid further damage, and it was then that I realized exactly where we were heading.

There, through the trees ahead, I could just make out the walls of Noorde Point. But the usual stoic brown gate was blackened and crumbling, the air above a swirling deep grey with speckles of oranges and bits of ash. I felt dread fill my chest as the smell of burning flesh made my stomach roll, vomit creeping its way up into my throat.

"Stop! Stop!" I screamed, reefing on the fur that had twisted its way between my fingers. However, Kalian ignored my pleas and continued to race towards the road, and I pulled again on the fur with all my strength only to receive no response. Finally untangling my fingers, I lifted my leg over his withers and tucked my body into itself as tightly as I could before pushing off from his back.

I thanked the Gods for the soft, damp earth as I landed, and I rolled through the mud gasping for breath before clawing my way up onto my feet. Running back towards the burning, I ignored the warning growl behind me. It was an obvious order for me to stop but I refused and instead charged through the gaping hole that should have been the gates.

My feet knew where to lead before my mind had even processed the destruction around me and I ran, not stopping until I was in front of the house I had been raised in. Only there was no house at all, but rather a pile of ash and soot. Swallowing a sob, I blinked through the tears that filled my eyes and searched for any sign of life, while carefully making my way through the wreckage.

The smoke was heavy and it burned in my lungs as I shielded my face with my cloaked elbow. Moving slowly as if not to disturb the pile of rubble, I tiptoed around what should have been my parents' room. My eyes scanned the area, searching desperately until something caught my attention. Glancing down at the toe of my boot, I focused on the pale, rough fingers that protruded out from under the stones that had once made a wall.

Three fingers—a pinky, ring, and middle, blackened with ash and smoke—became my only focal point as I fell to my knees, my own hand shaking as it reached out for them. With a sob breaking from my throat, my fingers slid over the skin. Even now I could recognize his hand.

It was the same hand that had brushed my tears away. The same rough, calloused flesh that had always stretched to hold my own as a child and though the silver ring was missing, I knew without a doubt it was his. It was my father.

Falling forward, I pushed and scraped at the rocks that were crushing the rest of the limb. My lungs heaved for air as my hands scrambled for purchase, my skin tearing as I tried to lift the wreckage. Unable to move the pile that lay across my father's arm, I brought my lips to the hand in front of me only to be hauled away by two strong arms. Then my body was being turned and pulled towards a solid wall of muscle as hands smoothed back my hair and I was folded into a lap delicately as if I were a child.

Fingers rubbed against my spine as I clenched my eyes shut, and it was then that I noticed a horrendous wailing echoing around us. It was a pained screaming—a howling, like some animal was being tortured. I couldn't help but to think that Kalian or Keyno should do it a kindness and put an end to its misery.

It wasn't until much later that I had realized that sound was coming from me.

Chapter 11

A hand stroked my hair gently while the murmured voices grew louder and louder from the other side of the room. The immortals had left me to my grief for days, but I had a feeling that graciousness was ending. Blinking at the blue wall in front of me in a daze, I tried my best to ignore those around me while another cup of tea was put in front of my nose in an offering. The hot steam fogged up my senses, and I turned my face into the pillow in refusal, doing my best to ignore the sigh of frustration. How could they continue to expect me to consume anything when all I could smell was smoke and death? The sickly scent of burning flesh was still trapped in the back of my nose and it made my eyes water.

Placing the tea back down on the nightstand beside me, Isla resumed her petting of my hair, and Kalian came to stand next to her shoulder. His silver eyes, which had been filled with pity, were now observing me closely.

It had taken both him and Leena to pull me from my parents' corpses once the Lupines had uncovered them. His strong arms wrapped around my waist while her gentle patient hands pried my fingers open one by one until my grasp had loosened enough to drag me away. I had been a shaking, shuddering mess, my sobs calming into deep heaves while Kalian did his best to comfort me. Keyno had dug two shallow graves near the edge of the woods at some point and placed what was left of my parents there. Once my legs had the strength to carry me, I had searched for Elizabeth, but her home had been unrecognizable. Kalian had only let me dig through the wreckage for so long before he stepped in again.

It had been pointless, I knew, but I couldn't help but feel it was my duty to find her. To give her a final resting spot as we had my parents.

When Kalian had finally been able to steer me away from the scene he turned to Leena, who had been gracious enough to carry me back to Denimoore while the two males ran ahead to scout for danger. Though she did not offer any kind words, her actions spoke instead. Isla had met us at the front entrance, tears in her eyes as she took in my appearance, and she waited silently as Kalian scooped me up from his sister's back before carrying me to the bed I had been given previously, his pack following worriedly behind.

And although that had been days ago, my eyes were still unseeing, and my mind was blank.

"Rest, dear Skylahr," Isla whispered as she tucked the blankets around me ushering everyone from my room.

Now alone, I was too afraid to close my eyes in fear of the visions I was sure to see. Instead, I pulled the blankets off of me, freeing me from their suffocating weight, and brought my knees to my chest before I buried my face in them. My eyes had been dry since returning to the Lupine territories, and even now tears refused to come, no matter how desperate I was to feel them. Taking in a shaking breath, I unfolded my legs before setting my bare feet onto the cold floor.

I wrapped the thick blanket around myself like a cloth shield, protecting me from the horror and guilt while I stumbled to the window. Pulling the curtains away from the glass, I exposed my face to the bright moon that hung in the sky. A view like this would have once pleased me, the beauty breathtaking and splendid. But now it brought the shadows to light, and the reality that my only family and friend were gone was too devastating to fully take in. Yanking the curtains shut with as much force as I could, I fell to my knees in a heap and then the broken sobs finally came. I had thought I would be grateful, but now I ached from their force.

Aware of how loud they were in the empty room, I lifted my hands to smother them. But because I was completely consumed with trying to quiet the wails, I had been oblivious to the door opening and the footsteps approaching me from behind.

A pair of large hands pulled at my shoulders until I was standing in front of him and then they slid up, his palms cradling my jaw, tilting my face to his. Kalian bent slightly, and his eyes were lowered to the level of my own, the deep silver soft in worry but unwavering while the fingers on my jaw gentled before dropping to curl over my shoulders again, clenching the blanket softly.

Holding my eyes in his sight, he grimaced before shaking me roughly, forcing my head to loll back and forth while blubbering wet sobs came from my mouth.

"Enough of this! Enough! Get yourself together!" His voice was a rough growl while my body rocked under his palms. Grabbing at my face again, he held my chin roughly.

"Breathe, damn it! Breathe!"

Confusion swirled in my mind until my lungs burned for oxygen. In my despair I had forgotten to inhale. I watched him closely and mimicked his own breathing until ours matched. We repeated the rhythmic pattern, and he stood there silently until my sobs quieted and then pulled me back to the bed. Lifting the blankets, he helped me crawl into them and waited for me to sink into their warmth and comfort before following me silently. Perching his large frame on the edge of the mattress, his bright eyes watched me as my own began to slowly blink. He waited until they finally closed, as I was forced to surrender to sleep.

The morning had come too quickly, and my heart remained heavy even in the sunlight. I pulled myself out of bed, dressed, and stumbled my way into the dining room only to find it empty with the exception of a plate filled with food and a piece of parchment with my name written across it. After sinking into the chair, I picked at my plate, managing to swallow a few pieces of fruit and a sip of tea before taking in my surroundings. The halls were quiet, and I grew more and more suspicious that it was because the servants had been told to avoid me. In the silence, I moved the rest of my food around my plate until the blackberries had turned to a black paste, and the sight of it had the smell of soot and burning fill my mind. Lifting a hand to cover my mouth, I raced towards the back balcony to empty my stomach.

Falling heavily to my knees, I winced as the sharp sound of contact echoed around me only to be outdone by the retching that followed. Then the light pattering of swift feet and skirts swishing came from my left and gentle hands gathered my hair out of my face.

"I'm so sorry," I croaked out, gesturing to the mess of fruit I had regurgitated on the stone floor.

"Don't be so foolish." The whisper was not the sweet voice of Isla but rather the deep smoothness of her daughter. Leena held my hair as another round of convulsions shook my stomach, forcing whatever was left out of me. Her hands soothed my back in wide, slow circles and then moved through my hair.

"I knew this would happen," I sobbed, falling back into her legs.

"The vomit? Then why did you bother eating?" she asked, irritated with me, and I didn't know if I could get the words out to explain my meaning.

"No. The—my parents. I knew."

Her hands paused in my bronze waves for just a second before resuming their pattern. She was silent for a long moment, weighing her words.

"How did you know?"

I was thankful that she hadn't immediately pushed the blame away from me, dismissing my guilt as if I was not at fault. Taking a deep, shuddering breath, I told her the secret I had kept hidden for what felt like ages. "I dreamt it. For weeks. Every night I dreamt it and then—" I broke into a sob. "And then a message was sent to me."

Leena's hands stilled, and I saw her come around my side in my peripheral vision, but I was too ashamed to look up. I instead studied the light grey flowers that had been stitched into her blue skirts. How could I handle meeting those cool, dark eyes when I had finally given her reason to hate me? After all, I had abandoned my parents, leaving them open to an attack.

Leena knelt in front of me, paying no mind to the bile on the floor. "Look at me!" Her voice was harsh and demanding while long fingers tucked under my chin, pulling my face up in her direction, her dark eyes blazing as they held my own captive. "You did not do this. That blame does not fall on your shoulders."

Holding my gaze, she waited until I nodded in agreement before standing back up, waving her hands at me to rise with her. "You are not this weak, Skylahr. You have had a devastating loss, but don't you dare let it consume you."

Nodding again, I wiped my tears from my eyes. I knew she was right. I needed to focus on what was next; I had to uncover the reason why this happened. Noorde Point had always been a peaceful village, not even a point on most maps. There was no reason for anyone to come that far north only to wreak havoc and kill so many innocents.

Long tan fingers circled around my wrist as she pulled me forward, and I dutifully followed Leena back to the dining table as I sifted through my memories, trying to pinpoint anything that may have been cause for concern. Besides the fever, nothing extraordinary had happened there, not as long as I had been alive at least. The only change had been the sickness and my journey to the Swallows. Violet eyes from my nightmares flashed through my mind, and I thought back to the witch, her warning, and our bull with my name carved into its head.

"Leena—" My voice broke. "Could the Goddess, the Seductress—" I felt foolish for even saying her name, but the woman in front of me had gone very still, watching me carefully. Deciding that was enough reason to speak of it, I continued.

"Could she have done this? Is that even a possibility?"

Leena took a deep breath before swallowing, and her pause caused my anxiety to rise. Her mouth opened and closed three times before she stood from her chair to pace back and forth in front of me, the threaded grey flowers dancing across the folds of her skirts as if in a spring breeze with each step.

"Leena," Kalian warned from the doorway, silently making his entrance while his eyes bore into his sister's before meeting my own. He smiled softly at me, his usual rugged face holding a warmth I had only seen directed to his mother. I dropped my gaze down to study the wood of the table as my eyes stung.

I had not seen much of him besides the visit to my room, but each time I glanced at him I remembered that it was his arms that had held me as I screamed for my family, rocking me gently until he had managed to lift me onto his sister. I had never been so weak in front of someone, and the thought of being in that state for him to see had me filled with shame and embarrassment.

Pulling out the chair across from my own noisily, he placed his hand on the table just far enough that the tips of his fingers entered my line of vision. They drummed one at a time, a dull rhythmic thud barely loud enough for me to hear, and I focused on the beat, letting it distract me from the memories that haunted me even now. Counting each tap, I tried to push down the suffocating wave of grief and blame that threatened to swallow me whole. But the panic won, and it bubbled in my chest until my breath caught, forcing me to rise abruptly from my chair when my need for air became pressing. Ignoring the startled eyes that followed my departure from the room, I rounded the corner out to the hall, my strides picking up the pace as I neared the doors. I could hear his footsteps behind me, but the walls began to close in, and I ran towards the yards.

Throwing open the doors, I bent and braced myself on my knees, gulping down air. The footfalls stopped behind me and I wiped my eyes before turning to him. "What is it that you want, Kalian?" I snapped, angry that I couldn't seem to control my grief.

"I was going to ask you the same." His eyes remained soft and I snarled at the expression.

"There is nothing that you can give me."

His head tipped to the side, his face serious before he grabbed my elbow and pulled. He led me down to the yard, his hand strong on my arm as he dragged me behind him, and I dug my heels into the frozen earth as I tried to slow him. But it was useless; I was no match for his strength.

Finally reaching the ring, I managed to free my arm and shoved him away from me with both hands. Tension rippled through my face as my jaw clenched and my eyes blazed in anger. He regarded me silently, and his lips pulled into a nasty smirk before he tossed a sparring sword at me, the wood landing in the wet snow with a splattering impact.

Never taking my eyes off of him, I bent at the waist and picked it up, fingers sliding over the wet hilt. And just as I straightened, he came at me with the first blow, nearly finding its mark as I narrowly blocked it with my own blade. The impact was so strong it sent painful vibrations through my arm up into my shoulder, and my mouth hung open in shock.

The wooden blades had only kissed for a second before he was pulling away to strike me down again, deadly in his precision, and I could do little else but block each attack. Using one long leg, he kicked out at me, taking my own move I had used against his sister, and I had barely been able to move at the last moment. Clumsily dodging his kick, I ended up losing my footing and landing on one knee. His blade pressed against my heated cheek while I huffed in exertion.

"Get up."

His order left no room for argument, and I stood watching as he took his position again. The second round was the same as the first, only ending when I landed on all fours and again, he pressed his blade against my skin, ordering me to get back on my feet. We went through this routine over and over again, his strength never wavering while my arms tired and shook.

Body aching, I lay sprawled on my back in the muddy snow, dazed and blinking up at the sky.

"Again."

"No," I whispered, pulling myself up, my chest heaving.

"Again," he growled at me, slapping my shoulder with his blade. Snarling at him, I lifted my blade and swung blindly, only for him to dodge it gracefully, forcing me to land in the icy mud once more.

"Again." Burning rage coursed through me as my nostrils flared, and I stood holding the wooden handle with both hands before using all my weight to charge at him. His chuckle was quiet as he lifted a foot to push me backwards and I fell onto my backside clumsily.

"Again," he barked at me, ignoring my spit that I aimed at him.

"I said," He paused, glaring down at me. "Again."

I felt humiliated as he played with me as if I were a mouse trapped between his claws. Using every last morsel of rage in my body, I let loose a scream as I came at him over and over, my blade swinging carelessly as I ran at him.

"That's it, Skylahr," he praised as he lifted his weapon. "Let it out, embrace it." I had no idea what he was talking about, but I took his encouragement.

I forced him back, my newfound strength surprising him with each lunge. I hadn't noticed I had begun to cry until his frame became a blur. My throat burned from the screams of anger and grief, and with one last strike, I knocked his blade from his grasp before pressing the tip of wood against his chest.

Standing still, I blinked at the wooden edge as my breath came in gasps and my anger melted into a fit of laughter. I had finally beaten him, I realised, and I giggled, high on the adrenaline of the spar. I wiped at my eyes, my body shaking from the peals of laughter, and Kalian stood mutely in front of me, his eyes wide as he watched me cautiously.

The deep, swirling pools of silver held shock and concern, and the latter slammed me back into reality when I was suddenly hit with the loss I had been consumed with. Catching my breath, I felt my knees give out, and there in the middle of the pen, Kalian followed me to the ground, kneeling before me while his hands stroked the tears from my cheeks.

"It was her, wasn't it? It was the Seductress," I whispered as guilt clawed at my heart again.

"Yes. I think so." His voice shook as he avoided eye contact.

I knew it had been, but hearing confirmation had sharpened the stabbing pain in my chest. That meant the witch of the Swallows had truly seen a vision and my dreams had been warnings. I had been right all along, and I had left my parents and Elizabeth to die.

Another wave of guilt crippled me as I thought about the time I had wasted waiting and wondering if leaving was the answer. Maybe if I had left earlier, I could have lured her away, or maybe if I had stayed, I could have stopped her.

As if he could read my mind, Kalian grabbed my jaw and forced me to look at his face. "You could not have stopped her, even if you had tried."

I knew that was most likely true, but it didn't take away any of my heartache. Sighing with exhaustion, I pulled his hands away from me. And when I straightened to my full height, I looked down at him, deciding if I would truly ask such a favour of him.

"I need to go south, Kalian. I need to find a way to end her." Before I could even ask, he replied instantly.

"Then I will go with you."

Chapter 12

Days went by and neither of us mentioned travelling down south again. Instead, Kalian avoided me, leaving me to my own devices for days on end, and both Keyno and Leena followed suit. In their absence I was forced to eat with Isla or wander the great halls on my own.

Deciding to bide my time until I could broach the subject again, I spent my days in the training yard, cutting down dummies, or reading in the extensive library learning about the people who had taken me in. The Lupines were such a beautiful group of people, full of history and culture. I browsed through art and poetry, completely entranced by them. By the second week I had managed to convince Isla to allow me to venture farther than the grounds of the castle but had not been able to talk her out of a chaperone.

I pulled myself from my bed and sat on the edge gazing out of the window. Today was the first day I had woken without painful eyes or a heavy chest, my mind too preoccupied with the anticipation of escaping the towering stone walls to notice much else. I tied my hair into a braid at the back of my neck, put on the clean tunic and breeches that had been left out for me, and grabbed the thick cloak before looking into the mirror that hung on the far wall.

The deep blue of the wool only contrasted with my pale face, highlighting the ashy tone that had lingered since we came back from Noorde Point. My eyes were dull, shadowed by the deep circles, and

I looked like a ghost of myself. Pinching at my cheeks, I willed for colour to bloom but soon gave up and instead threw a blanket over the mirror.

I smoothed down my tunic with my hands and opened the heavy wooden door, nearly colliding with a solid chest. Catching myself at the last moment, I rocked backwards, peering up at the annoyingly handsome face I had grown used to.

"You're finally gracing me with your presence. What have I done to be given the pleasure?" I snarked while rolling my eyes. His stare slid down to my toes before he hummed under his breath.

"I could show you pleasure, but you'd have to ask very, *very* nicely. After all I would be doing you a favour."

It would appear that the sympathy was long gone, and the infuriating taunts had come back in full swing. Groaning with frustration, I bypassed him, storming my way to the dining hall to meet the guard that had been organized for me. However, the Lupine alpha followed behind me, whistling obnoxiously, barely pausing for a second when I spun to glare at him.

Turning back, I rounded the corner of the entranceway only to be disappointed by the empty room. I had hoped to escape Kalian with as much dignity as I could muster, but it appeared that I would be stuck waiting. Sighing, I fell into a chair as my fingernails drummed against the massive wooden table, and Kalian leaned against the wall, smirking at me as more and more time passed.

Minutes dragged on and I felt my stomach settle into an uneasy swirling. I had longed to distract myself with new scenery, hoping to replace the black soot and swirls of smoke that still entered my vision anytime I closed my eyes. Kalian must have seen the grief cross my face and choosing to take pity on me, he pushed himself from the wall he was resting against before walking to the other side of the table, his hands cupping the back of the chair as he cleared his throat.

"I will escort you to the village." My own seat scraped noisily across the floor as I stood.

"Don't worry yourself, it was your mother's idea." I stalked to the doorway, and my arm was caught in his firm grasp as he pulled me back around to face him. The smirk that usually adorned his lips had been pulled into a frown as he cast his eyes down, his fingers holding me firm, though his thumb rubbed across my arm soothingly.

"Please, let me take you." His voice was soft, and I managed a single nod before he released me and stepped away while clearing his throat again. I stood there for a moment, fidgeting with my tunic nervously as I waited for him to lead the way.

Remaining silent, I followed closely behind, keeping my eyes focused on my boots as we weaved our way through the castle until we entered the courtyards. The smell of straw and horse wafted through the air, and a gorgeous stone stable with sprawling pastures had my lips lifting in excitement. My pace quickened as I matched Kalian's strides, ignoring his curious gazes as he took in my change of mood.

Horses filled the stalls, their heads poking out over their doors as they greeted us with noisy nickers and whinnies. A large grey horse with deep brown eyes reached for my shoulder as we passed, and I snuck a few scratches in under its chin while Kalian spoke to a groom. The two men continued down to the end of the aisle where the saddles sat on their racks, but I was too busy stroking the forelocks of the nosey animals who were pushing for attention.

"Lawnie will saddle the horses for us, and we will be on our way." Too focused on the dark bay who was now lipping at my fingers as I tickled his muzzle, I hadn't even noticed Kalian had come back to get me.

"Why do we even need to take horses? Couldn't you just—" I paused, blushing at my implication that he should carry me on his back again.

"Though I do miss the way your fingers stroke me so gently, I'd rather not wander my village nude. Sorry to disappoint *you*."

Blushing hotly, I realized I had forgotten that minor detail and felt foolish for even mentioning it. Rolling my eyes, I pressed my fingers to the bay's cheek, stroking the soft, gleaming coat as my blush faded.

"Would you like to take him?"

I turned to Kalian, eyes wide as he gestured to the gelding I had been petting.

"Really?"

"Of course." He waved the groom over and I watched in anticipation as they tacked him up. Once we were organized and ready, we mounted and trotted off through the thick woods that led us to the town.

I had never had the privilege of sitting on such a fine horse, and as the town drew closer and closer, I wished that we had more time to spend on horseback. I had ridden as a child, it was the only thing my mother and I had truly bonded over, and sitting astride the magnificent gelding, I longed to see her again. Blinking away the sadness that had gathered, I leaned down to pat the black mane and sighed before dismounting. Tying him to the post, I waited for Kalian to do the same.

"You ride well," he offered while busying himself with the reins.

"Thank you," I murmured under my breath, unprepared for the compliment.

He cleared his throat awkwardly, fingers still busy with the leather. "While you are our guest, the gelding is yours to use as you wish. As long as you have an escort."

Normally the idea of having a chaperone would irritate me, but I knew I had no right to argue, especially after receiving such a gracious gift. "Truly?" I asked, not quite believing him.

"Yes. Take him whenever you please." Finishing the knot, he turned on his heel, ignoring me as he walked through the town.

The streets were clean and tidy, the old buildings beautifully crafted and well maintained by their people, and the market was filled with happy faces and cheerful chatter. It was a welcome sight.

I observed Kalian closely as he led the way. Many people flocked to him, stopping to speak to him or to grasp at his hands. He paused for each individual, smiling at them kindly, always taking the time to ask them about their family or their business. This was unlike the Kalian I had dealt with these past weeks. Gone was the arrogance and ego;

now he was a kind leader who obviously cared greatly for his people.

Our day passed quickly, most of it spent talking to the townspeople as they welcomed their ruler with open arms. I had managed to hide in the shadows, avoiding attention, and focused on the lightness of Denimoore. Though Noorde Point had been happier before the fever, it had never been so peaceful, and my mind was at ease for the entirety of our trip.

Finally turning back for home, we mounted our horses again. This time walking back up to the stables, truly taking our time. And though I wouldn't say so, I was grateful for the small gift.

Rather than breaking the silence, I let myself be pulled into the lull of the rocking as I relaxed in the saddle ignoring the drop in temperature. Not even the cold bite of the northern wind could make me hasten my pace.

"Are you sure you still want to head south?" Kalian's deep voice drew my attention and I sighed in resignation.

"Yes."

"You could stay here. You would be protected, safe," he offered, his voice light as he gazed at me.

"But I would never be at peace." The village was beautiful, and I was sure I could find work, make some semblance of a life, but I would always long to find answers, would burn with vengeance for my family and friend.

"Looking for answers may lead you into a dangerous game, and getting killed will not bring you the peace you are longing for." He voiced my thoughts without warning, surprising me.

Scoffing, I turned in my saddle to face him. "I'm not afraid to die." My voice was steel, unwavering, though Kalian did not look impressed, only more displeased.

"You think that makes you brave, wanting to end your life?"

I frowned at him, anger pulling at my face. "You think that death is what I'm searching for? If that was truly my solution, I would have slit my throat the first chance I had." Pausing, I pulled the reins, halting my horse before searching for the right words. "I have never felt like

I was living for myself. I have always felt like there was something...
more. So no, I don't think it's brave, nor do I care. I care for others;
so, I will live. I will live to find the answers and save as many lives as
I can. I will stop the Seductress or whoever it was who burned my
home to the ground, and when I am done, I will go willingly if the
Gods wish it."

I slowly slid my gaze to his face, the air leaving my lungs as the
molten silver pools regarded me carefully. "Living for others is a
painful existence, Skylahr."

Dropping my gaze back down, I cleared my throat before nodding
my head. "It may be painful. But it's easy."

Kicking my heels into the barrel of the gelding, I cantered off,
leaving the alpha behind as we cleared the woods. Once entering
the stable, I untacked silently, refusing the help of the stable hands,
wanting to distract myself from the looming presence that now stood
behind me.

"If you are certain you want to travel south, we will go. I will
take you wherever you want. But you need to understand there is no
certainty that we will find what you are looking for."

Dropping the brush in my hand, I turned to him. "I'm not asking
you to come with me, Kalian. You owe me nothing."

He smiled softly at me, his handsome face warm as his lips parted.
"I know that."

"Then why come?" I asked, tipping my head to the side in confusion
as the alpha turned to gaze out the barn doors. His jaw was tight, and
I watched in silence as he seemed to gather his thoughts before he
turned from me. With a stiff spine, he looked back over his shoulder.

"Maybe I live for others too."

Chapter 13

Isla had found me after our return to the castle, her face pulled into a deep frown, and I knew that something serious was on her mind. But before I could reach for her, Kalian had stood in front of me, his massive frame blocking me from his mother, and they had a silent conversation all while my nerves ate at me.

Sighing in defeat, Kalian moved aside and allowed his mother to grab my wrist and tug me back towards her chambers. Isla had never gone this long without addressing me pleasantly or smiling at me and I had begun to worry. Isla pulled me through the doors to her room and slammed them shut before gesturing at the empty table sitting in the corner next to the window.

I watched as she grabbed a bottle of wine, removing the cork before bringing the bottle to her lips. Taking a long drink from it, she sighed and wiped her mouth with the back of her hand before holding the bottle out to me.

"Oh, I—" I stuttered as I lifted my hands in refusal.

"Skylahr." She had always called me sweeting or dear and I knew then something was terribly wrong. "Drink. You'll need it." I took the bottle from her hands, swallowed my own large gulp, and pressed back into my chair.

"You must understand why we have not told you. The Lupines are an ancient people, and our secrets are sacred to us."

I nodded my head before drinking another mouthful of wine.

"However, I feel that I owe you some answers, at least the ones I can give you. I hope perhaps they will bring you some peace." Anxiety filled me while Isla turned to the nightstand, opened the drawer, and removed a thick book.

Cradling it to her chest, she took in a deep breath before placing it face up on the table between us. I watched her, waiting for a nod of reassurance before my fingers traced the title that was carved into the leather cover. It was in the tongue of old and I looked back up to her face in silent pleading.

"It is the story of the Protector. The story of our people." Nodding, I flipped through the book, astonished by the beautiful writing and pictures that filled the pages, though not understanding any of it. My eyes scanned over each delicate piece of parchment until I turned to a drawing I immediately understood.

The colours had faded with age, but the purple irises were unmistakable. I had seen them every night in my dreams since my trip to the Swallows. A cold shiver ran down my spine and I blinked back up at Isla.

"The Seductress." Her voice was a whisper, and I nodded my head before peering down at the beautiful portrait. She had the same long dark hair I had dreamt of and her red lips were lifted in a frightening grin. My fingers trembled as I thumbed the corner of the page before finally flipping it.

"What does it say?"

Isla sighed and sat in her chair, her own fingers reaching for the leather-bound pages, turning the book to face her before reading the words to herself silently.

"You know the tales? You've heard the stories of the War of the Gods?" I knew our version of the stories, but I had never heard the stories from a member of the Lupine people.

"The Seductress was in love with the Protector, but when he mated with the Huntress, she killed them both," I summarized roughly while Isla smiled at me gently.

"I suppose that is a decent retelling from a southerner."

I grinned at her before cupping my chin in my hands and watched her as she began to recount the words of her people.

"What most forget is that it wasn't his love that the Seductress wanted, but power. She had spent hundreds of years trying to convince the Protector to rule alongside her, to overthrow the other Gods and their followers. She hungered for supremacy, not love, and when he and his mate finally fought against her, her rage scorched the earth. She had created her immortal army, had used her influence to twist their lust and devotion and controlled them completely, taking their choices and judgement away."

I watched as her fingers flipped to another page before pressing the spine flat against the table and then she turned the book back to me. The picture before me was one of gore and violence. There were two sides—one carrying crimson banners and the coat of arms that belonged to their Goddess, the others in green and black as they fought off the oncoming army.

"Though in the end our armies had been victorious in sending the Seductress into hiding, both the Protector and the Huntress had been fatally wounded. And our Gods knew that they had to find some way to preserve their magic in case she ever returned."

I stared in wonder as her fingers turned to a new page.

"The prophecy says that in her last moments, the Huntress sent her magic into the world, where it would lie dormant until the Chosen were born."

"Chosen?" I whispered, not understanding, but Isla just smiled softly, her voice dropping low.

"Five half-blood beings belonging to each of the Gods who will have the power to defeat the Seductress and her armies once and for all."

My mind spun as I blinked up at her gorgeous face. "Half-blood—" I gasped. "You mean halflings?"

The witch in the Swallows had been my only experience with a magical being. I had never seen another halfling or witnessed how they came to be, but I had heard stories. Stories of how some immortals would seduce the unsuspecting humans, resulting in a mixed-blood babe. A babe who would then be forced to spend the rest of its life hiding from the Crimson army. After all, the Seductress's troops were known to hunt for days just to find a single halfling, though no one knew why. I had always assumed it was to preserve their pure immortal blood.

Isla grabbed my hand as her eyes shone wetly. "Yes, that is why they are executed."

"So the Chosen? Have they been found? Are they alive?"

Isla sighed sadly before shutting the book tightly and standing to put it back in its place. "No one knows, sweeting. They may not even be born yet. They might not even be real. It all could be a grand tale."

"But they could be." I didn't wait for her answer as I stood from my chair, finally knowing what my next step was. "Isla, I have to know if they exist. If they're out there, they could stop her from harming more people."

Isla nodded her head, though she was watching me with worry. "Sweeting, I know how badly you want answers, I know how badly you want to avenge your family—"

I held up a hand to cut her off, not wanting to hear her reasons as to why I shouldn't.

"I am so thankful for everything you have done for me, but if there is even the slightest chance that the Seductress and her army were responsible for Noorde Point, if she and her Crimsons have murdered innocents, then I must find a way to stop them. And this may be how, the Chosen could be my chance."

Isla hung her head in defeat for a moment before striding forward and pulling me into a tight embrace. "Oh, Skylahr, how brave you are." Stepping back, she smoothed my hair from my face before grasping my hands tightly. "May the Protector be with you."

Sitting astride the black fur, I thought back to the difficult morning we had before departing Denimoore. Saying goodbye to Isla had been more testing than I had anticipated. Her face had crumpled in worry as she tried to convince me to wait a few more days. Although I understood her concern, I felt an irrational surge of resentment at her attempts of persuasion. I appreciated all the generosity they had shown me, but she was practically a stranger and my family had been taken from me. My resolve was unwavering even when she tried to have Leena and Keyno reason with Kalian. However, to my surprise, he dismissed them with one pointed glare and all arguments were silenced. I was grateful for his support even if I refused to show it.

A grumble below me pulled me from my thoughts, and I noticed we had reached what could only be the Lupine border. The forest opened in a beautiful archway, but the space between the trees appeared to have a glossy sheen, almost as if the entrance was covered with a glass curtain.

Dismounting clumsily, I approached the barrier, too entranced by the magic before me to notice the two shadows that lurked in the trees behind us. Kalian's rough human voice broke me from my daze, and I turned to find both Keyno and Leena dropping their eyes in compliance as they were scolded for their actions.

With a frustrated sigh, Kalian ran a hand through his hair before turning to me. Looking past his shoulder, I met Keyno's gaze just in time to see him smile apologetically at me.

"It looks like it will be a party of four," he rumbled before snarling back at his pack mates.

"Why would they come?"

"They're worried for us. Our kind has not been past the Lupine borders in years. They want to be here to protect us should things go wrong."

I nodded in understanding before looking back at the two as they approached us. "I appreciate the concern but can't ask you to risk your safety for me."

"It's not for you," Leena snarled, ignoring the nudge of Keyno's elbow. "We can't have our alpha down in the southern provinces without some sort of pack." Obviously, the kindness I had been besotted after Noorde Point was over and I was almost glad for it; I much preferred her anger and indifference over the pity.

Deciding to let them sort it out, I approached the shimmering air, reaching a shaking hand to it. As my fingers approached the glistening, I noticed that the air felt cold and prickled gently, almost in the same way a limb would when it had gone numb in sleep. Watching in fascination, I pushed my hand through carefully. It was like dipping into a clear stream, the stillness broken by ripples and waves swirling around the intruding object. A large tan hand lifted to join mine in the magic, jolting me out of my daydream. Glancing to my side, I saw Keyno standing next to me, twisting and turning his own large fingers with interest. Smiling softly at me, he nodded his head towards the siblings.

"They're still squabbling back there." His expression was filled with fondness and I wondered how he managed to put up with the two of them.

"Are they always so," I searched for the word. "Intense?"

"I think you mean difficult, annoyingly condescending, or obnoxious."

I grinned back at him before chuckling. It was obvious that he loved them both deeply. He was so warm and kind, like Isla, and yet, the siblings were anything but. Leena was cold and hard, only showing me kindness when we had left Noorde Point. And although Kalian was not nearly as unpleasant in the same way, he was constantly trying to aggravate me. Sighing, Keyno looked back at the pair.

"I know they aren't easy, but you won't find a better escort south."

Watching me roll my eyes, he placed a hand on my arm, pulling it out of the magic.

"I'm serious, Skylahr. They will protect you with their lives simply because they can, not because they should or have to." I blinked at him, one of my brows lifting in disbelief. "I grew up in the village north of Denimoore, a tiny poor little town called Clardin. I was an orphan and did not live a peaceful youth. I was cold and starving and had nothing to offer anyone and was just twelve when I met Leena and her father. They had been travelling through the northern villages, touring the lands together." His smile was sweet as he reminisced.

"One look at me and her father took me in and brought me south. Kalian and I grew to be brothers in arms over time, and he never treated me like the lowly boy I was. But I never had parents to guide me as a boy, so I was impulsive and rash, never thinking about consequences. And those traits almost cost Kalian his life."

Looking over his shoulder to be sure we would be unheard, he pulled me a step closer while he lowered his voice. "I had gone off on my own against his orders, only to be ambushed by a few Crimson soldiers. The minute Kalian realized I had been taken, he came to my aide, never once thinking about the risks for himself."

Keyno tugged me even closer and dropped his voice to a faint whisper. "By the time we escaped their clutches, Kalian was dying. His back had been split open and he was barely breathing. To this day I still have no idea what all they had done to him, he won't tell me."

My mouth dropped open in shock at his words. I had seen the evidence of that injury and could still picture that gruesome deep jagged scar that ran the length of his back. No one had ever spoken about it and now hearing the story I felt a pang of empathy for the alpha.

"Just under a year later we were out facing another breach on our borders. This time I was the one who suffered the brunt of the attack only to be saved by him again. He had gifted me—"

Suddenly he stopped and straightened, taking a step back before I realized that the two siblings had finished their argument and had come to join us at the edge of the border. Turning to his mate, Keyno wrapped her into his arms before pressing a sweet kiss to her brow. She, however, watched me with disdain. Rolling my eyes in annoyance, I pulled the hood of my cloak over my head effectively blocking her from my line of sight.

Kalian joined us, moving in front to cross through the border first, and I waited in anticipation. Just as my fingers had, his massive frame passed easily though the mirage. Leena and Keyno followed behind without so much as a second of hesitation, and then the three turned to me expectantly, waiting for me to muster the courage to follow. Although they seemed unharmed, I had a difficult time believing I would be so lucky.

"Going to stand there all day?" Kalian mocked me with a raised brow. "I know how much you love to stop and stare, but we really should hurry."

I wasn't sure if it was an act to get me to cross or if he truly was this annoying. But whatever his reasoning was, it worked.

Pulling my hood tighter around my face, I stormed across, only feeling the tingles on my face for a split second before I was through the veil. Passing the magic, I immediately noticed that the air on the other side of the invisible curtain felt heavier and dull, as if it was less clean, and I wondered if it always felt that way.

Walking through the dense forest, we began our journey south and surprisingly the three Lupines stayed on two feet rather than four for the first few hours. However, just as my energy had started to dwindle, Kalian huffed impatiently and shifted into his Lupine counterpart, bending for me to climb onto his back. It felt more awkward, almost wrong now that I had an audience. But when the other two also shifted into their wolven form, I was pleased that I would not have to worry about making small talk.

Kalian moved gracefully as he galloped across the northern land with complete ease. Our route had taken us to the northwestern coast, forcing us into the steep hills of the Elrin mountains. This far north we had little chance of running into any travellers, and it seemed to be a shame most would never witness the beauty. We travelled for hours and although I was not exerting myself, my energy was wavering as I felt my head bob, the harshness of the wind no longer having the ability to keep me focused. Kalian must have felt my balance teetering as he slowed to a light jog, moving his spine under me any time I leaned to one side or another.

By the time he slowed to a brisk walk, the sun had begun to set, casting golden shadows across the mountains, and as the last orange hues disappeared, the other two wolves split from the close formation they had kept the entirety of our journey. Keyno bolted west and

Leena sprinted forward, both leaving us as Kalian kept his pace.

After a long moment, a deep howl came from the west, causing Kalian to change our direction immediately, but he went no faster. Padding our way towards the noise, I could just make out the flicker of a fire hidden in a deep cave that was carved out on the side of a rock wall. Making our way to the entrance, I noticed both wolves were back on two feet, clearing loose rubble away to make space for us. I did my best to ignore their nudity as I slid off Kalian before tossing the pack at Leena's feet.

I moved closer to the flames, holding my palms out towards the heat, warming my fingers. In the corner of my eye I could see Kalian shrugging on a pair of breeches, not bothering to turn away or move into a more private area. The clear view of his muscular torso brought heat to my cheeks, and I was glad to have the fire as an excuse for it. Once dressed, he came to sit next to me and smiled smugly while he studied my face. Leena and Keyno, however, dressed and went back out into the night, Leena giggling while Keyno dragged her by the hand. My jaw went slack in shock at the foreign sound of her laughter only to snap shut moments later when a deep, throaty moan echoed from outside.

Clearing my throat, I stood, wiping my hands on my thighs before busying myself with the preparation of dinner. But try as I might, I could not hide my flustered reaction as more and more noise came from the couple.

"What's wrong, love? Does the sound of fucking offend you?"

I hadn't even noticed that Kalian had stood and walked over to me. Ignoring him, I knelt while I continued to dig through the pack with shaking hands.

"Or is it that the sounds actually interest you?"

Standing abruptly, I whipped around to face him. His body was so close to my own that I had to tip my chin up to meet his smoldering gaze. As our eyes clashed, his mouth lifted in that handsome smirk, the same one that made my blood boil with rage.

"Shut your mouth," I snarled, only to receive a deep chuckle in response.

"Don't be so sensitive. I'm sure if I drank enough of that wine in that pack of yours, you would be able to convince me to show you a thing or two. Who knows, maybe I'd like to bed a woman who could pin me down and take me as she pleases." He paused, his eyes studying me. "Or would you rather I make you feel like a damsel? Roll you under me and treat you like a proper lady?"

My hazel eyes burned with fury as I spat at his feet. I had always hated that I was not a dainty little woman, a true and proper lady. And now he had found my weakness and used it against me in such a cruel and horrid way.

His smirk wavered when he noticed the slump in my shoulders, and when he realized his mistake in crossing that line, he reached for me. But I moved and his hands met air as I dodged his reach. His lips folded into a thin line before he took a step back. "I'm sorry, that was unkind."

Although he seemed genuinely remorseful, the sour taste did not leave my mouth. I turned back to the pack, grabbing the blankets we had managed to stuff into it before spreading them on the cold floor of the cave. Kalian watched me with careful eyes as I pretended to smooth out the non-existent wrinkles in the cloth, only breaking his stare as his sister and her mate entered the stone walls again.

Avoiding eye contact with the both of them, I began to boil the broth and seasoning while they sat together near the fire. Keyno at least had the decency to look a bit embarrassed to have been so loud during their tryst. Leena, however, flicked her long hair over her shoulder as if her face was not flushed with a fine sheen of sweat coating it.

Dinner passed without incident as the two siblings ignored me completely. Keyno did his best to fill in the awkward silence with stories and jokes, only to be nudged in annoyance by his partner. I let her obvious dislike for me roll off my back as I ate quietly before packing away the dishes. I had decided it would be better to cause the least amount of annoyance possible while they travelled with me. Perhaps if I did not create any disturbance, they would aid my journey until we reached the safety of Carlon, our decided destination. Unfolding the other blankets, Leena volunteered me to take first watch, a position I gladly accepted, even if just to appease her.

Pulling my makeshift bed to the edge of the cave, I folded myself in half, knees to chest as I stared off into the black night. But only a few minutes passed before the cold began to eat at me, the frost causing my jaw to chatter against my knee no matter how hard I clenched it. Shivering violently, I wished I hadn't been so hasty in moving so far from the fire, and now my pride stopped me from moving back.

As if he sensed my inner turmoil, Kalian brought his blanket to me, dumping it onto my shoulders in a heap before he sat down next to me with a groan.

"Jester's balls it's cold out here!" he exclaimed, ignoring my dirty look at the choice of expression. Rolling his eyes at me, he lounged back on his hands, extending his massive frame to his full length across the ground. Choosing to ignore him, I brought my knees closer to my chest, unwilling to say anything he may mock me for later. We sat in silence for hours before I worked up the nerve to look over at him again. I turned my chin just enough to peer at him through my dark lashes, and my eyes widened in shock.

There before me was a creature more God than man. The glow of the fire flickered across his handsome face, catching on the sharp line of his jaw and cheekbones. His long, thick lashes cast a shadow across his golden skin, and his mouth was slightly parted, leaving him looking much younger in sleep than he did awake.

My tongue felt thick in my mouth as I swallowed, my cheeks burning in shame for ogling him while he slept. Swallowing again, I looked behind me to see if I had been caught. Keyno was awake and watching us carefully but remained silent. And when our eyes met, he motioned for me to end my watch and switch places.

Carefully standing up, I caught the blanket before it could slide off my shoulders. I debated bringing it with me, but the thought of taking it from the sleeping man who had left the warmth of the fire to keep me company seemed unfair. Instead, I knelt down next to him and spread it across his torso. Certain I would leave him undisturbed, I crept back to the fire. Smiling gratefully at Keyno, I curled on my side and tucked my hands under my cheek before I closed my eyes.

Morning came much too swiftly, and my body ached from sleeping on the cold stone. Sitting up, I stretched my arms wide as the smell filling the air in the deep cave left my mouth watering and I turned to the fire. Leena was kneeling next to the open flames, turning a spit with a rabbit on it, its meat roasting into a golden brown. Her dark gaze ignored me, and I searched for Kalian and Keyno, hoping they wouldn't be gone long. I wasn't sure I could handle Leena on my own.

I quietly rolled the blanket Kalian had discarded and pulled out the bread that had been packed. I was too cowardly to ask for some of Leena's catch, though I heard her huff of frustration. It was a sound I was becoming very familiar with and did my best not to let my surprise show when a roasted leg was pushed in front of me. Nodding at her gratefully, I picked at the meat, letting the flavour melt on my tongue. The smell must have summoned the men, as they both rushed into the opening of the cave before swiping at what was left of the cottontail.

Leaving the three Lupines to fight over the remainder of the meat, I wandered out to relieve myself and stretch my legs. I had slept more soundly than I had in weeks, but the cold had left me sore. Trying to walk off the stiffness, I made my way through the frozen tundra as the snow crunched under my boots. It was stunningly beautiful here; the great peaks of the mountains were so tall they kissed the clouds that swirled above them and left dark grey shadows dancing across the valleys between them.

It was cold, but the sun warmed my face and I tilted my chin towards it, a soft smile creeping across my lips. I had always hidden my face from the heat of the sun in fear that the light would produce more freckles across my skin, making my complexion even less desirable.

But the freedom of the northern wilderness had my usual insecurities scurrying back into the dark corners of my mind.

Throwing my arms out, I tipped my head back and spun beneath the cloud-covered sky, the warmth of the sun causing a great bubble of laughter to form in my chest. My mother would love the scenery here; I would have to try to sketch it for her.

Picturing my mother's smile of delight punctured that bubble of laughter that had lifted my spirits until a deep gasp was pushed from my lungs. The grief slowly burned away the picture of her grin until it melted into the blackened skull I had been left with. Bile rose in my throat as I remembered that my mother would never hear my stories, never see my sketches, never know the lengths her wild daughter travelled. How had I forgotten? How could I have been so happy when my parents were buried in the ground? Consumed and distracted by my guilt, I had not noticed the figure slinking behind the trees as it came towards me.

Chapter 14

A hand wrapped around my throat and pulled me to the ground roughly while my fingers clawed at air. Desperately trying to focus my mind, I lifted my fingers to scratch at the hand that pinned me while I kicked my legs as hard as I could. The stranger moved from my side to straddle my hips using his weight to pin my thighs while his hand crushed my throat. With my eyes watering, I fought for breath and swung my arm out to the side to grab anything I could use as a weapon.

My fingernails were sprawled and reaching until they scratched at a smooth, hard surface. The feeling of it would usually send shivers down my spine, but now it was a gift from the Gods. Grabbing on to the rock, I swung my arm with as much force as I could muster, slamming it into the side of the head above me.

Managing enough strength to knock them off my body, I used the opportunity to roll onto my knees, scrambling to my feet before I braced my weight, ready for another assault. Rolling to his feet, my attacker stood and pulled his long, pale white hair back and I took him in. He was slightly shorter than me, his lean build nothing extraordinary. His face, however, was beautifully delicate with full lips, a slim nose, high sharp cheekbones, and his eyes were a peculiar shade of deep blue.

Slipping a long, pale hand under his cloak, he produced a sharp dagger as a smile that could only be described as predatory slid across his mouth. My eyes focused on the blade as we circled each other carefully, waiting for someone to lunge first.

I didn't have to wait long as his impatience got the best of him, and he gracefully sprang forward. Anticipating this move I ducked down, avoiding his swinging arm, and waited until he was behind me before I swung one leg, swiping his feet out from under him. My advantage did not last, however, as he was back up on his feet before I had a chance to register it.

I had seen only the Lupines move with this speed, and it told me everything I needed to know. This was no ordinary nomad man; he was an immortal. Glaring at me in anger, he charged again, narrowly missing me as I dodged the dagger. We were in a deep game of cat and mouse, and I had a strong feeling that I would soon find myself caught. My breaths were shortening, and I burned with sweat but managed to avoid half a dozen more swings before my speed slowed, forcing me to take a hit to my shoulder. The blade was pushed in deep before being yanked out, leaving a searing-hot pain behind. Momentarily distracted, I had not noticed the other fire starting at the base of my spine. A blaze that I had felt before when my life had been in danger. Closing my eyes, I let my mind succumb to the flames before I was met with nothingness.

A loud noise was ringing in my head and Leena's eyes were mere inches from my own. Her mouth was opening, forming words I couldn't understand, and I squinted as I focused on her full lips while I waited for my brain to process what was being shouted at me. Slowly the ringing faded, and I could hear another voice blaring behind me. I turned my head towards the noise.

The pale immortal was screaming, his voice cracking in fear as he crawled away from the monstrous black beast who stalked him. The black furred body was low to the ground as his lips pulled over his teeth in what could easily be mistaken for a vile grin. The white-haired man began to beg, pleading for his life as the wolf rocked back on his haunches, preparing to pounce. I could hear Leena calling my name again and I felt her fingertips grab at my face to turn it, but I was solely focused on the scene before me.

"You know what she'll do if you harm me, dog!" the man screamed as he looked at me wildly.

Silver eyes flickered to mine for a split second before he sprang forward, jaws closing around the white hair before yanking harshly. A sickening crack echoed in the valley and I knew there would be no saving the immortal. Closing my eyes, I turned back to Leena, not willing to witness any more as she pulled at my shoulders helping me to stand before leading me away from the gruesome scene.

Once we were in the safety of the cave I sat down slowly, my eyes wide with shock. I had never been ignorant to violence. I had seen the injuries received during the tournaments at home, and I had often helped Elizabeth while she tended to grown men who had slashed and cut at each other over a drunken brawl. And though the smell often turned my stomach, I prided myself on my lack of aversion when it came to blood and gore. But watching Kalian's beast decapitate that man had been more than I was prepared for.

As if my thoughts had conjured him, a nude Kalian was running towards us. His deep silver eyes held my own as he came closer, only to pause an arm's length away as if he was asking me permission to enter. Swallowing, I checked with Leena before nodding my head. But he did not approach me, and instead grabbed a blanket from the floor, wrapping it around his waist before sitting next to the fire. Keyno was not far behind and he too paused at opening, not entering. His dark eyes narrowed as his gaze turned to steel, for once no ounce of warmth swirling in the depths. Not understanding, I turned to his mate, but she too held the same expression.

"What? What is going on?" My voice was high with anxiety as their silence ate at me.

Leena was the first to break the tension, turning to her brother with a plea. He, however, lifted a hand to silence her before focusing back on my face. His eyes searched for something I was unaware of before he growled at the other two to leave us. I wanted to plead that they stay but was too cowardly to question him.

"Do you know what happened back there?" His voice was hard, lacking its usual teasing. It was the voice of a man who had led for years, demanding and ruthless, and it made my throat feel like it had closed as my heart stuttered.

"You killed the immortal." My own voice was a weak whisper.

"Before that." The words snarled out of him and I felt my chest tighten in panic.

"He attacked me, I was stabbed, and—"

Pausing, I lifted my fingers to my shoulder where his dagger had been lodged. I felt the damp cloth, but there was only a tiny indent in my flesh. The skin was hot and raw, but there was no weeping wound, and Kalian watched my hand drop back down to my side.

"And?"

"And nothing. That's the last I remember."

Angered by my response, he stood, clutching the blanket around him before kneeling in front of me. His hand reached out, the tan fingers holding my jaw still as he examined my face.

"And how long have you known that you were a halfling?"

Chapter 15

My jaw hung open in his grasp while I tried to ignore the tightness of his fingers against my skin. His eyes narrowed in on mine before his hand softened, and I took the opportunity to pull my jaw from him as I leaned back to look up into his face.

"Halfling?"

It was obvious that he did not believe my disbelief as his face was drawn in anger and he stood, massive arms crossing over his chest. When I didn't follow his lead, he reached down and pulled me to my feet.

"Do not play games with me, girl."

"I'm not playing at anything and I have a name, you brute," I snapped as I yanked my arms from him.

A deep, low snarl shook his frame before he turned on his heel to march across the cave. He paced in front of me, back and forth like a caged animal, only to stop midstride and spin towards me before stalking back across the space between us.

"How could you not know? There had to be signs before this. When we found you, you were covered in blood and yet unharmed. And now I know why."

Swallowing nervously, I looked away from him. He was right, of course, there had been signs that something was wrong with me. My wounds healed at an incredible speed, and I lost hours' worth of memories, but being a halfling had never crossed my mind. It just wasn't possible. Both my parents had been mortal so how could I have immortal blood in my veins?

"You really didn't know." It was a statement rather than a question, and the air around us went from hostile to awkward. Crossing my arms over my chest, I studied the ground under my toes as he took a few steps back before dropping down into the dirt next to the fire. I peeked at him through my lashes, watching as he ran a hand through his hair in frustration. Following his lead, I too dropped onto the ground in a heap. The frigid stone was cold against my backside, and it was the first time that I had noticed how truly exhausted I was. Closing my eyes, I sighed heavily.

"That happens when you ignite. Your body needs time to recover."

"Ignite?"

"That's what we call it when the power of your immortal side takes over. When it burns through you."

I sighed again before rubbing at my eyes. It was a good way to describe it; I certainly felt as if my being was consumed by fire each time the flames licked at my spine.

"What happens when someone ignites?" I was almost afraid of his answer.

"Well, from what I can remember, at first it feels like an out-of-body experience. Some people have no recollection of what happens during it, at least not until they learn to harness it. But your immortal blood takes over and you become stronger, faster, more powerful."

"That's a possibility? Using the power consciously, I mean?"

"Yes. It takes time and a large amount of discipline. But it is. Healing, however, is done unconsciously and your rate of healing is quite shocking." His eyes roamed over my shoulder and paused on the blood that had stained the fabric.

"Shocking? Why?" My eyes flickered to the same spot and studied the torn shirt.

"I never mended as fast as you do when I was a halfling. If I didn't know better, I would wonder if your immortal half is in the name of the Healer."

My attention focused back on the Lupine and I pondered his words.

"Halfling?" My brows pulled together in confusion as I studied him closely. "But you're an immortal."

"I was born a halfling, Skylahr. My father was a human."

My mouth fell in surprise and I gaped at him in silence. Rolling his silver eyes, he shuffled closer to me before leaning back on his palms, which he stretched out behind him.

"It was quite the scandal, my mother falling in love with a southern human soldier. Both his heritage and lack of immortal blood were frowned upon by our people. Especially considering her father had been the alpha in the Protector's army before he fell in battle."

"So you're a halfling?"

Shaking his head, Kalian stood. He dropped the blanket that had been wrapped around his waist and dragged a pair of breeches up his legs while he smiled at my pinkened face. "Not any longer."

I grew frustrated as he spoke in riddles and half answers and glared up at him. "What does that mean?"

Kalian laughed at my irritation, his teeth bright in the dingy light of the cave, and he gracefully sat back down, his long legs crossing.

"I was eight and twenty when my heart stopped, and the eternal ceremony was performed. That was over three hundred years ago." His head tilted to the side as he grinned at me before pivoting to turn his back to me.

Even in the shadow of stone, the scar that ran across his back left me speechless. I leaned forward, my hand outstretched as one of my fingers followed the jagged edge of flesh that had lifted. His muscles strained under my fingers, but he let me trace the entirety of the old wound before he turned to face me again.

"Our territory had been breached by the Crimson army. There was an uprising after the war when they had learned of the prophecy of the Chosen and they thought they would remove the threat. They planned to start with the Protector's halflings." He paused and took a deep breath while staring out into the winter scenery before us. "Keyno and I had been young and eager to show our worth. We were reckless and stupid."

I remembered Keyno telling me a similar tale the day before. "But you saved him."

His eyes were endless pools of regret as they flickered to mine. "Yes. I saved him."

"So your back—" I broke off, not sure how to continue my question.

"The Crimsons are as merciful as their Goddess, it seems. They nearly tore me in two and when Leena and Keyno had finally managed to bring me home I was on my deathbed."

"And the ceremony you mentioned? It saved you?" Nodding, he cleared his throat.

"It can only be performed by someone who was born an immortal or has been given the gift directly by the Gods. The halfling in question also must be of age. Immortals reach maturity in their twentieth years, usually around two and twenty. That is when their powers take hold. It is the same for halflings, the immortal blood lies dormant until then."

Two and twenty. I had reached my twenty-second year just a few weeks before my trip to the Swallows.

"And this eternal ceremony, it can just change a halfling?"

His smile was tight, almost sad as he shook his head. "It's not so easy. The mortal side must be dead before you can begin, and there is only a tiny window of time to complete it before the being is too far gone. Not to mention it's not always successful. My mother had three other sons before me, all gravely injured in the war and none of whom survived their ceremonies. Only Leena and I lived."

My head spun with all of this new information. "And you are sure I'm truly a halfling?" There was no possible way I could be half of anything like these magnificent beings.

Kalian's fingers grabbed at my palm, flipping it over and tracing the smooth flesh before pulling at the shoulder of my tunic to show me my closed bloody skin.

"It isn't just your healing; I suspected it when we sparred but couldn't be sure. That is why I pushed you so hard."

I remembered his taunting that day, his encouragement to let it loose, and now it all made sense. However, I still did not understand where the immortal blood had come from. I had witnessed my parents injure themselves on our farm. Both had never shown an immortal ability and they most definitely aged. So, if I was a halfling, how did that come to be?

"Is there any other way for a halfling to be born?"

"What do you mean?" Kalian's brows fell as his head tipped in confusion.

"Besides an immortal lying with a human."

His lips lifted in amusement and his expression made me duck my head in my embarrassment. "Do you know another way for a babe to be born?"

I stuttered, trying to find a way to mask my inexperience. Clearing my throat, I lifted my face ignoring his raised brow as he delighted in my embarrassment.

"I just thought maybe magic could—" I paused, suddenly feeling very stupid.

"No, love, magic can be a wonderful thing, but it can't do that. Though fucking certainly does have its own sort of..." He lowered his eyes, watching my mouth closely before his voice purred out, *"Charms."*

Heat flooded my face, and that strange tugging sensation had returned in my lower belly. Sitting back, he straightened his spine, but the simmering that boiled in those silver eyes did not fizzle out. He held me with his stare until I could bear it no longer and I turned away.

"Kalian, do you think that's why—" I paused, gathering my thoughts. "Were they looking for me when they came to Noorde Point?"

Kalian stayed silent, but I did not miss the way he had almost flinched at my question. "It's hard to say for certain."

Without another word he cleared his throat, greeting his beta, who had snuck in, before standing abruptly, ending our discussion without so much as a second glance. When he pulled Keyno aside, I breathed a sigh of relief at the interruption and busied myself with my pack while Keyno and Kalian spoke in low whispers, throwing glances my way occasionally.

Leena had followed behind, but her deep scowl kept me from approaching her. So, I sat alone while I was gossiped about. It was not an unfamiliar position for me to be in, but it stung more than anticipated. Leena must have seen the hurt on my face because she huffed in irritation before coming to me.

"So, you're a halfling after all?"

"You knew?"

"I had my suspicions." She shrugged, looking bored as she picked at her fingernails, a habit I realized she did when she put on the façade.

I thought maybe she was bluffing, that she just wanted to feel superior in another way, but I decided not to press further. We still had a long journey ahead and I didn't want any more animosity between us than we already had. Looking over my shoulder, I noticed that Keyno had been left to tend to the coals alone.

"He had to hide the body. Where there's one Crimson, there's more."

I had no reason to feel the guilt that riddled me, after all I had not been the executioner for the immortal, but I wished I hadn't forced Kalian's hand.

"I'm sorry for the mess I have made. I should have been more aware of my surroundings." They nodded their heads in acceptance, and we continued in awkward silence while packing the rest of our things.

Fiddling with the buckle of my pack, I thought about the new information given to me, and soon my thoughts turned to my parents and home. I wondered if my blood was to blame for the destruction. I wondered if they knew what their daughter would become at the age of two and twenty. But most of all, I wondered if they cursed me in their last moments, or maybe cursed themselves for raising the halfling that may have cost them their lives.

"Leena?" I asked, my voice timid.

"What?" Blinking, she eyed me warily before exhaling noisily.

"Do you think my parents—" I swallowed my anguish. "Do you think they blamed me?"

Her dark eyes softened as they read the sadness that covered my face. Her voice was gentle as she hummed under her breath, but she made no other move to comfort me. "I think they loved you and they took comfort knowing you were somewhere safe."

The rest of the morning was uneventful as we discussed our plans. I had done my best to reassure them that I truly did not need an escort now that we were in the southern provinces, but Kalian wouldn't hear of it and insisted that they accompanied me to Carlon's city limits before returning home. Just as we had the day before, we travelled for hours, even as the sun began to set. We continued well into the night, only stopping when the smell of smoke filled our lungs.

Bounding up a rocky ledge, Kalian found an overlook that hung off the side of the cliff and surveyed the area. Down below was what would have been a tiny village, its size similar to Noorde Point, but it had also been burnt to the ground.

Rage filled my stomach, and I shook with anger while Kalian growled at the sight before sliding his way down to the scene. Once we were at the bottom of the hill, I dismounted and took in the heavy loss of another village while I searched for any sign of life.

The same stench of burning was heavy in my nose, bringing visions of my parents with it. I pulled the collar of my tunic over my nose to dull the smell while continuing my hunt for any of the village folk. Leena had changed back to her human form and dressed in a long tunic before she joined my effort, and together we lifted burnt wood and stones away in hopes of finding survivors.

"They didn't even stand a chance," she growled under her breath, kicking at the soot that lay around us.

"I honestly don't even know where we are," I admitted, searching for anything that would be familiar to me. I had little knowledge of the communities this close to the western coastline, and as far as I could tell, this one was too small to be a trading partner with Noorde Point.

"It was called Rushander. Not very big, maybe less than a hundred people. I have no idea why anyone, let alone the immortals, would bother with it," Leena whispered.

The complete disregard of life enraged me, and I looked at my surroundings in despair, the feeling of helplessness weighing me down again. Gazing back at the two wolves, I continued to the outskirts of the destruction only half ignoring the black beast who followed me silently.

"This will continue, won't it?" I whispered before turning to the wolf. Kalian's own eyes looked haunted as he took in the scene. "They will burn down everything in their path until they find whatever it is they are looking for." This time it wasn't a question; I already knew the truth of it. Kalian growled low in his throat in response, a yes.

"We have to try to stop them."

Chapter 16

Days began to bleed into nights and nights into weeks as I lost track of just how long we had travelled for. Little else excitement happened after passing through Rushander, and I had begun to feel the tension grow between the four of us over the last few days. Whatever kindness Leena had felt towards me in the cave had been replaced by her usual dislike, and Keyno had been oddly quiet. Kalian, however, was as obnoxious as ever, always in a state of undress even in the frigid cold, and that smirk had become a permanent fixture on his handsome face.

Wiping my brow roughly, I took in the dry, dusty mountains and desert landscapes while the strain around us began to reach a boiling point. It had been my suggestion that we travel as humans now that the cover of trees had disappeared, but gazing at the man in front of me, I regretted that choice.

Kalian had stripped his tunic off, and his tan skin and muscles glistened with a fine coat of sweat. Distracted by the shapes and angles of his shoulders, I stumbled over my own feet, causing me to curse loudly. The stupid, distracting man had the audacity to laugh out loud at my lack of coordination. His amusement only caused my irritation to grow, and I thanked the Gods that we were nearing Carlon soon, then I could send Kalian and his pack back north.

Throwing a glare at Kalian, I shoved my way past him with a glare and scouted the area ahead. Gazing across the landscape, I released a

breath of relief at the tiny group of grey speckles in the distance. We had finally reached our destination, and I turned smugly to Kalian, pointing at the village in the vastness of the dusty hills.

"We've made it." Following my pointer finger, Kalian narrowed his eyes, squinting in the sun before smiling at me.

"That's not Carlon." His voice barely contained his laughter, and I felt my shoulders lift in annoyance.

"What?" I asked, frustration colouring my tone.

"That's Celinde. A small mining village."

Sighing, I looked back out to the town while the disappointment filled my chest and continued down the sandy hill, ignoring the heat from the sun and the shimmering eyes that followed me.

An hour had passed by the time we had reached the main road and my feet ached, both heels blistered and bleeding, while my tunic stuck to me like a second skin. My long waves had matted in the knot I had tied back, and I winced as the strangers filling the streets watched us silently. They looked at the three Lupines in wonder, their jaws slack at their beauty. But when their eyes slid to me, they widened in surprise before turning away, and I felt my self-consciousness grow.

Ducking my head, I followed behind Kalian carefully as we stepped into a building off the main road, away from the prying eyes. Once we made it through the door, I realized I hadn't paid enough attention to what the establishment was, and I took in the dark walls while wrinkling my nose in disgust. By the smell of it, it was the local tavern.

Finding a corner in the back, we sat around a table, and I found myself lost in my thoughts, not noticing the serving girl until her delicate dark hand reached out to pat my own. Shaking my head, I smiled gently at her as she lifted her black eyebrow in question.

"What will you have?" Her voice was smooth and relaxed, her words coated with a western accent, and I watched as her full lips pulled over brilliant straight white teeth in a gorgeous smile. Swallowing thickly, I fidgeted under her dark gaze and moved my eyes to my lap.

"Ale, please," I croaked out, my cheeks heating at the gurgled noise that came from my mouth.

"Alright, and for you three?" I watched her carefully as she turned to my companions, waiting for the inevitable shock at their prettiness, but it never came, and I wondered if that was because beautiful people became less impressed with each other. She smiled kindly at them before her gaze lingered on Leena. Tucking a tight black curl behind her ear she grinned again at the female Lupine before her voice dropped suggestively.

"If you need anything you just give me a wave, the name is Ella."

Leena's eyes widened before she turned to the snickering males, who were trying to hide their laughter as they watched the normally poised Lupine become flustered. Her face was pink, and she swatted at her mate in frustration, obviously not used to such blatant attention from the same sex, and I wondered how that could be. How could she still be surprised by the wanting of others after hundreds of years? Turning my eyes away from the group, I gazed over my shoulder to take in the other patrons.

The room was fuller than I had expected, and I guessed the fever had passed by now or perhaps this town had remained untouched. There were groups of men scattered across the room, some drunk and disorderly, others gambling with dice, their voices rising in anger. Sliding my eyes around the space, I noticed a few older travellers pawing at the serving girls rudely and I felt my body tense, preparing to step in. However, just as I was about to rise from my seat, I noticed another man step between the group, escorting the drunks back to their table before turning to me.

He was tall, almost as tall as me, and broad. His skin was the same rich dark colour as our server, a trait most had in the west. He had a strong jaw with full lips and a wide nose. He was handsome in a rough way and still much nicer to look at than most. His ebony eyes caught my own before he smiled at me. His teeth were a blinding white in contrast to his dark skin, and the warmth of his grin had me dropping my gaze once again.

Studying the table in front of me, I shifted in my seat, remaining silent until I heard Kalian clear his throat. It was then I noticed the rough sound of boots on the floor. Turning my eyes up, I was met with a large hand stretched out in front of me, and my vision followed the rough skin up the thick forearm, over a dark grey tunic, only to stop on the same eyes that had held mine from across the room a mere moment ago.

"Hello. My name is Dane." His voice was deep and heavy, and I had been too distracted to notice he had motioned with his hand again, an encouragement for me to shake it. I grinned with tight lips as I tried to hide my awkwardness and slid my palm over his, before holding his fingers tightly in my grasp. I waited for him to flinch at my strength but instead he squeezed his grip, almost as if he was meeting my challenge.

"Skylahr."

Pulling away from him I waited for the others to introduce themselves, watching Kalian and Keyno as they too shook his hand roughly. Not fazed by our less than warm welcome, he drew up a stool and sat next to me.

"You lot look like you have travelled quite a distance. Where are you from?"

I turned to the Lupines, knowing they would be able to tell a tall tale easier than I, and watched as Leena and Keyno easily made up a false retelling of our travels. It was told so well I was almost caught up in it, only to be pulled back to reality by the frothing cup of ale that was placed in front of me.

"I see you have met my half brother, Dane."

I looked up at Ella as she shot a dirty glare at her brother, obviously disapproving his presence at our table, but Dane shrugged her off before turning back to the two men, totally enchanted by their presence as anyone would be. Ella huffed in irritation at the dismissal, turning on her heel with a swirling skirt and stalking back to her other customers.

"So you and Kalian then?"

"I'm sorry?" I hadn't noticed Dane had turned back to me.

"These two are together." He motioned to Leena and Keyno. "So are you and Kalian? Are you together?"

I opened my mouth to answer, only to be interrupted by a scoff. Narrowing my eyes at Kalian, I waited for him to say something nasty, but he instead lifted his ale and swallowed a mouthful. Following his movements, my eyes traced the foam coating his perfect mouth before he lifted a hand to wipe it away and he smirked at me.

"No, though I'm sure she has been dreaming of it. In fact, I am certain of it." He threw me a wink, as he referred to that night in Denimoore, and my face warmed with both rage and embarrassment. Standing from my seat, I excused myself, unwilling to accept his teasing for a moment longer, and nodded at the group before striding out of the tavern.

The town of Celinde was quaint with its small wooden shops and homes. It bustled with busyness as the locals went on about their daily tasks and the chaos made my heart ache for better times back in Noorde Point. Back when sickness hadn't been anything but a distant concern, and my only worries mediocre. Noticing a small armoury at the end of the main road, I felt my curiosity pique and ignored the whispers around me as I made my way to the entrance.

The smell of boiled leather was almost as welcome as the sound of water hissing across hot steel. It had been so long since I had been in a shop filled with weapons and armour and I felt elated to find such a lavish one. The sound of my heavy footfalls must have alerted the blacksmith, and he pulled the back curtain away, his catlike grin falling as he took me in. I was not the clientele he had been hoping for, that was for certain.

"What do ye want, girl?" he huffed at me irritably.

"I'm sorry to disturb you, sir, I was just looking."

"Well, look elsewhere, this is no place for the likes of ye."

His quick rejection was not unpredicted, but I felt annoyed that I would once again be shunned because of my sex, never mind the fact I was built stronger and bigger than any man I had seen walking down the street. Just before I could think of a rebuttal, I heard another person enter the small shop.

"That is no way to speak to a lady, you old prick." It was the same voice that had made Leena pinken, and I turned to Ella.

Looking at her, I smiled gratefully before ducking my chin. The blacksmith was not taken aback by the insult and instead stomped into the back angrily, the curtain sliding shut with a force that shook the rod it hung on. Laughing quietly under her breath, Ella grabbed on to my sleeve and tugged me back out of the door.

"You don't want to spend good money on that horse shit anyway!" She cupped her hands over her mouth, shouting loud enough for everyone around to hear, and then laughed loudly when she heard him cuss at her. Still holding my sleeve, she led me back down the main road, pausing to smile and nod at the few folk who greeted her.

"So, are you going to tell me what my brother said to have you storming out so suddenly?" Not wanting to embarrass myself by repeating Kalian's taunts, I swallowed nervously. I could only imagine the pity that would paint itself across her pretty face.

"It was nothing."

"It couldn't have been nothing, you were blazing mad by the look of you."

"He just asked if Kalian and I were..."

"Ah," she replied with a nod of her head. "Did you two not want anyone to know?"

"What?"

"The two of you, is it a secret or something?"

I stopped midstride to stare at her with wide eyes. "No. We are not together; you seriously couldn't have thought we were."

Her curls bounced as she tilted her head in confusion, her full lower lip pulled between her teeth. I moved my eyes around the street as she assessed me carefully. "Well, he certainly is prettier than most, but that doesn't mean he doesn't want you in his bed."

"He doesn't trust me. He could have anyone; he doesn't want a beast of a woman."

"A beast of a woman? Heard that one before, have you?" I nodded my head, and she sighed before pulling my arm, forcing me closer.

"You may not be pretty or delicate per se, but you have long legs and you sure look strong and sturdy. Plus, you have the prettiest eyes I have ever seen. If I thought I would have a chance, I sure as shit would try my hand."

I had never met someone so forward and my mouth hung open in shock. Taking my silence as answer enough, she continued. "Plus, my brother sure looked interested if the other one isn't to your liking."

Dane had been kind and friendly, if not a little too pushy, but I would have never thought that was his reason for approaching us. My cheeks were hot again, and I started to worry my face would be permanently red after tonight. Noticing my discomfort, she continued back towards the tavern with me in tow, pulling me along as if we were lifelong friends.

The three Lupines were still there with Dane, but this time a pretty dark-skinned woman sat across Kalian's lap, and by the look of it, his tongue was in her throat. For some reason I felt taken aback at the sight of it. Although Leena had insinuated that Kalian had other partners besides Nadine, I did not expect him to flaunt it so openly.

Clearing my throat, I sat back down in my vacant chair, ignoring the disgusting wet sound of kissing to my left, and smiled softly at Keyno and Dane. I listened to their heated debate over which combat weapons were most efficient while Leena looked bored, only breaking her façade to throw the occasional dirty look at her brother.

Hours went by but it wasn't until the woman and Kalian excused themselves that I noticed just how late it had gotten. I was well into my cup of ale, and the warm buzzing was a welcome distraction from the small pit of jealousy that sat in my gut as I watched the Lupine alpha lead his newly acquired friend upstairs. Ella had arranged three rooms for us, and I felt a sharp twist of envy watching the couple giggle their way to the doors, knowing they would have something tonight that I would not. They would not be alone.

As if he could sense my longing, Dane pulled his chair closer to mine. Normally I would have shied away from the closeness, but with the liquid courage of ale simmering in my stomach, I felt braver than I ever.

Tugging at my hand, he flipped my palm over, cradling it in his own before tracing the lines across the skin. I realized the action was eerily similar to how the witch of the Swallows had moved. Trying to tamp down the nervousness, I watched him carefully.

"My ma taught me to read palms as a boy, you know. I could read yours now, if you wanted?"

"Really? And what would it say?" My voice was deeper than I was used to, and it surprised Dane pleasantly if the heat in his gaze was anything to go on.

"Well, let us see. You'll be a magnificent warrior, strong and brave."

Snorting in disbelief, I rolled my eyes at him.

"What?"

"Your sister told you where I had wandered off to, you're using that information."

"Okay, fine, you caught me. How about this line?" He paused, tracing the crease that went right across my palm.

"You'll have a lifelong lover."

Tugging my hand, I pulled him closer to me. "You're full of shit, aren't you?"

He smiled at me, dipping his chin low so that our faces were inches apart. "Maybe I am or maybe I have a gift."

His eyes were glazed from the ale as he studied me, and I watched as he lowered his face closer and closer to mine. I knew that if I waited, he would kiss me. It would be pleasant I was sure, and he wouldn't be able to push me for more in such an open area, but still I felt apprehensive.

My throat was dry, and my palms felt like they were covered in a cold sweat. His own hand that was still wrapped around mine burned the skin, and it was all I needed to pull my focus back. At the last second, I turned my face away, leaving him my round cheek to kiss.

His lips were warm and rough against my skin and the pressure was barely there before he pulled back. Sighing with nervousness, I faced him again. He didn't appear angry, just disappointed, and I wished I had an explanation as to why I couldn't let him kiss me.

"I'm sorry if I had—"

Placing my hand on his arm, I interrupted him with a shake of my head, dismissing his apology.

"No, I'm sorry. It's late. I should really go to my room."

Accepting my rejection, he nodded, standing with me as I caught my balance. He walked with me to the bottom of the stairs before lifting one of my hands to kiss.

"Goodnight, Skylahr."

I nodded my head before climbing the stairs slowly, counting each step as I made my way up the steep incline only to pause at the top. Flickering my eyes up, I took in Kalian as he leaned against the wall. His hair was wild and his tunic was undone, opening wider when his arms crossed over his chest while he regarded me with bright burning eyes. I hated that he had the audacity to look so perfect, even now, and chose to ignore him as I sidestepped around his body. However, just as I was about to pass him, a long thick arm shot out and blocked my path.

"Did he hurt you?" Kalian's voice was deep with a simmering anger and the tone shocked me. Tipping my chin towards him, I inhaled swiftly before narrowing my eyes.

"No." I meant for the word to come out with heat, but it was barely audible as I felt his warmth seep into me while he held my stare.

"Did he say something cruel?" His body moved, his chest grazing the curve of my own, and I blinked through the daze he was putting me under.

"No, he's not you." The words were out of my mouth before I could stop them. I watched as his face turned cold and vacant, and I wished desperately that I could take them back. Without another word, he lowered his arm and allowed me to pass.

Straightening my spine, I marched forward two steps only to turn on my heel in anger. Striding towards him, I closed the space until I was back in the spot I had vacated, and I lifted my face with a tight jaw.

"What?" he asked, his eyes dropping to my mouth before holding my stare.

My lips opened but no sound would come out. As if I had no control of my own body, I rocked forward capturing his mouth with my own. It was clumsy and rough, my lips crashing over his full softer ones with no response from him. I realized he remained still, and dread curled in my chest, the feeling threatening to stop my heart. I leaned back, separating my mouth from his. When I was only a mere hair away, two large hands cradled the back of my head, his fingers twisting in my hair and tugging me forward. His warm, sweet breath fanned across my face and he growled out my name before lowering his lips.

This time his mouth held mine prisoner, parted and at his mercy. Heat pounded through my body and my breath quickened as I felt the sharp sting of teeth pull at my lower lip only to be soothed by his tongue a second later. He repeated this pattern twice before he dipped into my parted lips, his tongue running across my own teasingly. He then directed my head to tilt slightly, giving himself a better angle.

Completely consumed by him, I hadn't even noticed that he had spun us until my back was pressed against the wall, pinned there by his sheer size. My arms, which had been hanging uselessly at my sides, were now folded across his solid shoulders, pulling at his tunic as a needy whimper broke from my chest.

Kalian's answering groan was more than I could handle, and I forced my mouth away from his, panting in his ear as his lips kissed across my jaw and over my cheek. My lungs were still burning when he captured my mouth in another searing kiss. This one was more demanding than the last as his tongue ran across mine, coaxing it to life. My fingers found purchase in his thick, soft hair, holding it gently before tugging on it experimentally. The reaction was immediate as his hips rocked into my own, forcing my thighs apart involuntarily but invitingly.

And just as I felt one of his hands lower to my thigh, we were interrupted by a slamming door. Startled by the sound, I pulled my face away to turn towards the disruption.

Keyno stood before us, his jaw clenched in anger as he glared at his alpha. "I think it is time we all get some rest, don't you, Kalian?"

I took a step back, my arms fell from Kalian's shoulders, and I crossed them over my chest protectively before I ducked my head in embarrassment. Whispering a goodnight to the two men, I pushed past the alpha and all but ran to my designated room before slamming the door behind me.

Once I was within the safety of the four walls, I leaned against the solid wood and ran my fingers through my knotted hair while I tried to catch my breath. My lips were hot and swollen as I touched them gently with my tongue, still tasting Kalian there, and a small part of me prayed that I would remember this night for the rest of my life.

Chapter 17

My stomach twisted at the cold eggs that had been shovelled onto a plate in front of me, forcing the ale to bubble in my gut at the smell. I truly hated the fact that both Keyno and Leena seemed unbothered by the daylight and the pounding noise of the people around us.

Stupid perfect Lupines, I thought to myself while I sipped on tea carefully. Kalian had yet to make an appearance and the anticipation was slowly killing me. I had no idea where we stood. Though it was for me, that kiss was far from his first, but I was sure he must have felt something similar to what I had. Getting lost in the memory of those feelings, I was jolted back to reality when Leena kicked my shin under the table, drawing my attention to her dark eyes.

Her brows lifted at me before she tipped her head towards the stairs. Following her direction, my gaze fell on the tall frame of her brother, who was currently pushing his bed mate against the same wall I had been pressed against the night before. My head spun and I felt the cold wave of rejection fill my lungs. I shouldn't have been surprised; I knew that. After all, I had been the one to kiss him with no warning, it had been me who took that step, and yet some part of me had still hoped that he wanted me in the same way.

I stood from the table, my chair scraping against the floor loudly, and out of the corner of my eye I could see that the noise had startled the alpha from his female partner. Not paying them anymore attention, I grimaced at Ella in greeting before exiting the tavern.

The sun was hot and bright, making my head pound, but I was grateful for the distraction. Rounding the corner of the tavern, I headed back to the shop from yesterday. My sour mood and wine sickness would be just enough to keep me from feeling embarrassed, and I was determined not to be turned away before purchasing one of the blades I had admired yesterday.

The door swung open with more force than necessary, and I ignored the startled face of the smith as I grabbed on to the hilt of the blade that had caught my eye. Inspecting it closely, I walked to the counter he stood behind before unsheathing the metal. Running my finger down the cool silver, I flipped it back and forth looking for any sign of imperfection before swinging my arm out, slicing through the air with precision.

I could tell the man was impressed even if he didn't voice it, and I fed on his awe as I continued to twist and turn with the blade in my hand. My blood sang at the weight in my right palm and heat licked at my spine as my heart raced. My long bronze waves flew through the air as I whirled on my heel, extending my arm until just the tip of the sword was tucked gently under the man's fat chin.

"I'll take this one." My voice was deep and hard, harsh even to my own ears.

The man's jaw lowered, shaking against the steel as his eyes widened in shock. Holding the cold metal there for a moment longer, I pressed with the barest of pressures before pulling the blade carefully away from him. Without the threat of injury, his face became cold as stone and his fury rose at my antics.

"The hell ye will! Who do ye think ye are stormin' in here like some knight makin' demands of me?!" He pointed a thick finger at me. "Ye may be as big as a man but ye are still a woman and no woman will have one of me blades, damn you!"

The rage at his dismissal was an inferno in my body. Waves of fire crackled under my skin and I wanted so badly to gut him, to smack my fist into those dark, crooked teeth before kicking them in for good measure. I would show him just how good I was with a blade.

Tightening my fingers on the handle I raised my arm, ready to strike, but just as I was about to give in to the heat and unleash my fury, a strong arm grabbed my wrist, forcing it back to my side.

"I would highly suggest you watch your mouth, sir, or I will let her test out your work."

My jaw clenched as I looked over my shoulder at Keyno. He, however, only focused on the man in front of us, who cowered against the curtain behind him. Grabbing at my fingers, Keyno unwrapped them from the hilt and sheathed the metal before tossing it at the smith's feet.

"We'll be leaving now." His tone was harsh, leaving no argument, and I felt the air leave my lungs in embarrassment.

"She nearly killed me!" the smith yelled out at us before shrinking back at the heat of Keyno's glare. He studied the man for a long pause before fishing in his pocket for the sack of silver. Opening the pouch, his long fingers grabbed at a few coins, tossing them onto the floor before the smith.

"I think you are mistaken, sir; she was just testing a blade. That is all. Though I am sure you may find yourself a few fingers short if a different story were to spread." The threat was not idle, even if the words had been spoken in a calm, low voice, and for the first time since meeting Keyno, I realized just how dangerous he could be to the wrong person.

Without pause, Keyno grabbed on to my arm and hauled me from the shop, pulling me off the main road and back up to the secluded hills that surrounded the small town. I staggered behind him, my mouth opening and closing like a trout as I tried to form a coherent thought. Stopping once we were a ways away from prying eyes, he shoved me to the side before pacing in front of me.

"What in the fuck do you think you were doing?" He whirled on me, his jaw clenched in rage.

I stared at him wide-eyed as he began cursing under his breath before pacing again. I knew that I had made a mistake allowing my rage to get the better of me; I had never been so out of control. "I'm sorry, Keyno, truly."

He waved off my apology in anger before turning to me again. "You're certainly apologizing a lot lately, but have yet to take accountability for your actions. You cannot ignite here! Especially in front of a stranger who would be happy to sell a halfling for a few silver! Do you want to get yourself killed or expose us?!"

I hung my head in shame as I realized what the burning rage truly was.

Igniting.

I felt foolish for letting the current of flames take over again when it resulted in nearly revealing not only myself but potentially the Lupines as well. It was a crass, careless mistake that could have been devastating if not for Keyno stepping in.

"Truly I'm sorry, I won't let it happen again. If I had known it would happen that easily, I would never have left the tavern."

Keyno studied me closely then settled on the ground cross-legged. He ran his hands through his black hair before staring up at me. Gesturing to the space beside him, he waited for me to sit before relaxing back on his arms.

"No, I'm sorry. I forget you have no control over it right now. I remember how hard it is at the beginning and we have not given you the guidance you need. We should have talked about it these past few weeks instead of ignoring it. I guess we wanted to give you time to come to terms with it all, especially after Noorde Point. But looking at it now, I know we underestimated your strength."

The mention of my home brought a burning sting to my eyes, and I swallowed the grief before looking up into the cloudless sky. Taking in a shuddering breath, I mimicked the Lupine next to me and reclined back on my arms. We sat there in silence while the warm western breeze rustled against us. Even in winter, the western province was warmer than a northern midsummer. Enjoying the quiet for a few more moments, I gathered my thoughts.

Even if I hadn't lost total control today, the threat was still there. I had no idea how to stop igniting once the spark was lit, and I worried next time I would have no one to step in and save the day.

"Keyno?"

"Hmm?"

"Would you be willing to help me, with igniting, that is? Could you teach me how to stop it from happening?"

He sighed loudly before sitting up. "You can't stop it. Once you've ignited, you can't stop. But I could teach you how to control it. How to be present while it happens."

"You would do that?" I asked in wonder.

"Yes. Of course, Skylahr, that's not even a question."

"How do we start?" I asked impatiently before standing in front of the Lupine.

Chuckling at my eagerness, he pulled himself up with a groan, dusting his hands on his breeches before smiling at me charmingly.

"Well." He paused, a glint of mischief in his eyes. "The easiest way to get you to ignite is to piss you off. Anger brings it forward the fastest, but I never seem to be as talented in that as Kalian is."

The mention of his name left a tang of annoyance in my mouth. I knew it was childish of me to be so upset over a kiss, and I truly had no reason or right to be jealous. But perhaps it was because I had little experience, and I had thought that the kind of kiss we shared was only possible if both parties felt attraction for one another. Maybe I was misguided, and Kalian had taken pity on me but felt nothing else. He had been more than clear on what he thought of me in the past, and I could never compete with Nadine or the woman from last night. Had I taken advantage of him?

My lips pressed together tightly as I crossed my arms over my front, slouching in self-consciousness. I suddenly felt like a complete and utter fool for actually believing this morning would be any different than the others that had passed. Kalian had never shown any interest in me other than the teasing offers he had made mockingly.

"I don't think he will want to spend much time with me around after—" I stopped, looking at my feet in embarrassment.

"Why is that?" Keyno looked puzzled as he watched me.

"Because of what I did to him."

"I'm sorry, what?" Keyno asked, one brow lifted as he crossed his arms.

I tucked my chin in shame before whispering, "I kissed him. We were drunk and I kissed him."

"Yes, I was there, if you remember." Then he paused with his brows furrowed. "Did you not want to kiss him?" The tightness in his voice made his anger evident and I wished I hadn't said anything.

"No, I didn't mean me. I meant him. He didn't want it."

His sudden burst of laughter made my heart jump and my jaw fall open. Keyno held his stomach as he chuckled behind a hand. Breathing in deeply through my nose, I tried not to let my agitation show.

"What?" I demanded. "What is so funny?"

"You cannot seriously think you made him do anything he didn't want to?"

Not answering him, I turned away, hiding my hot face.

"You really think that?" Nodding my head, I waited a breath before peeking over my shoulder at him. Keyno smiled softly at me, his eyes gentle.

"Skylahr, Kalian has never done anything he didn't want to, and as for what I saw, he wanted that kiss as much as you did." Suddenly feeling flustered, I cleared my throat.

"Can we talk about something else?" I begged. "Please?"

Keyno nodded before placing a warm hand on my shoulder. "Of course, but just one thing. You need to be careful with your heart, Hazel." He hadn't called me that in weeks and I suddenly realized how serious he was being with his warning.

"I love Kalian and I respect him. He is my alpha above all else, but it would not be fair if I did not tell you to be cautious with him. I worry that you may be in over your head."

None of this came as a surprise, and although I wished I could deny him, I knew that in the end I would be the one hurt if I let it go too far. As of now it was just attraction, but I had always been fiercely loyal and cared with everything I had, and it could be my downfall.

I had once fallen for a boy in our village just before my sixteenth birthday. He had been the son of a traveller and had been the first and only to ever show any interest in me. We had spent weeks riding and sparring together and then he tried to kiss me behind our barn. When my nerves became too much, and I turned him away, he became enraged. He had been so angry that I was fearful of him and ran. It was two days later that I had learned about the bet. It had been a wager between the village boys, a game to see just how far I would let him go. A kiss was worth three silver, my maidenhead—ten.

The mere thought of the cruelty of those boys made my blood sear and I felt the beginnings of the ignite in my body. Turning to Keyno with a clenched jaw, I waited for him to instruct me. After watching me for a moment, he moved to grab my shoulders.

"Don't let it consume you, Hazel. Breathe through your nose and lean into it."

I closed my eyes in concentration, bracing my body against the heat with little luck. My spine burned and black was entering the edges of my mind.

"Breathe, breathe and let it in. Don't resist."

I held my breath until my lungs burned and slowly released it. Focusing on one limb, one muscle at a time, I relaxed and released the tension. The fire spread, crawling through my fingers and toes, flooding my veins and meeting in my chest. It was excruciating, the blaze of heat that wracked my body from the inside out, and I couldn't stand it. I had to let it go. And then it was—

Gone.

My eyes fluttered open, squinting in the sunlight as I sought Keyno out. "Did I do it?"

He smiled at me. "Close. You were close, but you managed to swallow it. Not quite what we wanted but still very impressive."

Sighing in disappointment, I studied my hands, unclenching my fists before turning my palms over. The crescent moons that indented my skin slowly faded as I watched them closely. Sure, I was in control. I lifted my face towards the Lupine.

"We'll try again, Hazel, but we have been out here for a while, and we should check on the others."

I pulled at my sweat-soaked tunic self-consciously and attempted to smooth my unruly hair before following Keyno back to town. Stepping through the doors, I watched as he greeted his mate with a bruising kiss before whispering silently in her ear, and her dark eyes widened before capturing mine.

"I'm impressed."

I smiled at her gently, pleased to have done something right, and sat back down at our table. My wine sickness had finally settled, and my stomach cried out for the broth and bread that littered the table. Spooning mouthfuls sloppily, I swallowed the warm liquid down, ignoring the chatter between the couple as they gazed at each other lovingly. Just as we finished our meal, their alpha appeared.

A new woman was draped across his arm as he smiled at us, and Keyno narrowed his eyes at him before lifting his feet onto the vacant chair beside me, a clear indication that he and his new friend were not welcome to dine with us. Other than a nasty glare, we were not given another greeting as they slid past us. Leena scoffed under her breath before turning to me.

"My brother is an idiot, Skylahr. Ignore him and his puores," she hissed.

"Now, my love, do not go calling those women that name," Keyno chided.

"They are only with him because he is handsome and appears to be wealthy. They are just a warm body to pass the time."

I looked to Keyno before swallowing, suddenly nervous about chiming in.

"I think that if they both enjoy their time together, they should be free to do as they wish—without our judgement."

Leena watched me with a wide gaze, surprise evident on her face before she nodded reluctantly.

"Alright, if you don't mind that he is chasing other skirts, I won't say anything else on the matter."

I smiled at her before excusing myself from the table. I was exhausted and wanted to escape before the ale and wine made its way to the table. Walking to the counter, I flagged Ella down. She too looked exhausted and irritated, her dark eyes glaring at the men who reached to touch her skirts before making her way over to me with a smile.

"What will you have, dearling?" she asked while leaning across the bar.

"Can I have a warm bath drawn for me in my room, please?" I knew the task would not be easy and I laid a silver on the counter. Ella scooped it up and tucked it in the bodice of her dress while smiling gratefully at me.

"Yes of course! I'll have that ready for you, my lady." Leaning closer to me, she placed her full lips near my ear. "Just so you know, your pretty boy is watching."

Choosing to disregard her warning, I straightened before nodding and turned for the stairs while ignoring the luminous eyes that followed my every step. I refused to acknowledge him and swore to myself that tonight would be the start of my indifference for the handsome immortal.

It had to be. I didn't have a choice; my heart depended on it.

Chapter 18

The tavern was quiet as I crept down the stairs, my bare toes nearly silent on the wood. My skin still felt warm and dewy from the steam of my bath and my muscles had loosened from the heat. Sighing heavily, I pulled my robe tighter around my middle and snuck my way to the bar, which was occupied by Ella as she cleaned up for the night. Her dark eyes lifted, and she smiled prettily at me while I folded my body into a short stool in front of her.

"How was your soak?" she whispered before pouring a glass of wine for me then one for herself.

"Wonderful," I exhaled sleepily before taking the glass she offered. We sat in comfortable silence as she wiped down the counter and I let the swirl of the cloth lull me into a tired daze, only startling when she flicked some water at me.

"Are you alright?"

I waved off her worry before crossing my arms on the wooded edge in front of me, perching my chin on them. My body felt loose and tired as the fire crackled in the corner and the warm hue only added to my relaxed state. The bath water had been tinged with rose oil, the smell of my mother's favourite perfume, and it was an added comfort I didn't know I needed. Lost in my thoughts, I hadn't noticed that Ella had stopped her cleaning to watch me in amusement.

"You look like you are a thousand miles away in that head of yours."

I nodded. "I'm just thinking of my mother."

"She's well, I hope?"

I smiled sadly. "She has passed."

Ella reached forward to pat my shoulder gently in support before climbing onto the bar next to me. "Did it happen long ago?"

"No, she and my father were in our home in Noorde Point when it caught on fire."

Ella's eyes widened before she took a long swig of her drink, swallowing it down noisily. "Nasty business that was. I'm sorry. Those Crimsons had no right to be doing that."

My brows rose as I repeated her words in my mind. "You know about it?"

"Word reached this far south in a matter of days; we spent a week preparing for our own visit from them."

"They never showed?" I asked, my voice shaking.

"No. We had a few travel through but no large groups, no banners." I wasn't sure if I was comforted by that or angry. No one had shown the northern villages that kind of mercy, so why would they not come after the western towns?

"No one has guessed what they wanted?" My eyes focused on my hands as they curled around my glass before I lifted it to my lips.

"Well, they were probably looking for a halfling like you."

The wine burned the back of my throat as I choked on it, spluttering and coughing into my fist while Ella smacked my back to help loosen the tension. Catching my breath, I tried to affect a mask of indifference, ignoring my racing heart.

"What?" Ella threw back the rest of her wine in one gulp before placing the glass down next to her. She took her time gathering her thoughts and I couldn't help but wish that I had come downstairs armed.

"Don't worry, I won't be saying anything. I'm not the type to rat on my own kind." My mouth fell open as I gaped at her.

"You're a—"

She interrupted me with a quiet chuckle before grabbing a knife and slicing the smooth skin of her forearm. I watched in wonder as she wiped away the blood that seeped from the gash before the skin began to stitch itself together. "You couldn't tell? Some halfling you are." She laughed gently. "You should have sensed it. I sensed you coming from miles away."

"Sensed it?" I repeated dumbly.

"Aye, even if I couldn't sense the power, there is no way the like of you is pure northern blood. You don't have the hair, much less the eyes. That dark boring brown they all seem to be cursed with. It is a wonder how you ever managed to make it up there."

"Can other people sense me? How can you hide so easily here? Why didn't the immortals notice you?" My mind was spinning as more and more questions formed.

"Not as far as I can tell, dearling, but I had been worried when you stormed out of here the other day. That's why I went after you. As for me, I look as if I belong here, and I've practiced embracing my ignite and now no one gives me a second look. Not to mention the fact that I do not have three immortals in my party."

I studied Ella closely, searching for anything out of the ordinary that would point to her halfling blood. Her dark skin was smooth and soft. Her tight black curls shone and bounced with fullness, she had long lashes and perfect gleaming white teeth. She was one of the most beautiful mortals—or rather, halflings—I had ever seen, but nothing else seemed different.

"So you could tell just by looking at me?" I asked, hating that I felt a sharp sting of self-consciousness.

"No." She paused, tipping her head as she studied me. "It is not your looks that give you away. Well, other than your eyes, there's something about them." Her dark gaze held my own for a moment before she continued. "It's your strength. The force you carry yourself with. There is a simmering just under the surface and it is obvious to those who look hard enough. It is something you'll need to fix if you want to stay undetected."

Keyno had said something similar the day before, and I knew that I was a liability for the Lupines in my current state. Ella had never come across in any way that made me think she was out of control, even when angered by the drunken men who groped at her. Maybe she was older than I had thought? Maybe centuries? If we healed, maybe we didn't age the same way either.

"How old are you, Ella?"

Her head tilted to the side in question. "I'm six and twenty, why?"

"Oh, I had thought— Never mind." I closed my mouth tightly, suddenly embarrassed by my naiveness.

"We are only half immortal; we age the same as any human, Skylahr. We also die."

"But the healing?"

"Ah, healing is a wee bit trickier than you may think. We can heal from most injuries; we won't get sick like humans. But a lethal blow is still lethal. Healing takes time for us, the worse the wound the more time it takes, and sometimes the blood is faster than the magic. So, don't go getting yourself run through."

"Is it the same for immortals?"

Ella sighed in thought. "It might be. I know that they can die in war and immortals can kill each other, so perhaps a human could too if they had the chance. But they are strong, and they are fast. We don't even compare." I hung my head in disappointment. "You weren't planning on going after that group who did that to your family, were you?" Her brows rose in question.

"I've been more focused on stopping their Goddess. I was hoping to find answers in Carlon first."

"Carlon, why there?"

"Are the scriptures not hidden there?"

"Aye, that is what I've been told, but they are in the language of old. Excuse me for saying it, but you don't look like the type to be fluent in the old tongues."

I felt like an idiot as all my plans unravelled. I hadn't even thought that far ahead and really had nothing else to go on. The Lupines had come with me to keep me safe until I reached Carlon, but I hadn't even thought to ask them about the scriptures or what we would do if we did come across the Crimson armies. My parents were dead, and I had nothing to help me avenge them, to help me stop the suffering of any other innocent souls at the hand of the Crimsons' wrath.

I was a silly girl playing knight.

"Dear Huntress, I am a fool." I cradled my head in my hands as tears of frustration filled my eyes. "What am I doing?"

"Now, now," Ella chided. "Don't go feeling sorry for yourself. Not all hope is lost, thank the Jester that you found a halfling who just happens to be fluent in both tongues, old and new."

My hands combed through my hair as I lifted my chin in surprise. "What?"

"I'm not just nice to look at, you know."

"Why would you help me?" I asked suspiciously. "You barely know me."

"Same reason as why those three immortals have. You are brave and strong, anyone can see that. And it is about time someone does something about that Seductress. If no one else will, I guess it's time I try."

A throat cleared behind us and I turned to the pair of bright steel eyes I had been avoiding. Kalian stood at the bottom of the stairs, shirtless and perfect as he stuffed his hands in the pockets of his breeches.

"So you told her then?" he asked Ella, his deep voice a gruff rumble in the quiet room.

"Aye, thought what harm could it do?" Ella answered, grabbing our glasses and hopping down from the counter. I watched as she cleaned up the rest of the tavern while I silently stewed beside the man I had promised myself I would avoid.

"You're angry with me," he accused, not lowering his voice.

"I'm not."

"You regret throwing yourself at me then?" I turned to glare at him, my mouth pressed firmly shut. He smirked at me with glee before folding a large hand under his chin, our eyes remaining connected until I forced myself to glance away.

"Must you always make everything so humiliating for me?" I

demanded, my voice rising harshly as I leaned away from his warmth. I felt foolish for kissing him and his pestering did nothing but add to my anger and embarrassment. Finally having the decency to look ashamed, he lowered his eyes.

"Skylahr. I'm sorry, I shouldn't have said anything." When I refused to look at him, he sighed. "Truly, it was not kind of me. But you have no reason to be ashamed, ale makes people do foolish things all the time."

I wondered if he was also regretting his response to my touch, using the ale to dismiss his actions. Whatever his reasoning, I was happy to take the out that was offered.

"Of course," I agreed. "A drunken mistake."

I knew that I would never forget the feeling of his weight against me when he pinned me to the wall. I would dream of it for the rest of my life, but it was better for it to be swept away as a foolish moment for both of us. I had not come all this way only to be distracted by this immortal man. I needed to get my priorities in order.

"Right, well, if you two are done, how 'bout we talk about the next step?" Ella's voice immediately broke us from our conversation, forcing us to lean away from each other once again.

"Which would be?" Kalian's voice was a lazy drawl, and he pulled his eyes from my face to look over at Ella, the cold grey steel assessing her carefully.

"Well, I think Skylahr here and I should continue on to Carlon, while you lot stop at Suideign Shores. I hear there may be a few of the Healer's immortals there, they may be convinced to help us."

"And how would you know that, ale wench?"

I lifted my hand to swat at his insult only for it to be caught midair by his larger fingers. He ignored my huff of frustration while his eyes turned cold, watching the dark-skinned beauty carefully.

"I overheard a few of the soldiers talking about it before they headed north." Ella seemed unbothered by the fact she was on the receiving end of such a nasty glare and continued to fiddle around behind the bar.

"Right, and you just happened to be close enough to overhear it?"

"Aye." She nodded, her own eyes narrowing in anger.

"And so we should just leave Skylahr to travel with you to Carlon. Unattended."

"I don't like what you are implying. If I wanted to harm her or reveal you three, I could have already."

"Or maybe you were biding your time. You're waiting for an opportune moment." The tension around us was coming to a boiling point and I pulled my hand out of Kalian's grasp before pushing against his chest. They had gotten closer and closer in their disagreement, and I could barely wedge myself between his massive frame and the bar.

"Okay, you two, relax. No one is implying anything."

"Actually, I am. She is insane if she thinks I am going to let you travel with someone you just met."

"Like she did with you, Lupine?" My head whipped towards her in surprise. I knew there was no hiding the fact that the three were immortals; you would have to be blind and senseless to not recognize their splendor for what it was. But I hadn't thought anyone would be able to tell that they were in fact the creation of the Protector.

Kalian ignored her blatant accusation. "She is safe with us. We have protected her."

"I don't think she needs your protection, but I can promise you I would not harm her."

I was getting frustrated; being talked about rather than talked to was becoming more and more bothersome. I felt like a plaything two children were fighting over. I was not defenseless, and although Ella had a point, I had gone with them willingly, I had never felt any true fear following them. In fact, it had always felt like I had finally found my fate. I was too embarrassed to voice it, however, worried that it would sound desperate and pathetic.

"Kalian, I don't think we have anything to be concerned about. Ella could have hurt me several times if she wanted to. She stopped me from igniting the other day and she has kept your secret."

She smiled at me softly. "You don't have anything to worry about." She nodded before lowering her voice. "I'm the only halfling here and my half brother doesn't even know. I've been a coward, hiding here in this tiny town, but I don't want to sit by and wait while more people die. I should have done something sooner, I know that. But I can't go back now. So please, let me help."

I turned to the Lupine with pleading eyes. I knew how hard it could be to be courageous when you felt as if you were on your own. It had taken a fever for me to even consider leaving the safety of my village walls, and I had no idea then that I was anything but an ordinary girl. Had I known I was a halfling, I couldn't say for certain if I would have left. Ella finally felt as though she had the chance to fight back; could we really judge her for wanting to take the opportunity?

"Kalian, if we really plan on stopping the Seductress and the Crimsons, we need all the allies we can get." I knew I was close to convincing him when he let out a loud sigh, the tension in his shoulders lessening.

"Not to mention, I would have an easier time blending in without you three and if I can get my ignite under control, we wouldn't have any issues I'm sure."

Ella seemed pleased by my reasoning, but Kalian still watched her warily.

"Kalian." I placed my hand against his chest, waiting for those glittering eyes to flicker down to me. "Please."

"We travel together until we reach the city limits, then we'll set up camp in the mountains and wait for you two there. But listen to me, halfling." His eyes slid back to Ella's face and the steel burned with warning. "I will tear your pretty face apart if you betray us."

A shiver slid down my spine at the threat, and I pictured just how easily he could do that.

Ella seemed to understand the promise in his tone as she nodded silently. "You have my word."

Kalian took a step back, finally defusing the tension, and it felt like I could breathe again. I watched as he turned to make his way back up the stairs, only to pause at the top. Captivated by the grace in his movements, I had been completely unaware of the shock on Ella's face until her horrified gasp echoed around us. Turning to her, I noticed her usual radiant skin had become ashen and a hand covered her mouth. Her dark eyes were focused on Kalian, or rather the skin of his back, where the deep scar was on full display.

"Healer help us, they tried to split him," she whispered under her breath.

Split him?

Looking back at Kalian, I noticed the stiffness in his frame, and I wondered if he had heard her. Without another glance back, he stormed into his room, slamming the door behind him with enough force that it shook the walls. The noise seemed to awaken Ella and she blinked out of her daze before swallowing.

"I think I upset him. I'm sorry, I didn't mean to." Her voice cracked as she gazed up at the closed door.

Leaning over the bar, I dropped my voice to a whisper. "What did you mean, Ella? When you said split him?" He had mentioned that they had almost torn him in two, but I thought it was just an expression.

Ella gave a heavy sigh before slouching onto the bar in front of me. "It's a barbaric thing. Something the Crimsons have done for centuries to their hostages." Her eyes slid back up to the door quickly before she pulled me closer. "It's a way to torture their captives. They do it when they are looking to get answers. They start at the shoulder and cut down, opening them up slowly before pulling out their spine. If the hostage lives that long, that is."

My throat was dry and my stomach churned at the thought. "Why would they do that to him? What answers would they have been looking for? Why didn't the skin heal?"

"It's hard to say, it was probably years ago, back when they thought the Chosen were hiding in the Lupine territories. As for the scar, some magic doesn't ever heal fully. You'd be smart to remember that."

"But the Chosen might just be a myth. None have ever been found." At least that was what Isla had told me.

"Aye. But those damn Crimsons have never stopped looking and the hunt for halflings has escalated these past few months. Obviously, they know something is coming."

"Will the scriptures in Carlon be able to tell us how to find them?" I asked, hope filling my voice.

"I don't know. But I'll be honest with you, Skylahr, don't be betting on it. If the Chosen are truly out there, they would be hiding for their lives. I can't see any old book being much help in locating them."

I peered up at Kalian's closed door again before bowing my head in prayer.

Please, Gods, let us find them.

Chapter 19

The impact of my tailbone hitting the hard ground had me hissing out a curse, and I winced as I pulled myself to my feet. I could hear Ella and Keyno snickering while Leena pranced around me with grace, poking me irritatingly with her blade. Swatting at her, I braced myself for another attack. We had been at this for hours with no end in sight and my strength was wavering. My arms had grown tired and there was still no sign of my ignite.

Kalian circled us, watching each move carefully. He had been cross with me all morning, only grunting instructions at me harshly. Always critiquing, always pushing, and I had never disliked someone the way I did him. Him and his golden perfectness. Blowing a strand of bronze hair out of my way, I lunged for Leena.

"Too slow, halfling," she taunted while twirling out of my reach before throwing a wink at our spectators.

Kalian seemed less amused and sighed before crossing his arms. "Stop dancing around, Leena, and fight."

His sister glared at him before taking position once again. This time, however, she charged at me.

The vibration from the impact of steel ran painfully down my arm, rattling the bone from wrist to elbow. The pressure lifted for a moment before she swung again and again, forcing me away with each hit until I was flat on my back with her blade pointed at my throat.

"I yield." My voice was hoarse with frustration, and I could barely make eye contact with the alpha as I rose slowly. Leena seemed as tired of this game as I was and threw her blade at her brother before falling gracefully into the dirt next to her mate.

"You try, Kalian, I'm done."

The Lupine glared at me with disappointment before picking up the discarded sword.

"Your head is not in it, you're not even trying. You need to focus, Skylahr." Without any further warning he struck out, forcing me to dodge clumsily to the side. He was relentless in his pursuit, swinging with speed and force I had not anticipated. We had fought only once before, but this somehow felt more severe, and in half a dozen more swings I was on the ground unarmed again.

Cool silver eyes narrowed at me, and I felt enraged looking up at him, waiting for another jape at my lack of grace or poor sword handling. Not giving him the chance, I swung my leg out quickly, swiping at his own boots, only for him to easily avoid the blow and growl at me angrily.

"That was a cheap shot and you know it. I expected more from you."

Childishly I mocked him under my breath while hauling myself up again.

"You truly think you'll be able to do anything for your family with this skill level? You'd be better off if I slit your throat here and now."

All laughter behind us ceased immediately and the air became cold. Leena and Ella looked shocked, their mouths open and eyes wide. Another time the expressions may have been comical but now, standing before the Alpha of the Lupines, nothing felt humorous. I had only seen this side of Kalian when he had accused me of being a halfling, and I swallowed nervously before looking at Keyno for guidance on how to handle this sudden change in his brother.

"Don't look at him for help," Kalian snapped, directing my attention back to his hard face. "He'll be no good to you if you are caught by the Crimsons. No one will. Do you know what they'll do to you if they get their hands on you? Do you know the pain they will inflict?" His voice dropped as he circled me. "You should be grateful that your parents perished in that fire. It was a blessing from the Protector. A blessing you will not be so lucky to be given."

My throat felt tight as my fingers closed into a fist. "I think that's far enough."

The smirk that stretched his lips was not full of its usual arrogance. No, this one looked positively feral.

"Kalian," Keyno warned from behind us, his voice quiet and unsure, but the only response he was given was a deep growl that had my heart racing.

"Hear that, girl, my brother thinks you can't handle the truth. He thinks you're weak. Fragile. Perhaps he is right. Maybe this is a waste of time and I should cut my losses."

His complete disregard for my feelings hurt more than I expected, and I felt shame burn its way through my mind. Hanging my head, I closed my eyes, willing the tears away.

"I really have no idea why my mother thought you were worth protecting. Did you know she had to beg me? I thought surely a creature such as you would have little worries when it came to predators, but she pleaded with me. 'Please, Kalian,' she whimpered. 'Please go with her, she's just a girl.'" He paused, his lips curling into a cruel grin. "'Girl' she called you. I think that was more than generous though."

"Kalian," Leena whispered angrily, but I could barely make out the words over the heartbeat pounding in my ears.

"Come on, Leena, we all can see the reality in my words. Though now she truly is unwanted. A little orphan, all alone."

A deep roar of fury broke from my chest, and the burning went from a spark to an inferno before I could fully grasp the feeling. Throwing myself forward, I wrapped my arms around Kalian's torso, slamming him into the ground. Pinning his thighs down with the weight of my hips, I pressed one forearm into his throat.

"Shut your fucking mouth, dog," I hissed, my voice deep and unfamiliar to my own ears. His mouth opened to retort only to be snapped shut with the force of my fist that slammed into his jaw. Two more blows came swiftly before a pair of arms hauled me off him.

Rage shook my frame as I watched the alpha cover his bloody nose with a hand, his eyes wide but never leaving mine as I struggled in the hold of my captors. Trying to fight my way back to the sprawled Lupine form that still lay on the ground, I glared as he watched with wonder as I was dragged farther away.

"Easy, Hazel. Easy." A warm hand grabbed on to my chin, turning it to face Keyno. His dark eyes were fearful as they watched me pant for breath. I mimicked his own breathing, and my heart settled slowly, but the fire still flickered in my veins.

Certain I wouldn't turn back to his alpha, Keyno released me before holding his palms up in an obvious sign of peace. He genuinely looked nervous of me, and I was pleased at the thought.

Good, he should be afraid.

Quiet footsteps crept forward from my left and I turned on my heel positioning in a defensive stance, ready to attack, but Leena ducked her head and averted her eyes in submission, halting where she stood.

"Not sure you can call her Hazel when her eyes are that terrifying blue colour, my love." She laughed awkwardly before taking a step closer.

"Leena. Stop," Keyno ordered when he noticed how tight my jaw had become as I narrowed my eyes at his mate. I knew full well she wasn't a threat to me, and yet I could not seem to convince my body otherwise. I felt like a cornered animal and my instinct to fight was surfacing rapidly.

"Leena, Keyno, move away."

I turned to see their alpha striding towards us, his face solemn and eyes soft. A stark contrast to how they were just moments ago. His siblings looked doubtfully at him, neither moving as they watched his approach towards me.

"Kal—" Leena started only for Kalian to hold his hand up at her, silencing her immediately.

"I'll be fine. But if she does decide to rip my throat out, it would be well deserved, I pushed her too far." My lips curled up at him in disgust as he reached for my cheek. Choosing his battles wisely, he settled for my shoulders and cupped them gently before lowering his eyes to the ground. My jaw was tight, teeth grinding as I observed his face. His nose looked no worse for wear, but I was pleased to see the stain of blood on his lips and chin.

"Skylahr." His voice broke on my name, and he cleared his throat before continuing. "I am sorry for what I said and the pain my words caused you. I didn't mean them. I wanted to push you, but I crossed the line."

I stood there silently, my eyes narrowing before I shrugged his hands off me. "You can't pick and choose what words you truly mean. Why should I believe what you say now?"

Silver eyes softened and then his shoulders sunk down, making his frame seem smaller. With a swift inhale, he fell gracefully to his knees, kneeling close enough that his breeches lightly grazed the toes of my boots while his black hair blew in the breeze. Bowing his head low, he rolled it to the side and exposed the length of his golden throat for me completely. I heard Leena gasp in shock.

Confused by her response, I lifted my eyes to the Lupines and noticed both had mimicked their alpha and lowered themselves to their knees. Watching as their eyes remained fixated on the ground, I finally understood. Kalian was submitting to me, fully, in the only way he knew how.

The great Lupine alpha was throwing himself at my feet in hopes of forgiveness.

Making him wait there silently on his knees, I ran my fingers through the soft, thick strands of his hair. The ignite gave me confidence I would not otherwise dream of having, and I twisted my fist, pulling his head back until his eyes were forced to meet mine. Holding the silver irises captive, I stared down at him.

"I should make you beg like a true dog," I snarled, my voice still unrecognizable. "If you ever speak to me like that again, I will find a way to kill you." Giving his hair one last sharp tug, I released him and stepped away.

Turning back to where we had left Ella, I fell down onto the earth beside her. The fire was slowly crackling to embers under my skin, and I took in a deep breath before I turned to her.

"I just have to say that was the most arousing thing I have ever seen. Nothing is better than watching a strong woman put a man on his knees." She laughed while patting me on the back.

My own lips turned up in a smile, and I chuckled with her while the three Lupines slowly made their way back to us. The rage and anger had all but dissipated, and I was left feeling exhausted and empty. Kalian had yet to look away from me, his own face pulled into a frown at my silent dismissal as I ignored them.

I could understand why he had said the things he did, but the words had cut me deeply, even if he did not truly mean them. They were my own worst fears and thoughts thrown in my face. Logically, I knew that I had to be pushed to the point of rage to ignite, but I couldn't help but feel those things had come from some truth. Had Isla truly begged him to come with me? Did he truly think of me as nothing more than an undesirable nuisance? I was pulled from my thoughts when Ella tugged on my arm. Looking at her, I watched as her gaze flickered back and forth from my left eye to my right.

"C'mon, Skylahr, I think we're good now. The hazel is back and I'm sure you could use a drink." Wiping my hands on my thighs, I stood and linked arms with her as we continued to ignore the Lupines the entire way back into town. I was pleased to have an ally in my anger.

Finding the table in the farthest corner, I noticed Dane was silently sipping on a glass of ale, ignoring the others until we made eye contact. A bright warm smile lifted the corners of his lips and he gestured for me to join him.

I pulled myself into the seat next to his and took his offered glass gratefully before swallowing the remainder of the cool liquid. I let the warmth settle in my belly and then I motioned for Ella to bring two more. Dane seemed surprised but stayed silent as I drank another glass, only stopping me when I reached for the third.

"Slow down there." He laughed. "Pace yourself."

I smiled tightly at him before agreeing. I knew I had been desperate to drink off the remainder of my ignite that now settled low in my gut, but he was right and I chose instead to half listen as he began telling me of his travels to a nearby town. Nodding my head at the appropriate times and humming under my breath, I watched Kalian as he sat on the other side of the tavern. He and his pack were drinking their ales peacefully, only throwing me the occasional glance to be sure I was alright, and I couldn't help but feel annoyed that they still thought of me as a responsibility.

The night continued in much of the same fashion as the one before, only the Lupines headed to bed quite early, nodding at us in greeting as they passed. Kalian was the only one to linger, and he paused at our table as if he wanted to say something. However, he seemed to think better of it and continued on his way at my angry glare. I told myself I had forgiven him, but I knew I wasn't ready to forget.

Finding myself at ease without my companions, I slid closer to Dane as he told me about a merchant he had come across earlier in the day. I really had lost track of what he was saying, so I focused on his gleaming white teeth and tongue that would occasionally poke out to wet his lips. He paused, his own eyes dropping when he noticed where my focus had been drawn to, and gently brushed my hair back behind my ear. His fingers were rough and warm and this time I did not let myself pull away when he leaned forward.

His kiss was much more tentative than Kalian's. It was warm, slow, and sweet, though clumsy, and I let him kiss me lightly for a few moments before I pulled myself closer. Feeling bold from the ale, I ran my tongue across his lower lip before nipping it playfully, the same way Kalian had done to mine. Dane's reaction was instantaneous as a deep groan left his throat only to be captured by my lips before he hauled me closer to him.

Feeling light-headed from the ale and lack of air, I lifted my mouth from his, angling my chin away, giving him access to the delicate skin of my throat. He kissed his way down to my collarbone, nosing the neck of my tunic aside to give him more room, and my own fingers twisted into the fabric that stretched across his shoulders. I pulled it tightly, and warmth filled my belly as one of his hands crept its way up the back of my tunic. His big palm spread across the skin of my lower back while the other was tangled in my hair.

Was this what it felt like to be desired? He certainly seemed pleased with me, and I couldn't help but find some comfort in that.

Pulling away from my neck, he lifted his mouth to my ear, whispering hotly under his breath, "Do you want to continue this upstairs?"

I didn't give myself a chance to second-guess myself as I stood from my chair, pulling him up behind me before leading him to the stairs. We laughed quietly as we raced up the steps only pausing when we were in the privacy of my room, and when the door shut tightly behind us, I pulled Dane to me again. His lips were eager as he misjudged the distance and sloppily kissed the side of my mouth, but I did not let the awkwardness stop us. I tipped my chin, lining our mouths correctly, before kissing him back.

I wasn't sure if it was the inexperience or the ale, but the next few minutes all happened so quickly, and I was surprised when my back hit the mattress. Gasping, I froze while Dane wedged himself between my thighs, his hips grinding into my own as he moaned into my mouth. His weight was warm and heavy against me, and the feeling pushed all coherent thoughts from my mind.

And then fingers were tugging at the laces of my breeches, hands fumbling until the front gave away and the fabric was pulled down my legs. For a moment his weight was gone, leaving me cold and frozen while I panted for breath. But then the dark hair was back in my line of vision and the pressure on my hips returned. Gazing at the man above me, I smiled tightly as he looked down at my face with a gentle grin.

"Are you sure?" His voice was hoarse as he watched me closely, and I nodded my head silently. We had already come this far, and he obviously wanted me, what more could I want?

"Are you really sure?" I smiled at him again while running my fingers down his back, grabbing on to his tunic only to tug it up over his head.

"Yes."

"Thank the Gods," he groaned before crashing his mouth against my own. I felt him struggle with his own laces before he was pushing my thighs open.

Fingers touched my sex clumsily, and I closed my eyes and willed myself to relax. Breathing deeply through my nose, I bent my knees, granting him more access. When the slickness grew, I felt a hand steady my hip, and suddenly he pushed into me, moaning into my neck before pressing his lips against the racing pulse there.

The horrid pain that I had always been warned about never came, though there was a sharp pinch and an awkward full feeling. I looked at the space above his head as he moved slowly inside me. Running my fingers down his spine, I held my breath when his rhythm changed into a quick tempo, and I tried to match his movements. Lifting my own hips, I forced him deeper, and just as we gained momentum, a deep groan was pulled from his chest and he collapsed onto me. Blinking up at the ceiling in confusion, I froze as Dane puffed forcefully against my skin.

His breath was hot against my skin, and he pressed a soft kiss to my neck before rolling off of me and onto his back. I remained in my spot, frozen and unsure of what to do as his snores filled the room. My breeches were still uncomfortably wrapped around one ankle and I sat up silently, sliding my other foot in the fabric before pulling them up to my waist. Grabbing my cloak, I clasped it around my shoulders and tugged it across my torso before curling on my side. Lying in the silence, I listened to the rumbling next to me and suddenly I realized that I felt more alone than I had in weeks.

Chapter 20

I shifted awkwardly on Keyno's back for what had to have been the dozenth time as I tried to find a comfortable position, and Ella threw me a sly grin from her spot perched on Leena. When I had finally snuck out of my room, I had not planned on running into Dane's sister, let alone in such a disheveled state. Thankfully Ella had not said anything about it, only offering me a bath in an empty room and a pouch of contraceptive tea leaves, and once again I was grateful for her kindness.

Her brother had avoided me the rest of the morning as we packed our things, only kissing his sister goodbye quickly before ducking out of the tavern. To my relief, the Lupines paid him no mind and I prayed to the Gods they would not find out about my first coupling, even if just to spare me from their teasing. I, on the other hand, burned with shame, cursing myself for my rash decisions and disregard for the virtue my mother had always told me to protect.

Not seeming to sense my inner turmoil, the Lupines focused on planning our best route to Carlon before leading Ella and me to a vacant spot up in the sloping mountains that was hidden away from any mortal eyes. There, Kalian had shifted and bent down for me to mount, but I had turned pleadingly to Keyno. I felt unable to be so close to the alpha who had hurt me deeply the day before, his words still stinging when I thought about them, and I truly could not stomach sitting astride him so soon. Especially not after what had transpired with Dane following our argument. Seeming to sense my anxiety, Keyno bent down while ignoring the low growl rumbling from the black beast and took the lead without so much as a second glance.

That had been hours ago, and I could still barely look at Ella. Each time her dark eyes caught my own, my face would burn, and hazy memories of the night before would fill my mind. Unwilling to catch her gaze again, I focused my eyes to the fur below me and began braiding the strands between my fingers.

"Oh, look! The ocean!" Ella exclaimed, and I looked up as she pointed excitedly, her eyes big with wonder.

The air around us had cooled considerably in the last couple hours, and the wind was damp with the smell of salt, though I had no idea we had been so close to the shoreline. The Lupines below us seemed to have a silent conversation with themselves before turning in the direction Ella was facing. And then all at once they bolted, racing through the sand, their paws thundering against the dry ground as they barreled towards the shore.

My hair whipped behind me flowing through the damp wind as I laughed loudly at Keyno's competitiveness with his mate. I could feel him pushing himself harder and harder as he tried to outrun the smaller wolf. I leaned down against his withers, making myself as small as I could to help him pick up speed. When his ear flickered back, I leaned close to it.

"C'mon, Keyno, don't let your tiny mate outrun you," I goaded, snickering when a deep growl vibrated from him before his stride lengthened. Passing Leena quickly, I threw a smug smile over my shoulder only to bite my lower lip trying to smother my laughter. There rocking clumsily with Leena's movements, sat a very ashen and sick-looking Ella. Her eyes were wide as she scrambled to hold the fur surrounding her, and the pull of her hand distracted the smaller wolf from the race. With three more strides we reached the waves, and a shrill scream broke from my lungs as Keyno threw himself into the cool tide with a yelp of giddiness.

Sliding from the Lupine's back, I too splashed and ran through the surf, my face stretching with a smile. I had never been far enough south to enjoy the ocean; the coast near Noorde Point was too frigid to swim in, and we rarely had days warm enough to enjoy the shallow lake just south of the village. Soaking in the southern warmth, I spun in the sunshine while Keyno pounced and jumped at the waves like a dog would.

"You two have lost your minds!" shouted Leena, her stunning face glowing in the sun. Sliding my eyes from her, I sought out the tall frame that stood a few feet behind. Kalian's mouth was pulled down in a frown as he watched us, and I quickly averted my eyes before glancing at Ella. Her petite body was sprawled across the sand, and I snickered as I watched her fold herself sluggishly before ducking her head between her knees.

Wading my way through the tide, I headed back to shore before throwing myself into the sand.

Ella lifted her head before narrowing her eyes. "I hate you right now."

The corners of my lips lifted and she groaned before leaning her head against my shoulder. I ran a hand down her back in comfort, and we watched as Leena ran into the waves after her mate. The couple was joyous and loud as they romped around, and I observed them for a while before standing. Wiping the sand from my wet breeches, I then pulled Ella to her feet unsteadily.

"Come on, you don't want to see a naked Keyno. Trust me," I joked as I pointed at the now human man.

"Ugh, you're right, I don't need to witness that." She shuddered before following my lead back up the hill where Kalian had begun to set up camp.

As the sun set, we lay the blankets out across the sand and watched the beautiful sky turn from brilliant oranges to dusky pinks and purples, silently taking in the wonder of it. Leena and Keyno sat huddled close together, lost in their own world, and Ella had curled up beside me, dozing off while the sea breeze lulled her to sleep. Kalian had agreed to take first watch, though he sat back up on the hill behind us, not coming any closer even as the rest of the group slept. Turning my head, I peered at him over my shoulder.

Settled with his legs crossed, he looked stunning in the soft light of the moon. His high cheekbones and strong jaw glowed in the pale light, and my gaze traced over his features until they met silver. However, the normal molten seemed cool, and his eyes almost appeared sad. Taking pity on him, I smiled awkwardly and nodded my head before settling next to Ella, letting the waves soothe me.

Days passed without much change, and the landscapes had begun to bleed together while the awkwardness between Kalian and me continued. Try as we might nothing seemed to ease the tension, and even the smallest conversations seemed to make it worse. Looking for a buffer, I had turned to Ella, and she and I had become closer. Her laughter and smile had brought a warmth into my life that was strangely familiar to Elizabeth's, and I was grateful to have her.

When we paused in our travels, Keyno and I continued my training, but we had little success with igniting, and no one was willing to push me the way Kalian had. And though I was thankful for the patience, I had begun to feel like a failure and wished I hadn't made such a scene before. Maybe if I had been stronger and less sensitive, I would have mastered ignite by now.

Sighing, I rolled the stiffness from my shoulders, washed my hands under the warm stream of water pouring from the wineskin, and took in our surroundings. We were nearing Carlon's limits, and cleaning myself had been a distraction from the anxiety brewing in my gut. Ella thought we would find the scriptures in the city, though she couldn't be certain they would help us find the Chosen or defeat the Seductress. I could feel doubt slowly settle in my bones.

Handing the wineskin to the halfling, I pushed away my uneasiness and walked over to Kalian, who was scouting the area. His spine stiffened as he sensed my approach, and I exhaled, trying to release any tension I had been holding in. I had begun to miss his teasing and arrogance in our interactions, and I honestly had no idea how to handle this reserved version of him. We had not known each other for long, but I had grown accustomed to his haughtiness and our group felt odd without it. Stepping forward until our shoulders aligned, I looked over the horizon.

"See anything of interest?" I offered, quietly gazing off into the dark night, unwilling to look at him but still extending a peace offering.

"There's a few immortal soldiers walking the perimeter but no sign of crimson banners. Though I find that odd, given that Carlon is such a large city."

My eyes slid to his face before I cleared my throat. "Would they usually come from Wahstand if there was no threat?"

His answering smirk lifted a weight off my chest. "I don't know, but I'm sure in a few hours they will wish they had." He paused, cupping my arm gently. "Because now there is a threat."

We had headed back to the rest of the group, sitting quietly while we planned our entrance. The three Lupines would stay here, hidden and waiting, while Ella and I entered the city. The gates had been open all day to travellers—obviously the city was not concerned about the fever any longer—and we would take advantage of their hospitality.

Ella looked flawless in her cloak and tunic, her dark skin shining brilliantly in the moonlight, and I, on the other hand, felt clumsy and awkward next to her. Fidgeting anxiously, I drew the attention of Kalian. Cupping my chin in his hand, he steered my face to his. "Breathe."

I took in a deep inhale before blowing it between us. We hadn't been this close since our kiss, and I begged my heart to slow before he heard it beating in my chest. "We aren't far, and we will be there the moment something goes wrong. But if you can't relax, you'll draw attention to yourself."

I nodded before turning to Ella, watching as she bounced on her toes in excitement before pulling her hood up over her head then doing the same to mine. Then she strapped a sword to my hip before offering her arm, and I linked our limbs together as she steered us down the slope of the hill we had hidden behind.

The glow from the city burned bright as we approached, and the tension in my gut twisted as we drew closer to the gates. Two armoured guards stood on either side of the entrance, only sparing me a fleeting glance before they took in Ella, who remained silent, her eyes widening. Casting a glance over my shoulder as we passed, I noticed they had both turned their heads to stare after her in awe, and I wished so badly I could tell them how out of luck they were. Ella seemed oblivious to their leering and continued to drag me down the street as she searched her surroundings.

"Where in the fuck is the temple?" she whispered angrily before pulling me down another alley. The buildings of the city were far more elegant than those of Celinde and Noorde Point, but the streets reeked of piss and filth. Wrinkling my nose in irritation, I too searched for any sign of the sacred Temple of Fate and Fortune.

"There!" Ella exclaimed, pointing to the west. She ushered me along hurriedly and we all but ran to the stone steps that led to two great wooden doors. Pausing there, we scanned the area and then walked around the gardens that acted as a border for the temple before finding a way around the right side. Creeping around the corner, Ella grabbed on to my arm and directed my attention to a partially shattered glass window that sat halfway up the wall.

"Even if we get you in there, Ella, how would you get out?"

She huffed at me before shrugging. "Don't know, but it's the best we got."

"I don't like you going in there on your own."

Rolling her eyes, she leaned into my side. "Don't you worry about me; I can handle myself. You just stand guard."

Sighing in resignation I bent down and linked my fingers together, waiting until her small boot was secure in my palms before rising.

Pausing at the window, she looked down at me with a grin. "Don't think I'm not going to ask about you and pretty boy. I've noticed those sad looks he's been shooting your way." My mouth hung open as she snickered at me before hoisting herself through the window.

Once alone, time seemed to drag as my anxiety heightened. I had crouched down, willing myself to be smaller as a couple people passed. Most of the townsfolk had headed to their homes, turning in for the night, and only the light sounds of a few were still echoing through the empty streets. Finally certain we would not be caught, I began to stretch out my long legs, only to pause as my attention was drawn to two quiet approaching voices.

"They left yesterday, and if we get through that border those Lupines are fucked. I wish I had gone with them, I'm in need of a new fur rug." A rough voice chuckled as they came closer.

"I hear their women are nothing like we've seen. My brother promised to bring one or two home for me when he was done with them."

My breath left my lungs and I listened to them go on about the raping and pillaging planned for Denimoore. I so badly wanted to run my blade through them. Waiting until I could no longer hear their laughter, I stood, praying to the Gods that Ella was done.

When all remained quiet, my concern grew as there had yet to be any sign of Ella. I waited for a minute longer before I decided I had to check. Standing on my tiptoes, I grabbed the ledge of the window before hoisting myself up to peer into the darkened room, but there was no sign of her. Concern pushed at my chest, and I tried to pull myself through the tight hole, kicking my feet against the stone as my boots searched for a ledge.

Distracted by my efforts, I had not registered the other presence until I heard the scrape of the blade leaving its scabbard. I dropped to my feet, ducking just in time to miss the blow directed at me. The sharp steel slid across the stone, leaving a trail of sparks in its wake. I turned on my heel to face my attacker, noticing immediately that he was dressed in fine crimson armour, and his pale face was covered by an elaborate helmet. With only his eyes visible, he examined me closely before covering the distance between us.

He was quick footed and sure in his pursuit as he backed me farther and farther away from the window, and I tried to keep enough space between us to study his moves before reaching for my own blade. His eyes widened for moment before he smiled cruelly at me and then he lunged, throwing his weight into his assault as our metals clashed. The sound seemed to echo around us in the dark, and I worried that the commotion would draw more attention to us. Deciding to change my tactics to the defensive, I moved my body out of his range while drawing him nearer to me in hopes of finishing this as quietly as possible.

Remembering a specific move from my training with Keyno, I lifted my left arm just as he stabbed forward and came down on his forearm, trapping it. Holding my own blade tightly, I pushed the metal into the small gap between his armour and into the exposed flesh under his arm. Confident I had lodged the steel deep enough, I pulled it swiftly from him and covered his mouth with my hand as he groaned in pain before lowering him to the ground.

His deep green eyes were filled with hatred as they held my own and I could hear how labored his breathing was as I leaned forward next to his ear.

"May the Gods be there to see you home," I whispered before bringing my blade to his throat. I, however, had been careless in my actions and had forgotten to disarm him completely, leaving me exposed. Just as I began to run the steel across his throat, his hand had grabbed at his dagger and he used his last moment to pierce the skin of my left side. The tip dug deeply into my body before it was pulled out and his life left his body.

Gasping in pain, I lifted myself away from the soldier and stood on wobbly feet as I stared down at the lifeless face while my hand pressed against my tunic, pushing against the wet heat there. Realizing the amount of blood that began to pool, I lifted the hem and tried to inspect it, only pausing when I heard Ella's voice softly calling for me. Running back to the window, I lifted myself up into the opening and searched for her in the empty hall.

"Ella!" I whispered into the silence of the temple as my eyes adjusted to the blackness and I scanned for any sign of her.

"Ella!" I was about to try to shove my shoulders the rest of the way through the tight space when I heard the quiet pounding of footsteps on stone.

"Skylahr!" she called as she ran through the room, a piece of paper clutched in a fist, her face tight in panic. Behind her I could hear shouting, and I was just able to make out the silhouettes of a few men. Quickening her pace, Ella leapt up with her arms raised, and I clutched her wrists as I hauled her to me. Pulling her across the opening, I ignored the sharp sting in my left side as I passed back through the sill.

We crashed to the ground roughly before we scrambled to our feet and raced back to the entrance of the garden walls. My lungs burned and my tunic clung to my left side but I willed my feet faster. Ella had begun to struggle at my pace and I all but carried her towards the gates of the city that were now left unattended.

Not bothering to wonder where the guards had gone, we continued to run, only pausing in our speed to check behind us sporadically. The route back into the hills seemed as if it was twice as long, but perhaps it was because of the ringing in my head and the heaviness in my lungs.

Once we had found cover behind the first foothill, I paused, bending at the waist to cough wetly into the dirt. Rubbing my back, Ella pulled my hair from my face only to gasp in shock and as she wiped at my mouth. Moving her hand away, I noticed she had a deep red colour painting her palm and I grew concerned that she had cut herself. Wiping the blood away with my fingers, I turned her hand over.

"It's not mine, Skylahr," she whispered tearfully as she cupped my face. And it was then that I noticed the thick salt that coated my mouth.

"We have no time, I'll be fine. The Crimsons are on their way to Denimoore, we have to warn Kalian," I heaved through my wet throat before grabbing Ella's hand and pulling her up the slope that led to our camp.

"Kalian!" Panicked, I began to call for him as we rounded the last bend. We had been careful not to be followed but my concern for the

Lupines made me reckless with the volume of my voice.

"Kalian!" I called again, scanning for the alpha and his pack, but Ella's fingers tightened on my arm as she pulled me to face her.

Turning, I gasped for air as I eyed all three Lupines kneeling in the dirt, each shadowed by an immortal guard. Keyno's and Leena's heads were bowed as a blade was pressed to their necks. Kalian, however, kept his chin raised and watched me with glowing eyes while his guard smiled at me.

"Well, if it isn't the halfling bitch I've been looking for. And look, boys, she brought a friend."

Chapter 21

I gripped Ella's hand tightly as her other pressed against my side, pushing my tunic into my skin, and Kalian's gaze followed the movement. His bright eyes widened for just a moment before they became cold steel again and I glanced at the immortal behind him.

"What do you want?" my voice rasped, and I tried not to wince at the pressure on my side.

"I thought that was clear, or are you as stupid as you are ugly?" My eyes narrowed at the Crimson. He was a high-ranking soldier, perhaps a lieutenant or captain. His deep red armour was grander than the others', and his dark brown hair was braided with threads of matching ribbon. Noticing my growing rage, Kalian drew his brows together in a harsh frown as he cautioned me silently to not react to the insult. I tried my best to release as much tension from my frame as possible.

"As if your filthy blood wasn't enough, you killed one of my guards, halfling. Though I suppose it makes us even now. A guard for your parents sounds like a fair deal to me."

A shattered gasp bubbled from my throat as my heartbeat stuttered in its bone cage. Ella braced for my grief as I staggered into her side. Keyno, who had remained stoic, snarled viciously as he tried to rise to his feet, only to be pushed back down on his knees with a firm hand.

"Now, now, Lupine. We wouldn't want one of these blades to slip, right?" The Crimson patted Keyno on the head before focusing back on me.

"You're lucky Kal here is so gifted. Had it not been for him, I would have found you sooner. With that pathetic amount of control over your ignite, you would have been easy prey." His head tilted as he studied me. "But for some reason he finds it necessary to protect you. He is so well trained, tell me, how did you manage it?"

The Crimson's eyes met deep silver and I shivered as they clashed violently before I moved my gaze to Ella. Her own eyes, however, were tracing across the guards and I realized she was searching for an opening, some sort of weak spot. Following her lead, I too took in our options. The Lupines were not in a position to move, and I was too weak to try to fight off all of the guards. Moving my attention across the group, I shuddered as a smile stretched across the captain's face.

It was cruel and haunting, and my fingers slid under my cloak for my weapon as I tried to focus on my fleeting strength. But there was no sign of flames, not even a hint of a spark, and I became more and more desperate as time went on. Gripping on to Ella's hand, I tried to picture the corpses of my parents, their skin black and charred, or the smell of burning flesh that had surrounded my village.

However, my feeble attempts were interrupted by a cold, inhuman snicker. "What is it, halfling? Too weak to ignite?" he taunted as his friends laughed. "What if I told you of your mother, of how she cried for you. Cried and wailed for us to spare you. She knew it was you we were searching for, you see, she knew the instant that gate came down." The immortal moved from his position, circling around the kneeling alpha until he was an arm's length away.

"And your father, pitiful man that he was, begged. He bowed on his knees, lips to my boots, and begged for your life. Though looking at you now, I can hardly understand why."

Keyno growled again as he attempted to rise to his feet, but I could barely hear the noise as the ringing in my ears grew in volume. Ella pulled me closer, supporting as much weight as she could before my legs gave out and we both toppled to the dirt. Landing on my knees with a hard thud, I stared dazed at the black-covered knees in front of me.

I could feel Ella leaning into my side, and I noticed Kalian's tan fingers were clenched into the earth while his eyes focused on my face, but it was as if my mind was no longer connected to my body. Now, it was racing through every memory, every image it could conjure of my parents.

I could hear my father's warm voice as he wished me goodnight, and I could see my mother's bright green eyes that shone so brilliantly, they captivated everyone around. The way her fingers would trace patterns across my back when I would seek comfort after a hard day of nasty whispers from the other girls. How my father would spar with me in the barn, pushing me to be the best I could be only to sweep me up in his arms when I felt like I could no longer pretend to be more than I was.

Every laugh, every smile, every tangle brushed from my hair, every kissed scab, and my mother's whisper: *Love is the most powerful healer.*

They had been extraordinary parents, better than I had deserved, and they paid for it with their lives. Blinking away my dizziness, I held on to the fury that was now burning in my gut before I lifted my eyes to Kalian. His own face was hard, his sharp jaw clenched, but he gave me no sign of what I should do next. Frustrated, I looked to his captor.

The harsh line of his jaw and the edges of his face had dulled as he gazed down at me in surprise before covering it quickly with a mask of indifference. Examining him closely, I plotted my next steps, and I knelt silently as he stood before me.

He moved with confidence and held himself with an arrogance that surely came from years of experience. However, I watched as he moved his blade teasingly, and I noticed just a slight sluggishness to the swing. I looked back at Kalian to see if he had noticed the faint fault in his movement as well.

"Tell me, Captain, why was such a high-ranking official left in this shithole of a town with only a handful of soldiers if you are so important? Surely, they had a use for you elsewhere?"

My eyes widened at Kalian's tone. I was surprised by his overconfident demeanor when a blade was a mere few feet from his neck. He, however, looked bored and unbothered, a disguise I had come to recognize.

"It is none of your concern, dog."

"Well, I'm just pointing it out. Not to mention this whole unnecessary business you have going on here. If you want the halflings, take them. I'm not willing to die for them, especially not one that looks like this." He gestured to me with a hand before sighing loudly. Ella tensed beside me, her hand holding my side so tightly I winced before grasping at her blood-coated fingers.

"You really think I believe you, Kal? If that was true, why have you been protecting her?"

"Protecting her? I wasn't protecting *her*; I just wanted to avoid all this drama. I'm bored and starving so if you could please just get on with it rather than taunting the poor girl about her misfortunate parents, I would appreciate it." He paused, his eyes flashing to mine. "I personally can't understand why she's so upset. Sounds like you gave them a shred of mercy."

My lower lip trembled at the harshness of his voice and I whimpered softly. He had seen what they had done to my people. He had pried my father's hand from my fingers and yet could talk about it so casually. How could he do that?

"I do have one suggestion for you though. If you truly want to impress the others, you really should make more of a valiant effort. Holding her party hostage while you berate her isn't a good look for you, now is it? Doesn't exactly scream powerful captain." My mouth tightened as I watched the alpha carefully; his own silver eyes were gleaming as he smirked back at me. "This halfling is quite the swordsman, you know. She has beaten my pack more times than I can count over the last few weeks. Perhaps you should have a go?"

The Crimson seemed to run over the words carefully in his mind before tracing his eyes up the length of my body, pausing on my wounded side before he snorted. "She is injured, what fight could she give me?"

"So it will be an easy defeat. Don't tell me you're not willing to try." Kalian chuckled.

Watching the captain as he made his decision, Ella and I scrambled to our feet, still leaning together as he approached, his right hand lifting his sword at me.

"Well, go on, girl, let's see what you've got."

Ella gasped beside me before turning to the Lupines for help, but no one said anything as both lower-ranking Lupines looked murderously towards their alpha. Focusing on the threat approaching, I shoved Ella gently out of harm's way and lifted my own sword while ignoring the burning stretch on my left side. Blood no longer coated my mouth, but the skin felt as if it had been closing, only for me to rip it open when I lifted the metal over my hip.

Pointing the tip at the immortal, I willed my arm not to shake under the weight of the blade. The blood loss had caused the edges of my vision to haze as I watched the opposing sword gently rest against my own, their edges gliding across each other in a kiss before he swatted mine away.

Turning to look at his friends, he laughed. "I don't feel right about taking on such a creature, she can hardly stand." He looked down at the Lupine alpha. "Are you sure you weren't lying, Kal? She can barely hold her weapon."

Taking the opening, I lunged forward, my blade ready to come down onto him, but he whirled around quickly, just managing to dodge my attack with a breath of surprise. The snickering from the other two Crimsons immediately ceased, and the air around us became silent and tense.

My eyes flickered to Keyno, and I watched as his dark gaze focused on my opponent's graceful footwork. He gestured for me to watch them closely with a subtle nod of his head. Staying fully aware of where his weapon was, I watched the captain repeat the same dance around me again and again. He cycled through it every time he struck, and it became a game of back and forth between us until I had moved right rather than left. Taking him off guard, I caught his right wrist with the edge of my steel, and I watched in fascination as red bloomed from the narrow wound. I was surprised that they could be so easily injured and realized that they truly were not the godly creatures they would have us believe.

Feeling a new sense of confidence, I squared my shoulders, watching him as he traced the river of blood with his tongue. He lapped at it before smiling at me. Glaring in response, I braced myself on bent knees, holding my sword with both hands, but the captain threw a glance over his shoulder at his comrades before passing his weapon into his other palm. Brows falling in confusion, I paused as the other two Crimsons laughed together before my opponent stretched his arms back with an exaggerated groan and then held his sword out in front of him.

His smile was wicked while he flicked his wrist around neatly, moving the blade masterfully and with ease, and I realized that he had fooled me. He had been using his weaker hand all along.

Swallowing roughly, I braced myself for his next assault, though I was not prepared for the power behind his swings. Our steel clashed loudly as he pushed me around in a circle, though never gaining the upper hand. We moved around each other, and I readied myself for his next move. Anticipating his swing to come from above, I lifted my sword to block only to be caught surprised by the sudden heat throbbing from my inner thigh.

Glancing down, I noticed he had knelt to the ground at the last moment, thrusting the metal into the soft flesh that had been left open. He smiled up at me before pulling the tip of the blade loose from my leg. Straightening to his full height, he touched the blood with his fingers before lifting them to his face. He smeared the red onto his cheeks just under his eyes and swung at me again.

Blood slid warmly down my knee and my leg shook under the effort of blocking his blows as he beat me farther and farther away from the Lupines. We moved quickly, and the fight went on, sparks flying while the metal blades slid against each other, and my hair matted to my sweat-slicked brow. Grunting in effort as he charged at me again, I was not quick enough to avoid his foot when it lifted to kick against my injured leg, his heel pressing into the wound, causing me to stagger to my knees.

"What a waste, I thought you would have more of your mother's fight."

I inhaled sharply at the mention of my mother and my jaw clenched shut as I hauled myself back to my feet.

"Shut your mouth!" I hissed.

"It truly was a shame she fought so hard. She forced my hand, and I had been so hoping to get a little taste of her. I wonder if she would have begged me then."

Rage shook in my very core and this time I embraced the fire that threatened to consume me.

Heat flooded my veins and the pain that had radiated from my side and leg now only tingled tightly. Grasping at my newfound strength, I swung at him, hacking at his body brutally with everything I had and I watched as he clumsily avoided each attack. He was forced to reel back, his mouth open in shock as his defense began to weaken.

Consumed by the threat in front of me, I had not noticed that the Lupines had used the distraction of my ignite as an opening. Keyno and Leena had waited for the perfect moment before shifting and then they turned on their captors. The soldiers hadn't even registered the impending threat before the wolves tore them apart and the captain shifted his attention towards the noise, unprepared for the demise of his party.

A cold smile stretched across my face as I used his own strategy against him. I kicked the captain sharply in the knee, watching as he went sprawling flat on his back. Looming over him, I grinned as he blinked up at me in a daze, his wide eyes glossy as his breath came out in desperate pants.

"Beg." I didn't even recognize my own voice as I pressed my blade to his chest.

"Beg!" I roared again as tears filled my eyes. "Beg like my father did! Beg like the piece of shit you are!"

His mouth opened but only a wet gargle broke from it, the blood blocking his voice. Gazing down at his pale throat, I pulled my weapon from his neck only to take an unsteady step back. My knees shook under me and I felt the air rush out of my chest as I collapsed into strong waiting arms.

Tucking my head under his chin, Kalian scooped me into his arms and held me tightly against his chest, his heartbeat a welcome distraction to the pounding in my ears. Sobs rattled my body as I pressed my face into the warmth of his jaw while he carried me to his bedroll before carefully placing me on the thick blankets. He pulled away, and his large, warm fingers held my chin delicately while his other hand brushed the tears from my cheeks. His bright eyes gazed into mine while he smoothed my hair back.

"I need to look at your leg, Skylahr."

I was still heaving loudly and could not understand what he was asking.

"What?" His fingers toyed with the frayed wet edges of the tear in my breeches as he waited for permission. Looking down, my eyes widened at the amount of blood that had soaked through the material before I nodded at him silently.

Pulling at the fabric, he ripped it open before tearing the pant leg off completely, and I watched as his fingers palpated the red skin carefully before he cupped the back of my thigh with one massive palm. The warmth seeped into the tender skin as he inspected the wound, and he blindly reached out with his other hand until he found the full wineskin. Bringing the cork to his mouth, he grabbed at it with his perfect teeth before tugging it free and spitting it out.

"This is not going to feel pleasant," he warned, pulling my leg into his lap before pouring the contents over my exposed flesh. His warm, tan fingers ran across the soft skin of my inner thigh, forcing a swooping motion into my belly while he gently traced the now healing wound.

"I'm sorry for acting like such a bastard. I needed him to believe I was indifferent to you."

"Are you not?" I whispered hoarsely, watching his fingers stroke my leg rather than looking up into the pools of silver that were observing me.

He cleared his throat loudly, ignoring my question before sighing under his breath. "I'm also so sorry for the things he said about your parents."

My heart dropped and I tucked my chin as a shudder ran down my spine at the memories that had filtered through me. "My mother used to kiss my injuries when I was a child. She used to say there was no healing power stronger than love. That was all I could picture when he spoke of her."

I didn't dare lift my gaze to his face in fear of the judgement that would be found there, instead my lashes fluttered closed as I willed the heartache away. My throat was tight, and my head pounded as we sat in silence, my leg still cradled in his hands. I had been so lost in my grief that I hadn't noticed the proud alpha had bent his neck down to my leg until I felt the solid press of lips on the sensitive skin. My eyes blinked open and I watched in shock as he ran his lips across the now closed wound, his own eyes peering up at me through his long thick lashes.

Pressing one last kiss on my pale trembling inner thigh, he smiled gently at me before pulling me further into his lap. Tucking my head against his shoulder, he wrapped me carefully in the blankets before his deep voice rumbled from his chest.

"Then you're healed, Skylahr."

Chapter 22

We packed our things in haste, worried that another party of Crimsons would be circling back at any moment. Kalian had stayed near me, his hands hovering in the air, ready to step in if I appeared uncoordinated. The blood loss had left my mind fuzzy, and I blinked away the haze as I rolled the blankets into a pack before helping Ella. Her dark eyes watched me worriedly as we worked in silence, the air tense around our group.

Securing the pack across my shoulders, she tipped my chin down so she could peer up into my face. "I'm glad to see the hazel is back for good."

"What else were you expecting?"

"Your eyes are always blue when you ignite but I thought they may stay that way this time." Ella wasn't the only one who had mentioned the blue that filled my irises, but I hadn't known that the colour could be permanent. Turning to look over at the alpha, who was now speaking to Keyno, I bent to whisper into Ella's ear. "Do you think that's what changed Kalian's to silver?"

"Maybe. His sister has dark eyes, usually that is shared between siblings." She nodded, agreeing before tightening her own pack across her back. I snuck a glance at the Lupines, smiling softly when Keyno's eyes met mine. He had been the first one to rush after us, assessing me as best he could while I sat next to Kalian. He had clapped me on the shoulder proudly before averting his eyes and pink face when he had realized that my leg was still bare and draped across his alpha's lap. Noticing his embarrassment, I had pulled my limb from the warm fingers that had been stroking the skin soothingly before excusing myself to find Ella.

The halfling had been more observant than I had anticipated and lifted her brows at my approach, while taking in my bare leg before she had quickly tossed me a new pair of breeches. Looking at her now, I dreaded the questions she would bombard me with as soon as we were alone. Avoiding her stare, I turned back to the two males who were still talking quietly with Leena hovering close by. None of them really acknowledged our presence as they decided our next step.

"I need to talk to you." Ella's western accent was smooth as she whispered in my ear, though her tone had changed, and worry built in my gut as I glanced at her frown.

"I'm pretty exhausted, El," I sighed while busying myself with the tie of my cloak.

"It's important." She urged me closer while throwing a cautious look over her shoulder to the Lupines. Sighing in defeat, I nodded my head and steered her a few feet away before blocking her with my larger frame. Checking to be sure she would not be seen, she reached into her cloak. Her fingers tightened around a faded piece of parchment as she took a step closer to me, unfolding the paper and smoothing it out.

Looking down, I recognized the tongue of old, but I couldn't make out any words. "What does it say?" I whispered.

"It's not what it says, it's what it shows—" Her brows lifted, and her lips parted in shock as she glanced over my shoulder before clearing her throat.

"What are you two whispering about over here?" Leena's bored drawl startled me, and I felt my shoulders lift at the interruption. Spinning on my heel, I tried to come up with a lie, only to gape at the beautiful woman stupidly. Luckily, Ella was much more versed in the art of tales and carefully slipped her fingers against my side before smiling at the Lupine.

"I was just making sure she really was okay. Had a nasty wound on her side before we ran into our new friends. I know your brother took care of her leg, but I just wanted to be sure she was alright is all."

Leena's eyes narrowed at us in suspicion before she turned on her heel towards her mate when he approached us. Keyno seemed unaware of any conflict as he wrapped one long arm across her shoulders before grinning at us. "Kalian agrees that we should travel on foot into the hills. There used to be a tiny town just west of here called Ferrii. It may not be there anymore, but it once had been friendly to the Lupines."

I glanced at Ella before searching for Kalian. I had warned him of what I had heard the guards talking about in Carlon and tried to convince him that they should head north to defend the border. He, on the other hand, seemed less concerned, certain that it was idle gossip and that the veil would hold for the time being if there was a threat. Determined that Ella and I needed them more, he assured me that they would head for home as soon as they were sure we were safe. I was grateful for their commitment, but we had little idea about where to go from here.

My eyes roamed, finally finding him standing a distance away with his muscular arms crossed in front of his chest as he observed our discussion. He had been quieter than usual after our private moment on the hill and it made me anxious.

"Skylahr." Ella waved a hand in front of my face before rolling her eyes in annoyance. "Time to go."

Our arms were linked, and I was pulled in tow as Ella settled into step with the others. Her fingers would graze my side every so often before she shot me a questioning look as if she was trying to reassure herself that I was truly okay. Nodding at her again, I looked ahead and caught myself watching Kalian more closely than I would ever admit. My eyes were transfixed by the way his shoulders moved under his tunic, and how his black hair curled at the base of his strong neck. My belly twisted in warmth while I longed to run my fingers across the skin there. Would he shudder? What if I traced my lips across his pulse? My mouth dried and I choked on the dry air loudly, not managing to cover my face in time to muffle the noise.

Turning to me with concern, he took in my heated face. His own eyes widened before turning into molten steel; he seemed to know exactly where my mind had wandered to. We had never talked about our kiss since he had dismissed it as a drunken mistake, but I wondered if he thought about it as often as I did.

My night with Dane had been adequate but it lacked something unknown, and now after feeling his mouth against my inner thigh, I questioned if I would have been more fulfilled if Kalian had been the one between my legs. Swallowing loudly, I felt shame heat my face and I avoided his questioning stare as I turned my attention to Ella as Keyno called her name.

"Did you end up finding anything helpful in the temple?" Her face grew ashen as her eyes darted to the Lupines before hardening.

"Nothing, just a few old books about Carlon's beginnings." It was a lie, a blatant lie. I knew she had found something, she had tried to show it to me, so why be dishonest?

"Oh?" Leena turned, looking at us questioningly. "Really? Nothing?"

"Nothing." Her voice was tight now and it left no room for argument as she tugged me closer to her before passing the mated Lupines. Her little legs were moving nearly at jog as she stomped forward, and it would have been comical if it were not for the sudden change in her attitude. Following along easily, I gave her another few yards before I pulled her to a stop.

"El, you don't even know where we are headed."

Her black curls bounced in the wind and she glared back at the others before looking up at me.

"We need to be careful," she whispered.

"Of what?" I asked quietly, my mouth frowning as I tried to understand.

"Them."

Closing her lips firmly, she peered up at me with pleading eyes before tucking some curls behind her ear. Keyno looked between us as they approached but his partner was less amused. Kalian, on the other hand, seemed troubled but remained silent.

"You okay, little one?" Keyno asked before ruffling her hair.

"Fine."

"Are you sure?"

Ella swatted at his hand before sighing in frustration. "I'm exhausted and starving. Us halflings don't have the same stamina as you lot. Plus, we've been through some very dramatic events today." They seemed to believe her plausible excuse, and we continued on silently, making our way through the dry valleys of the western hills.

Hours passed and I was thankful for travelling at night, if only for the drop in temperature, though I could still feel sweat pooling beneath my tunic. The two men had lasted only an hour before both were stripping off their own shirts, leaving their tan skin and muscular torsos bare in the moonlight. Leena and Ella had even fashioned their own shirts into a tied style, leaving their midriffs exposed, and I longed to have the confidence to do the same. I knew that petty jealousy should be the least of my concerns, considering what I had been through in the past few hours let alone weeks, but I couldn't stop my insecurities from rising. So, I chose to suffer the wet cotton as it clung to my lower back, no matter how many times I pulled it away.

"Would you please just let me tie it?" Ella groaned as she watched me shift uncomfortably again, and my face heated as Kalian quirked a brow at me in question.

"Ella, just focus on your feet, your tiny strides are slowing us down," I growled back before twisting my long waves into a knot at the base of my neck.

The sun was high in the clouds when Keyno finally pointed to a cluster of tiny run-down buildings, and I almost fell to my knees and thanked the Gods. It was agreed that the Lupines would shift and search the area first before we were to follow. Waiting for the all-clear a distance away, I turned to Ella.

"Are you going to tell me what is wrong?"

Her teeth sank into her full lower lip as she peered around me, searching for any eavesdroppers. "I just don't think they've been telling the truth."

"About what?" My brows pulled in confusion at her tone.

"Who they are."

"Who they are?" I repeated skeptically. I had seen who they were, I had been to Denimoore. I had lived inside their home for weeks. I knew them. "They're Lupines."

"But Kalian—"

"Kalian what?" His deep voice sent a warm shiver down my spine and I turned to face him.

"Nothing." A black brow rose, but he didn't press us any further while we followed him down the slope of the hill to the abandoned town.

Ferrii itself was just a few run-down buildings that had been thrown together at one time, and I assumed the population would have been nearly non-existent even in its prime. Beside me Ella exhaled roughly, and I watched as her nose scrunched in aversion as she took in the state of the structures.

"If this place is haunted, I will never let you hear the end of it," Ella grumbled and Kalian rolled his eyes at her before leaving us to find his family.

The town brothel had been the best choice to stay in, though it too was worn down and dirty. But it had the most rooms and beds, and we had even managed to find a few pieces of clothing tucked away. Picking the room farthest from the entrance, I set my pack down before meeting Ella in the common room.

"Kalian says there is a bathhouse in the back, if you want to go bathe. They just finished bringing the water in from the well. Thank the Gods it was still functioning."

Ignoring her change in subject, I narrowed my eyes at her. "I want to finish our talk."

"Later," she promised before glancing at Keyno as he came through the entrance. "I'm sorry, dearling, but you are filthy, and I really need you to clean up before you come any closer." With a gentle shove she directed me towards the hall that led to the bathhouse. Nodding in agreement, I made my way to the large empty room that was brightly lit with candles and a small fire. In the middle was a staircase that led down to a square pool, large enough to fit at least a dozen men, and the water was clear and still.

Tugging at my boots, I tipped them upside down while I shook the sand from them and then dipped my toe into the water, sighing in relief at the cool temperature. I was glad they hadn't taken the time to warm it as the air in the room was already stifling. I pulled my damp clothes from me, waded into the water until I was almost shoulder deep, and closed my eyes as the ripples slid across my heated skin.

Checking over my shoulder be sure I was alone, I took in a deep breath before dunking my head. I pushed myself to the bottom, sitting cross-legged in the bath as my hair swirled around me. The silence was welcome as I opened my eyes, watching the warm glow of the fire shimmer in the water. When my lungs began to burn, I unfolded myself and stood, breaking the surface before pushing my hair from my face.

"For a second there I thought you were going to shift into the Siren herself." Crossing my arms across my chest, I spun on my heel.

Kalian was standing at the doorway, his back turned to me, though I couldn't be sure how long he had been standing there while I was under. "What are you doing in here?!"

"Coming to bathe," he drawled lazily before turning to face me, and I sank down in the water until it reached my chin.

"Well, it's occupied." I glared at him.

"It's large enough for two," he teased while tipping his head to the side.

"Kalian," I warned as he smiled at me.

"We should be cautious about using all of our resources, Skylahr. And it will save us from hauling more water in." His grin grew twice in size before he winked at me.

I knew he had a point, and I didn't want him to think I was flustered or affected by him, so I nodded. "Fine."

My eyes roamed over his naked torso, taking in the sheer size and power of him before I swam to the far side and sat on the ledge that ran across the wall of the pool halfway from the surface. Sighing again, loudly, I made sure he knew I was truly annoyed.

His laugh in retaliation was warm and he smirked at me as his large, graceful fingers went to the laces of his breeches. Undoing the knot with ease, he tucked his thumbs in the waist and pulled them down.

My eyes widened and my jaw dropped as I turned from him. "Kalian!"

He laughed again and I could hear him enter the bath, the surface softly swelling at his added weight. "Still so innocent."

His tone was full of fondness, but I still threw one arm out to splash water at him. Only as my arm extended, my hand collided into a solid chest and I whipped my head towards him with a gasp. He had moved so quietly I hadn't noticed his approach.

My palm lay flat against the warm flesh coated in a fine dusting of dark hair, and my fingers spread as I unconsciously stroked my thumb across the muscle. Kalian inhaled sharply at the touch and I recoiled quickly while my face flamed.

"Sorry." The words were barely audible as I moved away, pressing myself against the ledge of the tub before I lifted my eyes to stare at the wall. Noticing my discomfort, Kalian backed away to the opposite side, grabbing for the bar of soap that had been left for me. I longed to watch him, longed to get as many glimpses at his shoulders and arms as possible, but the shame of my lust kept my eyes on the wall while I sank deeper into the water.

Reaching for the other bar of soap, I hissed sharply at the tugging pain in my left side. The wound had closed but an angry pink line remained, and it stung each time the skin stretched when I moved.

"Are you alright?" Kalian's voice was filled with concern, but I was too proud to turn. He had already witnessed my weakness so many times.

"Fine," I snapped while I dipped the soap into the water before roughly washing my left shoulder and arm. My skin prickled as I scrubbed until I could no longer put off switching hands, and I tried to move quietly to avoid alerting him of my struggle. But when my left hand grasped at the soap, I had to bite my lip to quiet the whimper of pain as I raised my arm. Cleaning my other shoulder and arm carefully, I moved to reach my back only to wince in pain, my fingers immediately dropping the soap into the water.

"Fuck." I blindly dropped my hands into the water, searching for the bar, cursing again as the soap slipped from my fingers.

"Let me help you. Please." My body froze as a warm hand gently pressed against my shoulder blade.

Glancing back at his silver eyes, I stiffened for a moment before nodding and releasing a breath. Turning away, I closed my eyes and willed the trembling to stop as his slick hands lathered the sweet-smelling bar into my skin. His fingers pressed into the tight knots of my back and my head tipped to the side as a broken moan pushed its way through my lips. The sound echoed around the empty room and the noise left me mortified and stiff. Stepping away, I curled my shoulders tightly, shrugging out of his reach.

"Shh, sweeting, come back." Kalian's voice was a deep rumble and my heart raced as he pressed his palm against my spine again. He pushed no further, giving me the option to turn him away, and though I was thankful for it, I swallowed my nerves and stepped back into his space.

"Tip your head back," he whispered into my ear, his hot breath tickling my skin.

Following his direction, I lifted my chin, my eyes closing as the cool water was spilled over my hair, soaking the roots completely. His fingers scratched gently at my scalp, cleaning the strands carefully before rinsing them. He was so gentle that the ministrations lulled me into a boneless state, and I had hardly noticed that he had finished untangling my long waves. Stroking the soaked stands, he began to twist them into a neat braid before resting his fingers against the nape of my neck. His thumb then traced my pulse softly, caressing back and forth, and I leaned my head against his chest.

The silence was calming as our breathing synchronized and I felt his hand slip around my waist, just under the curve of my breast, pulling me tightly back against him until our bodies were flush. Certain I wouldn't move away, he slid his fingers down my belly, tracing patterns over the faint lines that marked the skin around my navel. I was too distracted by the movement of his hand to notice that his nose pushed the braid away from my neck. He slid his mouth up my throat, his lips searching until they reached a spot behind my ear and the contact left me quaking.

"Kalian." His name was a plea, though I had no idea what it was I was begging for.

"Easy, love, I'm right here." His teeth scraped against the flesh behind my earlobe only to soothe the skin with his tongue gently. My knees felt weak, and had he not been holding me so tightly I was sure I would have sunk into the water.

Ignoring my trembling, he moved the hand on my belly lower, cupping one hip while the other grabbed on to my braid. Twisting it around his fist, he pulled my head back and exposed my throat to his mouth. Jaw falling slack, I whimpered again as his teeth pressed against the nape of my neck, biting softly before scraping the roughness of his jaw against the tender spot.

Was it normal to feel so much from just a single touch?

My veins filled with liquid heat and I so badly wished he would just touch me, truly touch me the way I had secretly longed for him to since I had heard his deep groan back in Denimoore. The warmth became a near unbearable inferno as the fingers below the water slowly crept to the tops of my thighs, moving at a snail's pace. I wished I had more experience besides my one encounter with Dane. Maybe then I would know how to ask for what I needed.

Lost in the daze his touch had put me under, I had been waiting for his next move and was completely unprepared for his warmth to suddenly leave me. My legs wobbled without his support and I was left confused and cold by his abrupt absence. I turned on my heel only to be shocked when I found him lathering the soap across his own skin while he ignored me.

Swallowing the hurt that bubbled in my throat, I lifted myself from the water and grabbed the nearest towel. Wrapping it around my body, I bolted for the door, rushing past a confused Keyno while I left Kalian and my longing behind.

Chapter 23

Ella met me in my room, her face painted in shock and concern as I slammed my door shut behind me. She rushed forward but my hand lifted, silencing her questions as I tugged on a new set of breeches. Holding the towel around my upper body with my teeth, I growled when the pant leg stuck to my damp calf. Hobbling on one leg, I pulled and cursed as the material continued to bunch around my limb, and I teetered awkwardly on my toes before I went falling back.

The wind was knocked out from my lungs and I shifted to one side, rubbing at the pain that rattled the base of my spine while blinking up at the halfling. Ella sat perched gracefully on my bed, her hands covering her mouth, and I knew her lips were fighting against the smile that pulled at them. Rolling my eyes, I rose to my feet and grabbed at the tunic she tossed to me before smiling at her gratefully.

Ella remained silent while I tugged the rough cotton over my head, her lips pursed as she bided her time. I still had yet to make real eye contact with her and instead busied myself with removing my hair from its braid with rushed fingers.

"Sky—" I ignored her, my hands becoming more flustered. "Skylahr! Stop! You're going to tug out half your hair!" Sagging in defeat, I crumpled onto the bed next to her before turning under her guidance. Ella's own skilled fingers lifted, and she began to sort through my damp hair while humming under her breath.

"Do you want to talk about it?"

I huffed in response, not sure if I could muster the courage to talk about the rejection I had just suffered. Ella already did not trust the Lupines, and I did not want to add to her animosity.

"Should we talk about that other thing instead?" I asked, and Ella's fingers froze in my hair for a moment before she pulled away and stood before me. Tilting my head, I blinked up at her, but the longer I gazed at her, the more I was sure I did not want to know what she was hiding. Whatever it was had hardened the pretty angles of her face, and she anxiously shuffled from one foot to the other as her eyes darted to the closed door and her mouth pressed into a thin line.

Taking pity on her, I stood, cupping her cheek before smiling down at her face. "El, if it really troubles you this much, share it with me. Maybe I can carry the burden." Dark eyes searched mine, but she never spoke a word. Instead, she smiled tightly at me and removed my fingers from her face.

"It can wait." Not wanting to force it from her, I dropped the subject and pulled her back to the common room where Leena and Keyno had been waiting.

The Lupines glanced up from their spots next to the fire, though it was only Keyno who graced us with a smile. Grinning back at him, we crossed the room and took the plates of food handed to us before settling into an easy silence as we sat at a nearby table. Travelling had taken a toll on all of us, not to mention the unfortunate run-in we had with the Crimsons, and so we relaxed quietly, finally finding a moment of peace.

Lost in my thoughts, I hadn't noticed the alpha as he made his appearance until the chair in front of me scraped across the floor. His damp hair fell across his forehead, and his skin was still flushed from the cool bath. Observing him closely, my eyes caught sight of a stray pearl of water, and I followed its path as it slid from his temple, down his cheek, until it dripped from his jaw.

"Sky?" A sharp nudge to my ribs brought my attention back to Ella, and I smiled in apology.

"How are the wounds?"

"They will probably scar, but they are nearly healed. The Crimson's magic wasn't as strong as I feared." My face flamed as Kalian's deep voice spoke for me, and I heard Keyno choke on his supper.

"And how would you know how she is healing, dear brother?" Leena's eyes slid back and forth between us, and I refused to help Kalian make up an excuse, even when his skin darkened in embarrassment.

"I—I—" The alpha seemed caught off guard, and I watched in fascination as he became more flustered.

Taking pity on the man, Ella sipped her tea before answering for him. "Sky's healing is strong, you two know that."

Kalian shot her a grateful glance before busying himself with his food, and Ella's fingers reached for mine under the table. Giving her hand a squeeze in thanks, I focused on my meal in silence until Keyno called for me.

"Hazel, I think we should take tonight to train. That is if you're up for it?" I did my best not to glance at the alpha while I nodded my head in agreement.

"Of course." Although I was both mentally and physically drained, I knew I needed to get a hold of my ignite. Waiting for another instance where I truly needed it without having the power to unleash it seemed foolish.

Keyno appeared to be pleased at my acceptance and guided me out the door, grabbing our blades before leading me to a field just outside the town. It started much the same way it always did. We began with a slow spar and built on our efforts until both of us were giving it our all. Normally we were well matched, but the remainder of my previous ignite still burned in my veins, and I could feel its power simmering just below my skin. I had managed to unarm Keyno three times before he finally surrendered and turned to our silent spectator, who had made an unnoticed appearance.

"She is all yours." Kalian's eyes were a burning steel as he took the blade from Keyno, who then excused himself and made his way back to the abandoned brothel.

Fluttering filled my belly, and my fingers shook around the pommel of my sword as I watched the alpha settle in his stance. Just as Keyno had, Kalian started slow and gentle in his pursuit as we crossed blades, though we remained silent in our practiced routine. Gone were the light jokes and smiles I had shared with Keyno, only to be replaced with hurt and anxiety.

Sensing my unease, Kalian slowed his moves while gauging my expression before trying his hand at an apology. "Skylahr, about the bath, I shouldn't have crossed that line." I didn't know what hurt more, the actual rejection or knowing that he regretted it.

"It's fine," I growled at him while I swung my sword in his direction.

Easily avoiding my clumsy attack, he sighed. "It's not fine. I didn't mean to hurt your feelings."

Angered by his ability to read me so easily, I narrowed my eyes before snapping at him, "There are no feelings."

"Really? Is that why you are hacking at me like a green squire?" I stopped in my tracks to glare at him in silence before tossing my blade at his feet.

"I'm not doing this. Either shut up and fight or fuck off."

"Ah, there's that sharp little temper." I knew he was goading me; I knew it and yet it worked. I bent to pick up my weapon and backed a few feet away before nodding at him. We easily fell back into our routine, swinging and dodging each other's assault until I became more frustrated at the care he was showing me.

"Could you please just get on with it? I'm not learning anything like this." Kalian's warm eyes became hard and he nodded with just a slight dip of his chin before he rushed me.

He was faster than I had anticipated, and I just narrowly avoided his first swing, though it was thanks to the Jester I was sure. Turning to face him, I raised both of my arms to deflect his swing as he came down on me with more force than he had ever used, and my eyes caught his for a second before he was releasing the pressure and moving to strike again.

Having anticipated his move, I ducked to the side, only to catch the closed fist to my ribs. The wind blew from my lungs in a gust as I stared up at him in shock. "Did you just hit me?"

"You gave me an opening and I took it. Just like any enemy would."

My hand rubbed at my ribs for a moment while I blinked at him. "So that's how this is going then? No rules?"

"Surviving isn't about rules and you didn't want to be coddled, you wanted to learn. Remember?"

That stupid smirk was pulled across his mouth and before I could blink my knuckles made contact with his sharp jaw, the same way I had dreamed about doing for months.

"Fast learner, remember?" I snarled at him before lifting my weapon and charging him. The sound of steel clashing made my blood sing, and I felt the beginnings of my ignite spark.

Noticing the change in attitude, Kalian grinned at me. "There's my girl."

Rage coursed through me and I glared at him. "I am not your anything." I could not believe the audacity of this infuriating man. He either spent his time insulting me or caring for me, and the constant change in his moods left my head spinning. I had no idea what I meant to him or what he wanted, and I hated that he could make me feel so baffled.

Harnessing my frustration, I used it to fuel my anger and soon enough the tiny spark that had been lit increased into a burning inferno. The fire swam in my veins, bubbling and scorching until it consumed me.

"That's it. Lean into it now." His deep voice was muffled over the pounding that echoed from my chest, but I did exactly that.

I embraced the fire.

I embraced it with everything in me, and slowly the burning melted into a soothing heat as it took over every inch of skin. Power came back into my tired arms, and my breathing evened out as I picked up my speed. My swings became more focused, more precise, and as I stalked Kalian, he smiled at me.

"That's it! That's it, Skylahr!" Normally the pride in his voice would have me blushing, but now it just angered me. Using every ounce of strength I had, I swung down onto his sword and watched as it flew out of his tan fingers and across the field. His head had turned to follow the metal as it sailed through the air, leaving him unprepared for my body to slam into him as I sent us both into the ground.

Moving my thighs to trap his hips, my now empty hands grabbed at his wrists until they were pinned against the earth beside his head. Silver eyes blinked up into my face in confusion and I sneered down at him. I was either going to kiss him or kill him.

"Sky—" The deep rumble of his voice made the decision for me and my mouth crashed onto his with enough force that I had muffled the rest of his words.

It was rough, hard, even violent as I used my weight to lean against him while my tongue curled over his. A different heat began to fill my belly as my hips rocked into his, pushing a groan from his mouth while my teeth sought out his lower lip. I nipped at it sharply, then soothed it with a gentle kiss before I trailed my mouth across his jaw and behind his ear, finding the same place he had in the bath. Air left him in a sharp gasp, and I chuckled roughly before dragging my teeth across the spot.

"Sky," he groaned again, and I pulled back to gaze down at his face before kissing him again.

His lips were sweet, warm, and yielding under my own, though I couldn't seem to get near enough. I needed to get closer. Moving my hands from his wrists, I slid them down his arms and his muscles tensed under my wandering palms. Smiling against him, I continued my exploration. Massive shoulders were firm under my fingers, and I traced the shape of his chest until my fingertips found the delicate laces of his tunic. Pulling my mouth from his, I panted above him while my fingers loosened his tunic.

"Skylahr." I ignored him, too focused on my task, growing more frustrated when I couldn't get the last lace loose. Warm hands lifted to cradle my own, halting my progress, and my eyes flickered up to his face.

"Stop. We need to stop."

"What? Why?" He had kissed me back, he had found me in the baths, he had kissed me first. "Do you not want to?"

He closed his eyes, his head falling back against the ground with a dull thud. "Yes, I want to, so badly. Can't you feel that?" He lifted his hips into mine and I could feel the hardness of him as it pressed against me. "But you finally embraced your ignite, and this happens."

"What happens?" My voice was stiff, and I grew impatient with his constant games.

"It's the blood lust. Igniting heightens all emotions, all wants, not just anger or sadness. This is a totally normal reaction. Which is why I can't let this continue."

I blinked down at him before taking in our surroundings. Glancing over my shoulder, I finally realized just how open the space was, and I felt humiliated that I had acted so loosely.

Feeling my cheeks tingle and pinken, I looked back down at him and mumbled out an apology before lifting myself off him. Not waiting for another word, I picked up my sword and ran back to the safety of the brothel.

Chapter 24

The cold, dusty bedding was a sanctuary for me and my embarrassment as I crawled under it, avoiding the group on the other side of the door. Both Ella and Keyno had stood to greet me when I came in through the entrance, the halfling's small hands cradling my face as she pulled it this way and that, examining it with wide eyes. The power of my embraced ignite still ran through me, and Keyno smiled proudly while slapping my shoulder in congratulations. And although I was grateful for their support, I couldn't shed the nerves or embarrassment that had followed. Wanting to avoid Kalian's entrance, I claimed I was just too exhausted to socialize and excused myself before jogging to my room. It hadn't necessarily been a lie; I was exhausted. Kalian, my feelings, and my confusion were all truly exhausting.

Now in the silence of my room I noticed how the old wood of the brothel groaned as the harsh winds pushed against it, like they were trying to flood the room with their power, and part of me wished I could be swept away with them. I was still coming down from the high of finally embracing my ignite but I realized how alone I felt.

When was the last time I had been embraced by my parents? How long had it been since I had seen Elizabeth's gorgeous smile or worried about the unwelcome stares in Noorde Point? Now my days were filled with death and hiding and plotting. I had always wished for more in life, but now, lying in the empty room of an abandoned town, I begged the Gods to take me back. Back to the simple life I had lived before. Before I had learned of the swamp witch, before I knew of my halfling blood and the total chaos it would cause in my life.

My bare legs shuffled, and I tossed and turned while I willed myself to sleep. But it was pointless; the wind was too loud, the heat was too stifling, and the memories from the day, hell even the last few months, were too much. Tossing the thick blanket off of me, I lay flat and closed my eyes while I concentrated on my breaths.

In and out. In and out. In and out.

Just as I was about to take in another deep inhale a quiet rapping echoed from the wooden door, and I groaned in frustration as I rose from the bed. Trying to keep the irritation off my face, I pulled my hair back behind my ears and straightened my tunic. Grabbing at the cold metal knob, I carefully unlocked it before throwing it open.

"Ella, I'm really not in the mood—" The words were cut off by my surprise in finding the tall muscled form of Kalian in the doorway. Both of his hands were braced on the frame, his fingers tightening around the wood as it creaked in protest. His bright eyes were narrowed, though they still held the same heat from before in the field.

Straightening my spine, I took in the rest of his face. Black brows were furrowed, creating a crease between them, and his usually smirking mouth was in a tight line as the muscles in his square jaw clenched. Taking a step back, I willed the wind to chill the space between us, if only for a moment of relief.

"You weren't in the common room." It was a statement, not a question, and his deep voice tore through me.

"I'm sorry to disappoint you," I snapped back angrily. This stupid, beautiful man was by far the most confusing, aggravating being I had ever met.

"I was disappointed." He sighed before rubbing his palms down his face. "I wanted to see you."

"I can't see why, you seemed uninterested in me before." My arms looped across my middle self-consciously as I tried not to curl into myself.

"Is that what you think?"

My scoff was the only answer I had for him before turning on my heel to stalk back to the bed. Perching on the edge of it, I watched him closely. Kalian stepped into the room and closed the door quietly behind him, only to lean against the wood, keeping the distance between us.

Looking around the room, he searched for something unknown before gazing at my bare legs as they crossed in front of me. His eyes left a trail of sparks as he traced the skin from ankle to midthigh.

"What?" I snapped, breaking his concentration.

"I'm not uninterested. I'm very, very interested." He paused and the change in his voice had me pulling at the hem of my tunic shyly.

"Then why do you keep stopping? First the baths, then the field." My voice was meek as heat filled my face.

"Because Keyno and my sister were right outside that room and if I had continued, he would have seen you bent over the ledge of that godsforsaken bath while I was buried in you." His throat bobbed while he swallowed. "And the field, you had just finally mastered your ignite. You were still burning with it and I couldn't take advantage of you by fucking you in the open." The explicit image had my face burning, and it felt as if I had swallowed a pound of sand.

"Oh."

"Oh? That's all you have for me, oh?" Pinching the bridge of his nose, he exhaled loudly before taking two long strides forward. When his toes were a mere inch from my own, he dropped to his knees. Warm palms slid across my thighs before the fingers tightened gently on them.

"I didn't want the first time I had you to be there, in that room or on the hard ground. And I really did not want any spectators. I want you and your desire for myself. For my eyes only."

My jaw fell and my eyes widened as I watched his fingers reach for me. Gently he cradled my cheek in the palm of his hand before stroking my hair.

"Do you want me now?" I croaked out awkwardly, my voice

catching in my throat. In answer he smiled softly, though his desire was plain.

"Yes." He nodded with certainty.

"Alright."

"Alright." He laughed before unfolding himself. I had anticipated that he would push me back onto the bed, but instead he sat next to me.

"Is this something you want?" I knew my answer immediately and nodded my head.

"I need to hear it." His voice was a whisper, but I could still hear the demand in it.

"I want you," I answered honestly, and Kalian turned my chin towards him before tipping my face to his. Just as his mouth grazed mine, however, I reeled away.

"Skylahr?" His voice was filled with concern, and I felt like an idiot for breaking the moment.

"I'm not a maid," I blurted as my chin fell to my chest while my hair became a curtain, protecting me from his questioning gaze. I should have told him sooner; I should have told him after it had happened.

"Oh, Ella's brother?" I nodded silently in confirmation before peeking up at him. The moonlight had filtered in from the tiny window, illuminating his beauty, and I so badly wished I had not said anything. I was not sure I could continue to travel with him any longer after this. I would not be able to bear his looks of disgust.

"Look at me," he demanded before cupping my face again. "Look at me." Sliding my eyes to his, I held my breath and waited for him to reject me. Again.

"I figured as much, Skylahr. I had assumed you two had spent some time together."

"What?" I knew there were obvious signs, but I had never said anything.

"It doesn't matter."

"It doesn't matter? But I lay with him, even after you and I kissed."

Kalian looked just as confused as I felt and we both just watched each other carefully.

"Why would it matter if you were a maid or not? I certainly am not untouched." I knew that, of course, but the men in our village had always talked about wanting a pure woman. How they wanted to be the first to lie with them, and a part of me had worried Kalian would be the same.

"Do you not deserve pleasure? Do you not deserve the same pleasure as me?" I stared at him blankly and watched as rage slowly seeped into his eyes as I remained silent.

"Did you want him? Did he ask? Did he force you?" His voice rose in anger and my head finally cleared enough for me to understand what he was implying.

"No! No, he didn't force me. He was—" I broke off, searching for the right word. "Polite."

"Polite?" The anger that had flooded his face now melted into humour as he smirked at me. "Polite, as in…?"

Rolling my eyes, I elbowed his middle sharply. "Agreeable. He was kind."

Chuckling gently, he turned my face back to his before capturing my mouth in a bruising kiss. His teeth tugged at my lower lip before soothing it tenderly with his tongue while his fingers cradled the back of my head. Pulling away just far enough that our lips still grazed each other, he sighed softly. "Let me make up for his lacking."

My voice was caught in my throat as his warm palms stroked my thighs, parting them before he stood smoothly. The motion sent me onto my back, and I blinked up at the cobwebs that had created glistening patterns on the ceiling above me. The calloused fingers that warmed my skin now moved to the backs of my knees, cupping them as he hoisted them up higher around his waist. The movement forced the hem of my tunic to fold back, exposing more and more skin. Silver eyes hovered above me as the bed dipped under his added weight, and I could feel the roughness of his breeches rub against my inner thighs. But the coarse material only added to the spark that was burning under my skin. Smiling softly at me, Kalian dipped his head, kissing my lips with enough force that my head spun.

"Give me your mouth." His voice was deep, pushing all focus from my mind as my lips parted of their own accord for his tongue. He kissed me with skill that I could not match, though he didn't seem to mind my clumsy rebuttal. Following his lead, I tilted my head to give him more access as my paralyzed fingers finally sprang to life and found purchase in his hair. Running my fingers through the silk-like strands, I tilted my head back as his mouth traced the lines of my throat, nosing at the collar of my tunic.

"I need this fucking thing off of you," he cursed, his hands now sliding under the cloth and around to the small of my back, crushing my chest against his as he hauled me closer. And just when it felt like I would somehow merge into him, he pulled away.

Snapping my eyes open, I realized I wasn't even sure when they had fallen shut, and I searched the room for him. He had toed off his boots and froze at the end of the bed, his gaze smouldering as he took in my rumpled appearance.

Striding over to me, he grabbed at my legs again, only this time he tugged me around and pulled me to the edge of the bed before dropping to his knees. "What are you—"

The rest of my sentence broke off as a quiet moan left me when his tongue traced the skin of my inner thigh before he hoisted my legs over his shoulders. Though confused, I watched him, intrigued, and his silver eyes held my own as his mouth dropped across my legs again in sweet, soft kisses. Gasping at the fluttering press of lips, I moaned as his mouth continued a path closer and closer to the apex of my thighs.

"Kalian." My voice was weak as his massive hands pried my legs farther open.

"Let me worship you." His voice was muffled, and the first touch of his tongue had my head tossed back as my fingers curled into his hair. I had never felt anything like this. My whole being was focused solely on the man who knelt between my thighs.

Closing my eyes tightly, I pried one hand out of his hair and instead fisted the thick blankets I was sprawled on. His tongue swirled across my wet sex, and I sobbed as he groaned against me, the vibrations muffled against my flesh. Digging my heels into his shoulders, I lifted my hips as his tongue pressed into me gently before he replaced them with one and then two fingers. He rocked them into me smoothly, and I couldn't contain the deep cry that slid from my throat.

The sound bounced off the empty walls around us, and my hand that had been preoccupied tugging at his hair slapped over my mouth in embarrassment. Noticing the movement, Kalian pulled his face from me, and his shining lips lifting into a smirk before he scolded me.

"None of that. Let me hear you." His free hand that had been resting on my leg grabbed at my fingers, pulling them away from my face before placing them on the bed. And when he was confident I wouldn't immediately move them back, he pressed his palm onto my lower belly.

"Now, be good for me and stay still." Heat bloomed in my cheeks, whether it was from embarrassment at his direction or from lust, I wasn't sure, but I could only whimper in need as he settled into the space between my legs.

Once again, I was at his mercy as he gently coaxed my body to coil tighter and tighter, only to let up and start all over again, never quite letting me reach that edge. I could feel tears leak from the corners of my eyes as the pleasure became too much for my body.

"Please! Please, Kalian," I sobbed, begging him, but to my horror, his fingers gently withdrew as he kissed my left thigh, then my right before standing. Curling my fists, I growled in frustration.

That was not what I wanted, and the damn smug bastard knew it.

As if he could read my mind, his lips twitched in a smirk and he lifted his glistening fingers to his face. "You taste divine, love. So sweet. So fucking perfect." He paused to suck the digits clean. "Now, what do you want, Skylahr?"

Kalian grinned and I wondered how he could expect me to be coherent enough to answer. I could barely hear anything over the blood pounding through my veins.

"What do you want?" His voice was rougher this time, deep and ragged, and I watched in fascination as those skilled fingers tugged at the laces of his breeches.

"Answer me." The authority of his voice had my eyes shooting back up to his face as I swallowed nervously.

"You. I want you."

Pleased with my answer, he tugged the material down his legs before kicking his breeches towards his discarded boots. I was too shy to immediately focus in on the part my eyes had been drawn to and instead fixated on the golden muscular thighs that were tightening with every step forward. Tracing the skin to his narrow hips, I then slid my gaze to his chiselled torso and then finally to the fine trail of hair that led to the massive thick length of him.

How would he fit? My gut tightened in nervousness, and it must have crossed my face because the moment his knees hit the edge of the bed, his hand cradled my cheek tenderly. "Have you changed your mind?"

I opened my mouth, but no sound came out. Trying again, I cleared my throat roughly and answered, "No, no, I haven't changed my mind."

The words were an awkward croak and my eyes widened as he grabbed at my hips, forcing me up before lifting me into his arms and turning us swiftly. Dizzy from the speed of the turn, I braced my hands on either side of his head while my thighs clenched the hips that they now straddled. My hair created a bronze curtain around us as our noses brushed against each other.

"We can stop at any point." I smiled down at him gently before sitting back on my heels. However, the change in weight had Kalian clenching his jaw as I slid wetly across the enormous length of him. Ignoring my own wave of pleasure that crashed into me, I rocked again, watching in fascination as his eyes closed and his jaw sprang open. He let me repeat this cycle three more times before his hands grabbed at my hips tightly and his eyes glared up at me.

"Take that ugly wool scrap off and let me see you." It was not a request, but a demand, and my breath came quickly as the nerves set in. Dane had not even bothered to try to pull my tunic off when he had been with me, and part of me had been grateful for that. I wasn't sure he wanted to see what was underneath, the hard muscled arms, wide shoulders, and rounded belly that was covered in faint lines. I was big in the wrong places and not at all delicate. Not like other women, not like Nadine was. And now, sitting above Kalian, I was sure he would be disappointed.

"Wouldn't you rather I leave it on?" My voice was small and quiet, and I looked down at his muscled chest rather than his face.

"No. I certainly would not. Why would you think that?" His hands eased off my hips and found their place on my thighs again as his thumbs stroked the skin soothingly.

"I don't look like Nadine." I so badly wished I hadn't spoken her name out loud, worried that the mere sound would have her image now engraved in his mind.

"Yes, Sky, I'm aware." My shoulders dropped and I went to move off him only to be stopped by his arms as he sat up. He pulled me closer to his chest, and I tried to ignore the warm feeling of him pressing into my bare thigh.

"Do you want to know what I see?" I twisted my mouth in a frown, unwilling to answer. But he continued anyway.

"I see smooth, strong legs. The longest pair I have ever laid eyes on, and I have spent more hours than I can count imagining them wrapped around me." His fingers trailed under my tunic to the small of my back. "I see round, wide hips, the perfect size for my hands to hold while I make you beg for me." Fingertips now traced my spine and shoulders causing my eyes to flutter closed.

"I see strong shoulders, built from years of hard work and training. I see a warrior. I see a fierce woman who is more than my equal." Testing to see if I would protest, he tugged on the material gently before pulling the fabric over my head. He tossed it to the side and leaned back until he was flat again, and his eyes widened as they took in my exposed skin.

His eyes filled with hunger as he gazed at my chest only to soften when they noticed the harsh pink scar that was still healing on my left-hand side. Sitting back up, he bent awkwardly to press a sweet kiss against the ruined flesh and then moved slowly as his mouth traced my shoulder, my clavicle, and then down to the roundness of my breasts. Gentle lips kissed at the tender skin, and when his mouth wrapped around a pert nipple my head flew back as I moaned his name. I had no idea a touch so soft could have such an effect and I squirmed on his lap as I felt myself slicken. Lying back down, he grabbed at my waist, positioning me carefully until I could feel him pressing at my entrance.

"Wait!" Kalian's hold immediately dropped from my waist and he lay perfectly still as he watched me in concern. "Wouldn't you rather be...wouldn't you rather me be under you?"

Noticing my discomfort, he stroked my thighs again as he smiled up at me softly. "I would have you any way I can, but this way you can control our pace. You can take as much or as little at your speed." My cheeks flamed as I realized he was talking about the size of his cock, and he laughed quietly at my pink cheeks.

"Ready?" Taking a deep breath in, I nodded before widening my stance and following his direction.

He was bigger, thicker than I had anticipated, and the tight stretch had me pausing halfway. Sensing my discomfort, Kalian brought his thumb to that spot above where he entered me and softly stroked until the heat in my belly was more prominent than the tension. Sensing my relief, he lifted his hips, easing more of himself into me with a long, slick slide.

"That's it, let me in. You're doing so well, love." The encouraging words had more of an effect than I thought possible, and suddenly I finally sank the rest of the way down. Falling forward on my hands, I panted with wide eyes as I took in the tension of his face. His jaw was tight as perfect white teeth sank into his full lower lip, and I blinked down at his glorious face while I settled on him.

I kissed the crease between his brows and waited until his eyes fluttered open. Silver clashed with my hazel and I nodded silently at him. Taking my cue, he sat back up and the change in angle hit something deep inside me that had me crying in need. His fingers dug into my hips as they coaxed me into rocking, forcing the air from my lungs as the other hand tangled in my hair, tugging on the strands until my back arched.

Lips trailing across my breastbone, he sought out as much exposed skin as he could find before capturing one of my breasts, trapping my nipple between his teeth. Soothing the tender flesh with his tongue, he moved on to the other one, giving it the same attention while I bit down on my lower lip, attempting to muffle the cry that was bubbling in my throat.

"Don't. Let me hear you." His mouth kissed my jaw tenderly before his teeth pulled at my lower lip, forcing my grip on it to loosen, and when he was sure I would not clamp back down onto it, he lifted his hips to press his cock into me with a sharp thrust.

My entire being was consumed by the Lupine alpha. I had no idea where I started and he ended.

Locking my knees, I lifted when he withdrew only to sink down as he thrust up, creating a pattern that forced my head to tip back as my lips parted. My voice was hoarse from crying out his name. One fist still grabbed at my bronze waves while the other curled around my neck, squeezing softly for just a minute until it slid past the valley of my breasts and down. Fingers smoothed over the curve of my belly and settled against the wet slickness of my sex, his thumb pressing against me roughly until, finally, I shattered around him.

Releasing my hair, two hands grasped at my tender hips, slamming the full weight of me down one last time before his teeth clamped on to the soft skin of my shoulder, muffling his groan as he finally came and spilled deeply inside me with a great burst.

Relaxing his jaw, he kissed the teeth marks before rolling us onto our sides and gently withdrew from me wetly. Sighing with exhaustion, I watched him while his warm fingers stroked the hair from my face, and I smiled softly when his lips captured mine in one final kiss.

Chapter 25

The wind still whistled through the wooded walls, and normally the noise would have woken me from my sleep. However, it was instead the heat from the chest that was currently pressed against my hips as rough kisses were scattered across my back. Sighing into the comfort of the bed, I crossed my arms under my chin, thoroughly enjoying the attention. Finding a particularly sensitive spot, I rocked my hips back as I muffled a squeal, drowning out Kalian's quiet laughter.

"Hmm, I wonder what other noises I can coax from you." Peering over my shoulder, I blushed hotly as I met his heated stare. Holding eye contact, he leaned back down, licking the small of my back before sinking his teeth into the top of my ass. The sharp sting had my hips rocking into the mattress below me, and Kalian seemed quite pleased with himself.

Grabbing a fistful of my hair, he softly tugged back until my chin tipped towards the ceiling. Keeping his grip, he slid his other hand into the space between my hips and the bed, fingers searching until they dragged through the wetness that now pooled there.

"You're already so ready for me, sweeting." Whimpering, I tried to nod my head, only to have him pull the thick waves a little harder. The hand that had been parting my wetness was now coaxing my hips up as his knees pried my thighs open. My lower lip was bruised and sore from my teeth biting into it while I tried to muffle the noises he forced from me with his teasing fingers as they continued their exploration. They were skilled and sure but never stayed in one spot long enough for me to really find the release I was so desperate for. He slid two of them into me, and my eyes fell shut. I was shocked when his teeth ran across the curve of my ear, his breath hot as it fanned across my face.

"Are you biting that lip? What have I told you about trying to silence yourself?" My thighs tried to clench shut around his wrist as his words vibrated against me.

I was so needy for him, embarrassingly so, and I was willing to do whatever he asked if he would only give me some relief. Sensing my desperation, he released my hair, coaxing my shoulders down onto the bed with a hand pressing firmly between my shoulder blades. The other hand moved from my centre, his fingers slick as they cupped my hips while he maneuvered them higher.

Once he was angled just the way he wanted, I felt him slowly ease into me. The hot stretch was still there as he bottomed out, but it was much easier than last night. And as he pressed even closer into me, my jaw hung open. I was so full in this position, he reached so far, and a deep needy pant burst from my lips as I shimmied my hips softly.

"Easy, sweeting. Easy. You take my cock so well." Kalian stroked my back soothingly and I grew more and more frustrated. I didn't need him to comfort me, I needed him to move. Deciding to take the initiative, I rocked back, gasping loudly as pleasure bloomed.

"Fuck, Kalian. Please!" I begged as my fingers curled around the bed, grasping for anything that would anchor me to these feelings. Kalian paused for two more heartbeats before he withdrew carefully with a long pull, only to slide back in with more force than I had expected.

"Yes!"

"Is this what you wanted, love? Like this?" He chuckled roughly. "Your cunt is so greedy for me." He didn't give me a chance to answer as he built a rhythm that forced every thought, every word but his name from my mind.

His hands moved up my back until one hand was tangled in my hair again, and the other slid back under me, fingertips searching until they found that bundle of nerves that sat just above where he was stretching me open. I pulled my head back again, and the force of his thrusts had stars filling my vision. My entire body tensed, clenching and tightening before sweet release raced through my veins.

Dropping back onto the mattress, I glanced over my shoulder just in time to see Kalian's jaw closed tightly as his own head tipped back. His hips began to lose their rhythm and I stared, entranced, as his mouth opened and his voice broke around us in a hoarse groan of my name as he spilled into me hotly, his seed filling me to the brim.

Falling onto my back, Kalian panted against my throat before pressing a gentle kiss over my racing pulse. We lay like that for a long while as our sweat-slicked skin cooled and our breathing slowed.

Taking in his handsome face, I wished so badly I could lift my hand to stroke his cheek, and as if he could read my mind, his eyes opened. Watching my face silently, he eased out of me and rolled to his side. The loss of him made me feel empty and I was grateful that he immediately opened his arms for me to crawl into.

I settled my cheek against his chest, and we lay in silence with our legs tangled. His fingers traced my back, softly following a pattern up and down until one of his blunt nails put just a bit too much pressure on the skin of my hips. Hissing quietly, I looked down at the rounded flesh and Kalian too sat up, moving slightly over me to have a better look.

"Shit, Skylahr, I'm sorry. Was I too rough with you?" Blinking down, I took in the red fingernail-shaped marks that had begun to bloom across my skin.

"It's fine. They'll heal and I wasn't complaining." Watching as his lips lifted into that godsforsaken smirk, I immediately regretted reassuring him.

"Is that so? Enjoy yourself?" I rolled my eyes before pulling away from him, searching for my shirt while trying not to wince at the soreness between my thighs as I stood on shaking legs.

Finding the pile of discarded clothes, I flung my tunic over my head in haste, fully aware of the silver eyes watching me, and I pulled at the hem to cover more of my thighs before tossing his breeches at him. Kalian caught them easily before huffing in annoyance. "Why are we getting dressed? Being naked is so much more enjoyable."

"Shouldn't you be leaving?" I asked while I crossed the room quickly before opening the door.

"Why? Is there a reason you want me to sneak out like a green boy who had his first romp with his sweetheart?" One black brow lifted but the rest of him remained still, naked and sprawled across my bed. My eyes drifted across the hardening length of him for a second before I lifted my eyes. "I rather not have you run into anyone in the morning."

"Why, Skylahr! Are you ashamed of me?" I didn't know how to answer him; I knew that the others most likely heard our coupling, but the thought of facing them tomorrow morning, validating their suspicions, made me more than uneasy.

"I don't need you to baby me. I know what this was." My arms crossed over my chest as I gazed down at the floorboards under my feet.

"And what is that?" His voice was closer than I had anticipated, and my chin rose in surprise.

"Can you just go?" I gestured to the door with an open palm, while I swallowed my embarrassment. Kalian watched me, his eyes roaming over my face before he took a step closer.

"I'll leave, but you should know, this isn't something that I will regret tomorrow or the next day." My eyes widened and my lips parted. Smiling gently at me, he bowed his head to brush a soft kiss across my lower lip, pausing for a second with his mouth parted. "In fact, I will envision this night, envision you begging for me, for a long, long, *long* time. Probably for eternity."

Embarrassment and anger flushed across my face, and I shoved his massive shoulders out of the room, slamming the door hard behind him. Crawling back into my bed, I pulled the blanket to my chin, and a slow smile spread across my mouth. My body was still ringing from his touch, and although he was infuriating, I was filled with giddiness.

Being with Kalian had been unlike anything I had ever experienced.

I had not anticipated the delight of having him in my bed. Sighing in the quiet of the room, I turned onto my side, burrowing my face into my arms while sleep finally took hold.

The air was sticky with humidity the next morning, and I groaned in frustration as the blankets clung to my damp skin. Peeling them from me, I stood from the bed and crept my way to the hall. I had just managed to silently close the door when two hands wrapped themselves around my hips.

"I was just coming to find you." His warm breath fanned across my cheek and my heart hammered in my chest as I turned to face him.

"You scared me," I whispered to him before peering over his bare shoulder to see if we had been caught. Kalian huffed before guiding my face back to him. He smiled down at me and I noticed his eyes were filled with amusement. When I was about to question him, his shoulders lowered, and his arms wrapped around my knees. A squeal that sounded much more like a pig than a human burst from my lips as I was hoisted over his shoulder and carried down the stairs.

"What are you doing?!" I squirmed and pushed myself up against his back. "Put me down! I'm too heavy!" My legs flailed and Kalian's warm palm smacked my ass in reprimand.

"Would you stop your squawking? You'll wake everyone and I would very much like another hour alone with you." With one more smack to my backside, he quickened his pace and turned down the hall to the baths.

Once entering the room, he dropped me to my feet and cupped my jaw in his hands before kissing me sweetly. He guided me to the pool of water, and his fingers played with the hem of my tunic, silently asking for permission, and I lifted my arms for him.

The fabric was pulled from my skin, and I watched as he tossed the shirt onto the floor before smoothing my hair and kissing my brow.

His silver eyes were soft in the morning light that glittered through the dust-covered windows, and I realized I had never seen him so at peace. The expression had desire racing through me and I leaned up, pressing my lips to his jaw while my fingers plucked at the loose laces of his breeches before tugging the waist down past his hips. He stepped out of them slowly and grabbed my hand, guiding me into the cool water.

Settling on the bench on the far side of the pool, Kalian pulled me into his arms before kissing me again. "How did you sleep, love?"

This time the term of endearment was just that. It was full of affection and warmth, and I eyed him suspiciously as he released me from his hold before dunking his head under the water. Waiting for him to surface, I watched as he wiped the water from his eyes before asking him, "Are you drunk?"

A deep, booming laugh broke around us, and I rolled my eyes at him, narrowing my gaze as his eyes heated before they roamed across my flesh. "No, I'm not drunk."

"Then stop with this silliness and be your normal prick self." I paused, glaring at him while he smiled warmly. "And stop looking at me like that!"

And just like that the smirk was back in place as he grabbed my waist and lifted me onto the edge of the pool. The floor was warm against my wet back, and I sank into the ground with a sigh while Kalian moved over me, his tongue tracing the drops of water that rolled from my body.

"Like what?" his voice rumbled as his lips roamed across my flesh in a flurry of heated kisses and scrapes of his teeth. I tipped my head back while lifting my hips in invitation. "Like the very sight of you lights my blood on fire?"

His teeth closed around one of my nipples while his hand pinched the other. "Like I want to consume you wholly? Like I want to bury myself so deep into you that I am all you can think about for days?"

A whimper was pulled from my chest and I squeezed my eyes closed before nodding. "I think it is time you see yourself exactly as I do."

Kalian flipped me onto my stomach, gathering my hair in a fist before tugging my chin up. I could feel him press closer, his muscular thighs hot against my own, and I nearly begged for him then.

"Open your eyes." My lashes fluttered open and my lips parted as I realized he had positioned me across from the full-length mirror that leaned against the wall. His eyes were bright behind me and he slid his free hand across my jaw, his thumb pressing against my bottom lip.

"I dream of those lips, so full and soft. I envision them wrapped around my cock while I fill your mouth. I long to see them parted around the sound of my name while you beg me to finish you off." Pulling on my hair, he lifted my torso from the floor, his hand sliding down my throat, squeezing softly before he moved to cup one of my breasts.

"I imagine your flawless breasts, their nipples that perfect shade of pink that would darken after I have teased them with my teeth." His fingers pinched the nipple they had cupped, the sharp sting only adding to my wetness that was now dampening my thighs. Lifting his hand, he cupped my jaw and held my face still as he slid his thick length into me, the stretch forcing my eyes to widen.

"And those eyes, my Gods those incredible eyes." I watched in fascination as his head tipped back, his jaw muscles clenched while he held himself still. "I want to see those eyes. I want you to watch me as I fuck you."

The first few thrusts were gentle and slow while he waited for my body to adjust, but as he moved through the slickness with ease, the tempo picked up and I was a groaning mess as he pushed himself into me roughly. His molten gaze never left mine, not once, not even when the force of his thrusts began to slide my body across the floor.

I was so full; he had pressed himself so deep I could barely breathe, and my fingers scrambled against the floor as they sought out something to grab on to, desperate to steady me as he fucked me roughly. The swirling heat in my belly began to travel and my fingers curled into fists as Kalian's hand travelled to my centre, the fingertips circling over the bundle of nerves until I was screaming my release. But his rhythm never wavered as he rode me through it, and the push and pull of his cock had me coming for a second time, my legs trembling as his hips snapped forward sharply. With three more twists of his hips, his voice boomed around us as he spilled into me. "Skylahr!"

I watched his reflection as his muscled torso fell forward, collapsing onto me while he buried his nose into my damp hair. His lips were pressed against the fluttering in my throat and I could feel them lift in a smile.

I waited for him to pull out of me and then rolled out from under him, slapping his seeking hands away. "I'm starving and I refuse to be distracted by you again."

After dunking under the water quickly, I waded back through the pool and crossed my arms over my chest. Ignoring his snort of laughter, I grabbed the fresh tunic he had left folded and pulled it over my head. With one last glance over my shoulder, I left the grinning alpha sprawled over the edge of the tub and smiled to myself as I made my way to gather something to eat.

Ella had been the first to rise and I smiled at her warmly as she settled in her chair. However, the halfling scowled at me and I spent the rest of the morning biding my time, waiting for her to speak to me or even just look at me, but neither happened. When Keyno and Leena met us, I thanked the Gods for breaking the tension and silently observed her poor attitude towards the Lupines as well.

Kalian had taken his time in the bath and finally appeared from the hall, sauntering through the room while swiping at the food on his sister's plate.

"Fuck off!" Leena snapped at her brother, her glare following his every move as he sunk into the chair across the table.

"You are awfully pissy this morning, sweet sister. Did you not sleep well?"

Leena huffed in annoyance before turning to her mate. The two Lupines spoke in heated whispers and I watched them carefully, waiting for either of them to say something to the rest of us. Kalian too noticed the quiet conversation and lifted a brow when Keyno finally turned to him.

"Kalian, we wanted to know what our plans are." My eyes slid to the alpha and I waited tensely for his answer.

"What do you mean?" I could tell by his tone that he completely understood what they were asking, but he was pushing them to say it out loud.

Keyno's dark eyes roamed my face and he smiled gently before focusing back on his pack mate. "We agreed to take Hazel south, and we've done that. But you heard what Sky said about the Crimsons, they are planning to get into our territory and I just—we just think we should turn for home."

He was apologetic when he caught my eyes, but I nodded my head in agreement. The Lupines had kept me safe and held their promise. They had done more for me than I could have ever expected, and I knew I needed to let them go.

"He's right, Kalian. You should be with your people. Even if the threat is not serious, you should be there."

"I'm not leaving you on your own." His eyes were hard as they narrowed at my face, daring me to argue.

"But, Kalian—"

"We don't need you." Ella's tone was harsh, and my head swung in her direction as I stared at her in disbelief. Her dark eyes refused to meet mine, and she stood from her place at the far end of the table before marching out of the room.

All three Lupines looked at me in question, and I shrugged before chasing after my companion. Her pace was hurried as she stormed through the abandoned town, not stopping even as I called for her. When she turned sharply towards the field Kalian and I had sparred in the day before I broke into a jog, reaching my arm out to grab her shoulder.

"Ella! What's wrong?"

Ella avoided my eyes, and my concern grew as she hesitated to answer.

"I'm worried about you, Sky."

Not expecting that, I faltered in my step and frowned at her.

"Me? Why?"

Dropping her chin so her voice wouldn't carry, she sighed. "I don't want you to be hurt and you two fucking has made this more complicated."

My face flamed in embarrassment, but I pushed her for an explanation. "What more complicated?"

Her jaw was tense as she tugged her full lower lip between her teeth. Scanning across her tight shoulders, I followed her slim arms down to her hands, and I noticed that her fingers had clenched into fists, one hand crumpling the piece of paper she had been carrying before. Grabbing at the curl of fingers, I pried them open before smoothing the paper flat.

None of the words stood out to me, and my eyes roamed across the wrinkled parchment. Not understanding I looked at her pleadingly before dropping my gaze back down again.

"Flip it over." Something in her voice had my gut dropping in fear, and my fingers shook as they turned the page over. Gazing down at the page, I felt a sharp pain, like someone had kicked me in the ribs and all the air left me as acid swirled in my stomach.

There in front of me was a portrait of a familiar face. Sharp jaw, high cheekbones, full lips, dark hair, and silver eyes. I didn't understand.

It was a portrait of Kalian.

"What does it say, El?" I whispered as my eyes traced the face staring back up at me. Ella remained quiet, her body frozen and fearful as she looked between my face and the paper. Grabbing at one of her hands, I squeezed once in pleading.

Ella's eyes focused on our hands, and I watched as her lower lip trembled. "I'm so sorry, Sky."

My brow broke out in a cold sweat, and I felt bile bubbling in my stomach. "What does it say?!"

"His mama said that the Chosen were nowhere to be found, right? That they have never been located?" I recalled the conversation Isla and I had all those weeks ago back in Denimoore and nodded.

"Then why does it say here he is the Protector's Chosen? Why is he lying to you?"

Chapter 26

Chapter 26

The corners of the paper flapped in the breeze as my fingers tightened around it. Thinking back on it now, it wasn't hard to believe that Kalian was more than just an immortal. Though he had shown no significant differences from his two pack mates, there was something about the air that surrounded him, something in his being that had always seemed different. Something more.

But why would they lie to us? Why would Isla conjure up an entire story about not knowing the truth of the Chosen and their existence? Protecting him was the obvious reason, but being a Lupine, not to mention being the alpha, already put a target on their backs, so what difference did his true nature make in the grand scheme of things?

We sat outside for a long while, both pondering on our next steps. I could outright confront him, but where would that leave us? If he wanted us to keep quiet, we could easily be disposed of, and though he and I had lain together, I was sure that didn't result in unwavering loyalty. The other option was to keep quiet and wait. But could I truly travel with them knowing I was being lied to? The paper was still clutched in my fingers, its delicate folds and creases weightless in my palm as my mind raced.

Grasping at a corner, Ella slid the parchment from my hand and unfolded it again. My eyes watched as she scanned the page. The shock of seeing Kalian's portrait had distracted me from observing the rest of the image below and I now took in the rest of it. It had probably once been vibrant with colours and details, but now the image of all six Gods was faded and dull.

Focusing on the portrait, my eyes moved over to the picture of the Protector and Huntress. They were drawn together in an embrace, the focal point of the illustration, and the pure beauty of the Goddess glowed against the dark features of her mate. Beside them stood the Healer in his white robes and modest cloak. His gentle kindness was obvious, even on the page. The Siren, Goddess of the seas, and the Jester, God of chance, were off to the side both looking as gruesome as their legends depicted. The Jester's short stature was dwarfed by the Siren's long scaled tail and webbed arms. Her face had been painted to include her gills at her throat and fangs that were said to eat a man alive. The Jester's face was given the traditional mask that always accompanied him, the cheeks bright red with a terrifying grin.

However, as my eyes roamed across the page, I couldn't stop the shiver that ran down my spine as I took in the sharp features of the Seductress. Her frame took up most of the background, and her violet eyes looked down at the others with hatred. They were the same eyes that had haunted me for weeks, and looking at them even now made my flesh break out in bumps. It was as if the purple irises had turned from the two lovers and instead followed my every move. Sensing my discomfort, Ella folded the parchment quickly and grabbed my hand.

"What do we do now?" she asked, her eyes holding mine before looking back at the brothel.

I wanted to say that I was sure I could ask him and that he would be honest and tell me the truth, but that wasn't the case. I wasn't certain about anything anymore.

"I don't know." It was an honest answer, though it cut at my heart to say it.

"Are you okay?" I nodded at Ella but her sharp look told me I was not convincing her, and she leaned against my shoulder, her thick curls tickling the skin of my neck.

"You care for him?" Her voice was muffled as I rested my head on top of hers, but I could still hear the true question in her voice. She was worried who I would choose if the time came.

"I won't let any harm come to you, just as I know you will protect me. We stay together," I reassured her, holding my hand out for her to take.

Linking our arms, I led us back to the brothel and counted each step as I tried to even my breathing. Panic and anxiety would not help my façade as I faced the Lupines; I needed to appear as unbothered as Ella if I was going to keep our secret for the time being. Pulling her along, I ushered her into the common room before sitting at the nearest table, and I waited silently for the Lupines. Leena came down first, eyeing us suspiciously before turning down the hall that led to the baths. Her mate was not far behind, smiling at us as he eagerly followed.

Kalian, however, was slow in his arrival, as if he was trying to gauge the room. His hair was tousled and his shirt unlaced, leaving him dishevelled but still unbearably handsome, and his silver eyes caught mine for a moment before I dropped my gaze to the table, ducking my chin. I could see his steps falter at my dismissal, and a pain echoed in my chest as he turned on his heel to walk back into the kitchens. Noticing my discomfort, Ella slid her hand across the table, squeezing my fingers in reassurance before she stood. She excused herself, and I watched her black curls bounce as she jogged up the stairs to her room, leaving me alone just in time for the alpha to re-enter.

Looking at him now, I could feel the accusations bubble up in the back of my throat, burning while I pushed them back down. I felt hurt by his dishonesty, tricked and played for a fool. I had thought we were allies, if not friends. He knew of my halfling blood, protected me because of it, so why wouldn't he trust me? Why couldn't he be honest? Doubt swirled in my mind, and I knew that I needed to build the wall that he had so carefully begun to tear down.

Swallowing my nerves, I glanced up at him as he approached me cautiously. It was odd to see such an earnest expression on his face when our eyes met, and he smiled coyly at me before striding to my table, his steps sure until I stood from my chair.

"I was just leaving. There's more breakfast over by the fire, if you're still hungry." I nodded my head to the pot that was hanging over the warm coals then cleared my throat awkwardly.

"Have I done something?" His voice was laced with confusion and I felt my brows pinch as I frowned at him.

"No. Of course not."

He took another step forward, his hand reaching out towards mine only to drop as I dodged his touch. "Skylahr?"

I smoothed my face before lifting my eyes to his. "What?" My voice was hard, and I clenched my jaw tightly.

"Why are you being like this?" His voice was almost a whisper and I nearly flinched at the sound.

"Like what?"

Silver eyes searched my face in question before he exhaled, his shoulders sinking in defeat. "You regret it, is that it?"

My arms crossed around my middle, shielding me from his scrutiny before I took a small step back, increasing the distance between us. "No, I don't regret it."

Kalian's gaze sank to his feet while his brow furrowed. "Then why are you pulling away?"

I ran a hand through my hair in frustration, tipping my head towards the wall to study the cobwebs that lined the wood before sighing. "I'm not doing anything. I knew what this was when you came into my room, and I know it now." I paused to swallow the lump in my throat. "I don't need coddling."

"Coddling?" His voice dropped harshly into a deep baritone. He was angry; I had obviously insulted him.

"Is that what I'm doing?" His teeth were a flash of white as he snarled at me.

"I know that last night and this morning meant nothing. I've seen how this plays out with you on multiple occasions. I wasn't expecting anything different for me." Kalian recoiled like I had struck him, and I was caught unprepared by the reaction.

"Perfect. I'm relieved to know that it was nothing but fucking." The sharpness of his tongue had my stomach dropping, and I felt my eyes mist over. "Oh, don't look at me like that."

I didn't bother replying as he made his leave, storming out the front door, but my pulse echoed in my ears, leaving me unaware of our audience until he spoke.

"You were not being fair, Hazel." Spinning on my heel, I faced the disapproving look from Keyno, his dark eyes hard as he gazed at me.

"What do you mean?" I snapped, my jaw clenched in anger.

"You know it was different between you two."

"Don't. Don't pretend I'm different than the other women he's been with. It's insulting to me and them."

Keyno crossed his arms over his chest, pausing to think about his next retort. "I just meant the two of you have more."

I rolled my eyes and smoothed my tunic down with my hands, picking a piece of lint from the fabric, feigning boredom. "More than him and Nadine?" I slid my eyes to his face, watching as his lips parted. "That's what I thought. They've been together for two decades. We had one night. Don't treat me like I am some lovesick fool."

I turned from Keyno in silence and climbed the stairs to Ella's room. Pleased to find her packing her things, I lay across her bed and watched silently as she unpacked and repacked her bag. Her black brows were furrowed as she cursed silently under her breath, pulling everything back out, smoothing the clothing only to refold them.

"Ella, you've done that three times now."

Her dark eyes narrowed at me as she blew a loose curl out of her face. "I fidget when I'm anxious." I nodded silently before rubbing my hand across her slender back. "I thought about it and I think we should go on our own."

"I just embraced my ignite, I don't even know if I have full control of it. Would it be wise to leave them?" I argued half-heartedly.

"I'll help you with your ignite. I learned on my own, I am sure I can help you, and we will draw less attention with just the two of us." She paused to gather her thoughts before dropping her voice down low, her eyes sliding to the closed door. "Something's just not right, and I think the longer we stay with them, the more we put ourselves at risk." I watched her nimble fingers work on the fabric, focusing on that rather than the nerves pooling in my belly. Shoving the last of her things into the bag, she turned to sink into the bed next to me.

"If what the scripture says is true, why hasn't he rallied against the Crimsons?" Ella whispered quietly. "Why is he sending us out on our own knowing he has the answers we are looking for?"

"I'm not certain I want to know why, but if he hasn't told me by now, he isn't planning to." My eyes closed tightly as I fought the stinging of tears. "You're right, we can't rely on him for answers, and I can't trust him to be honest."

Ella turned back to face the ceiling, taking in a deep inhale before clearing her throat. "What do we do?"

I could see the worry pooling in her dark eyes and I grimaced. Ella was usually so confident, and it was nerve-wracking to see her this spooked. However, I knew that if I decided to continue on with the Lupines she would grin and bear it for me, but I wasn't certain how long that could go on for. Kalian had held on to this secret for months, never showing me any reason to doubt him, but now that we knew, how could we coexist? And if he thought we were a risk to their safety, what ends would they go to to protect themselves?

Knowing my decision was made, I moved off the bed and smiled at Ella before returning to the common room. Kalian was straddling one of the chairs, holding his head in his hands while he ran his fingers through the black strands. And I could see from my place on the stairs that his jaw was clenched, signalling me that I should ready myself for a fight. My footsteps grew sluggish and heavy as I made my way down the wooden steps, announcing my presence. Silver eyes flashed to mine, his chair screeching across the floor as he stood, and I slowed my pace as I reached him, stopping a foot away.

"Ella and I have decided to continue on our own. Keyno is right, you need to go home. Your people need you." My voice was hoarse, and my cheeks flamed in embarrassment at the sound, but my discomfort did little to sway his irritation as his eyes narrowed at me, the silver becoming as sharp as my blade.

"Why?" he demanded, his voice sucking the last of the air from my lungs.

"I just think it would be best." I hated that my voice sounded weak and unsure, the shakiness revealing my tension.

"You're being petty."

Embarrassment rapidly turned to anger while I blinked at him, my eyes focusing on his face. "Petty?" I spat. "How am I being petty?"

"You are trying to hurt me. Though I have no idea as to why." Those tan fingers ran through the black strands again as he paced in front of me.

"I expected more from you, Skylahr. You may regret what we did, but you could at least have the decency to be honest!"

How dare he mention honesty when he had been the one lying to me all along? He had seen my entire world shatter, my loss and my heartache, and still could not just tell me the truth of his identity. He knew that we were searching for a way to stop the Crimsons. He knew that the Chosen were a piece of the puzzle, he was a piece of the puzzle, and yet he lied, letting me believe there was a chance that we were on a fool's errand.

Clenching my fists, I turned to him. "I'm not being *petty*. You got me past the border as you promised you would, and I am grateful." I paused, lowering my voice. "I appreciate all that you have done for me, but this is farther than what we had agreed to, and we don't need an escort. You have a home and people waiting for you. You should go back."

Steel eyes held mine before they darted up to the stairs. "Did Ella convince you to say this because of last night?"

I groaned in frustration while my fingers tugged at my hair. "This has absolutely nothing to do with last night. Last night was nothing."

"So you've said." I could feel the tension in the air crackle, and we had somehow managed to close the space between us unconsciously, the heat from his body warming the front of me.

"Then you know that moving on without you isn't about that." I gazed up at his handsome face, softening my own expression to appease him. "We don't have a solid plan; we've found nothing in Carlon," I lied before crossing the room to fall into his discarded chair.

"I know you are sure about the security of your border, but I just don't see any reason for you to continue on with us, do you? We have no inkling on where to find the Chosen, so unless you know something I don't, it seems pointless for you to continue with us." My eyes watched his face carefully, and I prayed that he would take the opening I had given him and tell me the truth.

"She's right, let's leave them be, Kalian." Leena's voice startled the alpha and I waited desperately for him to say something, but he remained silent while his sister continued. "We've been away too long and I'm ready to go home. So is Keyno."

I felt my stomach drop as I watched Kalian nod at his sister, and I exhaled shakily when I realized he was not going to say anything else. Desperate to escape the growing tension that was now surrounding us, I ducked my head as I passed them, climbing the stairs two at a time to gather Ella and leave.

Ella's expression was guarded when she opened the door and her eyes met mine, but I said nothing as I grabbed the pack she handed me. Following her down the stairs, I paused at the bottom to face the trio, who had gathered in the middle of the room. Keyno's eyes flickered back and forth between Kalian and me as he waited for one of us to say something, but I turned to Ella, silently begging her to step in.

Taking pity on me, she slid forward, her hand outstretched towards the Lupines. "Thank you for escorting us safely." Her voice was strong as she grasped Kalian's forearm, holding it for a few seconds before releasing it and doing the same to the other two. When they had finished, Keyno rushed forward and wrapped his strong arms around me, squeezing me tightly before ruffling my hair.

"Be safe, Hazel." Keyno grinned and I smiled back before turning to his mate.

"Thank you, Leena." Her dark eyes rolled in annoyance, and I peered over her shoulder when I noticed that her brother hovered behind her. His heated gaze locked on my face, and I froze when I realized I didn't know how to say goodbye to him.

For a long moment my arms hung awkwardly at my sides as we watched each other in silence until Leena cleared her throat. Taking the cue, Kalian cursed under his breath before striding forward and pulling me into his arms. His chest was warm against my own, and his breath tickled the shell of my ear when he pressed his face into my hair.

"I wish you would let me come with you." His lips grazed my skin softly and I trembled for a moment before pulling away from him.

I couldn't bear to meet his molten gaze and instead turned to Ella, staring at her while she finished fastening her pack across her shoulders. The atmosphere became stifling with awkwardness, and I shuffled my feet waiting until Ella gestured to the door for us to make our exit. Following behind us, the three Lupines stood at the door and watched as we began our journey.

Pausing once we were a dozen yards away, I turned back to face them for the last time. Keyno and Leena had disappeared from their spot, but Kalian was still as he watched us from the distance, and he lifted one large hand to wave goodbye. The sentiment felt oddly final, and the burning regret of not confronting him made my eyes water.

As if she could read my mind, Ella squeezed my arm. "It will be okay, Skylahr. We will find a way to stop the Seductress without him. I promise." We linked our arms together, and I let her pull me forward. I prayed to the Gods that she was right.

Chapter 27

Travelling without the Lupines was quiet, and the silence made more and more questions fill my mind, the most prominent being if I had made the right choice. I had been devastated and angry, and I knew that was a recipe for disastrous decision-making. I had taken Kalian's secrecy as a personal betrayal and although I knew I had a right to know, especially considering he was the very thing we had set out searching for, part of me wondered if I should have swallowed my feelings and stayed. After all, I had been travelling with a Chosen, or at least that's what the scripture Ella had found said, and yet I turned him away and wandered into the unknown.

"You're thinking too hard." I rolled my eyes at Ella before nudging her with my hip. "Seriously, Sky, you'll drive yourself insane if you keep questioning your every move."

"It's not my every move I'm worried about. It's travelling without protection and leaving the only person who has the potential to help us stop the Seductress." My tone was tight and the wounded look that reflected in Ella's eyes made me immediately regret taking my hurt out on her.

"I'm sorry, El."

"We can turn back, it's not too late." But I knew it was. Even if they had waited around for an hour or so, their wolven legs could easily cover more ground in a day than we could in a week. Shaking my head at her, I continued on my way, walking ahead so I could be left alone with my thoughts.

The sun had begun to set and with it went the heat of the afternoon as the air around us finally cooled. If the warmth hadn't been so heavy, I would have suggested we travel by night, if only to keep cool. However, there was no possible way either of us could manage to find any rest under the blazing sun during the day, and we would need to sleep if we were to carry on at this pace. Sighing, I grabbed one of the wineskins and took a sip of water before passing it back to Ella, encouraging her to drink.

"Thanks." Her words were meek, and I knew she was upset by my poor attitude, even if she wouldn't say as much.

"Ella," I called, waiting for her to look at me. "I truly didn't mean to snap at you." Her smile was full, and she nodded her acceptance of my apology before pointing up at a steep hill nearby.

"If we get up there, we will be able to scout the area better and it will keep us from being vulnerable." She was right, we would have an advantage by getting out of the valley we were passing through, though I dreaded the trek up we would have to take.

"Don't be like that," she laughed. "You've embraced your ignite, surely you feel the difference." She was right, of course. Despite the uncomfortable heat, I felt energized and strong. My feet didn't ache and the weight of my pack was barely noticeable.

Rolling my eyes, I grumbled while I followed Ella up the escarpment. With the sun having set we struggled to climb the hill as quickly as we had planned, just making it to the top by the time the moon hung near the middle of the sky. Unloading our packs, we made a small fire to help heat the leftover broth we had taken with us before we unfolded our bedrolls. Once we had settled for the night, I curled on my side and closed my eyes tightly, willing away the unease that had filled my chest as I finally found sleep.

The muffled shrieking should have been enough to alert me to the danger we were now in, but I wasn't fully awake until the swift kick to my ribs knocked the air from my lungs. Groaning, I wrapped an arm around my middle, coughing in pain as I blinked at the boots that stood in front of my nose.

"Did the Lupine alpha teach you nothing?" Lifting my eyes, I stared up at a smooth pale face, one very similar to the rogue soldier Kalian had killed outside the cave. He had the same pale hair, though his eyes were a light blue grey in colour as they regarded me with disgust. Pulling myself to my knees, I kept my mouth shut, knowing I was not in a place of power and our weapons had been gathered and tossed a yard away. We had been left defenseless.

Another muffled yell drew my attention from the pile of steel, and I searched for Ella. She was a few feet away, balancing on her knees as a group of Crimsons surrounded her. Her dark eyes were wide with worry and her mouth tried to open around the fabric that had been tied around her face. I scanned her for any sign of injury, and besides a cut to her forehead she seemed relatively unharmed.

"You two really should not have lit that fire. It was like hunting a wounded doe, easy and disappointing." My eyes stayed on Ella as the immortal walked to the burning embers before stomping them out with one of his boots.

"Now then, perhaps you could tell me where your guard dogs have run off to." I remained kneeling silentlyt, my eyes never leaving Ella, even when the immortal fisted my hair and pulled my head back.

"I believe I asked you a question, halfling." The hand curled in my bronze strands tightened and I shut my mouth firmly, refusing to answer.

"Fine. Daven, perhaps a little incentive will help our friend's shyness." The soldier he had called on took a step forward, his hand pulling at the dagger on his belt as he approached Ella.

"Wait! Wait!" The words tore from me desperately as I watched the soldier tighten his fingers around his dagger.

"Ah, that's what I thought." The hand left my hair and I stood on shaky legs as I turned to the leader.

"I will answer any questions you have, please just don't hurt her."

Amusement lit his grey eyes and the change in his face made my body shudder in fear. Smiling, he turned to his friends, and I then noticed just how many there were. A dozen soldiers adorned in crimson and steel were surrounding us, and I understood the very real possibility that this would be the end for us.

"I want to know where your friends are." Ella shook her head, which resulted in a kick to her back that forced her to the ground face first. Rage simmered under my skin as I watched her captor haul her back onto her knees by her tied wrists.

"We have no friends; I have no idea what you are talking about." I tried my luck at convincing the lead immortal, though I knew it was pointless. He already knew we had travelled with the Lupines, and although there was a chance it came to him by rumour, there was no way he thought the information to be false.

"I have little patience for dim-witted halflings, and the way I look at it, she only wants you." My heart raced in my chest while I watched in horror as the Crimson called Daven approached Ella again. Realizing what was about to happen, I ran to her. Screaming her name, I reached my hand forward, trying to get to her, only to be stopped by three of the soldiers who pulled me back.

Kicking and screaming, I fought and clawed at them, tears pooling as the glittering steel punctured the soft flesh of Ella's chest. Red bloomed around the blade and her eyes widened at me before dropping to look at the hilt of the dagger that protruded from her.

"Ella!" My voice was hoarse as I crawled across the ground, dragging two of the immortals with me as they tried to heave me back. But Ella had slumped to the dirt, her eyes shut, and I sobbed as more blood poured from her. "Ella!"

Her black curls blowing in the wind was the last thing I saw before the heel of the boot slammed into my head.

Piercing pain stabbed at my left temple and I squeezed my eyes shut, willing the world to stop spinning. It almost felt as if I was dangling in midair, my toes barely scraping the dirt while I swung gently back and forth. Squinting one eye open, I looked down and realized I was hanging. I tipped my head up to see both of my wrists cuffed and suspended from the ceiling. Flexing my fingers carefully, I noticed the motion forced a trail of blood to run down my arm, and I hissed at the sharp sting of the metal as the restraints bit into my skin.

"Ah, you're awake." My head lolled as I tried to face my visitor, and a cruel laugh echoed from the door. "Barely, I see."

He walked around my back, his fingers grazing the sliver of skin exposed by the tension in my tunic, and I held my breath as I felt one of his nails slice through my flesh with the lightest of pressures. Circling in front of me, he lifted his index finger to his mouth as his tongue licked across the red-covered nail.

"All of you immortals seem to have a fascination with my blood." His grey eyes brightened, and his grin grew as he lapped at the remainder of my blood.

"Is that so? And just how many of us have you come across?" His shining finger lifted, and he wiped his damp fingertip across my brow.

"More than my fair share," I growled out while tipping my face away.

"And what happened to them, I wonder?" His hand grabbed at my jaw as he pushed me to the side, causing my body to swing as it dangled.

"I killed them." His smile dropped from his chiselled face, and I grinned as I saw fury fill his eyes.

"You might be important to her, but I doubt a halfling like you has enough power to harm one of us. I bet the kills belong to your dog." I narrowed my eyes at him and I wondered what information he was looking for. Obviously, the location of the Lupines, but what else? Did he know about Kalian, about his true identity?

"Though I do wish you and your friend put up more of a fight. I so badly wanted to test out the strength of the northern halfling." The mention of Ella drained the blood from my face as I focused back on him, my eyes welling with tears.

"Where is she?" I snarled, lifting a foot to kick out at his legs, but he stepped out of my reach, his face lifting into the cruelest of grins.

"Still face down in the dirt, I would imagine. Unless the animals have gotten to her already." The vision of Ella, lying there dead while animals tore her to pieces, made my stomach turn, and I used every ounce of power in me to kick out at him a second time. Once again, my foot met air, but I was pleased when I saw the anger return to his face.

"Now, now, halfling, if you continue with that nonsense, my patience will wear thin." Sighing dramatically, he wandered over to the wall and tugged a stool across the floor and sat down.

"Now, let's play nice, shall we? Where are your friends?"

My ignite was boiling under the surface, and I looked to the ceiling while I attempted to smother it. For the time being I had to play this exactly right. "I told you, we have no friends."

"I don't like liars."

I glared down at him, clenching my jaw before I replied. "I don't like murderers."

Rolling his eyes, the Crimson stood before approaching me, his hairline just a mere inch or two lower than mine. Peering up through his white lashes, he held my stare. "Did he ever tell you the story of his scar?" My eyes widened against my will and I saw the glee he found in my response.

"That's right, halfling, I did that to him. I haven't seen the mark my work left across those delicious shoulders, but I can only imagine the magnificence of it." Swallowing loudly, I lifted my eyes from his face and focused on the wall across from me.

"Did you know immortal magic can do that? Can keep a wound from fading over time? Even a being as strong as the Lupine alpha cannot stop it." He took a few steps away from me, laughing quietly to himself before approaching a torch that hung on the wall. My eyes flickered over to him as I noticed his hand reach into the pocket of his breeches. His pale, delicate fingers cradled a small, rounded piece of metal, and he grinned at it before approaching me again.

"See this, halfling? This is the seal of our Goddess." His hand lifted the item and held it in front of my eyes. It was a seal matrix, and I recognized the impression immediately. It was the flaming heart of the Seductress. The three flames that peeked out from behind the heart lacked in detail, but it only helped draw my eyes to the two crossing swords that sat in the middle. Their hilts were carved to perfection, looking more realistic than I would have thought possible.

The immortal dropped his hand and sauntered back to the torch, pausing to grin over his shoulder before lifting the stamp to the flame. I knew instantly what he was about to do. Struggling in my bonds, I tried to use my weight to swing in hopes of breaking the chain, but they held fast, and I could see him turn back in my direction.

Fear coursed through me as he closed the distance, and I finally allowed my ignite to consume me. Leaning into it the way Kalian taught me to, I waited for my strength to break the bonds, but nothing happened.

"Those were made for immortals, halfling. Your ignite won't save you." His free hand grabbed at my chin and I ducked my head as my teeth snapped at his flesh. His fingers closed in a fist before he swung, hitting my jaw with enough force to leave me dizzy, and my head hung, giving him the perfect opportunity to cup it roughly.

Holding my face still, he lifted his other hand, and I could smell the burning flesh before the pain registered. Smoke slithered from my soft cheek and I screamed as he pressed harder, holding the seal there for what felt like hours before stepping away. Swinging from the ceiling, I felt my tears slip from my eyes, hissing as they made contact with the burning skin, and I gasped roughly. The smell was still wafting in my nose and the memories that came along with it took every ounce of strength I had.

"Don't cry, halfling. What's one little scar? It's not as if it's taking any beauty from you." His hand cupped my chin again as his thumb swiped across my ruined cheek, and he smiled when I whimpered in pain.

"Now that I've taken care of your face, let's see what other pretty marks I can leave." His cold fingers grabbed at my tunic before lifting it to the bottom of my rib cage, and I felt the cold press of metal on the skin of my bare hip for an instant before it was pushed into me. The cut was deep and smooth, sliced with precision, and he took a step back to admire his work before moving to the other hip. An identical slash marked my skin, covering a space that Kalian had kissed just last night, and I whimpered as the blood trickled down to my thigh.

"Hmm, pretty." He smiled at me before walking back to the torch. I watched as he lifted his hand and heated the metal blade, his eyes never moving from my face while he waited.

"You know, those eyes of yours are truly stunning. I think they take away from my mark." Pouting at me, he pulled the dagger from the heat. "I think we will just have to get rid of them."

He approached me slowly, his empty hand reaching for my jaw, and I closed my eyes, promising myself I wouldn't scream this time. But the pain never came, and I opened my eyes to gaze down at the immortal, noticing that his attention had focused on the door.

Holding my breath, I watched as fear clouded his face, and then suddenly the wooden door shattered and an enormous black body barreled into the room. Silver eyes searched for mine before they focused on the blistering cheek, and then Kalian's head swung towards my captor. His massive form slithered forward, his body low to the ground as he stalked his prey, and now that he was finally facing the Lupine, the Crimson trembled in fear. Watching as his face paled, I chuckled quietly, and his grey eyes flickered to me.

"I suppose I do have a friend after all."

Chapter 28

The immortal didn't even have a chance to scream before Kalian had his throat shredded, his blood splattering against the walls as the massive jaws clamped onto the pale flesh and shook. Throwing the corpse to the corner of the room, he turned to me, his eyes glowing before his body shuddered and quaked. Fur disappeared into tan skin and he rose on his two feet before rushing to me.

"Are you okay?" Big grateful tears pooled in my eyes, and I nodded at him silently, hiccupping as one landed on my burning cheek. His giant palms cradled my jaw, and he tipped my face away from him so he could look at my cheek.

"I killed him too quickly," he growled and a laugh bubbled from my chest as I tried to smile at him. Kalian's gaze softened as he blinked at me, and I was in a daze, completely forgetting myself until another drop of blood fell onto my check and I lifted my eyes to glance at my hands.

"Think you could get me out of here?" All at once Kalian was sent into motion. He sprinted to the dead immortal, his hands patting at the cloak until he managed to find a ring of keys. Racing back to me, he worked his fingers quickly, and my body suddenly dropped when the restraints opened.

Clutching at his strong shoulders, I let Kalian take my weight as my knees buckled, and I leaned heavily into him while his arms wrapped around me tightly. "Easy, love, I have you."

Warm hands circled around my wrists gently and he pulled them from his shoulders only to bring them closer to his face for inspection.

"Those might scar." He paused, his thumbs tracing the split in my skin before turning to the dead immortal. "He isn't very original, I would have thought he'd be more creative after all this time, rather than using the same cuffs."

His tone was light, but I could see the muscles working in his jaw and I knew his eyes would be filled with rage. "He said he's the one who hurt you."

Nodding his head, he turned back to me. "I had plans for my revenge. I had thought about it often over the years, but seeing you hanging there, smelling your blood, hearing your cries…" He paused, his voice breaking as he gazed at me softly. "I didn't know I could feel a fear like that. It consumed every ounce of vengeance I had. My worry for you consumed me wholly."

I blinked up at his face, noticing the tension that his jaw held, and I pressed my fingers against his cheek as my mind raced. I didn't know what to say and instead I dropped my eyes, breaking the pull between us.

"Sky—" I lifted my hand up while shaking my head, the motion forcing me to wince as the burning in my cheek grew. Noticing my discomfort, Kalian reached forward but I brushed his hand away awkwardly.

"Shouldn't we be leaving? What about the others?" There had been a dozen soldiers on the hill, and I was sure at any minute the rest of them would come piling through the open entrance.

"The magic of my barrier. He hadn't been paying attention, he was too busy planning your torture. If he had he would have noticed how silent it was outside."

I had so many questions, but I wanted to be sure there was no threat, and instead I turned from him and crossed through the shattered wood that covered the ground before peering out of the doorway. The smell of rust was heavy in the air. The ground was damp with blood and the only way to describe the scene would be to call it a massacre. Kalian had killed every single one of the immortals, leaving only torn piles of flesh in his wake. The brutality of it made my jaw drop.

"I couldn't spare them, you know that." Turning to face the alpha, I nodded my head silently. He was right, of course, and why should any of them be spared? They didn't deserve that kind of mercy.

"You were right though, Sky; we should be leaving. We need to get that burn and those wounds treated." My fingers lifted to my puckered cheek, trembling as they lightly grazed the destroyed skin.

"If we get it sorted out now it may not scar as badly." Dropping my hand, I ignored him and gazed out over the destruction of the immortal camp, my eyes moving across the ruined ground until I noticed a familiar dagger lying in the dirt.

My steps were hesitant as I came closer, and I dropped to one knee, ignoring the pain in my hips as I studied the silver pommel of the blade. It was the one that had been thrust into Ella, the same weapon that had taken my dear friend from me. I so badly wanted to stab it into every immortal who lay across the soil.

Swallowing the heaving sobs that threatened to collapse my lungs, I grabbed at the dagger, my fingers curling around the hilt before I stood. Kalian froze, his shoulders tense as he watched me enter the shed that I had been strung up in, and my feet led me to the immortal in the corner. Dropping to my knees in front of him, I thrust the dagger into his chest.

"You chose the wrong one to kill." I leaned down near his ear, shaking as rage crashed through me unlike anything I had ever felt before. "It should have been me."

Pulling the metal from him, I pressed the blade into him over and over. Not stopping until Kalian's hands grabbed at me, helping me back out of the shed as I sobbed for Ella. Tears blurred my vision, but I could feel the thick black fur press against me, and I clumsily climbed onto his back, wrapping my arms around his neck as he loped away from the camp.

Kalian had kept a steadfast pace, his paws thundering across the ground as he headed back into the cover of the hills. Time moved slowly as the sun had begun to rise, but the heat seemed non-existent compared to the cold weight that pressed against my chest. Shivering, I nestled closer into the black fur and sighed as he slowed to a walk.

When his body became still, I lifted my chest from his back to follow his line of vision. Narrowing my eyes, I could just make out the tiny camp Ella and I had made, and I slid from his back. Leaning against him, my legs suddenly too shaky to hold me up, I glared at him.

"Why would you bring me here?!" My voice quivered as I blinked back tears. Bowing his head, his ears flat against his skull, he pressed his snout into my back and nudged me forward.

"No, Kalian. I don't want to see her like this." His nose pushed me again and I dug my heels into the earth. "No!"

I couldn't bear to see Ella cold and lifeless. I couldn't endure the hurt another loss would cause me, and I so hated Kalian for bringing me here. Hated him for forcing this onto me when all I wanted was to imagine Ella bright and alive somewhere far away—somewhere safe. But he was relentless in his herding, and no matter how hard I protested, he persisted, his nose gently nudging me along. Shaking in fear, I focused my eyes on the black curls that were still swaying in the wind.

"Kalian, please," I begged again as I felt him creep closer. But this time warm hands cupped my shoulders and guided me forward.

"Trust me, Sky." With one last gentle shove I was standing over her, my eyes dropping down to observe my dearest friend in her final resting place. But after a long pause, I tilted my head to the side in confusion when I realized her dark skin still held its rich colour, though her eyes remained closed. Had I not known better I would have sworn she was sleeping.

Crumbling to the ground next to her head, I reached out for her. The backs of my fingers grazed her soft cheek, though I immediately recoiled when I realized her skin was not cold like it should have been. Blinking up at Kalian in question, I watched as his nude form knelt down next to me.

"I'm not certain it will work; I don't know if I got here in time." My mind was hazy, and I frowned at him before turning back to Ella.

"Why isn't she cold, Kalian? Why does she still feel like she's alive?" Wrapping one arm around my middle, he pulled me against his side before pressing his lips to my hair.

"If the ceremony worked, she won't just feel alive. She will be."

Chapter 29

I sat on the ground with Ella's head cradled in my lap, my fingers stroking her hair as we waited. Kalian had only ever performed one other ceremony, and Keyno had not been so far gone when the magic took hold of his body. So, we waited, unsure of what was to come.

Lost in thought as I detangled her soft strands, I hadn't noticed Kalian kneel next to me until a white piece of cloth was held out to my face. Looking up at him, I grimaced at the smell of the ointment he had piled on the cotton.

"We really should clean it up. Your body can manage whatever infection brews, but it will take more time to heal." I studied the runny green liquid that seeped into the fabric in reluctance. My cheek did ache and burn, its blisters stinging even when I sat still, but I couldn't bring myself to let the scar settle into my skin.

"Shouldn't we just cut it out? Why try to soothe it?" Kalian stared down at me before leaning away.

"Cut it out? You can't be serious."

"Surly you didn't think I would walk around with her mark on me?" The fact that my face was ruined really didn't worry me. However, I hated that it was her seal that I would be forced to carry with me for the rest of my life.

"Cutting it out will only make it worse. I have no way to stitch it, and I can't guarantee it will close. Not when immortal magic was used. We should let it heal before we look at a way to get rid of it. Perhaps we will find a healer who knows how." Sighing at him, I reached for the knife that hung from his belt on his breeches and unsheathed it before pressing it into his hand.

"I need you to get rid of it—now." When he made no move to stand, I closed his fingers around the blade. "Kalian, please. Put the knife over the fire and cover this. Don't make me wear her seal. Don't let them do that to me."

I couldn't explain it out loud, but the thought of having her mark on me, that people would see her flaming heart, made my stomach roll, and I couldn't carry that on my shoulders. Kalian seemed to recognize my determination and silently moved to the small fire he had lit. Watching me carefully, he pressed the blade into the coals. Waiting until the blade glowed, I then shifted out from Ella and came to stand next to him, tilting my cheek before tucking my hair behind my ear.

"Sky—" I knew the blade was ready, and the hesitation in his voice assured me that he was not willing to do this.

"Pass it to me," I ordered.

His eyes widened and he shook his head before stepping away. "We should wait, there might be another way."

"There is no other way! Hand me the knife, Kalian!" My tone surprised him but he did not argue any further as he pressed the knife's handle into my hand. Taking a deep breath, I lifted the metal to my face, feeling the scorching heat of it even with the inches of space I had yet to close. Shutting my eyes, I pressed the steel to my burn, holding it there as my skin sizzled against the steel.

"Sky!" I ignored him and pressed it harder, determined to be rid of her. "Skylahr!" His hand tugged at my wrist and the knife flew from my hand while his fingers tugged at my chin.

"Is it gone?" My voice trembled while my composure dangled by a thread. When Kalian remained silent, I turned to him. "Is it gone?"

Dread filled my chest when I noticed the pity in his gaze, and I realized it hadn't worked. I dropped my eyes from his face and allowed him to bring me back to my place next to Ella as he gathered a wineskin and another cloth.

"Please can I help you now?" No longer having a reason to refuse, I bit my quivering lip as he pressed the cool, damp cloth against my face. His touch was gentle and I observed him out of the corner of my eye as he carefully tended my burn before bandaging my face.

"For now, no one will see it." Tucking a strand of hair behind my ear, he smiled gently at me.

"I'm sorry I didn't get there sooner." His voice was barely a whisper as he turned from me, but I could hear the regret in his words.

"It's not your fault, thank the Jester you got there when you did." I dropped back to the ground next to Ella, checking on her again before looking up at the alpha. "How did you know we were in trouble?"

Kalian grabbed the cloth he had used to cool my face and wrung it out before looking over at me. "I sent Keyno and Leena back north but decided to track you, just to be sure you made it to safety," he reassured me. "I hadn't found you yet, Ella had done an excellent job of keeping you guys hidden, but I did spot a group of Crimsons. I was worried you two would cross paths with them, so I stayed in the area. I must have just been right behind them, by the time I got here—" He paused, his eyes tracing over Ella sadly. "Her heart was still beating, though barely."

He fell to the ground next to me and brought his knees to his chest before resting his arms on them. "I wanted to go after you, but I knew if there was a chance I could save her, you would want me to do everything in my power to make that happen."

I nodded my head in agreement before stroking Ella's hair affectionately.

"Thank you," I whispered quietly. "I was so stupid. I should have never dragged her along with me. She should have stayed in Celinde."

"As if you could have stopped her."

I smiled tearfully at him. He was right, there would have been no way I could have stopped Ella from doing whatever it was she wanted, but I still felt immeasurable guilt.

"You're right, but we should have never gone off on our own." Kalian's bright eyes watched me with uncertainty before he cleared his throat.

"Why did you?" The silent question was there, and his tone was unsure, and I wondered where the confident cocky alpha had gone as I regarded him for a moment.

"I told you it had nothing to do with that."

"Then what was it?"

Kalian had tracked us for hours, performed the ceremony on Ella, and hunted down my captors before rescuing me from their clutches, and the hurt of being lied to still kept me from being truthful.

"Skylahr, please, what happened?" Shutting my jaw tightly, I reached across Ella and pulled the wrinkled page from her pocket before slapping it against his bare chest. Looking down at my hand, he took the paper out from under my palm and opened it slowly, his eyes shooting to mine before tracing the page.

"Ella found it in Carlon. Is it true?" I watched his jaw muscles work and his eyes traced over his portrait before he stood and tossed the page into the flames.

"Kalian!" I shouted as I scrambled to the pit. But I was too late, the parchment had already caught, and I gasped as I watched his ink-drawn face slowly disintegrate.

"You should not have carried that with you!" he roared at me, his fists clenched at his sides. "Do you know what could have happened had someone found that?!"

I gaped up at him in shock before rushing to my feet. Standing toe to toe with the Lupine, I felt my ignite burn through me. "What? As if it's some secret?"

"It is! It is a secret, Skylahr! I have no idea how she managed to find the prophecy. I have no idea how she was able to avoid the magic that hid that godsforsaken book, but she shouldn't have taken that page!"

"What are you talking about?" My hands flew up in the air as my voice rose to meet his own.

"The Jester swore to the Lupines he would hide those damn

scriptures of his. That he would make it so no one would be able to come across that fucking prophecy he wrote. We wanted it destroyed but it was sacred to his immortals, so the Gods struck a deal. She should not have been able to find it no matter how hard she searched." His long finger pointed to Ella before he began pacing.

"I'm sorry, I didn't—we didn't know." Suddenly the rage and anger I felt for him for hiding such a secret had crumbled into guilt when I realized what the repercussions could have been.

"My own sister has no idea that I am the Protector's Chosen. No one other than my mother knows that prophecy exists."

"If I had known—"

"You what? You wouldn't have left? You wouldn't have risked my life, my family, or my people by carrying that fucking page around?!" He walked forward in three long strides before grabbing my shoulders.

"Who else knows!?" Rage burned through him, and I shrugged out of his painful grip before taking a step back.

"No one, no one else. I swear, Kalian. And no one will." But my reassurances did nothing, so I took a deep breath as I fell to my knees, cocking my head to the side. Holding my stance, I mirrored the same position he had folded himself into after that spar all those weeks ago. Dropping my eyes, I waited until I felt him take a step closer. "I promise, Kalian, no one else will ever know."

One warm fingertip touched my chin, and he lifted my face up to his. His expression was blank as he regarded me silently for a moment before he turned from me and began walking away. Clambering to my feet, I began to follow him until he threw a hand back at me, halting my movement completely.

"I'll be back. I just need—" He took a deep breath. "I need to run."

He turned away again, and his long legs began to sprint. He leapt into the air, his tan skin turning into black fur before he landed on all four paws and raced off. Crossing my arms around my middle, I turned and crept back to my spot next to Ella, my eyes watching the black wolf until he disappeared into the horizon.

"The rabbit is cooked. You should eat, and I need to take another look at that burn." Sitting cross-legged in front of the fire, I looked up as he approached. Kalian had returned a while ago holding two rabbits, but he remained silent as he cleaned and cooked the meat. His silver eyes had never lifted to meet my gaze no matter how hard I tried, and I hated that he was so angry with me.

I grabbed the meat that he had left for me and stuffed it in my mouth. Managing to eat half of what he had offered, I chewed carefully as he began to finger the bandage that covered my cheek. Pulling my face away from his touch, I glowered at the fire.

"The other wounds may be fine, but the burn was deep. It will be over quicker if you would just let me." I sighed in resignation, and my shoulders fell in defeat. I let him fuss over me until the cotton was changed, and he had decided it was good enough for the night.

Squeezing my shoulder gently, Kalian stood and pulled the neck of his tunic over his head. Free of the cloth he eyed me, and I realized I had been caught gawking at him—again. Scoffing under my breath, I turned away, ignoring his lingering gaze.

"No need for shyness, you've seen it all." I glanced back at him with narrowed eyes. "Do you want to undo my laces?" He gestured to his dark breeches but paused as he waited for my answer.

"I don't think you need any help," I grumbled at him, but I was secretly delighted by his teasing as the weight lifted from my chest. Teasing was better than anger.

"Maybe not, but I would so enjoy it." Turning away from him again, I tried to hide my warm cheeks and ignore the fluttering in my belly. My mouth had dried at the bare skin of his chest, and I grabbed at wineskin, taking a long sip before turning back to the Lupine.

"What exactly are you doing?"

He smirked at me before pulling at his laces. "You need sleep, and someone needs to keep watch. We would be safer if I was on four feet rather than two." Nodding, I took another long swig from the wineskin as I tried to ignore the feeling of disappointment, and when I turned back to him, I was met with the deep black fur of his wolf. Maybe it was a blessing; it would keep me from doing something rash. With a dip of his head, Kalian nodded at me before padding off a few feet and then dropping gracelessly into the dirt.

Repacking the wineskin, I then folded Kalian's discarded clothes before crawling onto the bedroll next to Ella. Settling myself into the material, I reached out a hand to grasp her wrist, my fingers circling her smooth skin while I pressed my fingertips to the slow, fluttering pulse. Reassured that she was coming back to me, I glanced over my shoulder. The big black wolf was sitting alert, his eyes focused on the western landscape, and when I was sure we were protected, I finally found rest.

Chapter 30

Halfway through the night the wrist that I had clung to suddenly stirred and the movement jolted me awake. Rolling towards Ella, I blinked down at her face. Watching as her eyes moved under dark lids, I held my breath while her long lashes began to flutter.

"El?" I whispered before turning to Kalian, waving him over when his silver gaze lifted to me. "Ella?" I called again.

Dark eyes squinted open and she lurched forward with a speed I had not been prepared for, resulting in our heads colliding with a sharp clap. Groaning, I pulled back and rubbed at the bump, the pain distracting me for only a minute before I gawked at her.

Ella's face was bright with colour but there were most definitely subtle differences. Her cheeks were less full, more angular, her lips were perfectly symmetrical, and her skin seemed to glow in a way only immortals could. Dark eyes peered up at me in shock, and I couldn't find any words as I turned to Kalian for help. The great black beast came closer before his body vibrated and then he was standing on two legs. Cupping my shoulder in reassurance, Kalian knelt down next to me and leaned closer to Ella.

"Ella, how are you feeling?" She gaped at him silently before turning to me, her eyes drifting back and forth between us before they focused on the white cotton that was tied to my face. Lifting her fingers slowly, she grazed the bandage, and her touch shook me from my astonishment.

"It's nothing," I assured her, grabbing her hand and holding it tightly. "How are you feeling?" Ella swallowed and I waited anxiously for her to say something, anything.

"It's much too hot." Her voice had a musical quality to it, different than how it was before, and I blinked stupidly at her until Kalian snorted.

"Yes, Ella, yes, it is." Ella's eyes slid from me back to Kalian, and they widened as she took in his state of undress. Curling her lip in disgust, she whipped her head away from him while shielding her eyes.

"Gods! Put some clothes on, Lupine!" Kalian laughed loudly before standing and grabbing his discarded clothes. Smiling fondly, I turned to Ella and rubbed her shoulder while I waited for her to focus on me.

"What happened?" she asked, still looking worriedly at the white dressing.

"What do you remember?"

Ella squinted for a moment before her hand began to claw desperately at her chest. Seeing her panic made my heart clench painfully, and I grabbed at her fingers before pulling her into a hug.

"Ella, you're okay. I promise." I waited for her trembling to stop before I moved away and held her shoulders. "You're okay."

"But how? They—and then—" Her mouth couldn't seem to keep up with her mind as she processed the events, and I waited until her wide, wild gaze settled on me.

"Kalian had been tracking us. He saw the Crimson party and followed them here. He found you." I paused, my voice catching in my throat. "He saved you."

"Saved me?" she questioned, her voice barely a whisper. Peering over my shoulder I noticed that Kalian had sat down a distance away, giving us some privacy, and I took it as permission to tell her about the ceremony.

"They call it the eternal ceremony. I don't know specifics, but I know it can be performed to save halflings. It doesn't always work, but he did it. He saved you." I smiled at her and turned to look back at Kalian. "Then he saved me."

Ella watched me with suspicion before grabbing at her pockets and

I knew what she was searching for. "Ella, it's gone. I showed it to Kalian, and he destroyed it."

"So he knows?"

"Yes. He knows that we are aware that he is a Chosen." I could tell her guard was still up, but she chose to let it go. For now.

"You said he saved you?" Her dark eyes had drifted over to the Lupine, watching him carefully as her hand reached out for one of mine.

"He found me at the Crimson camp. He came just in time."

Her free hand lifted to the knot at the back of my head and hovered there until I nodded. With nimble fingers she managed to loosen the material and it fluttered to the ground.

"Oh, Skylahr," Ella sobbed, her hand covering her mouth as she studied the burn. "They did this to you."

"It's okay, El, I'm fine." Grabbing her hand from her face, I squeezed it. "I'm fine. I swear."

Tears continued to fill her eyes despite my words, and I pulled her to my shoulder, savouring her warmth that seeped into me. Kalian observed us for a few moments before coming to us hesitantly, as if he felt like he was intruding on our moment. Leaning closer into me, Ella watched his approach. He seemed to sense her wariness of him and paused.

"You saved me, you saved Skylahr, and I will owe you for the rest of my life." His eyes narrowed at her and my spine straightened as I waited for her to continue. "But you lied to us."

"You're right, I did," Kalian admitted and yet held his head high without so much as a glimmer of guilt.

"Were you ever going to tell us?" Kalian's shoulders remained strong until his molten eyes focused on my face. He held my stare, and it was as if my gaze had knocked the wind from him.

"Ella, I don't know if the others live, or if they've even been born yet. It has just been me for three centuries, and it is my understanding that one of us isn't strong enough to take her down. It wouldn't be fair to give Sky false hope, so I chose to keep my secret until I knew more."

Pulling away from Ella, I stood, wiping my hands on my

breeches nervously while I stood in the space between the Lupine and the newly made immortal.

"Ella, I owe him my life. I won't tell you what to do or what you should feel, but I trust him." Ella exhaled in defeat, rolling her eyes, and I knew that for now, I had won this argument. Kalian also seemed to understand her silent acceptance and came closer, handing Ella some of the cooked rabbit.

"We should rest tonight, Ella. You'll need it." His voice was soft, and he ignored her answering scoff before turning to me and sitting down. Our shoulders brushed against each other's, and I ducked my head while peering up at him through my lashes.

"I'm fine with you travelling with us, but I refuse to watch you two stare silently at each other," Ella murmured through mouthful of meat and I blushed, dropping my eyes to the ground with my lower lip trapped between my teeth.

"And for the love of the Gods above, I better not catch you two fucking!" Kalian's booming laugh was so loud I could have sworn it would shake the hills around us, and I shoved him away from me. My face may have burned in embarrassment, but my heart was full of joy.

Our knowledge of Kalian's secret was out in the open, and although it lifted some of the weight, we were still left with so many questions. The immortal responsible for the destruction of Noorde Point was dead, as was Kalian's previous captor, but both of those Crimsons had been following someone's orders. Whether it was the Seductress herself or someone else, we had no idea. However, I knew that if someone did not intervene, more would die. Packing our things, we decided we would go to Wahstand as I had planned originally and search for a Chosen or something that would lead us in the right direction.

Now that plans were in place, the tension between my two companions had simmered, though it was often still tangible in the air thanks to Ella and her distrust and anger. Kalian, on the other hand, had been patient and kind, taking her nasty looks and short answers in stride while he tried to help her adjust to her new immortal life. Kalian assured me that this was normal, that the changing from a halfling to a full blood could wreak havoc on one's emotions and mind. He said it wouldn't last, and we should give her more grace than usual, though this just pissed Ella off more.

Sitting behind her while we straddled Kalian's wolven form, I could feel the tension coming off her in waves. Her spine was stiff, and she had spent the last few hours staying silent, even though I had done everything in my power to start a conversation. Angling my shoulders away from her, I tried to give her as much space as I could, even if only to keep the peace until we stopped to camp.

However, just as I had managed to create about six inches of space between us, Ella gasped, and her hand flew back to clutch at my thigh. Looking down at her fingers that grasped at my pant leg, I reached to take her hand, but her whisper of my name had my eyes peering over her shoulder.

In the distance stood a long wooden arch with three sacks of some sort blowing back and forth in the wind. Not understanding, I blinked down at Ella and watched in confusion as a single tear ran down her cheek before I felt Kalian stiffen under us.

"What? What is it?" Ella's fingers clutched harder at my skin as the distance closed, and I raised my eyes again, gasping as I finally understood.

They weren't sacks, they were bodies.

Three bodies hung from the wood and I felt bile rise in my throat. Two of them were women who appeared to be around my age, though it was difficult to tell given the state of them. But the third was a boy of maybe five and ten. He had obviously been the last to be strung up, and I could see from where we stood that his left cheek had an identical scar to mine.

"Halflings." Ella had lifted a hand and pointed the wooden sign that had been nailed to the arch.

Half bloods

I swung my leg over Kalian's haunches and ran to the base of the gallows, tears flowing from my eyes as I turned helplessly to my companions. With shaking hands, I searched for something, anything to cut them down with. Ella ran to meet me, her fingers grasping a dagger.

"That won't cut the wood." My voice broke as I wiped at my face in frustration.

"I can climb. I'll climb up there and lower them down." Nodding my head, I watched as she carefully held the dagger between gleaming white teeth before wrapping her hands around the wood and hoisting herself up the plank.

Confident she could manage, I turned to the ground and began clawing at the hard earth. My fingers scraped across the dirt as I dug and dug, my heartache making my movements clumsy. I had barely made a divot when a wet nose pushed against my shoulder. Sighing, I moved as Kalian's massive paws took the place of my hands and began to dig. When he had managed to create three shallow graves, I turned back to Ella, signalling for her to let the first body down.

One by one I carried the halflings to their final resting place, ignoring the stench of them while I gently covered their bodies with the loose earth. Kneeling with my head bowed, I leaned against Kalian and prayed for the dead while anger ran through me.

"That boy hadn't been up there a day. Whoever did this is close." I knew Ella's words were a warning, but they only added to my fury. Pulling myself to my feet, I turned to Kalian.

"Can you track them?" His silver eyes moved to Ella worriedly while his ears flattened.

"Sky—" But I shook my head at Ella's warning.

"Kalian, please." He held my stare for a moment before tilting his head in agreement and I exhaled roughly when he bowed down for us to mount him again.

His pace was much slower as his head lifted to the air every few strides, and in my rage, I prayed to the Huntress that we would find them. Moving my eyes across the hills, I searched for some sign of the crimson banners while holding my breath, almost as if I thought I could hear them if I stayed quiet enough.

Kalian paused for a moment and swung his head to the right. I followed his direction, noticing the smoke that weaved into the air. Preparing for the change in his gait, I held on to Ella tightly, readying myself for whatever was over the hill. When we reached the peak, Kalian slowed to a stop and a low whimper broke from his chest as his head swung towards me. Leaning to the side, I searched for what had caused his distress.

The rage that had consumed my being was overlapped with fear as I took in the row upon row of crimson tents that filled the valley below. But it hadn't been the number of immortals that had forced Kalian's reaction. No, instead it was the large metal cage that sat at the edge of the camp. A cage full of what I knew to be halflings.

"No." The word broke from my lips as my heart stuttered in my ribs. I threw myself to the ground, ready to spring forward, only to be stopped by Ella's strong hands.

"Let me go! Ella, let me go!" I screamed before another hand muffled my cries.

Moving to take Ella's place, Kalian grabbed my shoulders, and she came around to face me while cradling my jaw in her hands.

"Sky, you have to stop." My head shook frantically as I tried to rush forward again.

"Skylahr, Ella is right, you have to stop." Betrayal pressed against my chest and the feeling pushed the tears past my lashes.

"They're going to kill them, Kalian! We have to stop them!" I begged, my body flailing frantically as I tried to move closer to the camp.

"You're right, Sky, they will. But there is nothing we can do."

I blinked at him in shock before facing Ella, who too looked regretful.

"But we can! We're here, we can fight." The words were barely audible over my sobs, and I waited for one of them to agree with me. When neither moved I pulled from their grasp before making a run for the edge. But both immortals were faster, and this time Kalian scooped my body into his arms as he took us farther and farther away from the top of the hill.

I kicked and hit and thrashed with every ounce of strength I had, but even with my newly mastered ignite I was no match for the Lupine alpha. Continuing to move swiftly, Kalian ignored my nails against his skin as I clawed at him in hopes of loosening his hold, and he tightened his arms until we were half a mile away.

Deeming it a safe distance, he dropped me onto the ground before kneeling in front of me, effectively blocking my body should I try to crawl my way back to the halflings.

"Skylahr, enough!" His voice was harsh as his hands grabbed at my face and his thumbs tenderly wiped the tears from my cheeks, taking extra care around the burn.

"I know your heart is breaking. I know how badly you want to save those people. I know because my heart matches yours. But I can't let you go down there." Exhaling deeply, he smoothed my hair. "You are fierce and strong and magnificent, and Gods help me you are the bravest person I have ever met. I am not worthy to even look at your face. But you are not invincible; you are not capable of taking on the world no matter how much you wish you could." Ella's hand ran across my shoulders before she wrapped an arm around me, nodding her head in agreement.

"Skylahr." My name was a broken whisper and I peered up into the silver eyes in front of me. "There was a reason why they let you live on that hill. There was a reason why they took you back to their camp. Surely you must see that."

My brows pinched as I tried to understand what he was saying.

"The Crimsons wanted you, just you. They've been searching for you for weeks. Longer than that, they've been waiting for you since Noorde Point." Nodding my head for him to continue, I blinked the remaining tears from my eyes and watched as Kalian's mouth opened like he was going to continue. But it was as if the words had caught in the back of his throat, and I felt a shiver of panic run down my spine as his face crumpled.

"Sky—" he started, his voice a broken whimper.

"Shut up." I turned to Ella in surprise and watched as she studied the top of the hill with a frown, her eyes never leaving the spot until they flew to Kalian's in panic.

"Can you hear them?" Looking at the alpha, I watched as his face paled and my mind filled with confusion.

"Hear what?" I asked, my heart racing as I tilted my head to listen, praying that I might know what was happening.

"What? What is it?"

"They're coming. We need to go." Leaping away from us, Kalian had shifted midair before stopping just long enough for us to swing onto his back. And without so much as another pause, he darted in the opposite direction of the camp, all while my heart broke a little more with every step.

Chapter 31

Storm clouds rolled in rapidly, and it was as if the sky had decided to mimic the darkness that pushed at my heart. Stroking my back softly, Ella wrapped her free arm around my waist as she perched her chin on my shoulder. Giving her a reassuring squeeze, I loosened her arm from around me before leaning down over the black fur.

"We should find shelter before the storm reaches us." A low growl vibrated in his chest in agreement and he shifted his nose towards the empty fields coming up on our left. The heat had lessened as we travelled farther away from Carlon, but the vegetation was still very thin, and by looking at flat ground he had pointed his head towards, no crops had taken to the hard, dry soil.

Searching for the reason as to why the flat ground had drawn his attention, I realized the fields must have been tended to at some point, and I searched the area for a house or a barn. Spotting a run-down building tucked just in the corner of the farthest field, I nudged Kalian with my calf. Once we were near, Kalian stopped for us to dismount and went ahead to be sure the area had been well and truly abandoned. As we waited, I began to pace and Ella rolled her eyes at my concern before sighing in irritation. "Really, Skylahr, nothing is happening, we would hear something if there was."

As if her words had conjured him, Kalian's tall nude form waved at us from the entrance of the building, and my lips lifted just a bit when

I heard Ella groan before cursing. "Does the man have no shame?"

I linked my arm through hers as we approached the building, and I tried to push the heaviness from my chest. I focused on the bickering of my two companions and watched with amusement as she threw a pair of breeches at Kalian with violent force before storming to the stairs.

"We really ought to find her a woman. It may lift her spirits," Kalian called up the stairs, snickering when a door slammed shut. Passing him the breeches that had tumbled to the floor, I rolled my eyes and turned from him to search the house.

It had obviously been empty for a long time. The boards had begun to rot, and there was most definitely vermin of some sort occupying the space, but the firepit seemed usable and it would keep us sheltered for the time being. Squatting next to the pit, I sorted through the packs, rummaging for the remaining food before preparing dinner, all while silently ignoring the Lupine alpha as he observed me.

"Why don't you go rest? Ella and I can handle this. We do have more energy after all." I shrugged, not offering him any more of a response, and focused on the kindling that rested in my hand.

"Sky, please." His thighs brushed mine as he knelt next to me before emptying my hands and placing the kindling on the floor. Refusing to look at him, I went to reach for our packs again.

"I need to do this; I need to distract myself." He pushed the unruly waves from my shoulder and stroked my cheek with his thumb, the pad barely missing the scarred skin, and I froze.

"There was nothing you could have done." Pulling away from his touch, I glared at him.

"You don't know that," I scoffed, rising to my feet.

"Yes, I do. You would have been killed on the spot, or worse, taken hostage, and what use would you have been then?"

"At least I would have tried! There's honour in that!"

"There is no honour in dying because of stupid reckless choices!" Kalian's voice echoed around us, and I took a step back as I watched him with wide eyes.

"Stupid?" The words were a mere whisper. "Is that what saving a life is? Is that what trying to protect someone is?" He ran his fingers through his hair, tugging at the thick strands in frustration.

"You know that's not what I meant." But I didn't, because I would have gladly let those Crimsons run me through if it meant saving any of those halflings. And that did not seem reckless or stupid to me.

"This blind sense of honour will get you killed, Skylahr, and I'm worried you do not have enough self-preservation to realize how easily it will happen. That, or you just don't care." My chin wobbled and I sank my teeth into my lower lip.

"I care, of course I do." My tone was meek, and I hated how easily he saw through me, but it wasn't as if I had no regard for my own life, or that I wished to end it. That wasn't it at all. I just truly did not believe myself to be more important than anyone else. If I had the ability to help someone in dire need, should I not risk everything to do so?

"I think you're right. I am exhausted." I grabbed my pack and took the stairs two at a time until I was in the safety of the spare room. I fluffed my blankets across the floor, crawled into the middle of the pile, and held my knees to my chest as the thunder crashed outside. Now alone in the dark of my room, the image of swinging nooses filled my mind.

Hours later, something pressed against the wood of my door and I turned towards it, waiting for another sign of an intruder. When none came, I tiptoed to the entrance and inhaled deeply for a moment before throwing it open.

"Holy Healer!" a shirtless Kalian gasped as he sprawled over the threshold of my room and blinked up at me.

"What are you doing?!" I whispered before helping him up and shutting the door behind him. Kalian rubbed at his face tiredly before guiding me to the blankets.

"I didn't want you to be alone if you needed someone." He helped me back to the floor before pulling the corner of the fabric over me, and I watched him with interest. When he stood to leave, I called out for him, my previous anger and resentment from the afternoon forgotten.

"Stay?" I lifted my hand for him to take and pulled at his fingers when they slid across my palm before shuffling backwards to make room. Folding his body in half, he curled on his side and when he settled, I noticed there were still inches of space between us.

"What is it?" I furrowed my brow, not understanding why he was being distant, and his silver eyes softened as he studied me.

"Sky, I want to give you whatever space you need."

"I don't want space." The response escaped my mouth before I could process it, and I winced at my rashness. He seemed to think on my words before sliding his massive frame closer.

"Okay." Kalian's strong arms pulled me against his chest, and I nestled into the solid muscle while his fingers traced my spine and he hummed under his breath.

"Do you think they'll let any of them go?" I already knew the answer, it was a pointless question, but I still felt hope bloom in my chest.

"I don't know. If some appear useful, maybe. But Skylahr—"

I knew, and yet it still broke my heart to know those people would suffer, that they would die. Tears spilled from my eyes as I pushed my face closer to Kalian. He shushed and soothed me, his hands holding me tightly while he kissed my brow. Tipping my chin, I reached to press my lips the side of his mouth gently before moving them just slightly in order to kiss him properly.

His response was slow, hesitant, and I pressed my chest against his while tugging him closer to me. When he was bracing his weight over me, I lifted one of my legs to curl around his hip, using it to crush myself against him.

"Sky." It was a warning, though a gentle one, and I knew that he was worried that I was making a mistake. But I wasn't. I wanted him. I had wanted him since our last night in Ferrii and I so badly craved to feel those feelings again. To feel anything but this emptiness that was suffocating me.

"Please, Kalian." He pulled away from me and cupped my face in his hands. His eyes were still unsure and full of concern, but I needed this. I needed him and the comfort and distraction he could offer me. "Please."

His lustrous eyes searched my face for a long moment, and he must have found what he had been looking for because in the next instant, his hands were tangled in my hair and he was dragging his mouth across the delicate skin of my neck. I panted against the top of his head, my fingers clutching at his shoulders, my nails scraping across the scarred skin, and I whimpered when his teeth nipped at me in retaliation.

"Can I take this off?" His fingers slid under the back of my tunic before tugging at the hem. I nodded my head, desperate to feel his skin against my own. Bronze hair fluttered around me as the fabric was pulled away, and I shivered when his eyes gazed down at me in longing.

"The things you do to me." His voice was a deep rumble, and I dipped my chin away, showing him my unmarked cheek as I tried to shrug off his words.

"Don't," he ordered and I glanced at him. "Don't dismiss my words so easily. We've been over this." He pressed himself against me, and I could feel the length of him against my thigh. I leaned up to kiss him once more.

Sliding my hands down his back, I dipped my fingers under the back of his breeches and grabbed at the firm flesh of his ass. When his groan echoed in my ear, I clutched him tighter to me while hitching my leg higher over his hip. Kalian returned his focus to my skin, tracing his lips and tongue across my throat to my clavicle and down to my chest. Then warm hands cupped my breasts, his fingers rough against my flesh, and it made the warmth in my belly come to a boil.

"Kalian." His name was a broken whisper, my mind unable to focus on my voice when his mouth had taken the place of his hands. He was everywhere all at once but nowhere near close enough. My fingers slid out from his breeches to stroke his hips before tangling in the laces that held the material in place.

"Not yet, Sky. Patience." But I paid him no mind and continued to unknot the strings eagerly. His lips had paused in their ministrations, and he lifted his face to glare down at me.

"What did I say?" The gravel in his voice made lust burn through my veins, and my lips parted, feeling suddenly dry. Moving my hands back to the laces, I ignored him when one black brow rose, and he watched me for a moment before he leaned away from me and then his hands tugged the tie I had loosened.

Thinking I had finally won, I lifted my mouth in a smile, and he kissed me deeply while his hands grabbed at my wrists before pinning them over my head. Thoroughly preoccupied by the way his mouth had taken mine, I hadn't noticed the string wrapping around my wrists until it had tightened, and my hands were tied together above my head.

"I told you, patience." I blinked up at him in a daze before peering up at my hands. "If at any point we need to stop or you become uncomfortable, you tell me."

He stroked my scarred cheek gently and waited until I nodded before resuming his exploration of my torso with his mouth. Gasps and whimpers broke from me as I closed my eyes tightly, and I succumbed to the pleasure, grateful to feel so warm again.

Hands pulled at the waist of my breeches, and I lifted my hips to help Kalian ease them down. Once my legs were free, he threw the breeches across the room, and then his hands stroked up my limbs in long caresses, easing the tension before parting my thighs. Gazing down at him, I watched as he pressed his shoulders into the space between my legs, and I held my breath as his eyes locked on mine while his mouth descended.

At the first touch, my back lifted from the floor, and the hunger for release burned through me, but Kalian took his time. His tongue was playful as it teased me to new heights, only to stop suddenly. This game of his left me desperate and needy. The passion made my voice hoarse, and I called out for him over and over as he continued to taste me.

But the Lupine alpha paid no mind to my pleading, and instead lifted his lips from my sex and smiled up at me before sliding one, then another finger into me smoothly. Moving them softly, he curled the tips at the first knuckle and they pressed against me in the most delicious way, the motion making my pleading grow louder as I begged with even more desperation.

"Shh, love. Easy, relax." I glared down at him as he skimmed his mouth over my hip, his lips tracing the new scar before grinning. Frustrated by my need for release, I wrapped my bound hands into his hair and tugged in a silent demand. But he responded with a quiet chuckle that vibrated against my slick core as he resumed his game.

Seconds or minutes or maybe even hours passed, and my lower lip had been chewed raw in an attempt to quiet my sobs while he delighted in my exquisite suffering. His fingers were still pushing and sliding while his teeth and tongue tortured me into a quivering mess, and I was sure I had pulled out half of his hair by now. Releasing my fingers, I lifted my hands to the space above my head again while one knee nudged at a shoulder.

"I can't take any more!" My voice broke and his fingers finally pushed into me roughly.

Throwing my head back, I closed my eyes as the wave of heat swallowed me and I was left trembling from the delicious pleasure. Kalian kept his fingers in me, moving them gently as I rode out my release before his lips travelled back up my body. Caging my head in with his arms, he kept his weight off of me and smirked at my panting breaths.

"I think—" He paused, kissing me roughly. "You could have taken so much more." Fingers tangled in my hair before he tugged them back and exposed my neck to his lips. His teeth were sharp as they grabbed at the skin below my jaw before soothing it with his tongue.

"Are you okay? Should we stop?" I scoffed at him, thinking he was teasing. Surely, he knew I was too far gone now to even dream about stopping. "Skylahr, do I need to stop?"

His eyes were soft, gentle as they held mine, and his hands lifted to untie my wrists. Once my hands were free, he rubbed at the skin then brought them to his mouth to kiss them sweetly. "Sky?"

Lowering my arms, I slid them back down his back, my fingers skimming across his scar before I pushed at the fabric that kept him from me. Finally free of his breeches, I lifted my knees to his hips, and I wrapped my long legs around his narrow waist before kissing him deeply, tasting myself on his tongue. My hands cradled his sharp jaw, my thumbs stroking across his cheekbones, and I pulled back, taking in his beauty. "I want you. I want this, please."

Exhaling, Kalian surged forward, kissing my lips before he pressed his cock into me, slowly filling me so completely I was sure we were made of one flesh. Burying his face into the curve of my neck, I scrambled to grasp at his shoulders while he set a smooth, gentle tempo with his hips. He slid in and out of me, his rhythm becoming stronger and stronger with each thrust until my mind was blank.

Though he moved deeply, this was not the same fucking we had done that night in the abandoned little town. This was something so different that I felt it down to my bones when he murmured my name in my ear. His voice was soft, pleading, and I clutched him closer to me while my legs tightened around him. Trying to hold him as close to my body as I could, I pressed every inch of my skin against his while I let the heights of pleasure grow. And soon I was hurtling towards another release.

But he was still unrelenting, his hips snapping forward while one hand curled around my ass and lifted it, holding it at a higher angle for him, while his other hand grabbed at one of my own. Interlocking our fingers, he stretched our hands above my head, and the change in position pushed his cock against the same place his fingers had found. With the constant pressure, my bones melted, and I wailed.

"Kalian!" With one last cry of his name, I broke into a thousand little pieces under him. So consumed by the pure pleasure, I missed the stuttering in his hips as he lost his rhythm and filled me with his release.

His weight fell onto me and I clung to him while he panted into my ear. Caressing his massive shoulders with my palms, I closed my eyes and basked in the warmth of our bodies for as long as I could.

Because here, under him with the protection of his arms around me, everything would be fine. I could push away the cold and the dark. I could keep my head above the feelings that threatened to drown me, whether it be the guilt or the fear or the grief.

Here in this tiny little room while thunder and rain rattled against the old wood, I would find solace. I would find peace, even for just a moment while I hid away from the rest of the world.

Tomorrow would be a new day. It would be another chance to right the wrongs and to find honour and purpose. In the light I would put on another brave face while I searched for answers to my impossible questions. I promised myself I would go to whatever ends needed to stop the horrors of the world. In the morning I would vow to find a way to end the Crimson army and their leader. But as I lay there with Kalian's heart beating against my own, I swore to myself I would enjoy this little moment of tranquility.

Chapter 32

Kalian and I had spent the night tangled together and I couldn't seem to get enough of him. Though maybe it was because every time his warmth pulled away from me, I was left victim to the pain that chewed at my soul. I had only let him rest when the warm glow of the morning peeked its way through the gaps of the walls. Blinking in the light, I pulled from his arms before glancing back at the gorgeous man who slept soundly across my banket. His face was calm and relaxed, and I noticed his lips had lifted into a smile as he dreamt. Unable to resist, I pressed one last kiss to his mouth before I left to check on my friend who had been absent since our arrival.

I entered her room, curled around her, and smiled as she groaned in disgust. "You reek of...fucking."

Snorting in laughter, I pressed myself closer, running my smooth cheek against her in teasing. "Ew! Stop that! It's bad enough I had to listen to you all night." She pulled her face away, her dark eyes flashing before she threw her head back. "Oh, Kalian! Yes, Kalian!"

Her normally smooth voice squealed out in a poor imitation of my own and I shoved her playfully before a laugh broke from my chest, and I watched Ella smile in return. "Really though, you must be exhausted from all that—" She paused, taking a moment to find a word. "Activity."

Rolling away from her, I flopped onto my back and stared up at the ceiling as she shuffled closer, pressing against my shoulder, and in an instant, she was back asleep. Holding my breath, I listened to her soft snores as they puffed against my shoulder before I slithered out from under her weight and tucked the blanket around her. Certain she was still in a deep sleep, I crept downstairs.

The storm had passed long before Kalian and I had briefly paused in our coupling, but the smell of the heavy downpour of rain still lingered in the air and the break in the humidity was a welcome gift. Twisting my hair into a braid, I gathered wood for a fire and lit the kindling, blowing at the spark until a decent fire grew.

Boiling some of our water, I began to organize the rickety old table when Kalian sauntered down the stairs. He looked more God than human with his hair dishevelled and his breeches hanging off of his hips in the most alluring way. Approaching me eagerly, he pulled me to him and tipped my chin towards his face.

"Good morning, love." His voice was deeper, thick with sleep, and the sound made my pulse flutter.

"Morning. I didn't expect you to be up already," I replied shyly before he leaned down to kiss me sweetly. Something was different this morning, and I decided then I wouldn't run from it. Standing on my toes, I kissed him back for a long moment, taking the time to bask in his warmth.

"The hard floor didn't feel the same without you wrapped around me." His lips still brushed mine for another second before he pulled back and tugged on my braid gently.

Grabbing the boiling water, Kalian set the table, and when he finished, he admired his work with a grin before ushering me into a chair while he brought his own closer to me. He folded himself into his seat, and we ate silently, lost in our own little world until Ella stomped down the stairs. Seeing us nearly on top of each other, she rolled her eyes before sulking at the table.

"Listen here, Lupine." Kalian's eyes narrowed at her in suspicion while he waited for her to continue her idle threat. "I'm glad you two are so thoroughly enjoying each other, but please keep the racket of your fucking down." She grabbed at the knife used to cut the bread and waved it at him. "And don't you dare hurt her."

Glancing at Kalian from the corner of my eye, I watched as his lips turned down at the corners for an instant before he caught my staring. Lifting a brow, he smiled softly at me before cupping my head and kissing me thoroughly. Had I been able to think, I would have shoved him away in embarrassment, but he was just too good at this. Clearing her throat, Ella broke his spell and I pulled from him, lips swollen as I blushed hotly.

Grabbing my cup of tea, I took a long sip while Kalian popped some bread into his mouth before smirking, fully aware of the effect he had on me. I glared at him for a long moment before Ella called my name. "How is your face feeling, Sky?"

My fingers unconsciously lifted at the mention of the burn and I fingered the edge. It no longer stung, and it had healed, but the mark was still raised, and I had yet to find the courage to look at it in a reflection.

"Fine." My answer was clipped, and I saw the concern pooling in Ella's dark eyes. She knew it wasn't the physical pain, of course, as did Kalian, who was now stroking my back gently. But I was dreading seeing her seal on my face for the rest of my life. Leaving the topic alone for now, Ella focused on her breakfast and the morning passed without another word.

We packed our things and filtered through the door one by one, but once outside, Kalian stood tall, his shoulders stiff as he scouted the area carefully. I too looked around but found no concerns and turned to Ella to help strap her pack to her.

"We should stay off any roads, of course. Wahstand is still a distance but you never know who may be travelling." His gaze locked on to mine for a second before his eyes slid to Ella. "How are you feeling?"

"Good." Ella tilted her head to the side in confusion as Kalian grabbed at his dagger on his belt. Passing her the hilt, he nodded at her.

"You should be armed now that you've rested. We might as well take advantage of your new speed and strength." My eyes widened and I looked at Ella in wonder.

"She's faster now?" Other than her enhanced beauty, I hadn't noticed any change.

"Faster and stronger. Her senses are heightened as well. It comes after the ceremony, usually takes a day or two."

Ella spun the dagger between her fingers smoothly, and I watched in fascination at the speed her hand moved. Tucking the blade in her belt, she nodded at the Lupine before looking around her.

"Once we are in Wahstand, Ella will have to go in on her own." My eyes whipped towards Kalian and I began to shake my head.

"Skylahr, I can't go past the city gates, and you'll be recognized now that you have been marked." My shoulders tightened and I turned to my friend in pleading.

"He's right, Sky. I'll be able to slip past much easier, and I can read the scriptures. I'll find the temple, hunt for anything of use, and try to locate someone who may know the whereabouts of the other Chosen. Gossip spreads like fire in a city that big, there are ears and eyes everywhere. If there have been any whispers of anything, I'll hear it."

She was right, of course, but I still worried for her. Giving up the fight for now, I held my hand out for Kalian's tunic and breeches that he was now discarding. Once he had shifted, Ella and I climbed up onto his back, and I prayed to the Gods that we would all make it out of the capital alive.

The massive city was intimidating in size, its stone walls taller than any man-made thing I had seen, and behind them sat row upon row of buildings and houses, the structures crowded and identical in colour. At one time it may have been beautiful, but now the edges of the city appeared run-down and forgotten. The stone buildings were falling apart in the shadows of the castle that stood at the very north end of the city.

"That's it?" Ella's nose wrinkled in disgust as she took in the view. I understood her confusion; I had always pictured Wahstand as an elegant home of immortals, filled with ancient buildings that had been masterfully built.

"The immortals live in the north half of the city, closest to the castle. The south half is the housing for the slaves or humans. They call it Gutterend."

"How fitting," Ella scoffed. Smiling at her, I nodded in agreement before I helped her take off her pack. Ella stripped her breeches and tunic off, hastily pulling on the modest dress we had found in the brothel in Ferrii. She was stunning in the simple material, but I prayed that it would be enough for her to blend in with the other immortals. Kalian nodded his approval before passing her a small coin purse.

"Spend at least half of this. You need to appear as if you've been immortal all along and they are not known to be silver-pinching." Ella tugged on the drawstring of the purse before peering inside.

"That has to be more money than I've ever seen in my life! Where the hell have you been hiding this? You cheap bastard, you barely tipped me in Celinde!"

Kalian rolled his eyes. "Well, this can make up for my poor behaviour. Spend to your heart's content, but be sure to wait until you are in the north end, and do not pay the poor any mind."

I could tell the idea made Ella uncomfortable; she had grown up with little money and when her mother had passed, she was left with nearly nothing. That was something we had bonded over. So now seeing that amount of money, I knew it would be hard for her to not spare a silver to those who needed it. But charity was not something immortals believed in; it was beneath them.

Ella stuffed the purse into the pocket of her cloak before she lifted her hood. Taking a deep breath, she launched herself at me and I met her with open arms. She squeezed me tightly, and I gasped under her strength before pulling away.

"Easy, El! You'll choke the life out of me!" Lowering herself back onto the ground, she blinked up at me for a long moment before she turned silently and headed down to the road that led to the city gates. Sighing, I felt Kalian's warm hand cup my shoulder in support, and I linked my fingers with his, not moving from my spot until I was sure I saw Ella's cloaked figure make it to the entrance.

We made camp, though without the fire, and waited for Ella to return. The moon hung high in the sky, its light almost blinding in comparison to the black of night, and I watched as the shine bounced off the city below. Nothing catastrophic had happened, there had been no sign of a disturbance, and I took comfort in that even though I knew a single immortal woman would be little concern for the Crimsons that littered the city.

"She's okay." Kalian's warm breath fanned across my cheek as he pulled me closer to him. I turned my chin towards him and sighed heavily.

"But what if she's not?" Kalian kissed my brow gently and twirled a bronze strand around one of his long fingers as he encouraged me to lean against him.

"She would be pissed if she heard you doubting her like this." That was true; she would snarl at me if she was here. Settling against his chest, I continued to study the city below until Kalian pulled the blanket across my lap, and his steady breaths under my cheek lulled me to sleep.

Warm, delicate hands cradled my chin as Ella called my name urgently. Reeling forward, I focused on her face as she began to pull me to my feet. Scouting the area around us, I searched for the reason for her panic before realizing Kalian was nowhere to be found.

"Where is he?" I asked, my feet awkward as I tried to follow behind Ella's quick pace while she gathered our things.

"Sky, we have to go. Now." I didn't understand. When had she returned and where the hell was Kalian? Why was she so frightened? Digging my heels into the ground, I grabbed on to her arm and tried to slow her down. "Ella, what happened? Where is Kalian?"

She didn't answer as she pulled back with more force, her fingers painful against my arm. So, I called her name again, this time with more urgency. "Ella!?"

Her mouth opened but her eyes narrowed at something over my shoulder. I turned towards whatever it was that had distracted her. Silver eyes were wide, the whites bright around the shining metal colour, and I gaped in confusion as Ella put herself between me and the Lupine alpha.

"Get the fuck out of here!" Ella screamed, enraged, and I watched as Kalian's ears flattened against his skull. Trying to pass around her, I paused as Ella unsheathed her dagger before she sidestepped in front of me again.

Kalian's eyes shifted from the weapon, then to Ella, then back to me. They were pained and the sight of them pushed the air from my lungs. Our eyes locked for a second longer before the black fur on his shoulders lifted, and Kalian turned on his haunches to face the opposite direction.

Following his gaze, I could see the crimson banner rising over the sloping hill of the horizon and panic flooded my veins. Grabbing on to Ella, I clutched at my own blade that had been laid next to the pack Kalian and I had discarded on the ground, before widening my stance. We had nowhere to hide, not this close to the city, and I knew if we ran, it would be only a matter of minutes before they caught us.

My heart thudded frantically as the Crimson party closed the distance, and I watched as they calmly approached on horseback as if they were sure we were done. Once they were a mere few feet away, the soldier at the head of the group regarded Kalian with a sly smile. "Hello, Kal."

The shortened version of his name was oddly familiar, and I realized that the Crimsons who had found us outside of Carlon had called him the same thing. They too had known when and where we would be, easily finding us at the exact moment we were least prepared, and I knew then that there was no way it all had been a coincidence.

My fingers tightened around the pommel of my blade, and I could feel my blood pound in my chest as my gaze flickered back and forth between the immortals and the Lupine while I prayed for some sign that I was misreading this, for some sign that I was wrong. Focusing on the leader, I noticed him inspecting me closely, his expression changing from thoughtful to giddy before he turned to the black wolf. "I see you kept your end of the deal. She will be so pleased with you, Kalian."

Chapter 33

I took in the armoured men; each one was adorned in deep red metal and heavily armed, and I felt fear curl in my gut. The commander of the group was large in stature and well-muscled, though he gave me the impression he would move with grace. His skin was white, almost translucent, which only made his turquoise irises seem brighter. I felt his intense gaze as it inspected me thoroughly.

Ella's hand shook as she lifted her dagger, her other arm stretched wide as if she meant to protect me with her body. My own blade was raised in front of me while I stared at Kalian, waiting for some indication that I had misheard the Crimson commander. But his black head dropped low, and a deep whimper broke from his chest as he took a step forward. The sound made the immortals chuckle, mocking the Lupine, but my eyes misted over.

"Oh, dear, it looks as if our Lupine friend had played his role too well. The halfling truly thought he was a confidant." Those terrifying eyes narrowed at me while he tilted his head in consideration. "Or perhaps he was more."

A sob caught in my throat as I held the Crimson's penetrating stare, but refused to look away, promising myself I would not be so weak. Taking a step closer to Ella, I felt her own rage burn through her as she switched her attention back and forth between Kalian and the group, never focusing on one for too long.

"Shall I tell them, Kal? After all, we are at the end of your ruse." He growled a low warning through his snapping teeth, but the commander ignored him. "Come now, Kalian, no need for that. There is a freedom in telling the truth. Perhaps it will ease your guilt."

Ella pressed against me, herding us back a few steps as the immortal's grey horse was kicked forward, and Kalian watched him carefully, always keeping his body between us and the Crimsons. But now, I had no idea who he was actually protecting.

"Well, if you refuse to be a man of honesty, I will tell her myself." Dismounting, he clapped his hands together and smiled at me, his white teeth gleaming. The sight forced a shiver down my spine.

"We've been looking for you, halfling. For ages, years even. Did you know that?" His eyes narrowed as I clenched my jaw. I could tell he was goading me, pushing at me for a reaction, and I was pleased when I saw my silence irked him. Holding my stare for a moment longer, he grabbed at a blade on his belt, feigning boredom as he studied the knife he had unsheathed.

"You see, there was a prophecy, as there always is. There are always so many prophecies." He rolled his eyes as the metal blade spun between in his fingers. "But this one was different, or that's what I am told. It was said that there would be a halfling, true and fierce, whose bravery would match that of the Huntress herself. And that this single being would be the one to unite the Chosen and thus ending the reign of my mistress."

Ella's dark eyes had slid to my face, but I ignored her, too focused on the immortal who was now closing the space between us. "So, we began our search. But years passed with no sign, not even a whiff of soiled blood. We spent decades waiting and our mistress grew impatient, almost ready to forget the whole thing. That is until a baker's girl mentioned seeing the village castoff come from the forest one night. That the lumbering girl had blazing ice-blue eyes and not her normal hazel." Focusing on his words, I cursed myself for not being more careful with that girl. Ignoring my scowl, he continued.

"It was probably nothing more than gossip to her, a way to gain attention. Especially considering that she had told the story to our scout with such nonchalance, I can't see her truly knowing that she had divulged anything of importance. But it was what we had been waiting for." His voice dropped dangerously as his lips pulled tight, his grin growing twice in size.

"As soon as we heard about your little venture, we turned to our dear Lupine alpha. He had made a deal with our mistress long ago." He paused, his dagger lifting to point the tip at me steadily. "A halfling for his precious territory."

The captain sighed in delight before grinning again, his lips stretching so thin I wondered how the pink flesh hadn't cracked as they revealed more and more teeth. His eyes were bright with amusement as they moved swiftly to the black wolf before circling back to mine. "Though, my subordinates still ended up burning that village to the ground. I couldn't take that joy from them and lucky for us, Kal here had already found you."

My stomach fell and twisted into knots as my breath quickened. My vision felt like it had begun to blur around the edges while my gaze sought out the familiar silver eyes. But his head hung low and he studied the ground under his paws.

"Don't be too hard on him now, he didn't know how important you were to us. For him you were just another useless halfling, though I'd love to know when that changed. Perhaps when you spread your legs for him?"

Ella's hand grabbing at me forced my eyes to lift, and I realized that the commander had moved closer to us, his hand still curled around his dagger. His party had also slid down from their saddles silently and had readied themselves.

Holding on to Ella's palm tightly, I pulled her as close to me as possible while I shuffled another foot backwards. But they moved with us, their pursuit calm and confident, and I knew that there was no way out of this, not for both of us. Ella was faster, stronger now, and I had my ignite, but we were outnumbered and had no wolf pack to help.

"Don't you dare." Ella's whisper was full of rage as her fingers flexed around mine, and I tried to tug my hand away. "Skylahr, don't you fucking dare."

I could hear the fear filling her voice, and although it broke my heart to hurt her, I knew that I could not watch her die for me again. Squeezing her hand for a long moment, I prayed she knew how much I cared and how guilty I felt for leading her here.

"You do not harm her." My voice was unwavering as I tipped my chin, ignoring the growl and Ella's gasp. Pulling my fingers free of her, I tossed my blade to the ground and fell to one knee, head bowed.

"Wise choice, halfling. And I must say, our seal looks good on you." I could hear the dagger scrape against the leather case as he sheathed it, and I held my breath when his boots toed their way into my field of vision.

Refusing to look up, I waited for some sort of movement, but it never came. And then I blinked in confusion as I observed one, then two drops of ruby splatter against a leather toe. Reaching out with one shaking hand, I slid my finger across the wetness in wonder.

Blood. It was blood.

Alarmed, I raised my eyes, watching as Ella's dark hand jerked her dagger from the pale white throat, before stabbing it into the soft, delicate flesh under his cheekbone.

"You will never touch her," Ella snarled at him before grabbing at my shoulder. She then hauled me to my feet before pushing me forward, her hand firm on my spine as she steered me to the spooked grey who was now thundering in our direction. Lunging around me, she grabbed the leather reins before pulling on the horse's bridle with all her weight, spinning the creature in a circle as she ushered me up into the saddle. Scrambling up behind me, she kicked into the barrel of the horse, and I turned my eyes back to Kalian.

Everything was moving at half speed as the wolf turned away from us, his body shaking with a deafening roar that made the other horses scatter. And then the rest of the Crimsons who had seemed frozen in shock charged at the Lupine, their blades ready. I watched in horror

as he took down one then another before the group swarmed.

A scream bubbled in my chest for him and I grabbed at the reins ready to turn the horse around before Ella's hands closed around my own. "No, Skylahr, we can't. I am so sorry, but we can't."

Her words were just barely audible over the wind that raced past us, and my tears were pulled from my lashes by the gusts. Forcing my eyes forward, I choked on a sob while I kicked our horse faster, putting as much space between us and them, not looking back again.

When the grey of our horse darkened in colour from the foaming sweat that was now covering his coat, I slowed him to a walk. Ella was still gazing behind us, waiting for one of the immortals to make an appearance, while I swallowed the vomit that was sitting in the back of my throat.

Pushing my heels into the belly of our mount, I directed him towards the thick shelter of the forest that covered the land. I had no idea where we were or what direction we had ridden in, but I was thankful for the heavy woods that stretched for miles. When I found the most sheltered area, I slid onto the soft ground and looped the leather reins over a branch. Pulling the saddle off the horse, I distracted myself while Ella cleared an area for us.

"I'm sorry, Sky." Her voice was a whisper, barely loud enough for me to hear, and yet it caved in my chest. She had no reason to apologize; Ella had done nothing wrong. In fact, she had distrusted Kalian since Carlon, and I had defended him. What a fool I had been.

"No. I'm sorry. I put you at risk, I dragged you into this, and I didn't listen to you." Ella rushed forward to hug me tightly, and I pressed my face into her curls as I wiped the tears away.

"I chose to come with you, and I stayed because I wanted to. You have no blame in any of this." Pulling from her, I nodded before turning away.

"We need to let the horse rest and then send him off, they'll probably follow his tracks. When he's gone we'll go farther in and make camp. No fires this time." I tried to joke but it came out shaky and hoarse.

Ella must have sensed my need for space and began to empty the saddle bags, piling the supplies before detaching a bow from the saddle. Thanking the Jester for our luck, I looked over her findings. There was enough food and water to keep us going for at least a week or so, and the bow was beautifully made and in working condition. Searching the rest of the supplies, I was glad to see half a dozen arrows and some other weapons and clothing. At least I would be able to hunt if we were not able to find a town free of Crimsons, and we would be warm. Ella repacked everything neatly before strapping one of the leather bags around her and I checked on the gelding.

"I'm going to walk him to the edge and send him off." Clicking my tongue, I pulled on the reins as I walked the grey forward, following his previous tracks until we were at the edge.

"Thank you, my friend. Be safe," I whispered as I stroked his forelock before unbuckling his bridle and slapping him on his hide. I waited until he was out of sight, then I turned to the hoof prints that led to the woods, sliding my boots across the dirt in an attempt to cover them.

When I made my way back, Ella stood waiting for me, a soft smile full of empathy pulling at her lips as I approached. Weaving in and out through the dense forest, we were careful of where our tracks led while we searched for slopes and areas that would be too difficult for horses to manage. Had this been any other time, I would have appreciated the beauty of the way the sun broke through the leaves or how the woods were covered in thick green moss. But now I could see only silver eyes and wonder how I could have been so stupid.

The light in the woods had deepened into a warm glow, and I pointed Ella towards a spot that was elevated above the surrounding area. Pulling ourselves up the damp earth, we settled at the top before taking out a wineskin. "We shouldn't stay long, maybe get a few hours' rest before continuing." Taking a long swallow of the warm water, I nodded.

"How did you know?" My voice was a hoarse whisper and I kept my gaze down as I waited for her answer.

"I overheard a general bragging to his officers in the Capital. He said that the wolf had been spotted with the Chosen and their plan had worked after all. I just thank the Jester I made it back to you in time." Blinking through the tears that now burned my eyes, I ignored the questions that filled my mind and lifted my chin and smiled weakly.

"You should rest." I wanted to fall into her arms and let my heart shatter apart, but there was no time for that now, and the tension in her face worried me. She had to be exhausted and we needed to gather our strength before continuing on.

Ella observed me suspiciously before curling on her side, and I rolled my eyes before grabbing a crimson cloak that had been stuffed into the leather bag. Ignoring the colour while I draped it across her delicate frame, I waited until her eyes closed and breathing evened before I pulled my knees to my chest. Letting the weight of everything crush me, I pressed my forehead to my knee and tried to breathe through the pressure that sat on my lungs.

In the quiet of the forest, surrounded by Ella's soft breaths, my walls that I had so carefully built up slowly came crumbling down and I choked as the air left my lungs. I not only felt foolish and incredibly stupid, I felt ruined. Like the tiny pieces that had made me who I was had been traded, and now I was left with nothing but the wreckage of a stranger. A foreigner whose bruised, aching heart beat only for another.

The woods were full, green, and thick, but the lushness began to feel suffocating as the light grew dim around us. We managed to find higher ground, and I followed Ella as her sharper senses led us through the trees. We had kept a steady pace for a long while when suddenly she threw a hand back towards me, a sure signal for me to stop.

"Sky." Her smooth voice was filled with panic, and I peered around her shoulder with a questioning gaze. "Do you hear that?"

I couldn't hear anything over the rustling of wind or the light rain that had begun to drop from the heavy clouds that now hung above us. Pulling my hood down, I lifted my chin before frowning at her. "No? What is it?"

"I have no idea."

Ella bent her knees as she slunk down low, her body becoming smaller as she snuck through the branches. I opened my cloak's clasp and hurriedly shoved it into the pack, happy to be free of the added weight as I tried to keep myself from giving her away.

The green had begun to thin around us, and I waited for Ella to motion us forward. But she never did; instead her body stayed frozen in place as her long lashes blinked at the darkness that now edged its way through the forest. I watched her carefully, my breath tight in my chest while I waited for some sign of what she sensed.

"No, no." Her voice was soft in its pleading as her lower lip trembled, and I moved my chin near her shoulder in an attempt to spot whatever it was she had focused on.

"El?" But her eyes filled with tears before she pushed me back away from her. Her gaze narrowed on my face, filled with what appeared to be suspicion, though I could not understand why.

"Promise me you will not do anything stupid." I leaned back from her, recoiling at the harshness before trying to look around her again. But her fingers dug into my jaw when she pulled my face to her. "Promise me."

Nodding my head mutely, I waited for her to let go before asking again, "What is it, Ella?"

"Crimsons. But they're not alone. They have a helcyrbius."

The word trembled past her lips, the syllables laced in fear as she swallowed. I had never seen a helcyrbius, but I had heard horrifying stories. They were an ancient creature, though no one knew how they came to be. Several legends said that they were once a gentle creature, that is until the Seductress got her hands on them, breaking their bodies and souls into pieces before turning them into a creature of death and destruction.

Accounts of them varied, but they had often been described as having long extended limbs, fingers that had been sharpened into talons, and their faces were always covered in a wolf's skull. The most disturbing trait, though, was their hunger for human and immortal flesh.

"Why would they have a helcyrbius? Shouldn't they be worried that the creature would turn on them?" I whispered.

"They're using it to guard their halflings." Her finger pointed to a small cage that I could just make out, and I gasped as I realized it was filled with people. Eyes wide, I made a move forward.

"You promised." A hand grabbed me, pushing me back. Her words were heated and firm, and I sank back for a second before glaring at her. "You promised, Sky."

Had I known what I had sworn to, I would have never agreed to it, but now I knew I had to listen. I had risked Ella enough as it was. I had made her pay for my rash decisions, for my mistakes, and I owed her. I would not let her suffer by my hand again. Begrudgingly I nodded my head once before staying behind her, letting her set the pace as we crept forward. We circled widely to the right until we were close enough for me to make out the party.

Dropping the pack to the ground, I grabbed the dagger and followed Ella closely. Her shoulders were tense as a shriek echoed around us, and I watched in horror as the great beast lunged against its two chains that were fastened around its neck. Its limbs were long and thick, but not in the same way an animal's was. This almost had a human form that had hunched at the spine, its arms looking as if someone had stretched them out. Its hips were tilted high, and it oddly reminded me of when children would crawl on all fours, pretending to be a horse in a game of imagination. Its long legs ended with lengthy feet though the toes were tipped with talons, and its skin appeared to be dark, almost blue in colour.

However, the most terrifying feature of all was the skull that sat perched on the bulging shoulders. A skull that was now facing me, its bone mouth opening wide as a blue tongue swiped across a long line of sharp teeth before it appeared to lift at a corner, as if to grin at me.

"Oh, fuck," Ella gasped, her hand grabbing at my shoulder, but I couldn't look away from the bone head, my eyes trailing up the narrow nose to the two dark holes that were now filled with a burning violet. A violet that had locked on to my face for a second before the creature's jaws cracked open wide and another shriek shook the trees around us.

Chapter 34

Long blue claws reached out towards us as the beast pulled at the chains, its body surging forward a few steps only to be yanked back again. It repeated this process three times, each lunge accompanied by the shrill screech that had begun to echo in my ears. The sound must have alerted the Crimsons as one of them cursed at the helcyrbius before picking up a stone to whip at the creature and laughing with his friends. But the monster never dropped its eyes, its purple stare boring holes into my face as it lunged again, this time with more force.

"What the hell does it want?" the rock thrower growled before grabbing a sword and carefully scouting the forest while managing to stay away from the long, sweeping arms of their pet. Ella and I both ducked low, attempting to stay out of sight, but the immortal persisted in his search. Panic flooded my body as I scrambled to make my frame as small as possible, mentally cursing at the Gods for making me so big. Shifting carefully, I froze when Ella elbowed me softly and I stared at her as she mouthed two words at me.

Trust me.

Plucking the dagger from my hand, Ella twisted her fingers into my hair and pulled my head back. A wheeze broke from me as she pressed the tip of the metal against my throat before hauling to my feet and I could feel the muscles in my legs seize in panic.

"Who's there?" I could hear more metal slide out of their casings as

I blinked up at the night sky, praying I had not made the same mistake twice. That I hadn't put my trust into the wrong person. Again.

"I thought you may want another halfling to join your little collection there." Ella's voice was different, it was sultry and alluring in a way I had never heard, and I whimpered as she tugged at my hair with more force. Steering us far around the reach of the helcyrbius, her back never exposed to its eyes, she dragged me forward. Flickering my eyes over to the cage, I noticed the halflings pressing their faces against the metal bars, rallying closer to catch a better glimpse at the newest addition.

I could hear low murmurs rumble through the camp as the immortals crossed the distance, and I held my breath as Ella held the dagger to my throat with more force. Exhaling quietly in my ear, Ella counted the immortals just loud enough for me to hear.

There were seven total, more than I was comfortable with the, but the simple knowledge let hope bloom in my chest. If she was giving me this information, it must mean this was in fact a ploy. Thrashing in her hold, I grabbed at her wrist and pulled as I gave the appearance of a belligerent hostage. In response, Ella snarled and spat at me as she dragged me forward, kicking me in the back of the knee hard enough that I fell into a heap.

The men gathered in a circle as they watched Ella carefully. Only relaxing when they watched her hold the dagger to the back of my neck.

"Let me see her." One of them laughed while tipping my face towards the fire in order to get a better look. His fingers pulled my marked cheek closer to the light before he ran a finger over the seal. "Look at that, boys, she's already marked."

Blinking up at the immortal, I immediately noticed that the armour was not the fine detailed red that the others had worn, and I prayed that meant he had no idea who I truly was, or who was looking for me. Pulling from his hands, I glared up at him before spitting at his feet.

"You ugly bitch!" The backhand I received was sharp, but nothing compared to what I expected. Taking in his plain dark hair and round face, I smirked at him in return.

"Ugly? You're one to talk. Are you sure you're an immortal and not one of us?" I snarked at him, readying myself for another strike as he reeled his hand back. Taking the punch, I spat out the blood that filled my mouth before casting a glance at Ella. Her dark eyes burned with fury, but she kept them on my face, and it was almost convincing enough that I nearly believed her rage was directed at me rather than my attacker.

"This one can go to the helcyrbius. I already have a pretty little thing in the cage." Dread plowed into me as I cast a glance over my shoulder. I could see a few of the women from my spot, but none looked worse for wear. That is until they parted, and I noticed a petite, slender form curled in on herself. Her skin was delicate and pale, nearly white, and she had a head of short black hair. Her narrow eyes focused on mine as she trembled, and I noticed the gashes in her clothes.

My ignite burned in my veins, and I barely held myself together as I nodded at her silently. She would have her revenge tonight; I would make sure of it.

"You've lain with them?" Ella's disgust was obviously not understood, because the immortals laughed before muttering that any warm body, no matter the blood, was still a warm body. Distracted by their laughter, they missed the seething fury lining Ella's delicate face, too pleased with themselves for the pain they had caused, and I held my breath as I waited. "Who had that one?"

Ella had moved from behind me passing to my left, still aware of where the helcyrbius stood as she approached the cage. The halflings darted backwards, terrified by her advance as they curled into balls on the floor.

"Why, do you want a taste?" Ella's dark gaze narrowed on the brunette immortal and a sly smile pulled at her face. Lifting one finger, she crooked it twice as she beckoned him closer, and I knelt in place as his back faced me.

One of her hands slid into his hair, grasping at it passionately while she tugged his face to hers. A deep, muffled groan came from the couple and I felt my stomach turn over as the immortal seemed to succumb to her embrace. The rest of his party hollered and cheered, watching with glee as they continued to kiss.

However, I noticed the faces of the halflings, their skin pale and mouths slack as they observed the pair. Paying closer attention, I realized that Ella was holding the weight of the immortal up, his body had slumped into her, and she was oddly still. She tilted her head, her eyes slid open over his shoulder, and then they dropped to the ground before me, motioning for me to follow her gaze. The dagger had been left at my feet, just close enough for me to grab without anyone noticing, and my fingers slid towards it.

Arming myself, I kept my head bowed as I watched her face pull away from the immortal. Her lips were wet and dark with a shining red, and the man tumbled to the ground, his head lolling to the side. I realized his mouth was bloodied and his throat had been slit open. Moving my eyes back up to her face, I watched as a feral grin spread across her lips and she turned to the rest of the group who had still been celebrating and rough-housing with each other. None of them were aware of the turn their night had taken until she stalked towards them, her teeth gleaming against the maroon that covered her mouth.

"Who's next, boys?" she said, drawing their attention. There was a long, significant pause before all hell broke loose.

Grabbing at the first one to reach her, Ella moved with speed he obviously had not anticipated and blocked his blow with her forearm before slamming her closed fists into his stomach. The hit knocked the air from his lungs as he was sent sprawling back to the ground. The next two had been more prepared, arming themselves with their blades before pursuing her. However, the larger of the two had not realized how close he had been to the cage, and the halflings reached their arms through the bars, grabbing his legs and tugging him to the ground. Taking the opening, I ran at the immortal, sliding across the ground before straddling his hips and pressing my blade to his neck.

"May you burn in the darkest pits of hell." Sliding the metal across his flesh, I waited just long enough to be sure he was dead before moving onto the next. Ella had managed to finish two on her own, which left us with four. Grabbing at a discarded long sword, I rushed at the largest of the trio, my ignite burning through me as I locked eyes with him. Fear filled his features and I saw then that he knew exactly who I was.

Our blades crashed against each other in a simple dance. He had strength and speed as all immortals did, but I had the knowledge, and that was all I needed to finish him in half a dozen blows. Noticing the ring of keys on his belt, I turned to be sure Ella was still okay before I knelt and retrieved them. Tossing them to the halflings, I nodded at them before stalking the last three.

"You're her, you're the northern halfling." I smiled at the fair-coloured man, my grin full as I held his stare.

"Yes."

"The wolf should have brought you to us by now. You should have been destroyed, how are you still breathing?" The mention of Kalian and his betrayal had my ignite boiling through my veins, and my smile hardened as I circled them.

However, too bold in my pursuit, I had misjudged the distance and suddenly a sharp sting tore across my right shoulder. Glancing behind me, I moved with just enough speed to dodge the next swing as the long blue arm swiped through the air. Rolling onto my belly, I clawed at the earth as I moved to drag myself to my feet, but I had not escaped out of its reach, and four talons pierced the back of my thigh as the helcyrbius dragged me across the moss. I was no match for the creature's strength, and I felt my skin tear as it pulled me closer.

Moving onto my back, I ignored the pain in my thigh and watched as the bone jaws opened wide. It screamed at me, its other hand swinging to claw at my middle, but I had been waiting and I lifted my sword to cut at its moving arm. With one smooth swing, the metal tore through the dark flesh and blood soaked my forearm as the limb dropped to the wet ground.

But even with the loss of one of its arms, the helcyrbius paused for only a second before it was sliding its talons across my leg. It rushed forward against its chains, and the sharp claws found purchase in my hip. It pulled at my body until I was sliding across the grass, dragging me until I was close enough to feel the cold chill of its breath. With one last shriek, the long jaws opened as its head swooped down and I clenched my eyes shut as I prepared for the end.

Blindly kicking my feet in one last effort to ward off the helcyrbius, I noticed that the tugging of my body had stopped, and the piercing screech was now a deep growl.

Squinting my eyes open, I watched in shock as the black furred wolf tore at the hunched spine of the creature, his nails biting into the flesh of its sides while his jaw closed around the white bone of its head.

Holding my gaze with his silver eyes, Kalian clenched his jaw around the skull, his fangs piercing into the bone with a sickening crunch and then he pulled.

Chapter 35

The skull was flung across the moss, and I held my breath until the rest of the horrific body fell into a heap. Finally sure it was defeated, I lifted myself from the damp earth and ran at Ella.

Two men were left, and I watched as she fought them off brilliantly, her skill smooth and sharp as she cut at them. Seeing an opening, I charged at the one closest to me and cut through his middle as Ella knocked hers to the ground. Sure he was at her mercy, I backed away from them and turned to the cage. Noticing the halflings had opened the door but remained behind the bars, I took a moment to wipe the blood from my hands and face before walking to them.

All six halflings were women, young in age ranging anywhere from four and ten to midtwenties, and I prayed to the Gods that they had not suffered the same fate as the small pale one. Kneeling down in the entrance of the cage, I lifted my hands in surrender with my head bowed, waiting for some sign that they understood I was not a threat.

"Who are you?" The voice was high and sweet, and my gaze lifted to the dark, narrow eyes that had held my own before. She had come closer, though seemed wary of me, and I kept my hands up as I regarded her.

"My name is Skylahr." Her dark hooded eyes slid from my head to my knees and back again before she crawled closer. She was tiny, thin, and frail, and I wondered how long it had been since she had eaten.

Looking around at the other halflings, I took in each one. They all seemed to be in a similar state, small and malnourished, and it hurt my heart to see how immortals could inflict such suffering. Focusing on the one in the back, I nodded at her.

"They hurt you." It was not a question; I knew what they had done to her, but she nodded anyway. "Did that one hurt you?" I asked, pointing to the immortal who bowed at Ella's feet as he watched the black wolf with terrified eyes.

"He gave me this before he…" She paused for a long moment. "Before he hurt me." And I watched as she pulled at the collar of her shirt, showing me the skin of her breastbone. There, in the centre of her chest, was a seal matching the one on my face, and I felt my eyes water while I looked at the puckered flesh. Glaring back at the immortal, I offered her my hand and helped her to her feet.

"What is your name?" I asked while I wrapped my arm around her waist and encouraged her to lean her weight against me.

"Marissa," she whispered, her fingers grabbing at my arm as she stumbled forward. Ella stood, both hands holding a blade, while she waited for us patiently, never taking her eyes off of her prisoner. I took one of the weapons Ella offered us and pressed it into Marissa's hand, closing my fingers around her smaller ones.

"His life is yours, if you want it." Her dark eyes blinked at me, and I watched as they glanced down at the sword she held before focusing on her tormentor.

"Kiss it." Her honeyed voice was ruthless as she pressed the metal to his face, and I was shocked that her tiny arm did not shake under the weight of it. "Kiss it!"

The immortal held her eyes as he bent forward, pursing his lips ready to kiss the steel. But just as he shifted his weight, Marissa slashed at him and I watched as she cut into his face. The blow was swift and well-practiced, and I could feel my ignite burn with pride as the immortal fell to the ground, alive but gravely wounded. Without another breath, the tiny halfling launched herself at him, stabbing into his chest with the tip of her sword, killing him immediately.

She stayed in her spot, heaving with dry sobs as her slender frame trembled, and I knelt next to her, my hand hovering over her spine.

"It's over now," Marissa's musical voice whispered as her dark eyes turned to me, their depths swirling with the same hatred and rage that burned in my own. My lips lifted in one corner as I felt my ignite simmer beneath my skin again and I rubbed her back soothingly.

"Not yet. But it will be."

Keeping herself armed, Ella stood guard as she watched the wolf, her dark eyes never once leaving his face while I organized the women. The wonder that filled their faces as they watched the black creature would have been heart-lifting if the sight of him hadn't caused a deep agony in my chest. I avoided his glittering gaze while I tended to the women.

"Who is he?" one of the younger ones asked, her voice timid as she gazed at the beast from around my shoulder.

"He will not harm you." There was little more I could say without exposing my hurt, and I swallowed sharply before cleaning the grit from her face. Pleased with my work, I helped the others change into cleaner clothes and instructed them to collect the useful items.

"Skylahr." His voice called for me over Ella's scoff and I turned to his stunning face. His eyes were wary, and his face was pale, and yet he stole the breath from my lungs. Ignoring the gasps surrounding me, I collected a free cloak and tossed it at his kneeling form roughly before nodding at Ella.

"Gather the girls and head into the cover of the trees, I'll be right there." Ella didn't move and I crossed the space between us before pulling her into my arms.

"Please, I won't be long. I know you want to stay but I need to do this on my own." Stepping away, I smiled down at her sadly. "Go. You can't help me with this."

Watching as she herded the group of gawking women into the

bushes, I took in a deep breath and turned to the golden man. Biting my lip, I tried to muffle the sob that bubbled in my chest as I took in the tan skin I had memorized the last time he had held me.

His left shoulder was spilt at the joint, the skin still closing the jagged edges, and his right hip also had a deep puncture. He was still kneeling; his two massive hands tried to push his body to his feet, but his forearms shook under the weight before they gave out. He winced as his chest hit the ground with a muffled pained groan, and tears filled my eyes as my name broke from his lips in a devastated sob.

"Please, Sky." My eyes squeezed shut at the pain in his voice. "Skylahr, please."

Had I been stronger, I would have turned away and left him there, but I couldn't. Not yet. I needed to know why he lied, why he betrayed us, betrayed me. Tightening my fingers around the hilt of my weapon, I stood from my hiding spot and slowly advanced towards the beautiful broken man.

"What do you want, Kalian?" My voice was soft but unwavering and I watched as his strong jaw lifted, and his eyes focused on my blade for a second before he chuckled dryly.

"Good girl, always come prepared." I wasn't sure if it was a true compliment or jape but my teeth ground against each other as I clenched my jaw shut.

"Shut up." My voice betrayed me as it wobbled, and I blinked my tears away. "You don't say another word, not another word unless it is to tell me why."

One warm tear rolled down my cheek before I could wipe it away with my forearm, and I watched as his eyes followed its path. Dark lashes fluttered shut for a split second before he lifted his gaze, and I could see his own tears that were threatening to fall.

"Skylahr. I am so, so sor—"

"I don't want your apologies; I want to know why." My lower lip quivered, breaking the façade I was so desperately trying to paint. Pushing himself to his knees he held my stare and I waited for some reasoning that could take the hurt and fury away.

"Listen to me, what the captain said was true. I made a deal with them and alerted them when the whispers of a halfling spread through the north. But that was before." His voice caught and I felt the rage in my veins bubble.

"*Before*? Is that your excuse?" A cruel laugh broke from my throat as another tear fell. "Before what? Before we met, before you brought me to Denimoore? Before we fucked?" His head hung to his chest, and his hands gripped the earth beside him, his fingers sinking into the green moss before curling into fists.

"The first time I saw you, you were on your knees praying to the Huntress for protection, and I can't explain it, but I knew then that I could not harm you." The words rushed out of him, and my lips parted as I thought back to my first journey to the Swallows. It was the night I had forgotten everything. I had been worried about an animal stalking me before I lost consciousness. That animal had been him.

"When I found you the first time I never thought that you would be what they were looking for. I thought you had just been a foolish girl who had gotten lost, but then I caught your scent again in the Swallows and I knew it hadn't been a coincidence, so I followed you."

My lower lip quivered as I watched him, and I prayed for the strength I knew I didn't have as he continued.

"I listened to you beg that witch for a cure. You were willing to give her anything if she helped your people, and I was so amazed by your bravery, by your selflessness. And I wondered if you could truly be her, if you were more than just a selfless girl. So when I found you curled in on yourself covered in blood, I brought you back to Denimoore, and I waited for a sign. And when you ignited in Carlon and beat the soldier into the dirt, I knew that it was true. I knew that you were what they—what we had been waiting for. I could see the Huntress in you, and I was certain I could never hand you over to them." He finished, panting as tears slid down his cheeks.

Kalian had been there all along and had watched over me for longer than I knew, and yet I still could not shake my anger. He may have made that deal a century ago, long before I had been born, but he had still lied, still deceived me, and I knew my next question would be my last.

"Did you know they would destroy Noorde Point when you told them of what you had heard? Did you know my family would die?" My tears continued to fall as my pain curled into rage and I lifted my dagger towards him.

His eyes were wide and wet as he blinked at me, his lips just barely parting. "Yes."

Chapter 36

Though I was unsure if it was from the surprise of his admission or the realization that I had been well and truly wrong about him, my knees buckled under my weight and the air left my lungs in a gasp.

"Skylahr." Kalian dragged himself forward until his bare knees brushed mine and his fingers lifted my chin. "Please just let me explain. It's not what you think."

His face blurred through my tears, and there was a small whisper echoing in my mind, begging for me to dig the tip of my dagger into his chest. To pierce his heart in the same way he had stabbed my own.

Kill him.

Kill him, Skylahr.

Kalian's fingers pressed against my face and he frowned at me. "What is—"

But I interrupted him by shaking my head, pushing his hands and the voice away. He dropped his arms, and I froze as his fingers curled around the hand that was armed. He lifted it, holding the dagger directly over his heart, almost as if he had heard that voice too.

"Let me explain. Please just let me explain and then do whatever it is you must." His hand never wavered as it held my wrist, holding the steel against the tan muscle with such steadiness I wondered how he could manage it. Maybe he knew I really could never hurt him, not like that. Not like the way he had hurt me.

"I did know it was a risk, I knew that it was a very real possibility that they would come looking for you if word got out that you had breached the walls. And I now know I should have told you. But I had no way of knowing how or when they would come, and at the time, it was the farthest thing from my mind. Curse me or kill me, I am yours to do with as you wish." His thumb strummed against my pulse point as he watched me carefully.

"I know that my carelessness has cost you everything, but I truly did not know for certain they would come, and then after we had journeyed south, you were the only thing I was desperate to protect. You and what you meant for the rest of us, what you meant for me." His eyes roamed my face, searching for something. "You were what we had been waiting for."

"Waiting for?" My voice sounded far away, detached from me somehow, and I exhaled through my nose while trying to focus my mind. "Why do you keep saying that? That you were waiting for me?"

His half smile was sad as it lifted one corner of his mouth for a second before his free hand grabbed my chin. "Not just you, the Huntress's Chosen."

Lies. Lies. Lies.

The voice echoed in my mind again and I blinked away the splitting pain behind my eyes as I narrowed them at him. "Just because the immortals say it's real, it doesn't mean it's true. I expected you of all people to understand that," I snapped, pulling my chin free from his fingers. Kalian let his hand fall back to his side, though his eyes searched my face for a long moment, his gaze concerned as he attempted to reach for my cheek again.

"What is happening?" he whispered with a frown.

Angered by his worry, I slapped his hands away. "What are you talking about? And stop calling me her Chosen, I do not belong to the Goddess." Smiling sadly, Kalian studied the ground.

"Of course you do, there is no possible way the Gods made you an ordinary halfling, Skylahr Reed." Lies, more lies that were disguised as sweet words. Had he not humiliated me enough? He had pushed past my defenses, he had touched and seen and taken me completely. He had all but made me his, and yet he still could not do the decent thing and tell the truth of it.

"So that makes it better? Your decision to believe that I am of some great importance makes this all okay? You lied to me for weeks. My parents are dead, my friend and my people are dead. Innocent lives were lost and you could have kept that from happening."

"How would I have done that?" He glared at me, the sadness slipping into anger. "You are hurt and rightfully so, but you are choosing to ignore reality. I could not have stopped them even if I wanted to, nor could you." But he was wrong, he could have brought me to them as he had promised. He could have spared hundreds and that was what I could not forgive.

"You think I should have traded you, that's it, isn't it?" His voice grew angry and he tugged me closer to him, forcing the dagger from my grip before hauling me onto his lap. My hands pushed at his skin and I flailed in his grasp, my palm sliding across the drying blood on his shoulder. But his strength never wavered as he kept a solid arm around my hips and his other hand knotted in the back of my hair.

"I couldn't do that. I know that's what you would have done, but I could not." Tears were running freely down his cheeks now and my stomach dropped at the sight. "I have been waiting for you for centuries and I will not apologize for protecting you, for putting your life first."

"That wasn't your choice to make," I snapped, my teeth inches away from his face as I snarled at him before I dug my nails into his newly closed wound. The pain had surprised him enough to loosen his arm, and I pulled myself up from the ground, bending to grab my weapon before glaring down at the kneeling alpha.

"You obviously think you did what you had to; I can see that. But you chose wrong. You decided my fate for me, and it cost me everything." Pausing, I wiped at my face roughly before ducking my head. "I am sorry that my presence has forced you to make impossible choices because you believe me to be something I am not. But I cannot forgive you. I will always look at you and wonder what could have happened had you been honest. I will always second-guess your intentions and nothing will be the same. I can't trust you now."

Kalian's head fell, his muscled shoulders sagging forward, and my heart cracked as I watched him wipe at his face, his fingers wet as they left his cheeks.

"I need you to leave, Kalian. I need you to get up and I need you to go." I inhaled wetly, my throat constricting under the agony that was filling my chest. "You owe me. You owe me a family, a home, a life."

Silver eyes blinked up at me silently, begging me to understand, but I couldn't. I never would.

"You may have saved me, my life may be owed to you, it may be yours, but theirs were not. Their fate should not have been in your hands, and now I am begging you to let me choose this time. I am pleading with you, please leave me be." Tears had begun to run hotly down my cheeks as I backed away from him, my body forcing me to distance myself while I tried to reason with him. "Your people need you, Denimoore needs you, and I do not. Not anymore."

"Sky—"

"No. You know your lands are in danger, and you have little time before the Crimsons find their way through that barrier. You need to go home, Kalian. Ella and I will continue searching for the other Chosen. I won't stop until I have found a way to defeat her. But I don't need you, not now." I fell to my knees again, my hands cupping his sharp jaw as I tipped his face to mine. His lips were parted as shuddering breaths passed through the soft flesh and I wished so badly I had never learned the truth. Maybe then I could have comforted him the way I so desperately wanted to.

"Let me go, Kalian." Without another word I moved from him, dragging myself away from his warmth before turning on my heel. My long legs were weak as they sprinted back through the woods, only to buckle when the piercing howl echoed through the trees and I felt my heart finally shatter.

Ella must have heard the howl from her hiding place as she ran at me, her eyes wide and wild as they searched my body for any signs of injury. Grabbing at my shoulders, she checked me over twice before pulling me into the thicket that surrounded us.

"What the fuck were you thinking!" Her strong fingers shook my shoulders roughly as she scolded me. "Why would you tell me to leave like that?!"

My mind was spiraling rapidly, and I grabbed at Ella's delicate fingers before removing them from my shoulders and clasping them into one of my own hands tightly. "Ella, I'm fine. He didn't hurt me."

And he didn't, not physically at least.

"I am sorry. Truly. I didn't mean to worry you." I held her stare for a long moment, showing her how serious I was before I grabbed at her pack and bow, changing the subject. "I can carry these now."

It was the least I could do after worrying her. Holding them, I lifted my hood over my hair, hiding my face from her searching eyes, and I let her lead me forward into the thick cover of trees. The group of women had huddled together in the shadows, their arms linked together as they stood to face us as we approached. They obviously still distrusted us, and I could appreciate their bond. Trauma had a way of connecting people.

Using a gentle voice, Ella directed them carefully through the bush, and I ignored their questioning stares as I took up the rear. Marissa, however, had chosen to stick close to my side, her thin shoulders draped in my cloak as she tried to keep up with my long strides. Smiling down at her gently, I pointed to a clearing as Ella checked the area for any potential threats. Once settled, we passed out the food sparingly, and I wished I could have given them more. Guilt ate at me slowly as I turned to grab at the bow before calling to Ella.

"I'm going to hunt." The immortal looked at me carefully, and I knew she was letting me know that she did not trust me to not run off.

"I won't go far," I promised before grabbing a cloak and pulling up the hood.

Marissa's pale face whipped towards me as she noticed the tension between Ella and me, and her eyes narrowed at my immortal companion. Watching the suspicion fill her face, I remembered that these women had no knowledge of the ceremony or that Ella had once been a halfling, and I realized they distrusted her because she was an immortal, an enemy.

"It's okay, Marissa, Ella is not one of them." Ella's eyes widened at me, hurt flashing through her dark eyes. I felt the need to reassure our new companions that the dark beauty would sooner risk herself before she allowed any harm to fall on them. As would I.

Marissa seemed unconvinced though as she chewed on the dry venison, her eyes never leaving Ella's face, and I worried that she would refuse to listen to me. Kneeling down next to her, I handed her my own piece of smoked meat as a peace offering before sliding my eyes to Ella.

"I promise you, Ella has saved me more times than I can count. I would have been scavenger food by now had she not risked her life to save mine. And she has, countless times." Ella blinked down at me, her eyes soft as she smiled, and I knew that I should have spoken my appreciation for her more often.

Marissa sighed before chewing thoughtfully, her eyes still swirling with anger, and I waited in silence for her to say something. "You can control your ignite."

That had not been what I was expecting, and I stared at her, mouth open.

"Oh, uh, yes." I nodded dumbly while the rest of the halflings turned to me in awe.

"Could you teach us?" All six halflings stopped eating as they waited silently for my answer, their eyes were wide and hopeful as they peered up at Ella and me.

"Why don't you just worry about resting for now?" I suggested carefully before turning back to Ella. With one last smile I made a quiet exit from the group.

Slinking into the shadows of the trees, I lowered my hood and loosened up my shoulders. Now without the distraction of the others my mind began to wander, but always circled back to the silver eyes that no longer watched over me.

The loss of Kalian was raw and aching, and I felt my heart squeeze in my rib cage as I knelt down in the moss. Tears slid from my eyes as I took in a shuddering breath, and I knew what shattered me had not been the idea of him caring for me or us being something more than allies.

It was the idea that everything we had been through had been a ploy, a scheme to earn my trust and wield it in whatever way he saw fit. It was the humiliation that burned through me that left me wrecked. I had allowed myself to be his plaything, and that was unforgivable. Wiping at my eyes, I swallowed my pain and rage, promising myself that after this moment I would never allow him to hold this kind of control over my emotions again.

Pulling myself to my feet, I surveyed the area around me and took in one last shuddering breath before tipping my head back towards the sky. I threw all thoughts and memories of the Lupine into a cage and pushed it to the far back corners of my mind, never to be opened again.

Through the night the halflings had warmed up to us, and by morning they began sharing similar stories and tales of their past. Each one had known their true parentage, had spent their lives always running and hiding from the Crimsons while trying to find a way to live. As I listened to each story my heart broke a little more for them. I had been gifted over two decades of normalcy; I had a life, one that they had never been allowed.

Turning to one of the women, I listened as she explained how the Crimsons had come through her village, killing both her brothers before taking her captive. "The men they don't even bother to keep for any length of time, they are slaughtered on the spot. We are only kept for their amusement, if it suits them, before we are dealt with."

Her anger flared under her skin, and I watched as her light blue eyes turned icy, a true telling of the power that simmered in her being. Patting her shoulder gently, I offered my silent support, and we huddled together only to be interrupted by Ella.

"We really should be moving; we cannot stay here much longer. It's only a matter of time before other Crimsons pass through," Ella called from her spot a few feet away and I watched as fear blanketed the group.

"But where will we go?" a tiny, shrill voice cried with fear, and I looked over at the young girl. Her name was Alanna and she had just turned six and ten last month, though she looked to be younger. Her thin body had been starved and she barely came to my biceps in height. Kneeling down in front of her, I stroked her blond hair away from her face before smiling sadly. The poor girl wasn't even old enough to ignite. The only reason why she was found was because a neighbour had informed the Crimsons, trading the poor child for a few silver as if she was nothing more than a pig headed to market.

"We are headed south." Ella's voice drew my attention, and I could see her internal battle. She did not want to leave these women but travelling in such a big group came with risks and we were on a fool's errand.

"South?" Marissa asked as her eyes bounced back and forth between us. "Why south?"

I wasn't sure how much we should divulge; they had just as much reason to hate the Crimsons as we did, but filling them in on our travels could jeopardize our plans. If any of them were to mention our search for the other Chosen, the Seductress and her army would be able to track us, and they would know precisely where to look. Again.

Silver eyes flashed in my mind, but I shook the image from my head.

"It's the Healer's Chosen, isn't it? You're looking for him," Marissa called to me, her voice pulling me from my thoughts.

The Healer's Chosen.

The words were whispered in my mind, forcing a sharp pain through my temple for an instant and then it was gone, and I observed the halfling in surprise. She not only knew of the Chosen, she potentially knew of their location. Cursing under my breath, I glanced at Ella.

"Yes." Ella's voice was clipped, and she crossed her arms while glaring at the halfling. Ignoring my whispered warning, the immortal lifted her chin in challenge. "What of it?"

"Then you need to go to Suideign Shores. He is there."

Chapter 37

Ella and I did not bring up the Chosen again, and we did our best to steer the conversation away from the topic, though Marissa watched us carefully. The other women seemed unfazed by the tension between the three of us, and I wondered if they were as oblivious to the legend as I had been.

Ella pulled me aside once the halflings were distracted, her worried gaze watching Marissa carefully before focusing on mine. "Do you believe her? Should we really head to the shores?"

"Do we really have a choice?" It was the first solid lead we had, and now that I had sent Kalian north, we needed to find the other Chosen. Immediately.

"What do we do with them?" I turned to look back at the women, who seemed to have relaxed over the last few hours, their expressions lifting in the daylight.

"I suppose we find them a safe haven before we carry on." Focusing back on the group, I noticed Marissa's pale face observing us, her mouth pressed into a thin line. She pulled herself away from her companions before quietly approaching us, her shoulders hunched in nervousness.

"Are you alright?"

Marissa nodded before crowding herself close to me until her back was facing the others.

"I want to come with you two." Ella's brows pinched as she studied the smaller woman. "Please."

"Marissa—" I began, unsure of what to tell her, of where to start.

"Please. I know you don't know me well enough, but I promise I won't get in the way." Her eyes peered up at me pleadingly and I turned to Ella.

"Marissa, it's not safe." Ella reached out to cup the woman's elbow gently before giving it a gentle squeeze.

"I don't care about that. I know it will be dangerous, but I can't go into hiding knowing that I could help." She paused, taking in a shuddering breath before dropping her eyes. "My mother loved my father, even though he was married and an immortal. She adored him wholly. When he left, she was desperate for him, she spent years pining for him. Six months ago, she wrote to him in hopes of seeing him just once more, but his wife sent the letter to the Crimsons and they came to collect me. They slit her throat in front of me that day. Then they—" Her sob broke whatever resolve I had been holding on to, and I wrapped my arms around her gently, only closing them tighter when she returned my embrace, gripping at my back as if I was her lifeline.

Ella lay a comforting hand on her shoulder, her fingers delicate against the bones that stuck out against her skin. "It is not only dangerous, but it will be a long, hard journey. I'm just not sure your body will be up for it."

It was an honest statement. Marissa was weak and exhausted; there was no possible way she would be able to keep up with us and I could not risk being slowed down. Not now. Searching for a compromise, I sighed heavily.

"We will take you with us to Suideign Shores, but that's the farthest you can come." Pulling away from her, I peered down at her face.

Marissa seemed resistant to the idea but nodded anyway before she circled back to the group. I wished I could have had a different answer for her, but I could not have another life in my hands. As if she could sense my turmoil, Ella patted my back reassuringly before gathering the women together.

As they packed away the extra weapons and items, one of the women named Nellie turned to Ella with a grateful smile. "I have an aunt in the north just outside of Port Huronian. It would be a lengthy journey, but it is in the opposite direction we had been heading. I don't think anyone would search there, at least not before we found a passage east to Ustra."

The others turned to each other for a long moment, not saying a word, though it appeared they had all come to an agreement. I watched as they reached for each other's hands. It was a united front, a sisterhood of sorts, and the sight of it warmed my heart.

"Take the silver. All of it, and the pelts and clothing." Ella knelt down in front of them before passing off her own silver purse, and Nellie reached out with a shaking hand, her fingers just gripping the drawstring before she pulled Ella to her.

"Thank you," she whispered against the thick black curls as she peered over her shoulder, eyes locking with mine. "Thank you both."

We had bid farewell to the women and waited a few hours before we began to head south. Suideign Shores was nearly a week's journey away and travelling with Marissa would slow our pace significantly. Her body was tired, and we had made the mistake of both pushing her too hard and feeding her too much, which resulted in a delay after she had spent an entire night emptying her stomach.

Skidding down the moss-covered hill, I felt my own stomach turn as I reached the bottom. My head had been pounding for hours, the pain constant even as I swallowed mouthfuls of water and stripped down to my light cotton tunic. Ella had studied me with concern, but I waved her off in irritation, my temper seething though I had no idea as to why. Attributing my pain to stress and exhaustion, I pushed on, forcing my legs to carry me through the forest.

"Skylahr?" Ella's voice called out to me, and the very sound of it made my fists clench as I chose to ignore her. "Sky?"

A sharp pain radiated in my skull as she reached forward, her fingers just grazing my shoulder before I shrugged her off roughly. I could feel her hurt in the way she pulled back, and I wished I had an explanation for her.

"El, just leave me be." I had meant for my tone to be soft, but it came out nastily, vicious in a way I had never spoken to her. Her brown eyes widened as her mouth went slack in shock, and yet I could not bring myself to apologize.

"What's wrong?" Even now she regarded me warmly while her fingers cupped my check gently. But another stab of pain rang through my skull and I slapped her hand away from me with anger.

"I said leave me be!" My voice echoed through the trees, the noise forcing a flock of birds from their perch in the cover of leaves, and I watched as Marissa comforted my friend cautiously.

"Oh, Gods, Ella, I am so sorry." My fingertips rubbed at my temple as I blinked back tears, horrified by my actions. I had never even been so much as cross with Ella, let alone nearly violent, and my eyes misted over. "Ella, I'm so sorry, I don't know what's going on. I—"

Skylahr.

My knees buckled and I fell to the earth with my hands clasped over my ears. The sound of my name whispered through my mind brought a burning agony that had knocked the air from my lungs.

Skylahr.

I groaned as I clutched at the back of my skull, my fingers fisting my hair as the throbbing intensified. Clenching my eyes shut, I sobbed through my suffering. Warm fingers grasped at the back of my neck, but the usual comfort they brought had been replaced with a scorching that was so strong, it felt as if they were burning my flesh. As if I was being branded again.

Balor is coming.

He is coming for you and it will be the end of the Huntress once and for all.

Pressing my forehead against the moist earth, I closed my eyes, praying that the Gods would make the voice and pain disappear. I prayed and I begged until all that was left was the crimson smile and the purple eyes that flashed behind my closed lids.

Chapter 38

Ella stood a distance away, her eyes wide and confused as I dragged myself to my feet. The pain had faded just as quickly as it had come, and I blinked up at my companions in confusion. They both remained stock-still, Marissa standing just behind Ella, and I realized they were fearful of me.

"El, I'm sorry," I apologized again but she looked doubtful. How could I blame her? I had apologized over and over and yet I had still treated her poorly. Reaching out a hand to her, I waited for her fingers to slide across my palm, and then my eyes focused on her dark skin before I looked at her beautiful face. "Truly, I am sorry. I don't know what happened."

Her fingers threaded through my own, her grasp firm as she held my hand before turning to Marissa. Locking eyes with the smaller woman, I tried to smile reassuringly though it felt more like a grimace, and I wondered what they must think of me. What they must have felt when they watched me sobbing on the forest floor.

"Are you okay now?" Marissa was timid, nervousness sliding across her face, and I swallowed before nodding silently. I had no explanation, no reason for why or what had happened, and I was too uneasy to tell them of the eyes I had seen through the pain. Turning on my heel, I continued on, ignoring the way the women hesitated behind me. I was too focused on the voice still whispering in my mind.

The ache in my head was still present for days after the first incident. It was always just hovering there, in the space behind my eyes, no matter what I did to cure it, and with it came an unbridled anger that I was scrambling to control. I had tried to distance myself from the women, but Ella's troubled gaze never left me. I hated how she hovered, as if she was just waiting for me to crumble again.

Growling at the rabbit I had been skinning, I tossed my dagger and fisted the fur, holding it out for the immortal. "If you want to spend time standing around watching me, you could make yourself useful."

Her brows fell as she glared at my tone, but she snatched the rabbit from my fingers before grabbing at the dagger I had discarded. Turning from me, Ella squatted next to Marissa, taking the time to show her how to prepare the meat of the animal, and a longing echoed in my chest at the sight of the two of them.

The newly turned immortal had taken the halfling under her wing as my behaviour began to worsen over the days. My anger forced my companions to keep their distance, always waiting for me to snap or snarl at them for one thing or another. The first couple of times Ella had rushed to me in concern, feeling my face for a fever or some explanation as to why I had begun to act so out of character. But by now they just did their best to avoid me and my heated glares.

Rubbing at my forehead, I closed my eyes while trying to push the pounding away. Sleep had evaded me at night, and the exhaustion had begun to settle in my bones. Drowning in weariness, I hadn't noticed Ella pausing, her dagger midair as she tilted her head to the side.

"What is it?" Marissa called softly as Ella stood and retreated into the dark woods for a moment before scurrying back.

"Someone has made camp nearby."

"Someone?" I asked. "Or immortals?" Ella shrugged at me before packing our things carefully, leaving the dead rabbit on the forest floor.

"I can't be sure, but we should go." I stared at her mutely while the whispering filled my mind again.

Kill them. Find them and kill them all.

Rage began to swirl in my body and suddenly I was on my feet with the bow in my hands. "No."

The word broke from me before I could stop it. "No, I will not run." Refusing to flee again, I headed in the direction Ella had come from and raced through the trees.

The night was clear, and the moon lit my path as I scrambled through the branches that had sheltered us. Pushing through the brush, I continued until the smell of fire filled the forest, and when I could see the smoke, I quickened my pace, my hand grabbing at my bow that I had strapped to me after hunting. The orange flame was flickering in the distance and I ducked to the ground, crawling through the mud and leaves as I crept closer to them. There were three bodies curled in front of the fire, their backs turned to me as they slept peacefully, and my fingers wrapped around the wood of my weapon.

Kill them. Slay them. Destroy them.

The pounding was back and that voice that had been slithering in my mind echoed loudly. Completely consumed by the whispers, I hadn't noticed that my hands had lifted my bow, already taking aim at one of the bodies. My fingers shook as they held the weapon, but I couldn't release my hold, I couldn't stop.

Kill them, Skylahr.

Just as my fingers had begun to loosen, ready to let my arrow fly, a hand grabbed at my arm and pulled me back. Dazed, I blinked up at Ella's furious face, her dark eyes narrowing in on me before peering at the sleeping figures.

"What the fuck are you doing!?" she hissed at me before kicking my bow out of reach and I gaped at her. The pounding had vanished, as had the voice, and I was left confused.

"I—" My mouth opened, and I peered back at the camp before cradling my head in my hands.

"Those are humans, Skylahr! Humans, not immortals, not

Crimsons, and you were going to kill them." My eyes filled with tears as I turned to her helplessly.

"Something is wrong, Ella, something is happening." She knelt in front of me, her fingers hesitant before she cupped my face, her thumb running across my scar. Looking over her shoulder, I noticed Marissa had grabbed my weapon, her hands shaking as she held it to her chest, and I dropped my gaze in shame. I had nearly killed an innocent, had nearly ended a life, and I had no answer as to why. Tears spilled from my eyes as I choked back a sob.

"I couldn't stop myself, El. I don't know what is going on." I cried into her chest as she cradled my head against her. Her fingers stroked my hair gently as she hushed me. Taking in a deep, calming breath, I pulled from her before turning to the other halfling in apology.

Even though I was seemingly back to normal, I still felt unease as I realized I couldn't trust myself. Panicked that I would lose control again, I turned to my companions. "Tie my hands."

The words rushed past my lips, and I heard the gasp of surprise as Ella shook her head, refusing. "Ella, tie my hands. If I can't control whatever it is that is happening, I have to be restrained. Tie my hands."

But she stayed frozen, pain flickering in her eyes as she studied my own. Seeing the immortal's hesitation, Marissa knelt next to me. Her pale fingers pulled at a leather strap from the pack before they twisted the material around my wrists. Her eyes watched her hands work, never lifting as she tightened the strap until my wrists were secure, and then her gaze moved to my own.

"Thank you," I whispered to her, grateful that Ella was able to avoid the task. Rising to my feet, I looked over at the immortal and smiled half-heartedly.

"I'm okay." But Ella's expression never changed, and I knew she didn't believe my words. But then again neither did I.

The coast of Suideign Shores was stunning—deep rock cliffs dropped down to the shore and bright blue waves crashed against their walls. Everything was green and lush, and the salt air calmed the pain in my head.

During the entire length of our journey, Ella had continued to insist on releasing my wrists, but I held firm. I was not willing to put anyone at risk again, too fearful that I would harm her or Marissa. And now with the ringing in my skull, I was thankful that I had been so stubborn.

"Do we know where he would be?" Ella called over the heavy ocean winds, her hair blowing back in tangles as she searched the horizon.

"There is a cove just up ahead. It will be a steep climb down, but we will be well hidden. His house is at the bottom." It was an odd place for an immortal to live, and I grew doubtful as we journeyed closer to the ocean.

"I thought we were after the Healer's Chosen, not the Siren's." I turned my head to Marissa while she pointed to the path in the distance.

"I guess no one will look for him there." She shrugged before marching forward, leading us to the steep rock cliffs.

Marissa had been right, the narrow trail had been steep, and we all had nearly tumbled down the rock ledge numerous times before finally reaching the black sand of the shore. Running across the wet earth, Marissa ushered us along the coastline. Her strides were quick and sure, though the doubt grew and gnawed at me.

It's a trap.

The voice slid into my mind, and I clenched my eyes shut as I pushed it from my head. Ella must have noticed my discomfort, and she paused for a moment before grabbing at my bound hands, tugging me forward harshly.

"Skylahr, we have no time for this. We need to go."

Liar. Traitor.

I moaned quietly as the hammering continued, making me dizzy while I clumsily chased after them. Rounding a great wall of stone, Ella slid in the sand as she skidded to a stop, her arms stretched wide as she pushed Marissa behind her. Not understanding, I peered over her shoulder, my breath catching as I took in the monster that stood in front of her.

It was deep gold in colour, its legs long and muscled as it stood on all fours. It had a black mask that curled over its long muzzle, and the deep colour faded just below its brilliant bright ruby eyes. Watching the enormous dog carefully, I stiffened as its black lips curled over three rows of teeth and the fur along its shoulders stood on end.

"You didn't tell us he had a failinis," I whispered in suspicion as the giant dog approached us carefully, its eyes locking on my own as he stalked closer.

We waited, completely frozen as its long legs carried it forward with so much grace it appeared as if it was floating. My eyes roamed across its golden fur until I noticed a shimmer. With each step forward, silver bounced off its chest, as if a metal token was hanging from its neck. I narrowed my eyes on the item, ignoring the deep growl that rumbled from its throat.

"That is enough, Reif," a deep male voice called, and I lifted my gaze to the figure who had appeared. His thick dark curls blew in the wind as he lifted a hand to shield his eyes from the sun. He was well built, though not quite as tall as me, and unbearably handsome. His skin was a few shades darker than mine, and I watched as his eyes narrowed in on my bound hands.

"Are you—" His words stopped suddenly as he stared at my face, his eyes widening as the sun shone on my scar. "Gods almighty. It's you."

Healer.

The voice hissed and I watched as he approached me, his eyes wide as if he'd heard the sound. The dog, who had been guarding him, followed closely, it too only having eyes for me, and I held my breath as they closed the distance.

"Gaelon," Marissa greeted the man calmly, her voice warm with familiarity. "This is Skylahr."

But the man paid her no mind; he was too focused on my face. Grabbing at my hands, he unbound them quickly, and his touch almost seemed to sooth the pounding in my head.

"How long have you been suffering?" His voice was deep, and I swallowed as he rubbed his rough palms across my wrists.

"It was her idea, Gaelon. We were sure not to tie them too tightly." But again, he ignored Marissa, his fingers stroking my skin, and I noticed that the flesh under his hands tingled pleasantly.

"How long has she been in your mind?" One of his arms lifted, his fingers curling over my jaw as he looked up into my face, and I couldn't stop myself from nuzzling into his palm, seeking out the comforting touch that seemed to quiet the thrashing in my head. "How long have you been marked?"

But before I could answer him, my attention was pulled to the cold, wet nose that pressed against my hand as it hung limply at my side. I took a step away from the stranger quickly, fearful of the teeth that sat in his pet's mouth. "He won't harm you. He's here for you. We've been waiting."

Not understanding, I peered down at the dog, studying the great creature as it sat back on its haunches. Holding my eyes captive with his own ruby orbs, he lifted his head high, baring his chest to me, and I saw the shining again. Carefully kneeling down in front of him, I raised my fingers, holding them in the air for a moment before stroking its fur softly. The tips moved through the soft stands carefully until they caught on a metal chain, and I gently lifted it over his head before holding it in front of my face.

There in the sunlight hung a shining thick silver ring, its form spinning in a swift circle as it dangled from the delicate metal chain. I gasped when I realized what, or rather whose it was.

"What is it, Skylahr?" Ella knelt next to me, her hand reaching out to touch the ring softly.

"It's my father's ring."

Once the shock faded and I was able to move, Gaelon ushered us into his home quickly, paying close attention as I winced at the pain in my head. He pushed a chair at me as I wobbled on my feet. Falling gracelessly into the wood, I clutched my father's ring in my palm and glared at the man with suspicion. But he offered little explanation for both the failinis or how he came to wear that chain around his neck.

Instead, Gaelon seemed much more focused on the pain in my head. He sat next to me, his knees brushing my thigh as his hands hovered around my brow.

"May I?" He waited only a second before he pressed his hands against my forehead and with his touch came waves of soothing warmth.

"What are you doing?" Ella whispered from my side, and I peered at her from the corner of my eye.

"This pain in her is not just unusual, it's dark magic. When they marked her, they used the Goddess's power. The seal is not a scar, it is a window into her mind, connecting her to the Seductress herself."

Fools.

The word was barely a whisper, but I knew Gaelon sensed it too when his fingers flinched away from my skin. Fear pressed into me as I pulled away from the Healer's Chosen, my eyes wide in terror. "A window? She can watch us then?"

His warm brown eyes held my stare as he grasped at my fingers. "It's complicated, but yes, if she has found a way in and you're not careful, she can spy on you. She could even make you do things that are out of your control."

My eyes flickered to Ella as we both thought back to the incident with the sleeping humans and my anger over the last few days. "What do you mean find a way in?"

Gaelon leaned away as his eyes traced my face. "She uses a person's hurt and heartache to chip at their defenses. Sadness and anger can create a void in someone's mind and she waits for them to be lost in their suffering before she begins to sliter her way in ."

My eyes misted and I knew immediately how she had managed to find a way into my mind. I knew what had created a crack in my heart and now I hated him even more for making me weak. Sensing my distress, Gaelon reached for my hand and patted it gently before he smiled. "But a window works both ways, Skylahr."

"What do you mean?" I whispered, not understanding.

"She may be able to see into your mind, your heart, but you can change that. I can teach you to keep her at bay, to keep her from your thoughts. And I can also show you how to use this power against her. You can learn to enter her mind as well. You could learn to stop her. For good."

My mind spun, my vision blurring, and I heard the faintest of whispers.

We shall see, Healer.

Chapter 39

Gaelon had been patient with me and we had spent hours and hours trying to get my mind to focus on the Seductress, but all I had managed were flashes. Small pictures of random inconsequential things, and my frustration was building.

"You're not fully focused." Even though his words were meant to be scolding, his voice was still the same deep, kind tone.

Standing from my chair, I began to pace in front of him like some sort of caged animal. My strides were long and harsh, and I could feel her anger and rage building inside me.

Silly little fools.

Interrupting me, Gaelon grabbed at my face, brushing the tips of his fingers across my cheeks as he willed the thundering away with his touch.

"How do you do that?" I whispered, my eyes still closed as the muscles in my jaw relaxed. The tingling across my skin was gentle, and I pressed into his hands as he took a step back, unwilling to let the comfort leave.

"I'm the Healer's Chosen, it's my gift." Blinking my eyes open, I gazed down into his face.

"Do all Chosen have a gift?" *He* had been able to shift into a wolf, but so had the rest of the immortal Lupines.

"Who do you think created that barrier at the Lupine territory?"

I could picture the shimmering air of the border in my mind, and I finally understood why the Crimsons had been unable to cross it.

Not for much longer.

The voice had become stronger, more frequent as we had attempted to enter her own mind, and now I wished we hadn't attempted it. Pressing my cheek into Gaelon's palm, I pushed the whispers away.

"So you know about the Protector's Chosen?" I asked, refusing to use his name as I slumped back into my chair. The Lupine alpha had told us no one else knew, that it had been a secret. However, it wasn't as if he had been truthful with anything else so this lie should not have surprised me.

"I do." He nodded, his eyes watching me carefully. "Though I believe I am one of the few who are aware."

"And the shield protecting Denimoore, that is his gift?" I had seen the magic of the veil for myself, but I had never linked it to Kalian or the fact that he was a Chosen.

"Not just the border, Skylahr, he may also be able to shield those around him as well. Though it is much more difficult." My eyebrows rose in surprise and I tried to remember any mention of his shield having this power but when I pictured his face, a musical giggle echoed in my mind and I clenched my jaw in pain.

"When did this start?" Gaelon asked as his fingers stroked my brow bone.

When did this start? I wondered. Not knowing, I thought back through each excruciating headache I had been forced to endure and tried to pinpoint the first time I had truly heard the voice.

Kill him.

The only feeling that was stronger than the pain in my head was the sharp ache in my heart, and my fingers clawed at my chest as I remembered the first whispered words. Inhaling shakily, I dropped my eyes.

"When he—he—" Tears filled my vision and I swallowed a sob as I bent at the waist, pushing my head to my knees while cold flooded my chest. A warm hand caressed my spine and I gasped before unfolding my body.

"*Fix this,*" I begged and I grabbed for one of his hands before pressing it to my chest. My heart thundered under his palm and I wondered how that was possible. Surely it should be stopping if it was in this much pain. "Fix this. *Please.*"

His dark eyes widened as he finally understood. "I can't. I can't heal a broken heart." Lifting my hands, I grabbed fistfuls of my hair and clenched my eyes shut trying to block out the agony.

"Push her out, Skylahr. Don't let her see what hurts you." His breath was warm against my ear and I grabbed at him as her voice echoed.

Too late, Healer. I've already seen it.

Flashes of silver eyes and tan skin filled my mind as more and more memories crept forward. I could see the parchment with his face drawn over it, the words Ella had told me as she stared into my eyes, panicked. Then the muscled shoulders as they swayed above me, his head thrown back as he called out my name in passion.

I've seen it all, young Huntress.

Clenching my jaw shut, I closed my eyes and willed her from my mind as I scrambled to block the memories. Focusing on my body, I relaxed each muscle in the same way Keyno had taught me when we had practiced igniting. Starting with my toes, I worked up to my shoulders and quieted my mind. I could feel her anger at being pushed out and distracted by her rage, though she hadn't noticed she had left a link open. It was the barest of glimmers, but it was there, and I used everything in me to fling it open.

The image was blurry, as if I was trying to peer through some sort of fogged glass, but I could make out the shape of a man hidden in the shadows of the dark room.

"*Mistress, are you sure? Splitting your magic in this way is permanent. Creating a Chosen would mean he would not only have some of your gifts, he would be a part of you. A half of you.*" The voice echoed from the man and I could feel anger bubbling around us as her delicate hand lifted, nails scratching across his face in punishment.

"*Do not question me again, Luka. Creating a Chosen means that I will be able to preserve my magic. They will be fundamental in our plans.*"

The man's grey eyes widened before his hand lifted to wipe at the wounded cheek. Bowing his head sharply, he stepped away.

"Yes, mistress."

Things flashed quickly then. Just swift images one after the other, and I sifted through them to the best of my ability. None seemed of importance until I found one with a dark-headed man tied to a table. His mouth was gagged as he struggled in his bonds and he blinked up at me.

"It is necessary, my sweet Balor. In order for you to harness your true potential, you must be an immortal." The man watched as my pale hands grabbed at a blade, his body trembling in fear as I lifted it high above his chest.

"It will be over soon, and then you will be forever my Chosen. You will lead my Crimsons to Elrin and rid the land of the Huntress and her friends and then we shall find the others."

The metal plunged down and just as the tip pushed into his chest, the link was sealed, and I leaned back in my chair as I gasped for breath. Gaelon's fingers pressed against my cheeks, his eyes level with my own as he searched my face.

"What? What is it, Skylahr?"

My throat tightened as I swallowed twice and then I whispered the words.

"Balor, he's her Chosen. She's created her own Chosen."

Chapter 40

"Tell me again what you saw." Sighing in exhaustion at his demand, I sank deep into my chair as I thought back to the vision.

"I didn't see much, just flashes and bits and pieces. She told a man that she needed to preserve her magic and splitting it was fundamental. Then there was the dark-haired man tied to a table." I closed my eyes as I conjured the image in my mind. "Then she told the dark-haired man that it was necessary, and it would make him her Chosen forever and he would lead her forces. She called him Balor."

"And that was it?"

I glared at the Healer as I tipped my head back. "What else were you expecting?"

Gaelon paced across the floor as he ran his fingers through his dark curls. Ella and Marissa had both turned in for the night, their bodies huddled on the floor near the fire, and I was left with the Healer, who continued to berate me. Sighing, I watched as he moved gracefully while I stroked the golden fur of the dog who leaned against me. Reif had nestled against my thigh as he settled, and I was momentarily distracted by the great beast.

"Where did he come from?" Gaelon turned on his heel and narrowed his eyes at me for a second as my fingers scratched behind the dog's ears.

"Who?"

Gesturing to the dog impatiently, I raised a single brow. I knew it was poor timing, but the questions nagged at me.

"That's what you are worried about?" Shrugging, I looked at the Healer, and he frowned before running a hand down his face. "I have no idea, but we have more pressing matters, don't you think?" He was right of course, but I fingered the ring that now hung from my neck silently in thought.

"So he came with this?" I whispered before stroking the fur again, smiling as Reif snuggled against my legs.

"Yes, Skylahr. He did. Now can we get back to the task at hand, please?" His voice was exasperated, and I looked back up at his handsome face.

"Sorry, yes." Grabbing the chair across from me, he pulled the wood close and sat with his knees brushing against mine. Ignoring the warning growl that vibrated from the golden fur, he lifted a hand and pressed it to my temple.

"I will try my best to keep the pain at bay, but I need you to try to focus. Really focus. We need to get as much information as we can if we want to be prepared." Closing my eyes, I searched my mind for any hint of the link. There was no voice, no echo of words, and yet I did not feel truly alone.

"It's there, a presence, but I can't reach it," I whispered, flinching when his fingers pressed against my skin.

"Think of the window, Skylahr. It goes both ways, even if one side is fogged. Feel for an opening, any opening, and then push your way through it." But it wasn't that easy; the lock was not on my side, and the Seductress had been careful not to open the connection after I had seen her meeting with that man.

"How can we get her to check in on us?" I whispered as my lashes fluttered open. She had been a constant voice in my head since I had sent him away, surely she would linger if she thought there was something of interest, something that could help her cause.

"What do you mean?" Gaelon lowered his hand from my face and I searched around the small house.

"Well, she knows we have found you; she knows that I have now found two of the Chosen, surely she would want to watch me?" Nodding his head, he looked around the room as well, as if something would jump out at him with an answer.

"What about pain?" I whispered as an idea gathered in my mind.

"Pain?" Gaelon sounded doubtful and I reached for my dagger.

"You said pain was how she got in in the first place, right? Surely if she felt pain and thought I was injured she would check?" Not waiting for an answer, I closed my eyes and focused hard on that link. Holding my dagger tightly, I carefully nicked the inside of my forearm with the edge and waited. When nothing happened, I opened my eyes and groaned in frustration.

"I don't think a tiny cut will do it." He was right; the cut was already healing, and I knew she wouldn't be worried about that. Looking at my dagger, Gaelon grabbed at my wrist and hauled me closer, pushing the blade against his right shoulder before nodding. My mouth opened in concern, but words left me as he pierced his skin harshly and I groaned out in pain, and then there, in the back of my mind, was a tiny flicker of interest. I seized the opportunity quickly before she caught on.

I could hear the sound of waves and gulls, and I clenched my eyes shut and pushed at the link until I found her voice again. It was sweet and airy, though the sound still left my blood cold. I held on to the link with all of my strength.

"They've gathered at Suideign Shores and have found the Healer. We need to find the others, Balor, before they do."

The handsome man knelt before her, his head bowed as he studied the ground. Thin pale fingers tucked under his chin and she pulled his face forward. His hair was still dark but seemed to be longer and his face was stunningly beautiful though it appeared more delicate and feline than it had before.

I watched as violet eyes flickered to her face, softening as her thumb stroked his cheek. *"And what shall we do with the Lupine and his Huntress mistress?"* he asked, his voice calm and smooth.

"Ready the battalion and march to Suideign Shores. I know you won't fail me, Balor."

Preoccupied with the vision, I had not been prepared for when the link slammed shut, the force knocking me backwards. Pain radiated through my skull as I gasped for breath.

"What did you see?" Gaelon had grabbed at my shoulders, and I noticed both Ella and Marissa had herded in close behind. They all focused their eyes on my face as I caught my breath, waiting for me speak.

"They're coming."

The impending threat hung heavily over the shores, and Gaelon's concern grew as the days passed. After speaking to Ella and Marissa, we had agreed to stay and aid the Healer in any way we could. The week following the vision of Balor had been filled with a flurry of activity as Gaelon wrote letter after letter, sending each one out with a trusted messenger. It seemed that Suideign Shores had not only been a home to the Healer's Chosen, but to immortal allies as well, and with a quick message, they had rallied.

Reif's huge body pressed against me, his golden coat warm against my hip as he watched the newest visitors, and I leaned into him while Gaelon spoke to the other immortals.

"There are only seventy of them," Ella whispered to me, her eyes never leaving the massive dog's frame as she observed him fearfully. "Even if they are combat ready, we don't stand a chance."

Scanning my eyes across the crowd, I felt my stomach fall as I realized how right she was. I had caught glimpses of the Crimson battalion, and there had been nearly two thousand of them. Peering at the newest additions, I prayed that the Gods would answer my call and we would somehow find a way to survive this.

Stroking the fur of the failinis, I turned my face to Marissa and watched in concern as she huddled away from the group. Even though she longed to be here, I hated that she was so anxious and forced into such a difficult situation. She wasn't ready to be around immortals, let alone a group as big as this, and I approached her quickly.

"Marissa, why don't you take Reif inside and get some food? He could use a break, I think. He's uncertain of all these people."

She looked at the dog before nodding her head, the barest hint of a smile pulling at her mouth, and she reached a hand out for me. "Thank you."

Watching as the petite woman scurried back to the house, I turned to Ella. "We should make camp away from the others tonight. Give her some room," I whispered, motioning to the space around us. She too had seen how difficult it was for the young halfling and nodded her head in agreeance.

"How are you feeling? Has she said anything else?" I tried not to roll my eyes at the change of topic and sighed heavily. The Seductress had been quiet since she smothered the link between us, and though I knew I should be concerned, it had allowed me to relax as I finally felt like I was in control of myself.

"Nothing. My head is clear, but I wish I had seen where exactly they were coming from. It was somewhere on the coast, for all we know she's just miles away."

Ella's dark eyes scanned the ocean and shore around us. "But you said she was looking for the others. What did that mean?"

"I'm assuming she was talking about the Jester's and Siren's Chosen. *He* had said one would not be enough." Ella frowned when I did not mention the Lupine alpha by name, but she left it alone.

"And that Balor person?" I pictured the sharp face and bright violet eyes as I thought back to the vision.

"He is her Chosen." Gaelon had forced me to sit and explain in detail exactly what I had seen when I pushed through the link. I described the man as well as I could. I recited her words and what she had done to the man only to freeze when I saw how the Healer looked at me. It would appear that his scouts had been correct.

"Gaelon said that when she had learned about the Huntress and her prophecy, she began to search for a way to do the same. If what I saw is true, then she has found a way to split her magic and created him."

Sighing, I scanned the shore for Gaelon, seeking out his handsome face. He had been busy the last few days as he managed to organize his fellow immortals, planning and deliberating like a true war general while we had stood aside. It seemed he had been preparing for this day for centuries and I was overwhelmed by the very thought.

"How does it feel to be the Chosen of the Huntress?" Of course, it had been inferred but this was the first time Ella had spoken the words so plainly.

"It feels like I am going to be crushed into the ground with all of the pressure." I had been denying it, even when Gaelon had confronted me, refusing to believe I could be part of the legends, part of the Goddess my people had worshipped for hundreds of years. I tried to assure him he was mistaken, that they all were, but he wouldn't allow it.

"She herself called you Huntress," he had said. "It's time to stop running and accept it." It had been the first time he had spoken to me with severity and his tone left no room for my protests.

"Skylahr!" My name echoed around me, breaking my thoughts, and I lifted my face towards him. Gaelon stood, his hand lifted as he motioned me forward, and I turned towards him, taking two strides before the wind was knocked out of me.

Peering over his strong shoulder were a pair of deep brown eyes and their warmth filled my chest with hope as I gasped. Her pale face was lifted in a great smile, and I felt a sob of happiness push past my lips as I ran towards her. Spreading my arms, I pulled her smaller body to my chest, soaking in her rich laughter as her fingers gripped me tighter.

"Hello, Sky." Elizabeth's voice was soft as she kissed my cheek and my knees buckled, sending us to the sand as I crushed her to me.

Chapter 41

The immortals had gathered around us as I pressed my face into Elizabeth's hair, shielding myself with the curtain of brown while we sat in the sand. We held each other for what felt like ages, only pulling back when I sensed Ella behind me. Her concern was coming off her in waves, and I finally moved to smile at her tearfully.

"This is Elizabeth," I explained plainly, unable to form any other words, and I watched as her dark eyes widened before they turned to the woman I held.

"It's nice to finally meet you," Ella offered and Elizabeth smiled at the immortal, her face welcoming, and it was then I noticed the differences. Elizabeth had always been beautiful, but the last few months had not been kind and she seemed small and thin. Softening my arms around her, I pulled away as my eyes scanned her for any injuries.

"What happened? How did you end up here? How did you escape the Crimsons?" My voice was a hoarse whisper and Elizabeth's warm brown eyes glittered wetly as she swallowed before grabbing at my hands.

"Just before the Crimsons stormed the gates your father came to me. He told me I needed to run, I needed to leave immediately, and then he gave me this." Her fingers lifted to trace the metal ring that hung from my neck, and my head fogged with the news.

"I had just made it through the hole in the barrier when the Crimsons breached the wall. But I had no direction, no idea where to run to or where to find you until I remembered the Swallows. I thought that if I could find the witch, I could ask her if she had any idea as to where you had gone. It took me days to locate that godsforsaken cottage, but when I did Reif was waiting for me." Elizabeth reached out a pale hand and stroked his golden fur before focusing back on my face. "The witch, well, she was there too, though she was much more terrifying than you described." I wiped at my face before laughing softly and nodded my head in agreement.

"She knew why I was there and seemed to know exactly what was happening in the village. She told me to give the beast your father's ring and that she would send him to where he needed to be. Then she pulled a glass jar of blood from a shelf, stuffed it under Reif's nose, and spoke some words in the old tongues before ordering him away. Once he was gone, she told me to head south to the shores of Suideign and I would find the answers I sought."

"Did my father tell you anything else before you left? Did he know why Crimsons had come?"

Elizabeth sighed, her shoulders sagging as she studied my face.

"He told me that you were a halfling. He told me that your blood father had been killed only weeks after you were unknowingly conceived. That he and your mother were already half in love by the time she found out you were in her belly, and they married as soon as she had told him." My father and I had always been close, inseparable even, so the idea that he knew I was not only another man's child, but an immortal man's child stunned me.

"So Alden—" My words were cut off by a sob.

"He was your father in all ways that mattered, Sky, and he adored you." My lower lip trembled, and I rubbed at my chest as the weight began to crush me. Inhaling sharply, I gathered my courage and I finally asked the question that had plagued my soul since that day in Noorde Point.

"Did he blame me?"

Elizabeth's eyes widened in shock at my question, and I twirled the metal ring around in my fingers while I avoided her gaze.

"Blame you? Why would he blame you?"

Wiping at my eyes, I inhaled weakly but was unable to answer her.

"Oh, Sky." Elizabeth threw her arms back around my shoulders, her hand stroking my hair as she soothed me. "Your parents would never blame you. Ever. He was so thankful that you had left, that you were somewhere far from there. That brought him peace, and I know they loved you every minute until the very end."

We spent the rest of the evening together, lounging in front of the fire while the immortals turned in for the night. I had wedged myself between Elizabeth and Ella, my heart lifting as I gazed into the crackling flames. Gaelon sat across from me with Reif's head in his lap, though I can't say for certain that the Healer was exactly pleased about that.

"Tomorrow we need to organize everyone and begin training. There are whispers that the battalion have reached Siren's Cove. If that is true, they will be here in a little over a fortnight." I absorbed Gaelon's warning, and I felt my face pale in worry. "We will be as ready as we can. Let us pray to the Gods it will be enough."

His eyes were downcast as he gazed off into the fire and I looked at my friends in concern. We had all felt the weight of what was to come press into us, me especially now that the immortals watched me so closely, their whispers following my every move. My three companions had shied from the attention, their guards always up whenever someone approached us, and I wondered if they saw me differently. Now that we knew who, or rather what, I was.

Turning to them, I noticed how exhausted they truly looked, and I tipped my head to the tent that had been set out for us. "Why don't you three head off to bed? I'll be there shortly."

Too tired to argue, Ella and Elizabeth pulled Marissa to her feet, and I watched as they vacated the shore before turning to Gaelon. "Is there another way for me to reach out to her mind? A way to see just exactly what we are dealing with?"

His dark eyes held mine for a moment before he sighed. "If she hasn't opened the link again, I am not certain you will have a way in unless we continue to injure ourselves. Her powers are strong and her shield stronger. We were lucky she was fooled before; I'm amazed you even managed to catch a glimpse. I can't see her making that mistake again."

"How do you know all of this?" I asked in surprise. He seemed to be a wealth of knowledge and I wondered where he had learned all of it.

"My eternal ceremony was over two hundred years ago. You learn a thing or two over that amount of time." I had known he was a Chosen, but it had never occurred to me that Gaelon was immortal. Tilting my head to the side, I parted my mouth, ready to ask my questions, but the Healer lifted a hand.

"Not now, there will be another time to discuss whatever questions you have. For tonight let's just focus on rest. You look pale and nearly dead on your feet." His eyes were soft as they traced my face, but I crossed my arms over my chest in annoyance.

"You know, I hate secrets. Truly despise them." Gaelon's lips tilted up in the corners before he stood and smoothed out his tunic. Then his brown eyes lifted, and he studied me for a long moment before his calm voice broke the silence.

"Everyone has secrets, Skylahr. That's just something you'll have to learn to accept." Without another word the Healer turned from me, and I was left wondering what he could be hiding.

Chapter 42

"You're an asshole," I grumbled at Ella as she pulled me back onto my feet.

"And you are a complainer who is barely trying." She laughed as she dusted the sand from my jerkin. We had been at this for hours, waking with the sun, and my body, though stronger now, began to protest as our sparring went on. Turning my head, I noticed Marissa swinging a long sword clumsily, her weak arms overpowered by the blade, and I prayed that we would have enough time to strengthen her accordingly.

"Alright, let's go again," Ella called as she crouched near the ground, her weight on the balls of her feet with one hand splayed in front of her while the other hovered behind her back. She looked like a cat who had stalked its prey and was now ready to pounce.

"What the hell are you possibly going to do to me standing like *that*?" But just as the words left my mouth, Ella was charging. Her tiny body moved quickly and with precision and within a second, I was flat on my back, coughing for air.

"Never mind! Never mind!" I rolled onto my stomach groaning as I pulled myself to my feet. "Gods almighty, what in hell did that ceremony do to you?"

"This is fun." She clapped her hands together, bouncing on her toes. "Let's go again."

"Let's not," I growled as I spat the sand out from my mouth. "Go find someone else to taunt with your special talents, you little nymph." Leaving her, I approached Elizabeth and Marissa, watching silently as they circled each other. What Marissa lacked in strength she made up for with confidence, and I smiled as she lunged for her opponent.

"Good!" I praised as she dodged Elizabeth's blade. "Try again." Marissa swallowed and tightened her jaw before charging, but this time her arms held the metal steady and I watched in fascination as her skill improved rapidly.

"Her ignite is coming, looks like she will have mastered it very soon." Turning to Gaelon, I lifted my brows in surprise before focusing back on the pair. I had never seen another halfling ignite and it truly was fascinating. Marissa had gone from sloppy and slow to swift and refined all within a few minutes and she was now easily beating Elizabeth.

"She's good, now that she has more strength," he observed and my eyes never left the pair as I nodded in amazement.

"I'm glad. One less halfling to worry about now that we have our hands full with the new ones."

The words made my head turn, and I missed Marissa knocking Elizabeth to the ground. "New ones? What new ones?"

Gaelon's dark eyes slid to the rock wall that hid his small home, and I noticed two dozen women standing around the base of the cliff as they huddled together.

"Nellie?" I whispered as my eyes narrowed while I focused in on the familiar halfling before I sprinted over to them. Sure enough, it was the same women we had parted ways with before heading to Suideign Shores, although now the number of them had more than tripled in size.

"Nellie?!" I called as I grew closer, and the halfling turned to me with a blinding smile.

"Skylahr!" Running at me, she threw her arms around my shoulders and held me tightly. Patting her back I peered at the unfamiliar faces. The majority of the group looked to be halflings, but there were a handful that had the sharp features and beauty that only immortals possessed.

"What are you doing here?" I asked, pulling back from her.

"The Healer sent word to Port Huronian and now we are here to fight." The women around her nodded, though I noticed the immortals had fully focused on me, and I did my best not to fidget under their attention.

"And who are your friends?" I asked, smiling at them gently while I tried to hide my awkwardness.

"Halflings like us and immortals who fight for the Huntress." As soon as the words had left her mouth, the women sank to the ground and bowed their heads as they knelt before me. Flustered I turned to Nellie, but she too had fallen to the sand, perched on one knee.

Heat flamed in the skin of my cheeks and I grabbed at the halfling, hauling her to her feet. "There is no need for any of that. Please."

Suddenly feeling panicked under their watchful gaze, I wiped my hands across my breeches nervously and searched for Gaelon. Finding him across the shore, I waved him over and reached out as he approached. Grabbing at his shoulders, I pulled him close and shoved him in front of me. "This is Gaelon, he will get you settled and answer any questions you have."

One dark brown rose at me as he grinned, and I glared at him before making my escape. I had not been prepared for the show of devotion. The idea that they believed I was someone who was worth bowing to made my chest tighten as I strode across the sand. Noticing my discomfort, Ella dropped the wineskin she had been drinking from and crossed the space between us.

"What is it, Sky?" Her head tilted and I watched as she scanned the area, her eyes widening as she took in the newest group to join us. "Are they—" She broke off, her eyes searching mine.

"Yes, they came in the name of the Huntress."

Exhaling noisily, she took them in, her eyes roaming across the group swiftly. "And by the sweat across your brow, I'm guessing they know you are her Chosen."

"They *bowed* to me." The word slithered out of me tightly, and I scowled at the very notion. Ella laughed loudly, her head tilted back as her body shook. Crossing my arms over my chest, I waited for her to collect herself before I whispered, "It's not funny."

Wiping the moisture from her eyes, she tried to hide her amusement and bit her lower lip.

"Skylahr. Only you would be absolutely appalled at the idea of utter fidelity. These women are here for their Goddess, and they have been waiting for you for centuries. Of course they knelt before you."

Sighing, I looked back at the group. "How do I get them to stop?"

Ella's second round of cackling was louder than the first.

My body ached as I snuck out from the flaps of our tent. It had been a long day of sparring and drills, as we attempted to strengthen our collection of immortals and halflings before the battalion of crimson came. Unable to sleep with the stress that weighed heavily down on my shoulders, I decided to find peace in the dark water. Padding barefoot across the sand, I pulled on the laces of my breeches, and I shed them quickly before grabbing at the hem of my cotton shirt.

"Wait!" a voice called to me, and I whirled around, my knees bracing for an attack as I took in the form of the intruder. Relieved to see that it was Gaelon, I relaxed my stance only to realize the state of my undress.

"What are you doing out here?" I hissed as I pulled at the cotton in an attempt to cover my thighs.

"I was trying to find some peace now that the day is done. That is until some halfling decided to wander out and strip in the open."

"I thought I was alone," I grumbled while glaring at him.

"Clearly." His dark gaze lingered on my bare legs for a long moment before he cleared his throat and moved his eyes to the ocean. Free from his stare, I took in his features under the brightness of the moonlight. He had a strong jaw, straight nose, and smooth skin. His curls were windswept and thick, and I couldn't help but think that though he was incredibly handsome, he exuded a quiet gentleness that was unmatched.

"Were you headed for a swim?" Turning my eyes from him, I gazed out over the calm bay.

"I needed to clear my head." Nodding, he smiled at me.

"I had the same idea." Biting my lip, I looked around. The fires had dimmed, and the site was quiet. Everyone else had retired for the night, thoroughly exhausted by the training, and I considered my options for a minute before extending the invitation.

"The water is more than big enough for both of us, would you want to join me?" His eyes lit in surprise and he smiled, though this grin was not one I had seen. His lips had lifted to one side and it was a smirk full of teasing.

"I also tend to swim without pants." His lips curled in the corners as his grin grew, and I rolled my eyes as heat tingled in my cheeks.

"Then I'll turn around and save you some embarrassment." Spinning on my heel, my hands went to the back of my shirt, pulling it down to cover the curve of my ass as I waited for him to enter the water. When I heard the gentle waves of his entry I turned around. Gaelon had made it waist deep, leaving his back on full display in the starlight, and I let my eyes wander across his skin. His shoulders were thick and heavily muscled, the skin smooth and unblemished, and I couldn't help but picture a jagged scar that would run down from shoulder to hip.

Pushing the thought away, I grabbed at my tunic and lifted it over my head before running to the cold sea. The tide was high, and I had to go only a few yards into the cool water before the gentle waves were lapping at my shoulders. Dunking my head under, I swam another few feet out to Gaelon before surfacing.

The Healer's eyes slid over my face, focusing on my seal for a second before he smiled. "How are you feeling?"

I wasn't sure if he meant physically or mentally but both seemed too complicated to answer so I shrugged, dropping my chin into the water shyly.

"It has been a lot to take in. I never thought we would be here. That we would find you and rally together like this."

Casting a glance at the tents that lined the shores, he sighed heavily.

"Do you think we stand a chance?" It was something that had been plaguing me for days. Even with our new allies and friends, it still seemed impossible, and I worried that these people would be sacrificing themselves for nothing.

"I don't know, Huntress, but I know we have to try. Her army has been in power for too long, too many people have suffered at their hands, and it is time someone tries to stop her." He took a breath, and his face relaxed as he watched me. "Not to mention we have you on our side."

Rolling my eyes, I splashed water at him. "Not sure I'm that much of an advantage."

Gaelon's brows lowered as he frowned at me, his body stilling in the water. "Surely you see just how skilled your abilities are? How incredible your gift is?"

"What are you talking about?"

"I have never witnessed someone with such a strong second nature for combat. When you actually focus and truly let yourself go I would swear you are unbeatable. I've seen just glimpses of it here, and it's enough to convince me that no one would be your equal. Though I shouldn't be surprised, her power runs through your veins."

My lips parted as I stared at him, shock curling through my mind at his words. Sure, when I focused, I was a decent swordsman, and I could hold my own, but I would never have suggested I could be unrivalled. Taking a pause, I thought back over the last few months and my mind lingered on the brief moments I had embraced my ignite. Had I not felt her power when I knocked Leena to the ground in Denimoore? Or when *he* and I sparred in Ferri? Yes, I did, but I had chalked it up to luck, or maybe circumstance. Not once had I thought it was anything more.

Picturing that day in the empty field, I felt my heart crack just a little, and when I went to meet Gaelon's questioning eyes, a sharp shooting pain slammed into my mind. The ache was so strong my vision blackened and my legs collapsed under me.

Darting to my side, Gaelon lifted my shoulders from the water before towing me to the shore. Once the majority of his body was out of the sea, he bent to swing me up into his arms, cradling me awkwardly to his chest as he pressed his lips to my ear.

"Hold on, Skylahr, hold on." Running to our clothes, he set me onto the sand. Ignoring my nudity, he cupped my face in his hands and stroked his thumbs along my jaw.

"Breathe, Skylahr." His touch lacked its usual soothing, and I groaned as another piercing wave rocked through me. Clutching my head in my hands, I leaned forward, bracing my weight on my forearms as I gasped for air.

Enjoy his pretty compliments and attentions, Huntress. It won't be long until Balor brings me your head on a spike.

Chapter 43

Gaelon's eyes followed me all morning, never lifting from my frame for longer than absolutely necessary, and I had begun to feel stir-crazy. Stretching my neck, I loosened my muscles before picking up the long sword that had been set aside for me. Marissa had finally convinced me to spar, and I grinned at her in encouragement as she examined the pommel of her own blade.

"Ready?" I called from across the makeshift ring. Nodding her head, she took up her position, and I gave her a moment to gather herself before I lunged. Eyes wide, she had just managed to lift her steel in time to block my blow from above, and I held my position, pushing down with my weight for a second before I danced back and allowed her to regroup.

Taking in a deep breath, she staggered back to a defensive stance and nodded again. This time, I did not come from above but rather cut at her from an angle, using only half my speed in order to give her a chance to defend herself. But she had anticipated my steps and met me halfway, blocking my pursuit. Smiling at her proudly, I stepped back and waited for her to come to me.

Her attacks were quicker than they had been previously, and I was impressed at her handling of the sword. Realizing I needed to up my efforts in order to keep her at bay, I shifted my weight and met her blow for blow.

Picking up speed, we danced around the entire ring, moving across the sand gracefully as our swords clashed back and forth. Out of the corner of my eye I could see a crowd gather, and I noticed Marissa had faltered a step as she realized just how closely she was being watched. Pausing, I lowered my weapon and approached her carefully.

"Pay them no mind, they are nothing. The only thing that matters is me and my blade." Biting her lip, she dipped her head once and I resumed my chase.

Once she had righted herself again, I observed her movements closely. It was as if something had flipped in her and her attacks had begun to build in power and pace. I grinned at her as we continued, and I watched in fascination as her normally dark eyes lightened to a golden brown.

"That's it! Now lean into it. Embrace it!" I cheered her on as she lunged for me again, her strength surprising me as she came down from above. "Good! Now breathe!"

I heard her gasp shakily and then it was as if her body just snapped together. The air around us shook for a moment and I stood, astonished as the power surrounding her seemingly disappeared into her skin.

"Marissa?" I called for her and waited until her eyes focused on mine, the colour still the light golden brown, and she smiled.

"Did I do it?" Her voice was high and hopeful, and her eyes welled with tears as she swallowed. Grinning at her, I nodded my head while my chest filled with pride.

"You did it!" I ran at her, wrapping her smaller frame in my arms, and we jumped for joy together. Totally lost in our own world, we hadn't noticed the newcomers that had gathered until a familiar voice called from across the shore.

"Looks like I've been replaced. Who would have thought my little Hazel would make such an excellent teacher." My head twisted to the side so fast my vision spun, and I winced at the dizziness as I stared at Keyno.

Noticing my expression, Gaelon mistook it for something worse and jogged to me. Cupping my cheek in his hands, he directed my eyes away from the Lupine. "Are you okay? Is it her again?"

But his voice was just a muffled noise in the background as my eyes locked on to the bright silver irises that watched me from across the beach.

"Sky?" Gaelon's thumb tipped my chin back towards him and I pulled from his touch as if it had scalded me.

"Yes, I'm fine. If you'll excuse me."

Without waiting for his response, I turned back to the Lupine and ran at him. Keyno smiled brightly as he lunged for me, lifting me up and hugging me tightly for a moment before he was shoving me into the next set of arms.

Isla's dark head rested near my shoulder as she held me firmly. She pulled away just enough to see my face, and I watched as her dark eyes moved over my cheek. "Oh, sweeting," she whispered as her fingers traced the healed skin.

Grabbing her delicate fingers, I removed them from my face and smiled down at her. Though she was clothed in a loose tunic and breeches, she was still the elegant Lady of Denimoore, and I bowed just slightly in the space she had allowed between us.

Swatting at my shoulder good-naturedly, she stepped back, and I turned to face her daughter. Leena was stunning in her deep blue tunic and brown jerkin; her hair had been pulled high and swung out behind her like a banner. Looking at me, her dark eyes also sought out the seal, but she remained silent, only dipping her chin in a nod before turning to her mate.

"Where is the little one?" Keyno asked while searching the camp for Ella. As if she had been summoned, the beautiful immortal strode across the sand. Her shoulders were straight as she held her head high, walking towards us until she stood shoulder to shoulder with me in a united front.

"What are you doing here?" she asked, her eyes darting from the trio then over to the alpha, who still stood a distance away.

"The Healer called on us and so we came." Keyno's head tilted in confusion, and I could see his concern as Ella's rage burned through her. Clenching her fingers into fists, Ella stepped forward, only stopping as I cupped her shoulder.

"El," I warned softly.

"They shouldn't be here. *He* shouldn't be here." Lifting my eyes to Kalian, I waited for him to say something, anything. But he remained silent as he observed us closely, his eyes watching Gaelon for a long moment before flickering to me.

Marissa, who had not moved from her place in the ring, flocked to my free side, sensing the growing tension, and she stood as tall as her short stature would allow while she stared down the Lupines and I began to worry a fight may break out if someone did not step in.

"Enough, Ella. It was me who invited them. They are not our enemy and we need every last able body we can get." Gaelon's voice had left no room for argument, and my two companions begrudgingly nodded their heads before turning back to the camp. Sighing as the air around me grew lighter, I smiled tightly at the trio before turning to the Healer.

"I think that's enough for me today. Mind if I cut the training short?" I gestured to Keyno and Leena. "These two are much more capable than I am when it comes to training. They would be an excellent addition."

Gaelon grabbed at my wrist and pressed two fingers to my temple gently. "Are you sure you're okay? After last night I'm worried."

"What happened last night?" *His* deep, smooth voice echoed around us and sent a shiver down my spine. Holding my breath, I glared at him from the corner of my eye before focusing on the Healer's face.

"I'm fine, just exhausted. I only need to rest." Pulling away from the group that had gathered, I strode back to the tents and promised myself I would not look back at the silver eyes that followed me.

That afternoon the scouts had sent word that the Crimsons had made it north of the shores and were a day's ride away. The news had brought a hush over the camp and reality set in. We had been training for weeks, gathering as many supporters and allies as possible, but looking over at them all now, I wasn't convinced it would be enough.

Standing on the cliff high above the coastline, I overlooked the camp and felt an ache in my chest as I smiled sadly. Our forces had scattered across the beach, the group enjoying what may be their last night together. These people had come out from hiding, finally ready to face the world, and we had all but condemned them to a bloodbath. I crouched down and sat on the damp earth as my legs dangled over the cliff's edge.

"What are you doing up here, halfling?" Leena called for me, her hair blowing in the wind as she approached, stunning me with her beauty.

"Nothing." It wasn't a lie, not really. I just didn't know how to express my worries without sounding cowardly.

"I hear you are the Huntress's Chosen. Congratulations." Sighing, she fell to the ground beside me gracefully and scanned the beach.

"I'm not sure it's something to congratulate me for."

"No." She paused, tilting her head in thought. "But what you are doing here is."

Not understanding, I turned my eyes to her face, waiting for her to elaborate. Leena rolled her eyes before falling back, her hair spilling across the grass as she looked up at the night sky. "You've gathered these people; you've inspired them to risk their lives for a better world. No one has been able to do that. Not since the war."

Laughing dryly, I mimicked her position and blinked up at the stars. "You give me too much credit. I haven't done anything."

"You don't even realize it because it's just who you are. But people can sense your goodness, your love and loyalty. They don't need pretty words. They need an example and you've done that for them."

Narrowing my eyes at her, I rose onto one arm so I could peer down at her face. "Have you been drinking?"

Snorting with laughter, Leena shoved my shoulder. "No, you idiot,

I have not been drinking. But listen, if you tell anyone how nice I'm being, I will have my wolves rip you apart. And trust me I could. There are close to a thousand of them, I'm sure I could convince at least one."

Gaelon had mentioned the number of Lupines had exceeded his expectations, but I hadn't been told so many had come. I had yet to venture to the valley where they had camped in fear of seeing their alpha. Falling back into the earth, I blinked up at the night sky.

"A thousand? I had no idea."

"Our best soldiers, our generals, and most of the lords and ladies, with the exception of Nadine, of course. Mother wouldn't hear of it. Not with her officially being the future Lady of Denimoore and all." She scoffed in disgust before rolling her eyes. "Maybe I'll be too injured to make the mating rite."

"Mating rite?" I whispered, too afraid to assume what she meant.

"It's like a wedding, but there's more to it." Leena sighed as she closed her eyes.

"How could there be more to it?"

"The couple intertwines their very beings together. They truly become one, for life."

The words knocked the air from my lungs, and I froze for a long moment as I tried to process. Kalian planned to mate Nadine. He had held me, touched me, made me believe I was something of importance to him, and now he was planning a life with her. Sensing the change in my mood, Leena rolled to her side.

"No one told you?" I shook my head silently before dragging myself to my feet. "Oh, Skylahr, I didn't know. I'm sorry."

Waving her off, I wiped my hands across my breeches, suddenly feeling like my world was closing in. I had no right to be upset. I had no reason to feel this crushing hurt. He had never been mine, nor I his. He had betrayed me, and I sent him away. I was meant to hate him. So why did I feel as if my chest had split open?

"I should head back. Gaelon is probably looking for me." I turned back to the Lupine, knelt in front of her, and threw my arms around her shoulders. Holding her tightly against me, I waited until I felt her arms close in around my middle.

"Sleep well, Leena. If I don't see you tomorrow, please be safe." Without waiting for a response, I pulled away from her and ran down the steep path, putting as much distance between us as possible.

The waves were thundering as they crashed onto the sand, and I watched as the groups of people slowly disappeared into their tents. Deciding I needed a distraction, I searched the shore for my companions. Spotting Ella and Elizabeth, I approached them but froze when I noticed the dark hand wrapped around the pale fingers as Ella pulled Elizabeth towards her tent.

They giggled together as they crossed the sand, their bodies moving towards each other as if they were being pushed by an invincible force, and I smiled when I heard Ella's laugh echo across the beach. Though I was surprised, I was glad to see that they would not be alone tonight.

"Where have you been?" Gaelon called to me as he slowly approached. Seeing where my eyes had landed, he laughed quietly. "I'm surprised you hadn't noticed sooner; they've been making eyes at each other all day."

Turning to him in surprise, I was suddenly taken aback by his beauty. He was in a simple grey cotton tunic that plastered itself to his muscular chest as the ocean breeze blew around us. His dark curls were falling across his forehead, and the moon illuminated his sharp jaw.

"Sky?" I hadn't noticed he had called on me until his fingers jolted me from my daze as they brushed across my wrist. "Are you okay?"

I didn't know. Not truly. I couldn't remember the last time I had been. Maybe before the fever and the witch and her warning. Before my world had come crashing down and I was left alone. Before I had trusted, only to be betrayed. Before I had let the wrong person close, giving them my heart only for him to crush it into pieces.

"I don't know," I whispered honestly.

His lips rose on one side sadly and he nodded before lifting a hand to stroke my marked cheek. "Me either."

Something tugged at me as I watched his smile fall and before I could stop myself, I was cradling his face in my hands. Brushing my thumbs over his jaw, I tipped it up just slightly before bending down to meet him, slanting my mouth over his gently. It was soft and sweet and brought a glimmer of warmth to my chest, but nothing more. Pulling away from him, I stepped back and nodded my head silently before heading to my own tent. I was a coward for running, but there was too much rattling in my head, and I couldn't find the courage to stay and face him.

Crossing the sand quickly, I felt the heat of *his* stare and I knew the alpha had seen everything.

Chapter 44

The morning was heavy with rainfall, and the noise of it echoed through Gaelon's home as I studied my reflection. Isla stood behind me, her hands moving quickly as she twisted my waves into small braids before weaving them together down the middle of my back. Leena, who had remained silent, dipped her fingers into the black paint before running the tips under my tired eyes.

I sighed for what had to have been the tenth time, and I turned my gaze to my friends. The three of them were all huddled against the table, their faces pale as they fastened their breastplates and vambraces. The metal did not fit well, but it would offer them some sort of protection against the Crimsons' blades. And though that should bring me some comfort, I still shuddered at the thought that today they would face the Seductress's army.

"You look like a true warrior deity." Isla bent next to my head, smiling at me in the mirror, and I hummed under my breath. She was wrong, of course. I looked like a terrified, stupid girl who was playing pretend. Patting the hand that cupped my shoulder, I smiled at her.

"Thank you, Isla. For everything." Her dark eyes filled with tears and she squeezed me tightly before resting her forehead against my temple. Using one hand to comfort her, I reached for Leena with the other. The young Lupine eyed it warily before stepping forward, joining us in our embrace.

Blinking my eyes open, I met Ella's gaze and motioned the three women over, and there in the middle of Suideign Shores, in a tiny little home, I found myself surrounded by more friendship than I would have ever thought possible. I wrapped my arms around the group of women, holding them to me for a long moment before a pounding on the door disturbed us.

Turning my face towards the sound, I noticed a look shared between the Lupines, and my stomach dropped. Grabbing at the others, Leena led them out quickly, their bodies blocking the visitor from my sight, and I watched Isla with scrutiny.

"It is not just his gift, but ours as well. Please accept it," she whispered before pressing a kiss to my cheek. Not understanding, I stood and turned to follow her out, but froze when the dark head of hair ducked through the door, his frame filling up the entire entryway of the tiny house. Taking him in, I felt my throat tighten as his magnificent jaw lifted and his silver eyes bore into mine.

"Skylahr." My name sounded like both a plea and a prayer, and I inhaled sharply as he took another step forward. His tunic was soaked through, his hair dripping, and the bath in Ferrii flashed through my mind while I studied a pearl of water as it slid down his face.

"Kalian." It was the first time I had spoken his name out loud since sending him away, and the sound of it cracked my heart. We stood in silence; the air around us twisted with both longing and resentment, but I didn't know which one burned stronger.

"I've brought you something." His head dipped, gesturing to the roll of fabric that was cradled in his arms, and he moved to lay it across the table. I crossed my arms around my middle and refused to take a step closer as he unrolled the wool.

"It is from the elves in Braighdean, forged in their fires. They made it especially for you, their Huntress." Narrowing my eyes, I lifted my chin to peer at the package splayed across the table from where I stood. The metal was stunning, its colour a vibrant forest green with delicate gold details, and I took a step closer without realizing it.

It had to be the most stunning suit of armour I had ever seen, and

I raised my eyes to his in question. "Why?"

"Why?" he repeated. "Why what?"

"Why did you bring me this?" My eyes traced the shining metal of the helm. It was the same green as the rest with gold lining the sharp edges of the cheek pieces and nose guard. But the most astonishing part of the piece were the two twisted gold vines that protruded from either side, their shape forming antlers.

"I told you it was a gift." My fingers lifted to stroke the breastplate, flinching at the cool softness. It was unlike anything I had seen. It was not the same heavy thick metal I had associated with armour; it was nearly paper thin and supple, like it was made of magic. But then again if it truly came from the mythical elves in Braighdean, it was.

"I can't accept this." It wasn't just that the armour was more than I could ever dream, it was the fact that there were people just outside the door who had nothing. No helm, no breastplate, some barely had a weapon. We had to arm the majority of the immortals with daggers and scrap blades we had collected from the blacksmith.

"You can and you will." I opened my mouth to argue but Kalian glared down at me as he took a step closer. "You are the one with a target on their back. They are hunting for you and I will be damned if you walk into that battle vulnerable. I will not have it. Curse me, hate me. I don't care. Not if it means you have a chance of making it out of this alive." My eyes widened as he stared down at me, his silver orbs burning to molten steel, and my lips parted under his gaze.

"One more thing." Breaking the hold, he turned back to the table. Long fingers extended until they curled around a pommel of a blade and he lifted it from its wool cover. "This belonged to your Goddess."

I reached for the gold hilt, my fingers shaking as the tips slid across the cold metal. It was stunning. Its blade was long and balanced, the steel feeling as if it was an extension of my arm. I looked back at the Lupine.

"Kalian, I—" But my words were cut off as his mouth crashed to mine. He took the sword from my hand and dropped the blade to the ground before twisting his fingers into my braided hair. A searing heat bloomed through my chest as he tipped my head back, giving himself a better angle to slide his tongue past my lips, and I completely surrendered to him.

He kissed me thoroughly, and it felt as if he was savouring every second. I moaned as he bent to cup my thighs, lifting me to his waist before perching me on the table. Wrapping my legs around his hips, I slid my fingers through his rain-soaked hair, tugging at it when his teeth nipped at my full lower lip. Stroking his fingers up my thighs, they wandered across my hips and back until they cradled my face softly. His thumb caressed my scar as his lips eased away from mine, just whispering against the swollen skin, and I felt him sigh as he tilted his forehead against mine. Peering up through my lashes, I watched as his eyes studied me. His hands continued to stroke my face gently before his lashes fluttered closed.

"I couldn't go out there—couldn't risk dying without tasting you one last time. Without feeling your skin, your warmth." He paused as he swallowed roughly.

"Please, Gods, fight with everything you have." Leaning forward, he pressed one last sweet kiss to my mouth. "And don't you dare fucking leave me."

My mouth opened, though no sound came, and suddenly I was cold as he pulled from my arms. Turning to the door, he pushed his way through the narrow entrance, never looking back as he ducked into the rain. Shivering from the loss of warmth, I remained perched on the table, my hand grabbing at my chest as I attempted to keep whatever was left from shattering beyond repair.

Chapter 45

Gazing out across the group of us, I prayed that the immortals were right about their choice of location. Gaelon and the Lupine generals had met through the night and decided that we should cut off the Crimsons as they made their way to Suideign Shores, and now as I grabbed at my blade, I studied the earth around us. The air was heavy and dark as the rain continued to pour down. I observed the green field and wondered how many of my friends would be laid to rest here.

Isla's white fur pressed against me, pulling me from my worry as our steps sank into the mud. She had not left my side once we had gathered, even going as far as to offer to carry me into the battle, but I had declined. I didn't want her targeted and I refused to leave my comrades behind. I would stand with them, by their side until this fight was over.

"Don't get stuck in that head of yours," Elizabeth whispered as she took in the green armour with a soft smile. "You look like the Huntress herself. It suits you well."

Unable to form a retort, I silently dragged her to me, my hands grabbing at her shoulders and I held her tightly. Pulling away after a long pause, I watched her face harden as she took her place to my right. Moving my gaze from her pale face, I glanced down at the failinis, who had finally padded across the ground to stand in front of me. Stroking his fur gently, I watched as his ruby eyes focused on my friends for a moment before he sat at my feet and flickered his attention on the wet grass in front of us.

"I don't think he will leave your side," Elizabeth whispered as she reached out to stroke the golden fur. I knew her words were meant to sooth my concern, but she had misjudged my nervousness, and I so badly wished I could tell her to keep the animal for herself. A low growl interrupted my thoughts and I watched as Reif's hackles lifted and his giant body rose as he looked to the east. The Lupines who had gathered close also spun their wolven forms in the same direction and I held my breath as I waited.

Narrowing my eyes, I could just make out the crimson banners fluttering in the distance, the deep red fabric blowing in the wind as the soldiers approached, their war drums echoing. No one moved as we watched our enemy approach, and then suddenly everything swung into motion all at once. Gaelon began commanding from his horse, organizing us into a formation, and then we waited. Slowly line after line of Crimson immortals flooded the field, their pace never changing as they marched forward. The green of the valley slowly seeped into a brilliant red as they swept in.

"Ella!" Gaelon called from his horse and my eyes shot to him in question. "When you see the signal, go." Turning to face the immortal, I watched as she nodded and I grabbed at her hand roughly.

"What is he talking about?" Panic flooded my veins when her lips lifted in a mischievous smile and she winked at me.

"Nothing for you to concern yourself with, Sky." Patting my back roughly, she danced away from me, and I shot Gaelon an accusatory glare. But before I could move to question him, Elizabeth grabbed at a wrist and turned me to her.

"Sky, focus," she snapped, her eyes hard. "Stop concerning yourself with everyone else and worry about staying alive." Her eyes slid back to the sea of red, and I watched as they stopped, their drums silent as a striking black horse galloped to the front of the army. Even from the distance, I could feel his violet eyes on me.

Balor is going to enjoy bathing in your blood today, Huntress.

Gasping, I clenched my eyes shut and groaned. I had not heard her since the night in the ocean and part of me had been foolish enough to hope that the link was gone. Clamping my jaw, I took the opportunity and willed a different image through my mind, forcing it through the tie.

Green metal covering long fingers as it gripped the golden hilt. The silver edge thrusting into the Crimson body that lay across the grass as the light left his violet eyes.

"He will perish here under my blade. And one day so will you," I whispered into the wind before I used every ounce of my strength to slam the connection closed.

"Sky?" Elizabeth called, her words worried as she pulled me to face her while Marissa fidgeted at her shoulder. But my attention had drifted to the familiar black body I could just make out behind the women, and I exhaled roughly before swiftly moving my eyes back to Elizabeth's face.

"I'm fine. Let's end this." I could feel his silver eyes watching me closely as I took a step forward, but I ignored him while I moved to the front line.

It was time.

The Crimson perched on the black steed shouted something before circling behind the army, and I watched as the first three lines of men charged. Leaning forward, I braced my weight as I readied myself to take off at them but then I noticed Gaelon's gaze. He was watching the hooded figure in the distance who had come from the side, and I stared as an arrow was lit and pointed at the air before it was released.

My heart stuttered in my chest as I watched Ella's flaming missile arch over the field before dropping to the ground where the Crimson lines had reached. Holding my breath, I waited, and for a second, nothing happened, but then a great burst of heat slammed into us as the ground under our enemy exploded. Turning my wide gaze away, I searched for the Healer and laughed when his own dark gaze lifted as he smiled.

Screaming echoed from across the valley and I moved my attention back to the enemy, watching as Balor scrambled to organize his army. The thought of his panic made me grin.

"It's not done yet!" Gaelon shouted at me as he pointed to the next wave of Crimson who were closing the distance.

Waiting until the majority of the group had rounded the fire and cracked earth, we unsheathed our weapons and held our position until I could make out the faces of our enemies. Holding the gold pommel in my palm, I embraced the heat that pounded through my veins and then charged when I heard the blow of the war horn.

The impact of our forces colliding sounded like the waves against the rock cliffs and my head rung with the noise. It was chaos as steel crashed and blood sprayed, the splatters sticking to my skin hotly as I tore at the Crimson army. The immortals had been well armed and versed in the art of battle, and I fought with all my strength while I watched as they charged at my companions.

"Alanna!" The scream rang out, and I wedged my blade into the soldier in front of me before spinning towards Nellie. The halfling was pushing her way through the crowd as she tried to reach the young girl who lay crumpled on the ground, but from my place, I could see that it was already too late. Running at her, I grabbed Nellie around the middle and hauled her back, wiping the blood from her face quickly before yelling over the noise. "Nellie! Stop! It's too late! Stop!"

But her pale face shook as she blinked through her tears, one hand still reaching for her friend. Holding her at arm's length, I shook her roughly for a second before stepping back. There was a dribble of blood pooling at the corner of her lips and we both looked down to her chest just in time to see the silver that was now coated in red withdraw.

"Nellie!" I screamed but her body was crumpling to the ground and the attacker was rushing forward. Lifting my sword, I blocked his swing, and I backed a foot away, shuddering when he stepped on Nellie's body as he followed.

"You're the one we're after." He smiled, his pale face lifting with glee under the blood that soaked it, and our swords met, crashing against each other as he swung at me. Tightening my fingers around my weapon, I inhaled deeply before rushing him. My brain was hazy as my body moved through the motions, and I allowed the heat in my blood to sweep me away as I disarmed him before sliding my sword across his neck.

But where one Crimson perished another was there to take his place, and I could feel my will wavering as I realized they collected around me. Managing to fight off the group, I swung my sword tiredly as I hacked at my opponents. But my wide stance left me exposed and a blade found the opening in my armour just above the back of my knee.

The sharp push of it had my joint buckling and I knelt into the mud as another blade came at me, this time aimed for my jaw. Closing my eyes, I prepared for the impact. But the blow was never delivered, and I immediately recognized the sound of growling. Sliding my eyes open, I watched as Reif took down the immortal, his jaw wrapped around the soldier's throat as he dragged him away. Using the distraction to my advantage, I swung my sword again at another one of the men and the metal hit its mark as it sliced through the skin just under his plackart. And then as if they had been summoned away, the men seemed to scatter, and in my confusion, I could just make out that high-pitched screech that had haunted my dreams.

Turning, I stumbled back as the blood-soaked skull opened its jaws and its long blue limbs clawed at the earth as it charged at me. Lifting my sword, I waited as the helcyrbius raced towards me, but then suddenly it stopped, and the beast turned its violet eyes to its back leg. I watched as it swung one long arm at its attacker, but Reif dodged its blow before grabbing the leg again, his teeth sinking into the rough flesh.

Using his haunches, Reif hauled himself onto the helcyrbius, but it was not enough, and the beast kicked his back leg out, sending the failinis across the wet earth before running at me again. As it barreled closer, I could see the streams of steam burst from the bone nostrils, and I readied myself for the inevitable. But Reif was back and this time he hung from the jugular of the beast. His head whipped back and forth, his teeth tearing until the skin gave out, and with one last great splatter of blood, the creature was dead.

Finally free of the threat, I balanced on my uninjured leg and searched for my friends. The valley was mayhem and I couldn't find any of the women. Panicked, I ran through the mob until I found the Lupine alpha, and I watched as he struggled to snap at the man crawling up his back while a group of Crimsons circled. Racing towards him, I launched myself at the soldier, grabbing him by the shoulder before tearing him off of the black fur and finishing him.

Now free to concentrate on the others, Kalian tore the remaining Crimsons apart before his eyes darted to mine. They were wide and grateful, and I lifted a hand to stroke his pelt before nodding and continuing on.

The earth was soaked with mud and gore, and I slid in it as I continued to fight while I struggled for air. But each lungful was heavy with the smell of death, and it collected in the back of my throat as more and more of us perished. Losing track of just how many Crimsons I had killed, I prayed to the Huntress that it was enough and that we were nearly done.

Moving my eyes across the field, I took in the Lupines who were herding a group of Crimsons into the clutches of their pack mates, and I could see Gaelon and Ella taking down half a dozen on their own. Marissa and Elizabeth had stuck together with a few of the Huntress's immortals and too seemed to be victorious in their fight, but I could not find Balor anywhere. He and his black steed had never made an appearance, and my stomach began to twist in knots as I desperately searched for the Seductress's Chosen.

"Where is he?!" I screamed at Kalian as I scanned the valley. His eyes moved swiftly across the battlefield before they slid back to mine.

"I'm right here, Huntress, and I have a gift." A sweet voice echoed over the noise of the battle, and my gaze lifted to his face as he sat proudly on his black mount. Violet eyes met mine, and he tipped his chin towards his extended arm that he raised above his head. It felt as if time had slowed as I slid my gaze up, and I was sure the earth shook when the deep roar of pain burst from the black fur beside me.

Delicate rivers of blood ran down the fine metal of his armour and I watched as his pale fingers twisted in the white fur, their hold tightening on the wolf head. And as he smiled at me, only one word echoed through my mind.

Isla.

Chapter 46

The battle around us seemed to freeze, as if the very sight of the white fur was a flag of surrender, and I could have sworn my heart stopped. Kalian too stilled beside me, his coat blowing in the wind, and I watched as his front paws dug into the mud for a second before a roar echoed around us. The sound was so full of pain, I cried out as it rang in my ears, but Balor's answering smirk was sly and deadly. Holding my breath, I watched as he examined the alpha from his horse before tossing Isla's head towards us.

Refusing to witness it slide through the mud, I turned my face to the side. I couldn't bear the sight of the pristine white coat turning brown as it tumbled to us, and I closed my eyes as a whimper broke from Kalian. Reaching out to comfort him, my hand met air, and I watched horrified as Kalian bolted forward towards the Seductress's Chosen, leaving all aid behind.

Panicked that he was falling for a trap, I searched for Gaelon, weaving frantically between the bodies as I called his name over and over. My feet slid through the mud as I avoided Crimsons and their blades, only pausing to fight if I had no way around, and by the time I had defeated half a dozen, Gaelon was galloping to me, his face pale. Knowing my plan, the Healer shook his head frantically, but I began to reach for him as I attempted to hurry him from his horse.

"Sky—" He started to protest but seeing my determination he

dismounted, and I ignored his concern as I sheathed my sword and hauled myself into the saddle. Grabbing the reins, I spun the horse around and watched as Balor galloped away, a wounded Kalian struggling behind.

"It may be a trap!" Gaelon screamed at me, voicing my own concern, but I didn't care. I would not allow Balor to escape. Not now, not after what he had done, and I would not allow Kalian to face him on his own.

"He's wounded, Gaelon, and reckless. I have to go after them!" I shouted over the noise before I dug my heels into the animal. Taking off after them, I noticed Leena's own fur body running across the field, her legs pushing herself to catch her brother. Though I knew her loyalty was unwavering, the battle was back in full swing, and I was certain that the loss of even one more Lupine could be catastrophic.

"Leena, stop!" I screamed as I pushed my horse closer to her. "Stop! I promise I will protect Kalian, but I need you to stay here and help Keyno! Please!" At his name, her dark eyes turned back to her mate, widening as she noticed the swarm of Crimsons who had ambushed him. She slid to a stop, and her gaze sought mine for an instant before she turned on her haunches and sprang back to aid the grey wolf.

Sighing in relief, I leaned low over the mane, kicking my horse harder, until I closed the distance between me and the black Lupine. But now that I was close, I noticed that his back leg was dangling at a sharp angle, and the broken limb was slowing him down. I knew there was no way he would catch the Crimson Chosen, not in this state, and I ignored his warning growl as I thundered past.

I was only a few yards away when I felt my horse slowing, and I cursed the Gods as the space between Balor and me widened. Digging my heels into the soft flesh, I gritted my teeth as I tried to will my mount faster, my mind begging for just one miracle, one chance to end this.

As if the Huntress herself had been listening, my pleading was answered, and I noticed a golden blur coming in from my right. He ducked his head low, his impressive speed increasing, and ruby eyes fixated on its prey. Awestruck, I counted four strides before the giant dog was launching itself into the air and dragging the rider from its horse. The black muzzle held tightly to the metal arm, his canines puncturing the armour as he shook his head viciously.

"Reif!" I called, slowing my horse and dismounting, watching in horror as Balor smiled at me for a moment before he lifted a dagger from his belt and pierced the golden flesh of the failinis. Distracted by the wound, Reif released his jaws and yowled as he snapped at the hand that had curled around the hilt.

"Damn creature," Balor snarled as he pulled his blade from Reif only to stab him again. I ran at the Chosen, tackling him away from the dog as the golden creature whimpered off.

Our armour screeched as it slid against each other while both of us struggled to get the upper hand. But he was not a mere halfling, he was a full-blooded immortal and her Chosen, and my feeble attempts to get out from under him were pointless as he anticipated my every move. Finally securing my arms with one of his hands, Balor had managed to pin me to the grass, his forearm crushing my windpipe as he smiled.

"How very easy this will be." He grinned, his face just inches from my own. My eyes blinked through the rain that had begun to fall heavily, and I searched for some way out of this. Noticing my panic, Balor sneered in my face before leaning forward, his tongue skimming across my seal before he whispered in my ear.

"Will you scream for me, halfling? Will you call out to your Goddess as I ruin you?" His mouth slid over my earlobe before tracing his lips across my face delicately, almost like a lover would.

Holding my breath, I stilled while I waited until he was in perfect position. Balor had not noticed just how closely I had been watching him, and his arrogance left him unprepared for my teeth as they sank into his jaw, tearing at the flesh until I had managed to draw blood.

"You bitch!" he screamed as he scrambled away from my mouth, giving me the opportunity to throw him off of me and struggle to my feet. Grabbing at my sword, I paid no mind to how heavy it had suddenly become as I lifted the steel and lunged for him. But he moved with swiftness as he rolled to the side, and I was left with only damp earth under my blade. Heaving the weapon from the mud, my hand sweltering around the hilt, I backed away a few paces as I watched his fingers trace the already healing wound on his jaw.

"I'm going to ruin the rest of your face before I end you," he snarled, his violet eyes flashing. "I will show them how weak their Chosen truly is."

Running at me, Balor swung hard. His power echoed with every swing as he came at me blow after blow, violet eyes holding mine. The hilt of my blade simmered under my flesh as I lifted the weight of it, moving with just enough speed to defend myself against his attacks. We circled each other, our bodies smooth and fluid as we danced, and I watched as he studied my face closely, his eyes tracing over the scar.

Blocking an attack, he slid away from me and remained silent while he studied my blade, his gaze lingering on the design for an instant before he was coming again. "You think you can beat me, girl? Your soiled blood can barely wield that steel."

He laughed as he took a step back, his face lifting in amusement while I gasped for breath. He was right; my arms were quivering, and my hands burned as they curled around the pommel tightly. Digging my heels into the mud, I ignored the pain and lifted my arms again, ready and waiting. Grinning, Balor's angular face brightened as he observed my determination. "Fine then. Let's see how you do with this."

A sharp, cold pain stabbed at my chest, its force rattling me to the bones. I felt my breath catch as I heard my father call for me, *Oh, my sky and stars. I need to know that you are safe, that no one is going to harm you.*

Grief rocked through me when I felt the ghost of my father surround me, as if he were here next to me, holding me in his strong arms again. Blinking in confusion, I watched as Balor smiled before his eyes narrowed.

Then you are healed, Skylahr. It was Kalian this time, his voice warm as his fingers stroked my thigh.

Skylahr, you have to let go. They're gone. You have to let go. Tan, delicate hands unfolded my fingers as they clutched at my mother's ash-covered wrist. More and more voices and visions filled my mind. One after the other, and each memory cut at me like a knife.

I see you kept your end of the deal. She will be so pleased with you, Kalian.

Listen to me, what he said was true. I had made a deal with them.

I know my carelessness has cost you everything.

"Isn't it a neat trick? Her powers truly are unmatched, as are mine now," Balor's voice called to me though I could scarcely hear it over my uneven breaths. "I didn't realize how easy it was until I made that Liam boy send you the bull head. I had finally found a way to seep into his mind. Dirty little prick though, you should have seen the dreams he had about you. But that fear wasn't enough; my mistress still couldn't get into that head of yours. No, we needed our mark, and then our dear Kalian did the rest. He broke something in you and the last of your resistance went crumbling down."

I felt sick as wave after wave of grief pushed into me, and I could feel my burning fingers loosening around the gold metal of my blade. Seeing my fragility, Balor took the opportunity and swung.

The sound of blood splattering across the ground echoed over the rain, and I gasped as Kalian's silver eyes widened before his body slumped to the grass. Using his foot for leverage, Balor pulled his sword with both hands from the wolf's shoulder before laughing as the great wolf struggled to move. Watching in horror, I inhaled sharply as he lifted his weapon again, this time aiming at the back of Kalian's shoulders, and I ran.

Rage burned through me as I hurled myself over the fur, and I felt the smooth edge of his sword just catch the side of my neck as I brought the Chosen to the ground. Both of us sprawled across the mud for a second before we were scrambling again. But this time was different, something more than my ignite was coursing through me, and I moved with power I had never possessed before.

Hands and legs flailed as we tumbled through the mud, and I could feel his fingers as they slid across the wet metal of my armour. Kicking at him, I crawled towards my weapon, which had been dislodged from my grip, and I slid through the mud, my arm reaching for it. However, Balor had been anticipating my move and dug his hand into my healing wound in the back of my knee, pressing his thumb there until the mending flesh gave way and opened again.

Gasping at the sharp pain, I raised my pelvis and loosened his grip before rolling onto my back. Lifting my uninjured leg, I used all of my force to kick out, finding my mark as my heel met his chest. But it still was not enough time to arm myself, and the immortal was back on me in a second. His gloved fingers grabbed and pulled at my breastplate as he tugged me back underneath him, his knees pinning my wrists to the earth. Grasping at his belt, he curled his fingers around his dagger and plunged the blade into my right hand, the metal digging deep enough to pierce through the flesh and nail it into the wet earth below. Satisfied that I was trapped, he moved his hands to my cheeks.

"Oh, Skylahr Reed." He laughed weakly. "I cannot wait to gouge those pretty eyes from your face."

His gloved fingers slid across my skin, hooking under the edge of my helm before pulling it off. He cupped my jaw roughly, and his thumbs crept higher over my cheeks, their pads brushing just under my eyes, and I panicked as I realized what he was planning to do. Bucking wildly under him, I thrashed and struggled until I felt his weight shift just slightly, and I managed to free my left arm. Reeling it back, I slammed my fist into the side of his head with as much power as I could muster.

The force of it had been enough to knock him to his side, and Balor used one hand to cradle the side of his face while the other stretched out, his fingers reaching for the golden hilt of my blade.

Seizing the opportunity, I grabbed at the dagger, yanking it from my hand before crawling after him. I grabbed on to his dark hair and pulled until I flipped him back and lifted my body swiftly. Sliding my weight across his chest, I used my knees to pin him down.

Panicking, he lifted his arm above his head and curled his fingers around the gold of my weapon. But the metal hissed under his skin and he groaned in pain before snatching his fingers away. Moving

forward, I grasped at his wrists, immediately noticing that his skin
was freezing under my own, and I twisted each arm, pulling them
away from the metal. Clutching at the hilt, I linked both my hands
together and held the blade in my grasp, lifting it above my head
before thrusting open the link.

I warned you of his fate, Goddess.

No. No. NO! her musical voice screamed through my mind, and I
smiled at the wide violet eyes below me before I brought the metal
down with every ounce of strength I had. The strike into his face was
smooth and easy, and I held the sword in its place as his eyes dimmed.
Feeling her panic and pain, I pushed the vision of her dead Chosen
at her.

I told you he would die, Seductress, and you are next.

Chapter 47

My body fell forward, my palms reaching out to brace myself as I blinked down at the dead man below me. His unseeing violet eyes stared at the dark sky and I watched as the rain washed the blood from his pale skin. Sitting there for a long moment, I blinked back to reality when I noticed the sharp burning in my fingers. Hauling myself to my feet, I turned my wrists and gazed down at the deep red burns across my flesh, my brows falling in confusion.

"Skylahr." My name was a low whisper, but the very sound of it drew my entire focus to the Lupine who was shivering in the mud. I turned, my knees buckling as my eyes met silver. Kalian had shifted back into his human form, his strong arms and shoulders covered in blood as he tried to lift himself from the muck. The muscled limbs trembled under the strain and a sob broke from me as I crawled towards him.

"Kalian!" His name came out of me in a broken cry, and my hands shook while they smoothed over his back, my fingers flinching when they felt the thick warmth of his blood that covered his flesh. Lifting himself, he crawled up my thighs before slumping into my lap and I curled myself around him, using my body to shield his skin from the rain that was pounding into us.

"Sky?" he groaned, his fingers slipping against the metal. It took me a long moment to realize he was pushing me away. "You have to go! Go!"

Not understanding, I pulled him up higher against my chest until his face was nestled in my neck. But his hands still continued to flail as he sobbed into my skin.

"Go! Please, run!" he wailed. "You're not safe! I can't lose you too!" His words shook through me and I clenched my eyes shut at the pain in his voice. Wrapping my arms carefully around him, I shushed him tenderly while I rocked us.

"I'm safe. He's gone, Kalian. It's okay." But it wasn't okay; looking at his golden skin now, I could barely find more than an inch that was not covered in blood.

His leg was still twisted at an awful angle, and his body was shivering violently. Sliding my palms across his torso, I tried to take note of each injury, my fingers pausing when they edged a deep laceration. Pulling from him just slightly, I tipped my head to look at his ribs. The wound was narrow, but it was deep and black liquid was oozing out of it. The colour shocked me and I watched his skin struggle to knit itself back together.

"Kalian?" I whispered, my fingers palpating the flesh carefully. "Can you feel this?"

But as I pulled away, I noticed the heat of his skin, and the shine in his eyes. The normal sharp silver was unfocused and the sight of it was twisting fear in my gut.

"Sky," he sighed, his eyes filling with tears as he lifted a weak arm to cup my cheek. "Please. Go. Leave me here. Hate me if you must, but I need you to go." Grabbing the rough palm, I brought his fingers shakily to my lips, pressing against the knuckles before tucking his massive frame closer to me. Harsh sobs shook his frame, the breaking of his deep voice increasing my grief tenfold as his fingers scrambled for purchase on the slick metal of my armour. Resting my cheek against his hair, I stroked his back carefully.

"It's okay. You're going to be okay. You hear me, you stubborn, infuriating man? You are going to be fine." My words were barely a whisper as I clung to him.

"Skylahr—" He tried again but I shushed him.

"I'm not going anywhere, you idiot. I'm staying right here." His body shuddered against me, and I lifted my head to search the area for some way to get him back to the others. My horse had long since wandered away and we were miles away from the field. Kalian's teeth chattered as he clung to my body and I held him closer to me, praying that I could find a way to get him the help he needed.

"SKY!" My name echoed around us, the sound carried by the winds. "SKYLAHR!"

I pulled away from the Lupine and pressed a soft kiss to his heated brow before gently lowering him to the ground. Wiping the rain and mud from my face, I squinted through the downpour and searched for Ella.

"Sky?!" I could just make out her tiny form as she rode closer, her dark hair plastered to her face as she galloped through the storm. It felt like ages as I waited for her horse to cover the distance, but once she was within arm's reach, I helped her from the mount and hugged her tightly.

"Are you okay?" I asked as I pulled away.

Her dark eyes were wide for a second before rolling, and she too scanned my body for signs of injury. "You run off to fight the Seductress's Chosen on your own and you ask me if I am okay?"

"Sky?" I heard my name called, and I turned to Gaelon as he approached swiftly on another horse, his face pale with worry as he took us in.

"I'm fine! But I need your help, it's Kalian." Turning to Ella, I pulled her along with me as I returned to the Lupine. His back had been rinsed clean of blood from the rain, but his side was still open, and I knelt to the ground as I pulled him back to me.

"His side, it won't close and it's bleeding a black colour." Carefully adjusting the now unconscious Kalian on my lap, I lifted his arm to show the Healer the wound.

"Poison, some of the others have similar wounds." Gaelon's dark eyes fixated on the skin as his fingers pressed against the opening. "We need to get him back and clean it. His leg will also need to be set."

"How many of us are left?" My voice was weak as I stroked the Lupine's dark hair.

Both Ella and Gaelon remained silent, their faces pale as they moved to lift Kalian from me, and I knew I truly did not want the answer.

"We were victorious, Sky, that is what matters." Ella's voice was hard, and her jaw shut tightly as she pulled the Lupine up. She was wrong; that's not what only mattered. Not to me.

"How many?" But they both remained quiet as Gaelon guided his horse to the unconscious Lupine before helping the immortal lift him onto its back carefully. "How many!?"

"Not enough, Skylahr." Gaelon's voice broke when he finally turned to me, his shoulders curling as he gazed at Balor's body. "But Ella is right. We were victorious, you have defeated her Chosen." Tears pooled in my eyes as I watched Ella tug my weapon from Balor's corpse before wiping the steel across the grass. Deeming it clean enough, she held it out to me.

"No." I took a step back, my hands rising. "I am not worthy to hold that blade." Ignoring their concerned stares, I lifted myself onto the horse behind Kalian and directed us back to the destruction that was waiting for me.

The grass was littered with gore and casualties, the soil soaking in both rain and blood, and my heart dropped as I surveyed the valley. The Crimsons' bodies had been piled high, their forms stripped of armour before they were lit, and the smell of burning flesh made my stomach roll. Closing my eyes, I held Kalian to me tightly and pushed the horse through the battlefield towards the camp as I tried to come to terms with the loss we most definitely suffered.

Our own fallen had been lined across the ground, their figures cleaned and laid gently to rest. Choking back a sob, I tried to ignore the number of Lupine and immortal bodies that I had passed, only halting when I saw a peek of white fur creep out from under the blanket that had been placed over it. Blinking, I turned my gaze to the dead, searching for Leena and Keyno only to sigh in relief when I heard them call my name.

Both Lupines ran to me, their pace hurried when they saw their brother, and I dismounted before helping them take him into their arms. Leena's dark eyes filled with tears as she stroked his face softly, and then she pulled me to her, holding me tightly while her cheek pressed against my own as she wept.

"Thank you for bringing him back." Her voice was soft, and I held myself to her before stroking her matted hair.

"Leena, I am so sorry." I hiccuped. "Your mother—" But I couldn't finish my sentence as I felt her own shoulders shake with sobs. Pulling back, she cupped my face in her hands.

"She was so proud of you, Skylahr, and she believed in you. She wouldn't have changed anything, not even if she knew her fate. She wanted to be here, to fight with you." Turning to her mate, Leena helped carry her brother back to the tents, and I searched the area around me for Elizabeth. Small groups had gathered, their eyes lingering on me, but there was no sign of my friend. Beginning to panic, I ran back to the line of dead, my mind spinning as I pictured the worst.

"Skylahr?" Her sweet voice shook as she called for me and I spun towards her bracing myself for the impact of her body as she launched herself into my arms. "Oh, thank the Gods." Her pale hands smoothed my hair gently before she smiled at me, tears sliding from her eyes.

"Are you hurt?" My voice trembled. There was blood splashed across her face but I couldn't locate an open wound.

"A few nicks but I'm fine." Sighing in relief, I pulled from her arms and studied the bodies again.

"Marissa?" As soon as the words left my mouth Elizabeth froze and grabbed at my hand.

"She's in Leena's tent." Nodding, I turned to head towards the camp, only stopping when she pulled me back to face her. Her skin had paled, and her lower lip trembled as she hiccupped. "Sky, she's gone."

My eyes filled with tears while I watched her face crumple, and I looked around us helplessly. "But she's a halfling. Surely the ceremony could bring her back?"

Elizabeth's eyes shone as she shook her head roughly. "One of the Lupines tried already."

"So try again!" I ordered as I stormed away from her and into the tent. Moving my eyes across the space, I froze in the entrance. Marissa was barely recognizable with her pale skin tinged blue and her face bruised and bloodied. Gasping at the state of her, I stood on trembling legs before I turned to the two Lupines who stood off to the side. Their faces were sad as they watched me stare at the halfling, and I sobbed while blinking back the tears.

"Help her, please," I begged as I stumbled to the cot she had been laid across. "Please, help her!"

But the couple bowed their heads before the male regarded me sorrowfully. "I tried, Huntress, but it did not work. I am truly sorry for your loss." His head bowed low for a moment before he pulled the woman to him and exited the tent.

Now alone, I knelt at the halfling's side, my fingers caressing her cheek softly before I burrowed my face in my arms. Lost in my grief, I ignored the sound of the tent opening, only looking up when Ella's warm hands brushed across my shoulders gently. Pulling her close to me, I held her while we cried for our fallen friend.

I forced myself not to wince as Ella clutched my hand tightly, her palm pressing against the burns and healing wounds. Standing hand in hand, we watched as our friends were laid to rest, their bodies lowered into the shallow graves that had been dug by the Lupines.

Marissa was the last to be buried, her pale face peaceful as the dirt covered her inch by inch, but my own being was in turmoil. We had lost so many; only a few dozen of us remained and the guilt chewed its way at me.

Stepping from Ella's grasp, I ignored the bows of the survivors and turned to head back to the tents that had been given to the wounded. The attention was more than uncomfortable, and I lowered my eyes until I reached the camp.

Creeping past the cloth, I strode silently to the chair next to Kalian's bed and found some peace in the quiet that surrounded us. He had been delirious with fever the last time I had seen him, when I had held him to me as he begged for me to run. But now he slept soundly, his temperature was back to normal, and his colour was its usual golden tone. Taking one of his hands, I traced his fingers softly as I gathered my thoughts with a frown.

"I thought I warned you about the risks of such an expression back in Denimoore. I would hate to see that scowl become permanent." His voice was hoarse, but his smile was warm as he watched the disbelief fill my eyes. Tears leaked down my cheeks and I lifted my hand to his jaw to stroke the skin carefully.

"You did. But you've always been full of shit."

He chuckled quietly before grabbing at my wrist, bringing my hand to his lips only to freeze when he noticed the red welts that still littered the skin.

"Are these from her sword?" Nodding my head, I pulled my fingers free as I inspected my own palm. "I should have warned you there was a chance. The steel is made from magic, making it powerful and deadly. It was created for the Goddess herself, a halfling was never meant to wield it."

"At some points it felt as if it was taking every ounce of strength from me," I admitted shamefully, hating that I did not have the skill or the ability to harness the steel's power.

His eyes dropped to my palms and he blinked thoughtfully for a moment. "It was fashioned for the war, only to be used by her hand against the Seductress and her Crimsons. I was warned that you would be able to wield it because you are her Chosen, but in order to unleash its full capability, you may need to be an immortal."

My fingers curled into my palms and I placed them into my lap silently as I focused on the blanket that had been draped across him. The air around us grew tense with the silence and I didn't know how to say what I needed to; I didn't know where to start. Gnawing at my lower lip, I dropped my head until a warm hand tucked under my chin and lifted my face.

"You need to stop carrying the weight of the world on your shoulders, it will crush you." Kalian's voice was soft, his eyes earnest as he caressed my jaw with his fingers.

"Kalian, I am so sorry. Isla—" But his thumb pressed against my lips, forcing me to pause as he pulled himself up carefully.

"My mother would not tolerate you taking the blame for any of this. If anything, it was my own foolish actions that led us here." I watched as he sighed heavily before clearing his throat. "I made mistakes, Skylahr, so many mistakes." His brow furrowed as his voice lowered and my heart sank at the sight of him.

"Kalian," I whispered in pleading, my voice breaking as I watched tears line his eyes.

"I will live my life regretting so many of the choices I have made. But one I will forever stand by is loving you. You are the Huntress, and I am your Protector, and I love you, Skylahr Reed. I will never regret that." His head tipped forward, pausing for a second to give me the chance to pull away before his mouth slanted over mine. His lips sealing the words with a kiss.

Chapter 48

Sighing against his mouth, I combed my fingers through his hair for a second before tipping his head away. Leaning back, Kalian rested against the furs, and his eyes softened while he studied me. I slid my hands from the nape of his neck and moved them across his cheeks, my thumbs stroking the skin.

"Sky?" His voice shook as he waited patiently. I knew what he was waiting for, what he wanted me to say, but the words wouldn't come. I couldn't let them, even though they were burning in my chest.

"I'm sorry, Kalian. I'm sorry for any pain I have caused you, any pain I am causing you now, but I can't give you any more than what I have." His dark lashes fluttered closed as he exhaled heavily, and I could have sworn his frame shrunk two sizes.

"Sky…" His voice was a whisper, and he cleared his throat. "I understand, I knew that you—" But I interrupted him.

"You don't understand, not really." Crossing my arms, I willed myself to not to fall apart as my eyes roamed the tent, unable to look at his face while I tried to explain. "You think it's because I haven't forgiven you for the deal. But I have and the anger that filled me is just emptiness now. We have both lost so much, we have both suffered and grieved and fought, and, in the end, it has torn us to pieces."

I paused, taking in a deep breath, knowing that what I was about to say was true though it broke my heart. "You say you love me, but you don't. Not truly. What you feel isn't love, it's obligation."

When his eyes widened and he began to shake his head, I smiled sadly. "You think you and I are fated to be together, that it was destiny. But it's not true, we aren't them and I am not what you need. I can't be, not now. I can never go back to the way things were. I can never overlook what has happened."

Kneeling on the floor next to his bed, I took one of his hands and held it to the thumping in my chest. "There has been too much pain. Everything in here is twisted and torn now, Kalian. I can feel the sharp edges rattle in there, and I know that it would only be a matter of time before I cut you open too." Pressing my lips to his fingers, I gazed up into his handsome face. "I forgive you for your mistakes, but I am not your Huntress, and you can no longer be my Protector."

Closing my eyes, I felt a tear trickle down my ruined cheek. "Be with Nadine, Kalian. Go home to her and build the life your mother wanted for you." Pulling away from him, I ducked through the entrance, ignoring the whisper of my name that followed me.

Gaelon's fingers were careful as they wrapped my palms with the strips of cotton, the balm soothing the burns that still coated my skin. We sat in silence, his jaw tight as his hands worked. The Healer had been on edge since the burials, his eyes always watching me closely, and I began to wonder what he saw.

"What is it you are looking for, Healer?" The title made him flinch, and he dropped his hands as if my skin scalded him.

"I am waiting to see if that hurt and that anger is going to burn you up from the inside. I'm waiting to see if you'll let it." His eyes were sharp and knowing, and the force of his gaze made me swallow roughly.

"What were you expecting from me exactly? You thought we would fight against her Chosen, I would watch good people die and be okay with it?" The very memories made my skin crawl and my stomach turn.

"Of course not. But this darkness that is festering worries me, Skylahr." He was right, of course, there was something growing in me. Something that had been planted long, long ago that was just now beginning to bloom. But I knew it had nothing to do with the Crimson Goddess. This was all my own doing; it was a part of me.

"I hear worry can take years off a man's life, Gaelon." I laughed dryly, hoping to lighten the mood.

"Good thing I'm immortal." His eyes warmed just a little, and I kicked at his shin when he tightened the knot around my hand. He cleaned the table free of his supplies, grabbed a bottle of wine, and handed me glass. Sipping the ruby liquid carefully, I forced myself to ignore the colour as flashes of the battlefield threatened to fill my mind and instead finally brought up the topic we had been avoiding.

"I want to open the link." I had been thinking about it for hours, but the Healer's surprise at my words had him choking.

Patting his chest roughly, Gaelon fixed me with a hard stare. "Why?"

"Because I want to know how badly she suffers. I want to know what hole she crawled into and where she plans to slither off to next." Dark eyes narrowed at me, but I held his stare. "I want to try. I need to."

Sighing in defeat, Gaelon snatched at the knife that lay near the edge of the table, but my fingers beat him to it. Grabbing at the metal, I closed my eyes and searched for the shimmer of the link before plunging the tip into my thigh. The pain immediately drew her interest, but I managed to push her presence away as I searched for information.

I could hear the same sounds of the ocean as last time, but the air was much warmer than it would be at this time of year in Elrin. Gulls squawked and the wind was heavy with salt. But under the heat and humidity there was a coldness, a piercing chill that crept in my mind.

"How did they find that blade and how was she able to wield it! Balor should have been able to kill her, she should have been no match for him!" The grey eyes of the man lowered to the floor as he flinched away from her venom.

"And now I am weak! I am vulnerable and they have three Chosen!" The man scampered backwards, his hands raised to shield himself from her long nails as she swung at him again.

"The uprising of the halflings has increased and my support has all but vanished. I cannot win against them now! I will lose, I will lose everything! My only option is to retreat." Her rage flooded into me before it shifted into fear.

Sensing her power as it pressed against the link, I slammed the connection shut before she could turn it on me, and I kept my eyes closed for a long moment to be sure I had locked her away. Holding my breath, I felt a warm hand cup my jaw, and I leaned my face into the palm before opening my eyes.

"What did you see?" Gaelon's voice was deep with concern, and I pulled from his hand.

"She's scared. She's ready to flee." My lips lifted in a grin before I realized something. "She said there has been an uprising of halflings. What is she talking about?" Gaelon crossed his arms and leaned back into his chair while he mulled over my words.

"There have been rumours that small groups of halflings have rallied together to fight against the Crimsons, but I had assumed it was nothing but gossip."

"Gossip or not, it was enough to spook her." I smiled at him. "She feels powerless; she plans on hiding."

"And the link?" he asked, his eyes scanning my cheek.

"Closed for now," I murmured, turning my face away from his eyes as a knock at the door echoed around us. Gaelon strode towards it, his gaze darting back to mine before he opened it. Sipping on my wine, I watched as Ella gave the Healer a gentle nod before turning to me. Her stunning face was heavy with tension as she grabbed at my hand, giving my fingers a gentle squeeze.

"The rest of the Lupines have left for Denimoore. They give their regards." Ella had turned her body towards the Healer, but her eyes remained on mine. Kalian and his family had left late last night, only after the alpha had spent hours pleading to speak with me. Knowing he would try to break my resolve, I had run like a coward, taking a horse and Reif to the cliffs to hide away from him until Elizabeth had come to reassure me that they were gone.

Fidgeting under Ella's scrutiny, I tried to ignore the heaviness in my chest and instead watched as she handed a worn leather-covered book to Gaelon, her eyes never leaving mine.

"What's this?" he asked, his fingers thumbing through the pages.

"Turn to the marked page." With one last, long glance she finally turned to Gaelon. "I could hear your discussion about the link outside and figured now was as good as time as any." Sitting in the vacated chair, Ella held my hand and squeezed, her dark eyes empathetic as if she could see inside my heart.

"Where did you find this?" Gaelon's whisper was full of surprise, the tone drawing my attention, and I jumped when the book dropped onto the wood in front of me. The faded page had a sketch of the same seal that covered the right side of my face, its details worn but visible across the parchment. My fingers traced the drawing.

"One of the immortals brought it with them. They thought it might be useful after the battle." Ella's voice carried through the small room and I ran my hand across the page once more before turning to the Healer.

"What is it?" My eyes peered up at Gaelon as he grinned at me.

"A way to heal that scar. If it works, your face would be free of her seal and you would be free of the link." Turning to Ella, I watched as she too grinned at me, her joy blinding.

What they were offering had been something I had once longed for. I had been willing to cut it out of my flesh myself and yet now, I couldn't find the same desperation. It wasn't just that I had grown used to the lifted puckered skin and the link that I could now seem to control. It was a symbol. A mark the halflings had been forced to don in the last moments of their lives. Dear Marissa herself had borne it proudly. She had used it to light the rage inside her as she faced the world, faced those who had tortured and mocked and murdered. She never shied away from it and now, neither would I.

"No. Leave it be." I stood from my chair, unwrapping the

cotton from my palms before tossing the cloth on the table. "I will wear it proudly. I will show the remainder of her Crimsons that this seal shames us in no way and that it's time for things to change. That her reign is over." Leaving the pair behind, I slammed open the door and lifted my face towards the sun.

Chapter 49

Saying goodbye to Suideign Shores should have been easy. There was nothing left here but hurt and loss, and yet, as I curled my arms around Reif, I felt a part of me break off and bury itself in the earth below, that piece of my soul guarding those who had been lost here.

Burrowing my face in the golden fur, I sighed as the massive dog leaned against me. "What will we do with you, hmm?" I whispered as his enormous jaws opened and his tongue slid across my cheek. "Yes, thank you for that."

Laughing, I wiped my face dry with the sleeve of my tunic while pulling myself from the ground. Losing his spot, Reif glared at me, stretched with a low grumble, and followed at my heels as we headed back down the path to the shore. The failinis had been a constant companion, his presence lifting my spirits, though I had yet to convince Gaelon that he was not a nuisance. The dog's habit of curling on the Healer's bed was most likely the reason for that.

"Are you ready?" Ella called from her horse once I was in sight, her eyes warm as they looked back at Elizabeth. The pair had been inseparable the last few nights, and I had a sneaking suspicion it was partly due to the immortal wanting to get revenge for any lost sleep she had suffered in our previous travels. Elizabeth rushed to her, her pale arms curling around the immortal before she pressed her face to Ella's cheek. Kissing the dark skin loudly, the human then pulled back before sticking her tongue out at me.

"Oh, don't be so jealous. We still love you." Rolling my eyes, I tried to hide my grin as I tacked up the black stallion. I was so pleased that my two closest friends had continued to find joy in each other, though admittedly I was a little worried about being forgotten.

"Okay, you two, can we just focus for the few next hours?" Gaelon's rough voice called from the doorway of his home, his dark eyes narrowed at the couple as he passed me a cup of warm tea. "They were at it all night in the spare room. Between them and that incessant dog, I will never sleep again."

Nudging him gently, I smiled into my mug before swallowing the warm tea in one long swig. Gaelon had been exhausted since the battle, staying up all hours to use his expertise and Healer's gifts to mend the wounded. Now that the last of the immortals had returned home, the fatigue had finally caught up to him.

"You should have joined me on the beach." My face immediately heated as I realized how that sounded and I gaped at him as he choked on his tea. "I didn't mean that! I just—"

But Gaelon lifted his hand before smiling at me. "I know what you meant, and you're right. Now I know better."

We had never spoken about the kiss we shared, nor the devastation that rocked through me after the Lupine alpha had left. The Healer just seemed to sense that I needed space and peace, and I was grateful for his uncanny ability to know what I required without me having to ask.

"Where is it we are headed exactly?" Ella asked, finally pulling herself from Elizabeth. The two women had been adamant that we stick together after the war, refusing any other option, and I knew it was pointless to try. Though I wished they didn't feel obligated to stay with me. I worried that they would one day regret it.

"Hectoar is meeting us in Beilham. There had been an uprising there and the halflings had managed to capture and defeat a small party of Crimsons." After seeing the fear of the Seductress the last time I opened the link, we had investigated the rumours of the halfling rebellion, only to learn they had in fact been true. More and more halflings had come out of hiding and began to fight back, though more often than not it led to many villages' ruin. Now we planned to travel to as many as possible and help those who had lost everything. We would rebuild those towns that had been burnt to the ground or ravaged by the battles and try to restore a peace to Elrin that had been missing for over five centuries.

"Who is Hectoar?" I asked as I tightened the girth on my horse before hauling myself into the saddle.

"A fellow Healer's immortal. He and a few others had made it to the village in time to assist the halflings, though I have a feeling he is rather put out that he missed the action here." Dark eyes turned to me, his lips lifting in a smirk. "He is also desperate to meet the Huntress's Chosen."

Rolling my eyes, I whistled at Reif and urged my horse into a smooth trot up the hill until I finally settled at the edge of the cliff. Closing my eyes, I breathed in the salt air before tipping my chin so that the wind would carry my whispered promise to the valley where our allies had been laid to rest.

"Goodbye, my friends. I will carry you all with me. Always."

Hectoar was more than a gracious host. His tall, lean frame had jogged out to meet us before he pulled Gaelon from his horse to kiss both cheeks twice. The familiarity between the two men was obvious, and I smiled as the immortal teased the Healer endlessly on our arrival.

"You must be her." His voice was delicate and smooth as he finally directed his attention to me, and I tried not to shrink back from his emerald eyes as they scanned my body. "You are everything I pictured and more."

Pulling me to him, he pressed his lips to my face, paying no mind to my scar before he guided us through the village gates. A group of men had been stationed around what was left of the town, their spines straight as they watched us approach. I tried not to shudder as they fell to their knees once we neared.

"Huntress," the leader whispered, his head bowed. I turned to Gaelon for help, but his dark gaze held mine and he lifted one brow.

"Please, there is no need for all that." I moved forward to pull the men to their feet only to be stopped by Hectoar's slender hand.

"Huntress, you are the Chosen. This kind of respect is demanded for you." Smiling at me gently, he too knelt at my feet. His warm green eyes gazed up at me as he placed a hand over his chest. "We offer our honour and loyalty to you."

Unsure of what to say, I nodded my head silently and swallowed before turning to the other group. They were huddled close together, their eyes wide as they whispered about us, and it was obvious that they were in fact halflings. Thankful to find some of my own kind again, I walked towards them.

"Hello," I greeted them slowly, my lips curving into an awkward smile. But my voice spooked them, and they backed a step away, never returning my greeting. Unsure how to approach, I halted and waited for Gaelon, though they also seemed unsure of him.

"I'm Gaelon and this is Skylahr. We mean you no harm." One of the halflings was a tall soft-bodied woman. Her skin was a smooth ebony so dark it reminded me of the night sky in Noorde Point, and I was taken aback by her beauty. Her dark eyes regarded us carefully as her irises swirled with heat. They narrowed at the Healer before sliding to my own.

"You're the northern halfling? The Chosen of the Huntress?" Her voice was deep, almost soothing in a way. Or rather it would have been if it wasn't for the hostility.

"Yes," I choked out.

"Did you fight alongside Marissa?" My eyes widened in surprise, and I could hear the pain in her tone. Immediately wishing I had better news to share, I scrambled for my answer.

"I did." It was short, no explanation. I didn't know how to report something like this to a stranger.

"Does she live?" I didn't answer, but I didn't need to; I could tell she knew when her shoulders sagged under the grief. "Did she suffer?"

"No." Ella came forward, rescuing me, and she placed her hand on my shoulder as she regarded the halfling. "No, she did not. She fought brilliantly with no fear, and when she met her end, it was instant."

The woman considered Ella's words for a long moment before nodding at me. "Then she died for her cause. She died for her Huntress." The weight of her words nearly crushed my chest in as I felt panic flood through me. I shrugged from Ella's touch as I searched for an escape. Running from the feeling that began to close my throat, I retreated to the patch of woods that surrounded the town, my eyes refusing to meet the questioning stares that burned into my back as I fled.

I wasn't a Huntress. I was a coward, and soon they would all see that.

"Her name is Selbie. Hectoar says she's a fierce warrior. Strong and skilled, better than any immortal he's seen." Elizabeth sighed as she sunk to the ground next to me. Leaning against her shoulder, I took a deep breath in. "She did not mean to upset you, she's in pain and she's grieving. She's known Marissa since they were children."

"We are all grieving. It's all we ever do these days," I snapped at her before leaning away and focusing on the green of the trees. Sighing in defeat, I hung my head. "I can't do this, Elizabeth. I can't have these people swearing loyalty to me when all I've done is bring hurt and death to these lands."

"That's not what you are doing, dear Skylahr." Scoffing, I turned my face, flinching as her pale fingers reached for my own. Placing her hand back in her lap, she exhaled slowly. "You are leading, Sky. You are fighting and inspiring. You are doing things no one else has been able to do in years. Not since before the Huntress fell."

"I can't even use her blade without my skin burning. I'm not nearly enough to do all those things. I'm not her, Elizabeth." The words were bitter on my tongue as I acknowledged my reality.

"No, you are not. But you care in a way only she could." Pausing, she stroked my back gently. "If I could shield you from any of your pain, take any of the weight of it, I would in a heartbeat. But I can't, Sky. So you need to find a way to use it. You need to find a way to harness it to help you change the world." Cradling my head in my hands, I closed my eyes and soaked in her words.

"Let's not add any more pressure to the poor girl." Ella had been silent in her approach, and I nearly jumped out of my skin as she threw an arm around my shoulder. "We both know that she can handle it, but Gods, Lizzy, give the girl a break." Ella's smile was bright as she removed my hands from my face and kissed my cheek. Her warmth eased the shiver in my soul and I nearly teared up with gratitude at the interruption. Sighing loudly, Elizabeth clamped her mouth shut before scooting closer, pressing against my other side until I was sandwiched tightly between them.

"Plus, if you really want our Sky to agree to a coronation, you're going to need to lighten up a bit." I blinked at Ella, my mouth opening as I realized just how serious she was being.

"Coronation?" I groaned as my face paled.

"Oh, don't you start now, Skylahr Reed. You will put a pretty crown on that head of yours and you will do as you're told." Falling back into the earth, I clenched my eyes shut and groaned again.

"That means more *bowing*." The women burst into a fit of giggles and I let the harmony of their laughter sooth the pressure in my chest for the time being.

Chapter 50

My self-pity lasted for another few hours, only disappearing when we headed back to town and I really looked at the devastation around us. These people had also lost their homes, friends, and family, and I had no right to wallow in my own pain when so many others suffered and still carried on. Feeling ashamed, I threw myself into work as I helped the halflings clear the debris, and they slowly warmed up to me, though kept a cautious space between us. But even with time and distance, they continued to gawk at me as I moved the rubble and my face heated under the surveillance.

"You should probably drink something," Selbie called out to me, tossing a wineskin my way. Pulling the cork, I smiled gratefully at her before taking a long drink, using the break to gather my next words.

"I am sorry about Marissa. I did not know her for long but from what I saw, I know she was amazing." Selbie sank to the ground, crossing her legs slowly before tipping her head to the spot beside her. Taking the invitation, I settled next to her, passing the halfling the water.

"The last time I saw her was our twenty-second birthday. As children, we had bonded over the fact we shared the day so as usual we had dinner together." Pausing, she took a deep breath. "That was more than half a year ago. I had left our home in search of my blood father. But when I heard news of the attacks on the northern villages,

I was forced into hiding." Dark eyes slid to my face, their depths swirling as she studied me closely. "Then, word got out about a group of halflings who had slayed their captors, and when I had heard the whispers, I knew Marissa had been one of them. So, I turned back to her last known location only to learn that she had begun to travel with the Huntress's Chosen."

"How did you hear that?" I asked, shocked. We had been extremely careful with our routes, staying out of sight and never approaching strangers while we travelled to the shores. So I couldn't understand how she had learned of our location.

"A young halfling named Alanna told me. I had come across the group of them as they travelled to Suideign in hopes of aiding the Chosen." She brought her knees to her chest, rested her chin on them, and blinked into the space in front of her. "I so badly wanted to follow but I knew that there were Crimsons littering the land, and I had to be here to defend the other halflings who had sought safety in this village."

Lost in her voice, I listened to her carefully and realized there was this power that surrounded Selbie, this sense of strength that I was in awe of. I wondered if everyone else felt it too. Reaching out one of my hands, I gently cupped her shoulder and squeezed the soft flesh, though I was almost nervous to break the spell she had put me under.

"I am sorry I couldn't save Marissa. I wish I had done more to protect her."

Her dark fingers patted mine for a second before she shook her head.

"Marissa was strong and independent, and she would absolutely hate that you were taking any blame for what happened. She knew the risks and for her, it was worth it. You were worth it." Sensing my unease at the admission, Selbie rolled her eyes at me. "How many people have to explain this, Huntress? You may want to brush off your importance or what you were promised to do, but we can't. So, if you are unable to accept your role for yourself, do it for those of us who would give anything to make your prophecy come true."

Pulling from my touch, the halfling stood from her spot and

glared down at me. "Do it for Marissa and for the others who have died fighting for you. It's time you realize that some of us have been waiting for years for any sign of hope. We have been waiting for you and now you need to show us why." Without a second glance, the halfling turned away, leaving me behind to ponder her words.

We had spent weeks in Beilham as we rebuilt the village until it was deemed livable for its townsfolk. Once finished there, we continued north, our small party growing as more and more halflings and immortals joined our venture. Peering back over the group, I searched for Ella and Elizabeth and watched as they chatted excitedly to Selbie. The new halfling got along with them famously, and I was pleased to see her so comfortable in their company.

Deciding to keep to myself in fear of interrupting their lively conversation, I turned to the area around us, watching as Reif loped through the lines of thick trees, and I realized that the landscapes had morphed into those I was familiar with. The skyline was filled with the mighty mountains of the north and the smell of evergreens wafted in the air. Pulling my thick green cloak closer, my fingers then slid to the metal ring that hung from my neck.

Being so close to home made my heart ache, and I longed to feel my parents' embrace again.

"I miss them too, Sky." I hadn't noticed that Elizabeth had ridden up next to me, and I smiled at her as my eyes filled with tears.

"I wonder where we are going?" I asked. We had been bouncing back and forth between villages. Picking up the pieces that been left by the battles before moving on to the next. But there were few towns this far north and although the scenery was familiar, I had never really travelled prior to the Swallows and did not recognize the road we had turned on.

"We should be entering Noordeign's borders anytime now," Gaelon called from over his shoulder as he led the group. I had never been to the capital of the northern province, not even as a child, and I wondered what would be waiting for us.

"Were they also attacked?" Ella called from behind and Gaelon turned in his saddle to answer the immortal.

"Only just, but the damage was superficial." His tone was light, but I immediately grew suspicious as he turned back around.

"So why stop there?" I asked, frowning as Gaelon ignored me. Touching my shoulder gently, Elizabeth called my name and lifted her hand to direct my attention to the massive walls of the city that had appeared through the gaps of the now thinning forest.

The barrier was made of tall, pointed trunks, identical to Noorde Point, and I felt my stomach sink at the sight as memories flooded into me. Swallowing roughly, I chose to focus on the space between my stallion's ears as we passed through the gate, and I felt panic grow when I took in the crowd. The centre of the town had been filled with lines and lines of people, their faces blurring together as my mind spun only to be pulled into focus when Gaelon reached out to me.

"Breathe, Skylahr." His handsome face shone under the northern sun and his brown eyes glittered gold as they fell across the crowd. Following his gaze, I noticed that our audience had dropped to their knees, heads bowed, and I shook in the leather of my saddle.

"Breathe." He repeated the word as if it was an order, and I inhaled deeply. Sweeping my eyes across the bodies, I noticed a massive figure made of stone.

She was tucked behind the crowd, though I guessed on a regular day it would have been the centre of the square, and I traced her frame closely. Her long hair and delicate face stood out to me, and even though the details were minor there was no arguing that she was stunning. Her head was adorned with a crown of gold and the bow in her hand was dusted in emeralds. I had never seen a statue decorated in such splendor.

However, when my gaze lifted back to her face, I realized that the true treasure was her eyes. A pair of ice blue sapphires sat above sharp cheekbones and I could have sworn they followed my every move. There was something about them that made me believe she would break her stone casing and come alive at any moment. I shifted under her stare.

"The Huntress." The words were barely audible but Gaelon nodded.

As if in a trace, I dismounted from my horse, ignoring the way the crowd parted as I approached the stone. And when I reached the platform, I fell to my knees and stretched shaking fingers up to her carved cold toes.

Her eyes gazed down at me, their brilliance piercing my soul, and I knew right then, in that moment, the others had been right. I couldn't explain why. Maybe it was magic or maybe the Goddess herself was there somehow, but for some reason I was certain I had a purpose, a reason for being, and it was time to stop running from it. Bowing my head under the glittering blue, I swore an oath at her feet.

"I will find the strength and courage you have given me, and I will make you proud. Protect me, Huntress, and I will protect them. I promise."

A swift swat landed against my shoulder as I fidgeted for the hundredth time and I sighed in frustration. Ella and Elizabeth had been working on my hair for what felt like hours and I blinked at Selbie in pleading, willing her to step in and save me before they stuffed me in the monstrosity of green silk that hung from the wardrobe door. Eyeing it from my seat, I grimaced at the corset that lay on the ground next to it.

All eyes had been on me since our arrival, and although I struggled with it, I had managed to not shudder under the attention. However, the idea of squeezing my body into such fine fabric had my palms sweating. Wiping my hands on my robe, I focused on the reflection in front of me instead.

"Are we nearly done?" I asked quietly as Ella pinned half of my bronze waves back. Her eyes met mine in the glass and she smiled softly before turning to the small white cotton roll that had been laid gently on the bed. Watching her fingers unroll the fabric, I gasped as the metal shimmered in the light.

The delicate design of the comb was still just as beautiful now as it had been when I had first seen it in Denimoore, and I lifted a shaking hand to trace the metal edges as Ella held it out for me.

"How...?" I couldn't finish the rest of my question as I blinked back tears.

"Leena sent it. She mentioned that you had admired it when you were in Denimoore." Staring down at the silver, I brushed a tear away.

"When I saw it in Isla's hair, all I could think was that my mother would have adored it."

Elizabeth squeezed my shoulder in comfort as she nodded.

"Your mother would have loved it." Pausing, Elizabeth swallowed before passing me a small piece of parchment and I bit my trembling lower lip before unrolling the note.

Dearest Skylahr,

My mother would have wanted you to have this. I am sorry we could not be there today, but I know she is with you. Always.

Just as we will be.

Yours truly,

Leena

Passing the comb to Ella, I sat frozen as she pressed it into the back of my hair. She smoothed a few waves, and we sat there in silence for a long moment while I gathered my feelings.

"Ready?" Elizabeth held out a hand for me to take, and I rose to my full height and followed her to the dress. The rush of emotions had left me compliant, and I barely moved as the corset and dress were tied around me. Once finished, Ella and Elizabeth took a step away and grinned at each other before pushing me back towards the mirror.

The woman in the glass was not one I recognized. Her bronze hair gleamed brightly, and her skin glowed beneath the forest green material. The lace sleeves did not awkwardly elongate the arms they covered, and the tapered waist flowed out to a full skirt that was flattering in a way I had never seen. The pale skin of her face and the freckles that splattered across the bridge of her nose were familiar, but I had never shone the way my reflection did.

"You are stunning, Sky." Blinking back to my friends, I smiled softly before pulling them close.

"Thank you," I whispered, tightening my arms around them for a long moment only to be interrupted by a soft knock on the door. Stepping from their embrace, I crossed the room and smiled while Gaelon stared dumbfounded at me.

"Gods help me, you look—" He paused for a breath. "Radiant." I didn't have the words or courage to respond, and instead I linked our arms carefully and allowed him to lead me to the Temple of Light where I would be officially crowned the Huntress's Chosen.

"Are you ready, Skylahr?" Gaelon asked as he paused at the wooden doors. Closing my eyes, I lifted my hand to the ring that hung from my neck, my fingers tracing the cold metal for a moment before I hung my head gently and prayed.

Huntress, please guide me with your light as I lead your people. Fill me with your strength when I am weak. Feed me courage when I am afraid. Let me be wise and just as I defend those who do not have a voice, and above all else, let me be good.

Blinking my eyes open, I smoothed my skirts carefully before straightening my spine and lifting my chin. Holding my head high in the same way her statue had, I took a deep breath as I willed my body to reflect the Goddess's magic that ran through my veins.

"Yes, I'm finally ready."

EPILOGUE

The mud splattered across my boots with every step I took, the damp seeping into my bones as the gusts of wind made my eyes water. Watching my booted toes, I ducked my head as I crossed the burnt remains silently. Nothing had grown here, even as more and more time passed. I fiddled with the ring that thumped against my chest as I imagined the solid wood walls of my childhood.

"Skylahr?" Gaelon called from his place a few feet back. Lifting my eyes to his, I smiled half-heartedly at the Healer before waving him off.

"I'm fine," I answered, though it was a lie. Even after all this time, seeing the remnants of my village still crushed me.

I continued on, my feet never faltering as I weaved my way through what was left of the wreckage, and it was almost as if they were moving without my control, only stopping when I stood at the edge of their graves. Ignoring the tightness in my chest, I sunk into the cold earth, the freezing wetness soaking my breeches as I knelt there, stroking the earth.

"Hello, Da," my voice whimpered and I cleared my throat as I gathered my courage. "Gods, I thought it would be easier."

Laughing wetly, I pressed the back of my hand to my damp cheeks while a sob broke through my lips. I had spent the journey planning my words but now that I was here, I didn't know where to start. Dropping my gaze to the ring, I cradled it gently while my other hand pressed harder against the earth that covered my parents.

"I miss you both. So much that sometimes it feels like I can't breathe. Like my body will fall into a thousand pieces knowing you aren't here to hold me together anymore." Pulling the chain from around my neck, I pressed the ring to my lips for a long moment.

"I have spent so long wondering if you knew what I am, what I have done, and what I would do, and if you were somehow with me. But sitting here, I can feel your love and I know that you have never left. I was foolish to think you would. I want you to know—" My throat constricted again, and I shook in an effort to breathe.

"I want you to know that I am still your sky and stars and I always will be. I promise." Wiping my face roughly, I cleared my tears from my skin before digging into the wet earth. Certain I had gone down deep enough. I dropped the ring into the hole before covering it once again. "I love you both."

Unfolding my body, I stood on shaking legs and pulled at the wool of my hood. Shielded from the cold, my face pointed towards the woods that were no longer obstructed from view now that the barrier was gone. Scanning across the familiar thick green, I held my breath as I felt his warmth surround me.

"Kalian." It was a mere whisper, but I could hear his answering rumble as his shining black coat peeked out through the branches. Holding my head high, I waited for him to come closer as the cold breeze swirled around us and silver eyes finally found my own while we stood silently gazing at each other. We held our positions for a long moment, neither moving until I dipped my head in recognition. The black wolf's head tilted gently to one side in response, and his eyes blinked at me while I found the courage to say the final words I had been unable to form the last time I had stood in his presence.

"Goodbye, Protector."

Turning away from him, I jogged back through the rubble and mounted my horse without saying another word. Once settled in the saddle, I kicked my stallion into a gallop, letting the cold north winds drown out the sound of the howl that echoed behind.

And I knew it was his own goodbye.

$\mathcal{A}$CKNOWLEDGEMENTS

This novel has been nothing less than a labour of love. However, the burden of getting the story out into the world is not just mine alone and I owe a lot of people my gratitude.

First let me thank my very own Ellas and Elizabeths. Heather, Jenn, Shelby, and Ellen; you have been my supporters from the very beginning, and I could not have finished this story without you. I will forever be thankful for your opinions, encouragement and love.

To my hubsand, I am so grateful to have such a loving man who has always pushed me to follow my dreams no matter how crazy they may seem. Thank you for always standing in my corner. Thank you for reminding me that I can do more than I think I can and for always seeing the best in me.

To my incredible parents, you raised an independent and stubborn woman who sometimes has a hard time admitting when she needs help. In those moments you remind me I can do anything and that I will always have your support. Without you, I would have never believed in myself or followed my dreams. Thank you for always putting my happiness first. You love me more than I could ever put into words, and I hope you know that my success is your success as well.

Ralphie, you are the most majestic mutt and I am so lucky that you laid beside me every night while I typed my heart away. You have been the best companion and I will forever be grateful that you came to the shelter that day. You are my Reif and I will love you always.

To my angels Robyn, Charlie, Peter, Anna and Cora, I miss you every day but I know that you played a vital role in making me who I am today and without you, I would have been lost.

Thanks to my editors Lottie and Beth, you made my book into a work of art and I will forever be indebted to you. To Nat, thank you for designing such a stunning cover and for answering all of my ridiculous questions. You have the patience of a saint.

Lastly, thank you to my readers. I am so honoured that you read this story. I am so grateful for you and I hope you know that you play the most important role in making my dreams come true. Thank you from the bottom of my heart.

ABOUT THE AUTHOR

Author K. Godin lives in beautiful Ontario Canada, with her husband and four dogs. When she isn't hiding in her office typing away, she spends her time reading, painting, or daydreaming of the fictional worlds she gets lost in.

Her passion for writing started early, and she has always had a knack for it. She excelled in her high school English classes and decided to pursue a general arts degree after graduation. However, after her first year, she knew that college just wasn't for her and found herself working for a local animal shelter. After spending nearly a decade there, she decided to change her career path and started her own business all while creating those fantastic stories in her mind once again.

PRONUNCIATION GUIDE

Characters	
	Skylahr: Sky-lar
	Kalian: Kal-ee-an
	Keyno: Key-no
	Isla: Eye-la
	Gaelon: Gale-on
	Balor: Bay-lor
Places	Rushander: Rush-and-er
	Noordeign: Noor-dean
	Celinde: Cell- ee-nd
	Ferri: Ferry
	Wahstand: Wa-stand
	Ritari: Ri-Tary
	Suideign: Sue-dean
Other	Helcyrbius: Hel-seer-bee-us
	Failinis: Fail-in-is

Printed in the USA
CPSIA information can be obtained
at www.ICGtesting.com
LVHW031639080923
757263LV00046B/1419/J